"This is just supposed to be one night."

She reminded him quietly, but he saw it in her eyes. She didn't even try to hide it. She'd bitten off more than she could chew.

He had too and he was nowhere near done eating.

"Change of plans. A night and a morning and, maybe, an afternoon and, possibly, another night," he amended and her eyes got softer as her hand slid up to cup his jaw.

"I have to work," she told him.

"Call off," he told her.

"I can't. I own the joint," she explained something he knew. "And things are a bit crazy."

Things were always crazy for Lanie. The woman lived crazy, she thrived on it. If there wasn't crazy, she stirred it up because she couldn't breathe without it.

"Babe," he pressed his body into hers, "told you, got more I want to do to you."

Acclaim for Kristen Ashley and Her Novels

"A unique, not-to-be-missed voice in romance. Kristen Ashley is a star in the making!"
—Carly Phillips, *New York Times* bestselling author

"I adore Kristen Ashley's books. She writes engaging, romantic stories with intriguing, colorful, and larger-than-life characters. Her stories grab you by the throat from page one and don't let go until well after the last page. They continue to dwell in your mind days after you finish the story and you'll find yourself anxiously awaiting the next. Ashley is an addicting read no matter which of her stories you find yourself picking up."
—Maya Banks, *New York Times* bestselling author

"There is something about them [Ashley's books] that I find crackalicious."   —Kati Brown, DearAuthor.com

"Run, don't walk...to get [the Dream Man] series. I love [Kristen Ashley's] rough, tough, hard-loving men. And I love the cosmo-girl club!"   —NocturneReads.com

"[*Law Man* is an] excellent addition to a phenomenal series!"
—ReadingBetweentheWinesBookclub.blogspot.com

"[*Law Man*] made me laugh out loud. Kristen Ashley is an amazing writer!"   —TotallyBookedblog.com

"I felt all of the rushes, the adrenaline surges, the anger spikes...my heart pumping in fury. My eyes tearing up when my heart (I mean...*her* heart) would break."
—Maryse's Book Blog (Maryse.net) on *Motorcycle Man*

FIRE
INSIDE

*To all those wounded beauties out there who valiantly
battle their monsters every day and find the strength
to keep on keepin' on. This book is yours.*

Acknowledgments

The usual suspects...

Chas and Rikki, if you didn't take my back, I wouldn't be able to spend so much time creating my worlds. You know you rock. I know without you as my rocks, I'd be in some serious trouble.

Emily, your calm is infectious. But knowing I can live my days doing my gig with the understanding that you're out there, hard at work broadening my horizons, is even better. You're simply the bomb.

Amy, bathroom sex got better because of you. That's saying something! And I said they were wee gifties to you, but they were your wee gifties to Lanie and Hop. You know what I'm talking about.

And to Bob Seger, a man who can tell a mean story through a rock song. You're a god. Thank you for inadvertently helping me make some beautiful points by using your songs. But more, thank you for the hours of rock beauty you've given me while listening to them.

PROLOGUE

Complicated

HOPPER "HOP" KINCAID watched her wind through the loud, rowdy, drunk bikers and their groupies, heading his way.

Lanie Heron.

He didn't move. He kept leaning against the post that held up the roof over the patio area of the Compound, holding a beer and watching her move.

Jesus, she was one serious class act. Even when she came to the Compound to shoot pool or to a hog roast, communing with the brethren of the Chaos Motorcycle Club, she didn't dress down. Designer gear, head-to-toe. She looked like a fucking model except better because she was real, right there, walking right to him, her eyes locked to his.

She was also one serious messed-up bitch.

This was not simply because the woman was pure drama. Fuck, he'd seen her create a scene when the diet cherry 7Up she was pouring fizzed over the top of the glass.

No, Lanie Heron was messed up because she stood by her man.

Under normal circumstances, Hopper would find that an admirable trait in any woman mostly because he knew by experience it was a rare one.

It was not admirable with Lanie.

This was because, before Lanie's man, Elliott Belova, got shot to death, Belova had been even more messed up than she was. The proof of this was he was now very dead, and she had scars from the bullets her dead fiancé bought her because he wanted to give her some crazy-ass, out-of-season flowers for their wedding and he got involved with the Russian Mob to do it.

The fucking Russian Mob.

For flowers.

Not messed up, *fucked* up.

Before it all went down, Lanie had found out about her man working for the Mob. Being a woman, of course, first, she busted his balls. Then she made a tremendously bad decision and stood by him even after his shit got her kidnapped. Then she watched him die and nearly got herself killed in the process.

Fucked up. Your old man gets involved with the Russian Mob—this gets your ass kidnapped—once you get rescued you kick him to the curb. No question. You just do it.

You don't go on the lam with him and get yourself shot.

Hop watched Lanie move his way, thinking all of this, and at the same time thinking about the moment he first saw her. It was the night she found out her old man was making whacked decisions in order to buy her flowers. Even though, at the time, she was in full-blown drama mode—for once her drama being understandable—the second Hop saw her years ago, he'd thought she was definitely one fine piece of ass.

Watching her come his way, he had not changed his mind.

She was not his thing, normally. Too tall, too skinny, a nice ass but not enough of it for his usual taste. Also not enough tits and way too put together, with her designer jeans and high-heeled boots that had to cost a fucking mint.

But there was no denying her glossy, long, dark hair was fucking gorgeous. And her green eyes defined what Hop always thought was a stupid as shit saying but in her case, it was true: She had bedroom eyes. The kind of eyes any man with a functioning dick would want staring into his as he was moving inside her.

Fuck, her eyes were amazing.

After she nearly lost her life standing by her man, she'd taken off, moved from Denver to be close to her family in Connecticut, and she'd stayed there for a while licking her wounds. This while lasted too long, according to Tyra, Lanie's best friend and old lady to Kane "Tack" Allen, the president of Hop's motorcycle club, the Chaos MC. Tyra, known to the boys as "Cherry," flew out to Connecticut, reamed Lanie's ass, and hauled it back to Denver.

Lanie set herself up again in house and job and now she was a staple at Chaos gatherings mostly because she was Tyra's best friend. Also because the brothers liked looking at her so they didn't mind her being around, and even Hop had to admit her frequent dramas were pretty damned funny (when they weren't annoying). You had to give credit to anyone who was who they were no matter who was around and that was pure Lanie. She was Lanie; she didn't water that down and she didn't care what anyone thought of her.

This was the way of the biker, letting it all hang out, so men like Hop and his brothers could appreciate it.

That said, freaking out because your 7Up overflowed was over the top. Still, a bitch as gorgeous as Lanie Heron... fuck, you'd watch her sitting around and watching TV. Having a fit over spilled soda was definitely worthwhile. Especially if she did it like she did it, jumping around so that hair was swinging, those eyes flashing, and what little tits and ass she had moving right along with her.

As she got close, Hop tore his eyes off her and looked through the crowd.

Neither Tack nor Cherry were anywhere to be seen. This was not a surprise. It was late; things were getting rowdy but that wasn't why those two had disappeared. Hop knew they were either on Tack's bike going back up the mountain to their house or they were in his room at the Compound. They were married, had been together awhile; neither of them were anywhere near their twenties, they had two young boys, but still, they went at each other like teenagers.

This also wasn't a surprise. Tyra *did* have tits and ass, lots of hair, and a serious amount of sass. A woman like that was built to be bedded and often, and Tack took advantage. Then again, that was why Tack accepted her ball and chain. Actually, not so much accepted it as much as forced her to clamp her shackle on his ankle. Given the choice of waking up to Tyra Allen every morning, not many men wouldn't have accepted that shackle.

"Hey," he heard Lanie greet him and his eyes moved back to her.

"Hey," he replied.

Her head tilted slightly down, but her eyes never left his as she remarked, "Getting rowdy."

"Always does," he murmured, his gaze moving over her shoulder while he thought, Jesus, she was tall. She had to be five-nine without those heels. In them, she was six-foot-one. Nearly his height. They were almost eye to eye.

He didn't like this, normally.

Lanie…eye to eye with those fucking eyes?

Shit.

"Wanna fuck?"

At her question, his gaze sliced back to hers as he felt his body jerk in shock.

"Say again?" he asked.

She leaned in slightly, never looking away and repeated, "Wanna fuck?"

Hop stared at her. He'd just watched her walk to him, winding through loud, shitfaced bikers and their bitches, her gait steady. She didn't move like she was hammered, nowhere near it. Even now her gaze was clear as it held his.

Still, he asked, "You had one too many, babe?"

"No," she replied instantly and moved closer.

This was not good, because, when she did, he could smell her perfume.

Those eyes, bedroom eyes.

That perfume, fuck me perfume.

Jesus, he'd been catching whiffs of it now for years and it never failed to do a number on him. He didn't know what it was—the fact that it smelled expensive, the intense femininity of it that said, point blank, "I am *all* fucking woman," or the fact that it was elusive. If you got one smell of it, the woman who wore it owned you because you'd do anything to go back for more. Any time Lanie got near him, Hop hoped to catch her scent. Sometimes he would. Sometimes he wouldn't. But every time, he hoped for it.

Now, though, smelling her scent was a very bad thing.

"Not sure that's a good idea, Lanie," he told her, gentling his voice as he gave her the honesty.

"Why?" she asked immediately, and he felt his eyes narrow on her before he answered.

"Maybe 'cause you're best friends with Tack's old lady. I respect him, I respect her, and shit like this, babe, it gets complicated. Any complication sucks but a complication like this," he shook his head, "no one needs that."

She threw out a hand and declared casually, "It won't get complicated."

Okay, maybe she was messed up, fucked up, a drama queen, high maintenance, *and* a nut.

"Bullshit," he replied. "It always gets complicated."

She moved closer and, Jesus, her scent, that hair, those eyes, all so close. If she got any closer he'd physically have to set her away or pick her up and carry her to his room.

"Do you want to fuck me?" she asked. Her voice, sweet and feminine normally, was soft now, a little hesitant, a little excited, and that intoxicating combination was doing a number on him too.

"Babe, you looked in the mirror lately?" he asked back by way of an answer. "Man would have to be dead not to wanna fuck you."

A little smile twisted her pretty mouth, and he knew he was screwed because that was cute *and* fucking sexy as all fucking hell.

Shit.

She got closer and Hop braced. Any closer and she'd be cozied up to him. She was inches away.

"Do you like me?" she asked.

"Everyone likes you," he answered.

"I'm not asking about everyone, Hop," she told him and he held her eyes.

"Yeah, babe, you know I do," he finally answered when she didn't move or speak, just waited. "You're funny, you're cute, you're hot, and you got no problem letting it all hang out. That's why everyone likes you. That's also why I do."

To that, she returned, "Okay. Good. Then no complications, Hop. Just you and me and tonight. Tomorrow, I won't expect flowers. I won't expect a belated courtesy date. I won't even expect you to take me out for a cup of coffee. This isn't about that. I don't even *want* that. I just want you and sex. No expectations. Nothing but what we have tonight," she told him. "Tack and Ty-Ty, or anyone, they never even have to know."

He pushed away from the pole, reached out an arm to put his beer on a nearby picnic table, and took a huge chance straightening to her because it meant they were closer. But it also gave him the half an inch he still had on her when she was in those heels and he needed it.

"Don't wanna be a dick, lady," he warned softly, "but bitches say that shit all the time. Then, in the morning, they expect breakfast, coffee, and to come home from work to roses with a note sayin' the guy never had better. You got a man who thinks to buy you roses, says he's never had better, big chances are he's lyin'. He just wants it regular and he'll take it as it comes."

He knew every word out of his mouth made him the dick he told her he didn't want to be, but she needed to move on. If she was in the mood to get laid, she needed to find herself some, *not* on Chaos. Tack's woman, Cherry, had chosen Chaos but that didn't mean she wouldn't lose her mind if her best girl hooked up with a brother. She would. Hop knew it. But if that shit happened anyway, Cherry would want to handpick the brother who got in there and Hop also knew that brother would absolutely not be him.

"Then take it as it comes," she shot back, not appearing offended in the slightest, her words coming out almost like a dare.

"Lanie—" he started, but she leaned in and, fuck, if he moved his mouth a quarter of an inch, it'd be on hers. She was all he could see, all he could smell, and all he could think was that she was also all he wanted to *feel*.

"You know my story," she whispered. "You think I want

another guy?" She paused then finished with emphasis, *"Ever?"*

He got her. Her dead old man was a moron and she'd paid for his shit in the worst way she could. Her loyalty had bought her nothing but pain, bullet wounds, and heartache. Not to mention, her man might have been good at what he did for a living, the computer geek to end all computer geeks, but he was nothing to look at. So she not only gave love and loyalty but she stepped out of a zone no woman who looked like her had to step out of in order to give it.

So, yeah, Belova was a moron and she chose that. He could see her wanting to get back in the saddle but being skittish about buying the horse.

She just wasn't going to get back in the saddle with him.

Hop started to lift his hands to curl them around her upper arms and set her away, but she moved fast, lifting her hands to curl them around the sides of his neck. They felt warm. Her perfume assaulted him straight on and he stilled.

"I do not want that," she carried on. "What I want is... *you*. For one night. Just one night."

Fuck him.

Fuck him.

"Lady," he muttered but before he could say more, she kept talking.

"It was... I know you know where I was back then and who I was with and I know you had a woman then too, Hop, but still, that night I met you, I couldn't help but notice you were good-looking. But you're not with anyone anymore and I'm *seriously* not with anyone anymore and I've been thinking about it for a long time, just too scared to do anything about it. Now I've decided I'm doing something about it."

"I gotta say, I like that you're into me, babe," he returned gently. "Already told you that you're beautiful and under any other circumstances, I would not hesitate to take you up on an offer this sweet. So you gotta know it's killin' me even as you gotta trust me when I say this is *not* a good idea."

"I've had no one since him," she whispered and, acting on their own, Hop's hands came up and settled on her waist, giving it a squeeze. The move was intimate but comforting. The news that this woman, this crazy-gorgeous woman and all that she was, hadn't had a man between her legs in fucking *years* moved him even as it troubled him.

"Lanie, honey," he muttered, not having the first fucking clue what else to say.

"I've thought on it and decided it's you." Her hands at his neck gave him a squeeze and fuck him, *fuck him,* that moved him even more. "I understand why you don't want to, but I promise, Hop, *I swear,* no kidding, seriously, no strings. No expectations. Just us. One night. Tomorrow, it will be like it's always been. Like it didn't even happen. I promise."

Her hands slid down to his chest, but she didn't move away as she finished laying it out.

"Now, I'm going to your room and I'm going to wait there for fifteen minutes. If you don't show, no harm, no foul. I promise that, too. Nothing changes between us. No one knows anything." She sucked in a breath and took a half step back, her hands falling away when she concluded in a quiet voice, "But," she took a deep breath, "I really hope you show."

With that, not giving him a chance to say another word, she turned and strutted her narrow ass back through the loud, rowdy, drunk bikers and their bitches, her hair swaying, her arms moving gracefully, her scent still in his nostrils.

"Shit," he whispered when he watched her haul open the door to the Compound.

"Shit," he repeated when the door closed behind her.

He kept his eyes on the door and he did this a while.

That woman, that crazy-gorgeous woman, was right now in his room.

"Shit," he whispered yet again right before he made his way to the door.

* * *

Hopper broke contact with Lanie's hooded eyes, eyes that were a fuckuva lot sexier since he'd just come inside her, and he did it hard and he did it long, and he shoved his face in her neck.

All he could smell was her. All he could feel was her warm, soft body under his—one of her legs wrapped around the back of his thigh, the other one cocked high, her thigh pressed to his side but her calf swung in, her heel resting in the small of his back. Her arms were tight around him, one at his shoulders, one angled, resting along his spine. Last, he could feel his cock buried in her unbelievably tight, wet cunt.

He didn't know what it was. Maybe it was that she'd never had kids. Maybe it was because it had been so long since she'd had a man. Whatever it was, her pussy was close to virgin it was so tight. Luckily, it was also sleek. Luckier, it tasted like goddamned honey.

He'd been right when they were talking outside.

This was about to get complicated.

Her head moved and he felt her lips at his ear even as he heard her soft, tentative words. "Was that all right?"

Hop closed his eyes even as his hips reflexively pressed into hers, and he gently fisted the hand he had buried in her hair.

She was worried she was out of practice. She was worried it wasn't good for him. And considering the fact that, if she was out of practice, when she got into the swing of things, she'd be off-the-charts, her worry was both cute and sweet and, like everything else about her, it did a number on him.

Yes, things were going to get complicated.

He opened his eyes, moved his head so his lips were at her ear, and murmured, "Lady, I don't fake it. Not only because I can't but because, even if I could, I wouldn't."

All her limbs convulsed around him even as her cunt did the same and, Jesus, God, it felt seriously fucking good.

Then it got better when her body started moving under him and he heard her husky, low chuckle in his ear.

He lifted his head in an effort to watch her face in laughter through the dark. Once she got back to Denver, and Tyra got her hands on her, Lanie laughed a lot. He liked watching her laugh. It was always, every time he saw it, a good show.

It was better now because he could *feel* it. Even though he couldn't see much, the little he saw was still pure beauty.

Totally complicated.

He liked her smell. He liked her feel. He liked the sound of her low laughter. He liked her uncertainty. He liked how hard she made him come. And he liked how hard she came for him, her pussy tightening around his cock, her long limbs wound around his body holding on, her soft pants and moans sweet to his ear and, best of all, the look on her beautiful face when he gave it to her.

Totally fucking complicated.

He waited until she stopped laughing before he slid his hand out of her hair to her jaw and then rubbed the pad of his thumb across her lips while he asked, "How you feelin'?"

"Uh...good," she answered, her words meant to be an obvious understatement, her lips moving against his thumb tilting up even as she spoke.

"Good enough for another go?" he asked, his thumb

pressing in, pulling at her unbelievably full lower lip, and he felt her shift under him.

He knew what that shift meant even before her voice came at him, breathy, "Another go?"

He replaced his thumb with his lips. "Yeah, another go."

"So soon?" She sounded disbelieving.

"You're gonna have to work me up, lady, but...yeah. Soon as you're ready, my mouth wants more of that pussy."

She wanted that, too. He knew it because her body trembled under his.

"Yeah, I'm, um...good for another go," she told him, her sweet voice still breathy.

"Then don't move." He pressed his lips to hers before he lifted his head. "Gotta hit the can and I'll be back."

"I won't move," she whispered.

She better not. If she did, he'd find her and haul her back. He didn't care if she beamed her ass to Mars.

Fuck.

Complicated.

He knew it and didn't give a fuck as he slid out of her, kissed her throat, feeling her skin, smelling her scent, and rolled off her and the bed so he could make his way to the bathroom to get rid of his condom.

When he got back, she hadn't moved, but seconds later, she did because he moved her.

He parted her legs, swung them over his shoulders and didn't hesitate a second before he dipped his face into pure honey.

*   *   *

Hop exited the bathroom and saw Lanie sitting on the side of his bed, her back to him, putting on her bra.

"What the fuck you doin'?" he growled and, shit, that was it. He couldn't deny it. Even he heard it.

He *growled*.

She twisted and he felt her eyes on him in the dark.

"Ty-Ty and Tack are down the hall. They won't come up for air until the morning, but it's almost morning so I should be gone by then."

"You're not goin'," he informed her, putting a knee to the bed and moving her way.

"I'm...*oof*," she puffed as he hooked her at the belly, yanked her back onto the bed, and rolled on top of her. She blinked up at him through the dark and finished, "not?"

"Not done with you," he informed her.

"You're..." again with the breathy voice, something he felt in his gut, chest, and dick, "*not?*" and again with the disbelieving.

Totally disbelieving.

"I'm not," Hop confirmed.

"Is that even," a pause then, "*possible?*"

"Is what possible?" he asked.

"Three times in an, erm...night?"

Obviously, Belova wasn't only messed up, fucked up, and stupid, he'd clearly had no stamina, which was fucking insane. A ninety-year-old man had a shot at that beauty, he'd find a way to get it up and do it repeatedly even if it killed him.

"Yeah it's possible."

Hop watched her head tilt on the pillow. "I...No offense, Hop, but I don't believe you."

Fucking *excellent*.

He slid his hands up her sides as he dropped his mouth to hers. "Right. Good, then, babe. I get to prove it to you."

Close up, he watched her eyes get wide.

"Wow," she whispered against his lips.

"Don't say that now," he ordered. "You can say that later, like you did after I did that thing with my fingers the second time."

Her body shifted under his, her chest pressing up; she remembered something he knew she wouldn't soon forget, and she repeated a whispered, "Wow."

He grinned against her mouth and promised, "I'll give you wow."

"You've already given me three wows," she reminded him.

"Four," he corrected.

"Oh yeah," she murmured, her hands moving lightly down the skin of his back. "I forgot that one because it came so close on the heels of that other one."

Her hands made it to his ass, so he decided their conversation was over, and to communicate that to Lanie, he asked, "Are we gonna keep talkin' or do you want wow?"

She moved her head, sliding her lips from his, down his cheek to his jaw and finally his ear.

Once they were there, she murmured, "Give me wow."

With his mouth at her neck, he trailed it down to her collarbone then engaged his tongue and, after, taking his time and a lot of it, he gave her wow five *and* six.

*   *   *

Hop came out of the bathroom to see Lanie on her feet on the other side of the bed, panties on, hands twisted behind her back putting her bra on. Again.

He didn't say a word. He prowled to her, reached out an arm the second he was close, yanked her to him and fell to his back in the bed, taking her down with him.

"Hop—" she started, pushing her weight against his

arms, but he slid her off him then wasted no time rolling over her and pinning her to his bed.

"Sleep," he ordered when he caught her eyes in the weak dawn. "After rest, I'll get coffee, we'll juice up, then round four."

She blinked and breathed, "Four?"

"Got lots more I want to do to you," he informed her and watched her eyes go soft, sexier, then her teeth came out to graze her lush lower lip, also fucking sexy, and her arms slid around him.

But she asked, "What about Tack and Ty-Ty?"

"I'll make sure the coast is clear," he told her.

"But they'll see my car," she told him.

"I'll move it," he offered.

Her hand slid up his back, around his shoulder, and then to his neck where her thumb moved to stroke him. Her touch was light but, fuck, it felt good. He'd never had a woman touch him in an unconscious way like that, just a touch, a stroke, giving something that meant nothing at the same time doing it without thinking about it meant everything.

Shit.

Complicated.

"This is just supposed to be one night," she reminded him quietly, but he saw it in her eyes. She didn't even try to hide it. She'd bitten off more than she could chew.

He had too and he was nowhere near done eating.

She was cute. She was sweet. She was hot. She was better than he expected and he'd expected her to be pretty fucking good. All that wrapped in a package that gorgeous?

Yeah.

He was nowhere near done eating.

"Change of plans. A night and a morning and, maybe, an

afternoon and, possibly, another night," he amended, and her eyes got softer as her hand slid up to cup his jaw.

"I have to work," she told him.

"Call off," he told her.

"I can't. I own the joint." She explained something he knew, that she ran her own advertising agency. "And things are a bit crazy."

Things were always crazy for Lanie. The woman lived crazy. She thrived on it. If there wasn't crazy, she stirred it up because she couldn't breathe without it.

"Babe," he pressed his body into hers, "told you, got more I want to do to you."

He felt her shiver but her lips whispered, "Hop, I don't—"

He cut her off with a quick kiss then lifted his head and asked, "Where are your keys?"

"We shouldn't sleep together. Sleeping is bad. Sex is good, sleeping together is something else," she stated and she was right.

He just didn't care.

"Where are your keys?" he asked.

"Hop—"

"Lady, we're not sleeping, we're resting then we're fucking some more. Last time I'll say it. Not done with you, got things I want to do to you and I'm doin' them. Now, where... are... your... *keys?*"

She stared up at him, her gaze hot, her body bothered, shifting under his, and she whispered, "Jeans pocket."

Stretching out to reach a hand to the floor, he grabbed her jeans, got in the pocket, and yanked out her keys. Once he had them in hand, he went back to her and kissed her. He took his time, and it was wet, deep, and fucking brilliant.

When she was holding on tight and kissing him back like she never wanted it to end, he ended it. Lifting his lips to her forehead, he touched them there then dipped his chin and looked into her eyes.

"Rest, honey. I'll move your car and be back."

"Okay," she agreed quietly.

He touched his mouth to hers, rolled off, grabbed his jeans, a tee, pulled on socks and his boots and made his way to the door. He turned back before he slid through the still mostly closed door.

She was curled in an "S" in his bed, pillow to her chest, cheek resting on it, arms around it, hair everywhere. Her bare back was exposed, and he could see one leg and her ass in red lace panties. Eyes on him.

Fucking gorgeous, every inch, and she tasted and felt as good as she looked.

She grinned.

Gorgeous.

He returned her grin, slid through the door and went after her car.

When he got back, she was dead to the world.

He took off his clothes, dropped them to the floor, and slid into bed beside her. Carefully, he turned her into his arms.

She didn't wake. She just cuddled closer, her arm snaking across his stomach then holding tight, her torso pressing into his, her knee cocked and resting on his thigh.

This felt good, too.

She was right. They shouldn't sleep together. Sleeping suggested something more. A kind of togetherness neither of them wanted. Sleeping like this with her, it feeling so good; it was, with everything else, enough to make you want a fuckuva lot more.

So it was good, Hop thought, that they weren't sleeping, they were just resting.

On that thought, he fell asleep, Lanie curved close and held tight in his arm, her perfume all over his sheets.

*   *   *

Three hours later, Hop woke.

Lanie's perfume was still all over his sheets.

Lanie just wasn't in them.

*   *   *

That night Hop was stretched out on the fluffy cushion on the lounge chair in her courtyard, feet crossed at the ankles, eyes trained to the back door of the garage.

He had no idea how late it was. He just knew it was dark and he'd been there a really fucking long time.

Too long.

Long enough for him to get pissed.

Or *more* pissed.

He heard her garage door go up and didn't move when he heard its grind or when he heard the purr of her sweet ride moving into it. A pearl red Lexus LFA. According to word on Chaos, her father had bought it for her.

High class ran in the family. So did money.

He only moved off the chair when he heard the garage door going down.

He was on his feet when the outside lights to the courtyard that separated her brownstone from the garage came on, but he didn't move from his spot even as the door to the courtyard opened.

She strode out, sex on stilettos; tight skirt, tailored blazer that was unbelievably feminine, hair out to there; slim, shiny, expensive briefcase in her hand; trim, small designer purse over her shoulder.

A *Cosmo* girl tricked out in business gear.

"Yo," he called when she shut the door. He watched her jump and swing around to him, face pale, eyes huge.

"Oh my God, Hop. You scared me half to death."

He didn't reply.

When he remained silent, her face lost its pallor. Her head tipped to the side and her brows knitted as she asked, "What are you doing here?"

"Told you, I wasn't done with you," he answered, and her head immediately righted with a snap.

"Hop—" she started.

"Told you that," he cut her off. "Still, you snuck outta my bed and slunk away."

She took one step toward him, her body moving like she was going to take more, but she suddenly stopped.

"I said just one night," she reminded him.

"And I said I wasn't done with you," he fired back.

"I—" she began but he interrupted her again.

"You had dinner?"

Her head jerked in surprise then she answered, "Yes, a business dinner. New client."

"Good," he grunted. "Upstairs. Naked. Now."

He felt it coming off her in waves.

She wanted that.

Bad.

Then her head moved again like she was forcing herself to do it, shaking it side to side. "We agreed. One night."

"I think we also agreed, though the words weren't spoken, one night's not enough."

"This can't get complicated," she reminded him.

"You keep your mouth shut, I keep my mouth shut, we're smart, we contain it, no one finds out, and we stick to the boundaries, it won't."

"I don't think—"

"Lanie. Upstairs. Naked. *Now*."

He saw her breath come fast, her chest moving with it and, Jesus, fuck him, he could taste her excitement and he was five feet away.

"We shouldn't—"

"Fucked you on your back. Like to look in your eyes when I'm inside you. Done that. Now I want you on your knees, gonna fuck your face and your cunt and I can't do that in the courtyard. It'd shock the shit outta me, class act like you gets into that, but if I get you naked, you're all mine. I don't share with the neighbors."

She stood stock-still, her eyes riveted to him. The only thing moving on her body was her chest, rising and falling with quick breaths.

"Lanie," he leaned in, "upstairs. Naked. Right...fucking...*now*."

She took off toward her sliding glass door.

Hop didn't move but he did smile when she dropped her keys, cursed under her breath and crouched in that tight skirt to get them.

Second go, she got in and left the door open as she hurried inside.

Hop stared at the door before taking a deep breath and walking to it.

He got inside and saw it was a big kitchen, living, dining area. He saw the clock on the microwave said it was ten forty-two.

He took no more in.

To make sure something that could get complicated didn't, he understood that this wasn't what he was going to take or what she could give. He didn't get to look at her shit, check out pictures in frames, see if she was clean or messy, read what he could in how she decorated.

He didn't get that.

He got what was upstairs, naked in her bed.

He turned slowly and slid the door closed. He locked it. Then he moved through the dark space.

He found the blazer on the carpet of the stairs. A camisole on the landing. Her skirt on the next flight. Panties, bra, and shoes leading him to a room where dim light was shining.

He was hard by the time he made it to her room.

He didn't look around there either. Not because it wasn't what he got from her but because she was on her ass in her bed, knees to her chest, chin to her knees, arms wrapped around her calves, ankles crossed at her ass, hiding everything but still cute as all fuck.

His dick started throbbing.

"Fuck me, I'm gonna come just standing here looking at you," he muttered and watched her eyes close slowly, something moving over her face making beauty so beautiful, it was almost impossible to take it in. Like staring at the sun; if he saw that look on her face for another second, he'd go blind.

She opened her eyes, pushed out of her pose, and gracefully moved to the edge of the bed. Feet to the floor, naked, her eyes to his, his going everywhere that was her. She moved to him and stopped so close he could smell her perfume.

Instantly her hands went to his tee and she yanked up.

Hop lifted his arms. She pulled the shirt away and dropped it.

Then her mouth went to his chest, her hands followed, moving, licking, sucking, touching, then down.

On her knees, she unbuckled his belt, pulled it open, unbuttoned his jeans, not looking at him through this. He got nothing but the gleaming hair on top of her head.

He knew why when she reached right in, found him, pulled him free and slid him deep inside her mouth.

She had something she wanted and she was concentrating on getting it.

Fuck.

Fuck.

His head dropped back, his fingers slid into her hair, and his voice was hoarse when he ordered, "Baby, up. Woman like you does not get on her knees."

She wrapped a fist around him, slid him out and he looked down just in time to see her tip her head back, those eyes, those fucking eyes, hooded and turned on, looking up at him.

"I like it, honey."

"Suck me off in bed. Not on your knees. Class doesn't hit her knees."

"Hop—"

"Up, Lanie. Get in bed."

"But—"

He jerked his hips back, she lost purchase on his dick, and he planted his hands under her arms. He pulled her up and then swung her into his arms. He took four strides and tossed her on the bed.

He bent, yanked off his boots, his socks, his jeans and he joined her there.

He pulled her into his arms, rolled to his back, rolling her on top.

"Right, *now* you can suck me off," he told her.

"I get to go back to what I was doing later," she told him and he grinned at the look on her face. She still looked turned on. She also looked miffed.

Cute.

Adorable, actually.

Fuck. It was going to take a serious amount of work for this not to get complicated.

"Maybe," he lied. "Now back to work."

"Ty-Ty told me you guys take bossy to extremes and do whatever it takes to get your way. That was why I snuck out of your bed this morning. I told you we shouldn't sleep together. It seemed you weren't going to take no for an answer so I had to get creative," she shared and there it was.

Cherry blabbed so Lanie was prepared.

He'd have to take that into account in the future.

"You're telling me this instead of going down on me because...?" he prompted.

"Because I want your promise I can finish what I started later," she explained.

"Lady, you can do it now. In fact, I'd be obliged if you would," he told her.

She scrunched up her nose. "Like we were before."

Hop shook his head. "I said, no. Not like that."

Her hand came to his cheek and her face got close. "Hop, what you said was sweet and I liked that, but I also liked what I was doing and—"

He rolled on top of her and he moved his hand to her cheek, thumb to her lips, pressing in and his face got close.

"I'm guessin' you get what this is. We played with fire, we got burned, now we gotta contain the blaze, but sayin' that, I got no intention of puttin' it out and, babe, I'm gettin', since you left me a trail of breadcrumbs to this room, you don't either."

She tried to turn her head to get away from his thumb to say something but Hop kept going.

"We get it, we don't gotta talk about it. We know what we got revolves around bein' naked in a bed, so you shouldn't get what I'm gonna give you right now. But I'm gonna give it to you. Never had class. Never had beauty. I'll repeat, never…had…*class.* I'm not gonna fuck over Cherry, who I care about, or Tack, who's my brother, and I know you don't wanna do that either, so this is what we got for as long as it's good. But it's a clean, pure beauty the like I've never had, I'm gonna respect it like I feel like I gotta and you're gonna let me."

He paused, bent his face closer to hers and dipped his voice lower.

"So, no, Lanie, you are not gettin' down on your knees like every biker skank or groupie or drunk, high piece of ass before you dropped to hers and sucked me off. You go down on me, you do it like who you are. Respect. You don't want that, you're looking to play with rough trade to get you off, find another guy to make you skank. That is not what you're gonna get from me. Now, are you gonna finish givin' me a blowjob or are you gonna fight me on this?"

She laid there and stared up at him, not saying a word, so Hop gave her an alternate option.

"Or are you gonna lie there and stare at me?"

"I think I need to lie here and stare at you for about thirty more seconds," she whispered and Hop felt his lips twitch.

Then he offered quietly, "Have at it, baby."

"Though, while lying here staring at you, I'm just going to say, I really like your mustache," she told him.

"Good to know," he muttered, his lips still twitching.

"It's badass biker cool," she went on.

"Right," he kept muttering, now through a grin.

"And it feels good on my neck and, well…other places," she continued and his grin turned to a smile.

"Also good to know."

"I think I'm done staring at you," she announced.

"So, you gonna get busy?"

She'd lied.

She wasn't done staring at him. He knew this because she kept staring for a beat before she lifted her head and touched her mouth to his.

"Yeah," she whispered.

He grinned against her mouth before he kissed her, rolling her with him as he turned onto his back.

When he broke the kiss, she got busy and sucked him off in bed.

Like class.

Like a lady.

*   *   *

Dressed and sitting on the side of her bed, Hop shifted the soft, heavy hair off Lanie's neck, leaned in and put his lips there.

"Tickles," she murmured. He lifted his head and caught her eyes. "In a good way," she finished.

"Good," he murmured back and dipped his already close face closer. "Sun's up, honey."

"Yeah," she whispered.

"Later," he said.

"Yeah." She drew in breath then asked, "Tonight?"

"You want that?"

She nodded her head on the pillow.

Excellent. He did too.

He lifted his lips to her temple, kissed her there, moved them to her ear and said softly, "You got it."

Then, without another look at her in her bed, sleepy, sexy, and sated, something he knew he couldn't walk away from, he walked away from her, through her house, and out the sliding glass door, putting Lanie Heron out of his mind.

Until tonight.

CHAPTER ONE

Cheese Whiz

I WAS ON a hand and my knees. My other arm was straight out, hand flat against my cream linen padded headboard, Hop behind me, fucking me *hard*.

I was close. This was good, the best.

The best I ever had.

Then he did what I knew he'd do—four nights, no matter how many times we did it, he always ended it the same way.

He pulled out and my head jerked around, my eyes went to him and I pleaded, "Hop. Please don't. I'm close."

He dropped to a hip at my side and pulled me over him. Head to my pillows and, God, *God,* he looked hot, all that messy hair, that biker 'tache, his badass gorgeousness framed by my pale pink pillowcase.

"Ride me, lady," he muttered, and I didn't make him ask twice.

I lifted up to straddle him, wrapped my hand around his cock, guided the tip inside and slid down until he filled me.

My head dropped back. I loved this, I missed it. He'd been pounding inside me not ten seconds before, but having him back, it felt like I hadn't had him in years.

Hop shifted then I felt his fingers slide into my hair so

his hand could cup the back of my head. He tilted it down. I opened my eyes to see he'd knifed up so I was staring into his, close.

His eyes were intense. Always when we were like this, they were intense in a way I never felt before. Like he could read my thoughts. See into my head. Touch my soul through a gaze.

"Move, Lanie," he murmured, and again, I didn't make him ask twice.

My gaze held captive in his, I wrapped my arms around his shoulders and moved. His arm snaked around my waist, holding me close so my body slid against his as I rode him, his hand cupped to my head pulling me down so my lips grazed his. Through this, his eyes held mine, not letting go.

My soft breaths whispered against his lips as it built again, just as his deep groans sounded against mine.

I was getting close. This was good, the best. *The best.*

The best I ever had.

His arm around my waist moved so his hand could glide over my belly and down. Suddenly, his thumb hit the spot and, God, *God*, perfect aim.

Elliott couldn't do that. Because I was me and more than a little crazy, I'd done the math and Elliott had hit the spot on his first try one out of every four times.

Hop never missed.

I closed my eyes as it shot through me, my head automatically arching back only to be caught in Hop's grip, forced forward, my lips to his, my moans sounding in his mouth. I kept moving, faster, faster even as it shook me.

The best I ever had.

I finished and kept moving, my rhythm not breaking, needing to give to Hop what I'd just had. Needing to get it back. Needing it like a drug.

Hazy from my orgasm, I watched his face get dark, hungry. He was close.

Then he shoved my face into his neck as he shoved his into mine, his arm clamped around me, holding me down on his cock as he groaned deep, the sound vibrating against my skin.

Absolutely, bar none, the best I ever had.

Every time.

Damn.

After he came down, he loosened his arm around my waist but still held me close as his mouth worked my neck, his mustache tickling, making me shiver.

I returned the favor, gliding my lips along his neck, my tongue snaking out so I could touch the tip to his earlobe. When I did, his arm around me grew tighter.

I ran the tip of my tongue down his neck to his collarbone.

His arm again grew tighter.

He tasted good. He smelled good. Both man. *All* man. I couldn't describe it. He didn't wear cologne but his scent was spicy. Intoxicating.

It was . . . *him.*

His head went back, his hand in my hair relaxed and my head came up.

His eyes caught mine.

God, badass biker beauty.

Every inch.

"Climb off me, beautiful," he murmured, and I didn't want to but I nodded, maneuvered up, sliding him out of me, and I moved off him, dropping to my side next to him.

That was when he did something that I was trying not to process. Something sweet. Something un-biker (or what I expected a biker to do). Something thoughtful.

Something gorgeous.

He pulled the sheet around my nudity and yanked a

pillow down to shove it under me right before he bent deep
and kissed the hair at the side of my head.

Damn.

I struggled. It was hard not to let his sweet actions pen-
etrate and every night, every time he did something like that,
it got harder.

Do...not...process, Lanie!

Curled around the pillow, my leg tangling in the sheets
and comforter, straddling them, I managed to shove how I
felt out of my head. Instead I watched him walk to the bathroom thinking that I liked how tall he was. Elliott hadn't
been taller than me. I'd towered over him in heels. I told
myself I didn't mind this and when he was alive and sweet
and always being Elliott, I didn't.

But having a tall man was fabulous.

And Hop's sculpted ass made it all the more fabulous.

He hit the bathroom, the light went on and he disappeared.

I closed my eyes.

It was Saturday night. We'd started this at the hog roast
on Wednesday.

Only bikers would have a blowout hog roast on a Wednesday night, but then again, most of them had jobs where it
didn't matter that they showed up late and/or hungover. And
their hangers-on had jobs in bars or strip clubs; their shifts
didn't start until late so they had time to recuperate.

As for me, I came back to Denver and was greeted
warmly (and in some cases with relief) by a number of old
clients, so I made the mammoth decision to be my own boss.
That was, the boss of an advertising agency, which was not
conducive to having sex all night long and dragging into
work the next morning. And Hop and I had been going at
each other all night long, from dark to dawn, every night for
four nights. I was exhausted.

Still, I wanted him to come back so I could have more. I was just going to have to inform him that he needed to do all the work.

He would not quibble. Unlike Elliott, Hop had staying power. He actually *liked* taking over, dominating, doing the hard work. Sure, I rode him on occasion but he didn't lie back and enjoy it. He participated fully, like just now.

Elliott could start giving it to me, but then he'd stop, panting and grunting, and ask me to take over and I always did. I didn't mind. I liked the top.

Then again, I'd been in love with Elliott, and you do stuff like that when you're in love. You shove to the back of your head little things that bother you. Things you had before that you missed. Things like having a man who was all man fucking you until you ached but ached in a good way.

In my experience, which wasn't vast but it also wasn't limited, a man who was all man was usually a total jerk and an asshole and took both of these to extremes.

I felt Hop's presence, opened my eyes and watched him walk back into my bedroom.

The back view, fabulous.

The front, God...*staggering.*

Never, not ever in my life, would the man I was staring at right then be a man I would expect to be in my bed.

But he was and he was, for the first time in my life, in my bed on my own damned terms.

When I met Hop years ago, I'd been in a drama because I'd just learned my fiancé was *whacked.* Even so, Hopper was the kind of guy that his looks, his charisma, all that was him, and there was a lot, could cut through anything. I was engaged to be married and in the throes of a crazy situation that only got crazier, so my mind didn't go there but it did process all that was him. It was impossible for it not to.

When I got back from Connecticut, with Elliott gone but Hop alive, breathing, and so freaking good-looking, my mind went there.

Again and again and again.

Thick, black, unruly hair that was long in front, often fell into his face and had little flips and waves all through it but especially around his neck.

Gray eyes with lines radiating out the sides, that stated not only did he not have a desk job but that he lived his life, didn't exist through it. Whether those lines were from squinting, laughter, or frowning, they were intriguing and took your attention to the gray that was a pure gray, not slightly blue, not dark to black, just a startling gray.

His mustache, facial hair something else I didn't like on a guy, was the epitome of biker cool. Thick along his upper lip and down the sides, bushier at either side of his chin.

He had no body fat in evidence, *at all*. He was tall, lean. There wasn't bulk to his muscle but the definition stated without doubt there was power in his frame and that power wasn't insignificant.

A dusting of black chest hair, not a thick mat. Short, rough, sparse but not meager, arrayed across his pecs and ribs, hair that felt crazy-good against my skin.

The best part, defined the center ridge in his six pack, where the hair got thicker, darker, leading in a thin line from the valley of his pecs to his navel, then got thinner as it led down to one of the best parts of him.

I loved his chest hair. I loved his height. I loved the power behind his body. And, if I was honest, I loved the beauty of his cock, perfectly formed, both thick and long, and it helped a whole lot that he knew what to do with it.

I also found that I loved his tats, something on other men I wouldn't like. The Chaos emblem on his back. Another one all the men had that Hop had had inked into the inside of his right bicep was a set of unbalanced scales with reapers, scythes, and the words "Never Forget" at the bottom. There were also black, yellow, and red flames dancing from wrist to elbow on both of his forearms.

Badass.

Hot.

Fantastic.

And last, Hop was the only man I'd ever had who wore jewelry. He wore a lot of it and, as with everything else, he looked good in it. Bulky silver rings on his fingers, sometimes two or three, sometimes five or six. Leather bands or silver bracelets at his wrists. A tangle of chains with medallions at his neck. Stud earrings in both ears, the same every day: a small silver cross in one, a tiny silver profile of a skull, the back of its head a set of flames, all this set in black in the other.

No man looked good in jewelry.

No man except a biker in a motorcycle club that had great chest hair, zero body fat, and flame tattoos up his arms could carry off that jewelry.

The man in my bed.

I watched as he came toward that bed then stopped, bent and tagged his jeans.

At that, my belly hollowed out.

He never left. Not until dawn.

Now it appeared he was preparing to leave.

I didn't lift my cheek from the pillow I was cradling when I asked, "What are you doing?"

His gaze came to me even as he tugged up his jeans. "Chaos business, babe."

I tipped just my eyes to the clock on my nightstand. Eleven thirty-six.

It was late and I could use some sleep.

I still didn't want him to leave.

Damn.

Do...not...process, Lanie!

I didn't process and therefore said nothing.

Hop dressed, yanking his black tee over his head, pulling it down, and I watched with some fascination as it sculpted itself to his torso as if by magic.

Nice.

Unbelievably nice.

He nabbed his boots and socks and sat on the side of my bed.

I didn't move.

He tugged them on then turned to me and bent in, his hand shifting the hair off my neck, his face coming close.

I wanted to ask if he was coming back the next night. Maybe the next morning. Whenever. I didn't care. I just wanted him to know whenever he showed, I'd be there.

I didn't say this. I *couldn't* say this. I wouldn't allow myself to say this. It would expose too much. It would give too much. I didn't have it in me. I had nothing left to give. Whatever I'd once had leaked out of my body in the form of blood on a floor in Kansas City while my eyes stared into the dead ones of my fiancé across the room.

So I just tilted my eyeballs up to look at him.

His hand moved to my cheek, the pad of his thumb gliding whisper-soft on the skin just under my eye as his eyes studied mine, not like he was looking in them but *at* them with an expression on his face that said, quite clearly, he liked what he saw.

This was another thing he did frequently that was something I was trying not to process. I liked that he liked looking at me. I liked that he didn't hide that he liked what he saw. He certainly wasn't the first man to do that.

What could I say? I wasn't blind. It wasn't like I didn't know God had been generous with me. It wasn't like I didn't appreciate it. But with every blessing, there was also a curse, and my curse was that I was a dick magnet.

Handsome men knew they were handsome, and it was my experience this did not skip a single good-looking guy. It was also my experience that they thought the world should throw roses at their feet just because they were hot. They definitely thought their women should bow down or eat shit.

If they weren't exactly handsome but still smart, confident, charismatic, and successful, they were worse.

Hop was good-looking, smart, confident, and charismatic. What he wasn't was a man who hid that he liked what he saw.

He could act the player. He could pretend he could take it or leave it. He could hide his attraction to me in order to gain the upper hand. He could even begin to lay the groundwork of tearing me down, making me feel less than I was, trying to make me feel lucky I had in my bed all that was him and, in doing that, embarking on a campaign that was usually scary successful, not to mention swift, to make me feel like I was nothing.

He didn't.

He liked looking at me, my eyes especially, like just then but particularly when he was inside me. I never came without my eyes to his and his to mine; Hop made it that way. I'd never had a man look me in the eyes so intently, so steadily, so hungrily, as Hopper.

I found my hand lifting even as the rest of me didn't move, cupping his jaw, my eyes watching my thumb trail the side of his 'tache, moving over the thickness of his whiskers at his jaw, and he muttered, "You really like that, don't you?"

My gaze went to his and I kept my hand where it was. "Yeah."

That was an understatement. It looked good on him. It felt good on my skin. It felt better between my legs.

Heaven.

"Before you, was thinking of shaving it off. Growing a patch." He lifted his hand, touched his middle finger to the indent under his lower lip and I took in his rings.

A plain silver band on his thumb and three rings, side by side, index, middle and ring finger, one that said "Ride," one that said "Free," the last said "Chaos."

Badass, biker, *cool*.

"I'll wait until we burn out before I do that," he concluded.

My eyes cut up to his.

I'll wait until we burn out before I do that.

His tone was light, his lips surrounded by that 'tache tipped up. He was teasing.

I didn't like it. Teasing, I could take. A reminder we would burn out, I couldn't.

I didn't tell him this mostly because I refused to process it.

"Not that you need it but you have my encouragement to grow the patch," I said instead then clarified, "*Along* with the mustache."

His face dipped closer, taking my hand with it, his eyes never leaving mine as he whispered against my lips, "Then I'll grow the patch."

I smiled against his mouth.

"Gotta go, honey," he went on, and there was one good thing in that. He sounded like he didn't want to.

"Okay."

"Okay," he replied but didn't move, didn't let go of my eyes, nothing. When this went on for a while, he prompted, "Forgetting something?"

"Uh..." I mumbled.

"Lady, kiss me."

Lady.

I'd been around Hop and all the Chaos boys for some time. They called women a lot of things, some of them good, some of them not so good.

Not one of them, not one, called any woman "Lady."

This was something else he gave me. Something gorgeous. Something I wouldn't let settle in my soul or I'd be lost, lost again. Not lost to a jerk or an asshole who played games or had to cut me down so he wouldn't feel I overshadowed him. Lost in what I'd discovered the hard way was worse. Lost to a dangerous man who could not only get me hurt but who could hurt me worse by getting himself that way.

I didn't share any of this either. I tilted my head, lifted it, pressed my lips to his, slid my tongue in his mouth and I kissed him. Hard. As hard as I could. As hard as I knew how. And I did it deep.

This lasted for a while then it lasted even longer when Hop's arms closed around me. He hauled me out of bed, across his lap, arched me over his arm, and he kissed me. Deep and long.

When he broke the kiss, he twisted me back in bed, pulled the covers up under my arm, tucking them around my back (something else sweet and gorgeous I tried to forget the minute he did it, though not entirely successfully, alas) and he bent in to kiss my temple.

"Later, babe," he muttered then pushed to his feet.

I bit my tongue so I wouldn't call, "Tomorrow?"

I knew it would come out eager or desperate. I wasn't about to be either.

Not again.

I'd learned that lesson the hard way too.

I just curled back around my pillow and watched him round the bed until he disappeared.

Once he did, I waited until I knew he was downstairs before I reached and turned out the light on my bedside table. Then I swung my legs over the side of the bed and got out, yanking hard at the sheet to free it from the end of the bed to take it with me. I wrapped it around my body, tucking it tight, and went to one of the two wide double windows that looked out to the courtyard of my house. Carefully, I slid up one side of the plantation shutters and looked out.

The courtyard was in darkness. My outside lights were not on, but the space was dimly lit by streetlamps in the alley. I saw him move through. I liked the way he moved, just walking. I liked the way he moved other places better.

He went through the back gate and disappeared down the side of my garage.

I slapped the shutters closed, leaned my forehead against them and closed my eyes.

"One night," I whispered. "It was supposed to be safe. Just one night." I pulled in a breath and let it out on a "damn."

I'd picked Hop because I was attracted to him. I'd picked Hop because he was hot. I also picked Hop because I figured he wouldn't say no and he'd also say yes to no strings, no complications, and no entanglements. All the boys were good ole boys, few rules and the ones they had were unwritten and pertained mostly to how they treated their bikes and how they treated their brothers. Anything else went. No. From what I could tell, *everything* else went.

It was not lost on me, however, that there were men amongst Chaos who fell hard and fast and not only didn't mind the fall but also got off on staying down. Tack, Ty-Ty's husband, was one of them. Dog, also a Chaos brother, was another. Brick got lost in every woman he was with. He just didn't pick good ones so eventually they took off, but they did it with him not wanting to let go even when they did it not nice stuff like stealing his money or making a pass at one of his brothers.

So when I decided I was going to approach one of them to get what I needed, what I'd let go on for so long, I was beginning to crave, I needed one who would break the seal and then move on without complications.

I picked poorly because I picked so damned well.

I sighed and banged my head lightly against the shutter.

What I needed.

What I *craved*.

Gah!

I opened my eyes, slid open the shutters, and stared out to the empty courtyard.

"You are seriously stupid, Lanie Heron," I told the window.

I did this because I knew what I craved.

A taste.

Just a taste.

A small, sweet, short taste, even if it was pretend, even if it was milk and I had to imagine it was a thick, rich, vanilla shake, a little sip of what Ty-Ty had with Tack.

I didn't have that with Elliott. I loved him, no doubt about it. I was ready to spend the rest of my life with him. I missed him even though he was totally *whacked*. I'd even made the decision to stay with him knowing he was totally whacked.

I loved him so much I'd taken bullets for him.

But I'd never seen anything like what Tyra had with Tack. I'd never seen a woman get that from a man. I'd never seen the naturalness, the ease of what she gave back. I'd never seen a man and woman able to be just who they were and yet make it so plain to each other and anyone watching they appreciated what they had more than anything.

Anything.

I wanted a taste of that.

"Boy, you got it, Lanie, you big, stupid, crazy, *idiot*." I kept beating myself up just as my phone rang.

My head twisted around to look at it and my eyes narrowed even as my heart skipped.

I knew who it was because this happened all the time.

Nearly midnight my time, wee hours of the morning hers.

"Shoot, shoot, *damn*," I mumbled as I wandered to the phone knowing I shouldn't pick it up. My sister Elissa always told me I shouldn't pick it up. *She* didn't pick it up. She'd learned years ago and stopped doing it, so now she'd stopped calling my sis and called me instead.

Exclusively.

Because I stupidly picked up.

I got to the bed, saw that the display on my phone told me I was right and still—stupid, stupid, stupidly—I picked up.

"Hey Mom," I answered.

"Lanie, baby, howeryoudoin?"

I switched on the light, turned, sat on the side of the bed, lifted my feet up to the padded footboard, knees closed, and dropped my forehead to my knees because I could hear it.

She was gone.

Sloshed.

Well past three sheets—she was five sheets to the wind and sailing.

I was "darling" when she was sober. When she had it together to keep up appearances. When she expended all her energy to be the Connecticut banker's wife and buried the Tennessee farmer's daughter. Even if that Tennessee farmer had enough acreage to build three malls and had been the richest man in the richest family in town, she was still a farmer's daughter and that didn't do, according to her, in Connecticut.

"Good, Mom. It's late. What's up?" I answered.

"Oh, nuthin'. Just wan'ed to talk to my lil' girl."

"You're talking to her, Mom, but it's nearly midnight here. I'm really tired and I should get some sleep. It's even later there so you should get some sleep, too."

"Doan need sleep but *you* need some fun, Lanie. What you doin' home? You shud be owd on the town, paintin' it pink or, bedder, on a date," Mom told me, a bit of what I thought was the cute, countrified twang she'd worked for decades to get rid of coming out in her voice.

This was a constant refrain even when she wasn't drunk out of her mind. Heck, she'd started in on me about five days after I left the hospital, after everything happened with Elliott and the Russian Mob.

Then again, she'd never liked Elliott. "He may be brilliant, darling, but men like him never get very far. Middle ground. My girl? My Lanie? Looks like yours?" She had flicked my hair off my shoulder before she finished by declaring, "Breeding and beauty like yours, darling, you deserve to be on the arm of a star!"

I shoved this memory down and replied, "I've had a tough week at work." This wasn't a total lie. "So I need a quiet weekend." That wasn't a total lie either.

"Okay, quiet is good," Mom returned. "Bedder than you rubbing elbows with Tyra's family. Whad she was thinking, I will nod *ever* know. Such a priddy girl, too. Total *waste*. Her parents must be devastated."

Suffice it to say, not only the Connecticut banker mom but also the Tennessee farmer's daughter mom did not approve of the Chaos MC.

"They're good people, Mom," I told her for the four hundred and fiftieth time.

"They're *bikers*, Lanie."

She said the word "bikers" like uttering those two syllables spontaneously filled her mouth with acid.

"Can we not talk about this?" I asked on a sigh. "Really, it's been a tough week and I'm exhausted."

"Okay, wad d'you wanna talk about?"

I didn't want to talk at all.

I didn't want a lot of things and I hadn't wanted most of them for a long freaking time.

I didn't want my fiancé to be dead.

I didn't want my fiancé to be dead by having been whacked by the Russian Mob.

I didn't want to live with the knowledge, and the guilt, that his antics with the Mob got my best friend kidnapped, twice, and the second time it got her stabbed. Repeatedly.

I didn't want to be alone.

I didn't want to be so damned lonely.

I didn't want to live like I was living—the nightmares, the fear, something no one would understand, something I had to hide so people I cared about didn't get worried.

I didn't want my mom to be wasted...again.

I didn't want to know she was sitting alone in the big house on all that land in that exclusive estate where I grew up, close to the country club, every single resident a snob.

I didn't want to know she was alone because Dad was either working or on a business trip.

I didn't want to know these were his ready and oft-used excuses, otherwise known as flat-out lies, for leaving Mom alone for a night, a weekend, a very long weekend, and all of this so he could be with his mistress of thirty years.

I'd seen him with her more than once. He wasn't careful. He was arrogant. He kept up the pretense of the secret even knowing it wasn't a secret and hadn't been for decades. He even gave Mom filthy looks when she was drinking even though she was drinking because the love of her life had two loves of his and he expected her to share though he'd never asked if she would. So she'd made the decision to do so because he was the love of her life but also because without him, there would be no big house close to the country club and she wouldn't be getting slaughtered on forty-dollar bottles of wine and top-shelf martinis.

"Mom, how about you call me tomorrow? We'll talk then. Now, I really have to get some sleep."

This got me nothing and I knew what that meant. She was pouting. When I was a kid, I wondered if Dad wouldn't have found another woman if Mom hadn't acted like a spoiled brat. It was only later, when I grew up, that I knew it didn't matter if she pouted or was spoiled. You didn't do that to someone you loved.

Not *ever*.

Elliott would never have cheated on me. Other boyfriends had and it hurt. No, it *killed*.

Elliott did not, would not. He didn't even glance at other women when we were out.

For Elliott, it was only me, and if I'd had him for the lifetime I was meant to have him, I would have lived that lifetime knowing, without a doubt, it would always *only* be me.

"Okay, baby girl," Mom slurred, bringing my thoughts back to her. "I'll call you tomorrow."

She didn't sound disappointed, she sounded crushed. She was hurting. She was lonely. She was wondering, as she had been for decades, where she'd gone wrong.

So, of course, I felt daughterly guilt. I should be there for her.

I just couldn't help. I'd tried. I'd failed. Taking these phone calls. Having gentle discussions trying to bring her around to talking about what she was drowning in booze, discussions she always firmly veered in another direction. Sensitive talks about how she might want to lay off the wine a bit, more talks she firmly took in another direction.

Years of it.

I had nothing left to give.

Still, I tried again, "We'll have a long chat, Mom. Promise."

"Okay, baby," she whispered.

"Love you, Mom, to the moon and stars and beyond," I whispered back what I'd whispered to her since I could remember, since I was little and she tucked me in my pink bed with my pink sheets and pink, filmy canopy, my stuffed unicorns all around.

"Love you, Lanie, to the moon and the stars and beyond," she replied quietly the words she'd taught me to say.

"Bye, Mom."

"Bye, baby girl."

I sighed, hit the off button. Then, with my fingers curled around my phone, I put my forehead to my knees.

My life *stunk*.

Every bit of it.

Therefore, I started crying and did it like I did just about everything. I let it all hang out and thus, got lost in it.

This meant, when a hand curled warm and tight around the back of my neck and I heard Hop mutter, "Jesus, baby, what the fuck?" I jumped a foot, screamed a little bit as my head flew up.

He was crouched in front of me, staring at me with his usual intensity, but there was more, a lot more, and all of that was about concern.

When my head came up, his hand didn't move. It tightened.

Warm.

Warm and sweet.

Do...not...process, Lanie!

I stared at him.

Then I blurted, "What are you doing here?"

"Wallet fell out of my jeans," he muttered, his eyes holding mine in a way that, even if I had it in me to try, which I didn't, I couldn't break contact. "Now, what the fuck?" he asked.

"What the fuck, what?" I asked back, trying for innocence. And failing.

His eyes narrowed. It was a little bit scary. Then they dropped to the phone in my hand and came back to mine.

"You're crying." He pointed out the obvious.

"Uh...I do that, like, for no reason. You know, like Holly Hunter in *Broadcast News?* I just cry but, unlike her, I don't do it at my desk at work. I do it at night, um...alone."

He stared at me.

He didn't believe me. This was wise since I was lying.

"It's just a release." I kept lying.

"You gotta wrap your hand around a phone when you do it?" he semi-called me on my lie.

"Wrong number," I lied again, and his eyes stayed narrowed, but this time his hand tightened a bit on my neck.

"At midnight," he stated, not hiding he didn't believe me.

"Someone at a party," I told him (lying). "They asked for Cheez Whiz." More lying. "It's the munchies hour." This wasn't a lie, exactly. It was the munchies hour if you were doing what one *should* do on a Saturday night, which was having fun. It was just that no one had accidentally called me erroneously to ask me to bring the Cheez Whiz.

Hop held my gaze.

I tried not to squirm.

Hop continued to hold my gaze.

I continued to try not to squirm.

Hop's mouth got tight.

I switched to trying not to think that was really sexy, then I switched to trying not to think how weird it was that I thought him looking annoyed was sexy.

He gave up waiting for me to admit I wasn't being honest and slid his hand from my neck while asking, "You done releasing whatever you gotta release at midnight, alone in your room?"

That sounded insane. Mostly because it was.

Oh dear. I was being an idiot.

"Yeah. All good," I lied again.

He didn't believe me and didn't hide that either.

"So, you goin' to bed?" he asked.

"Yeppers!" I answered fake-chirpily. His brows snapped together and his mouth got tight again.

Yeppers?

Yes. I was being an idiot.

"Yeppers?" he asked, and that word coming from his beautiful lips surrounded by his badass 'tache made me want to start giggling.

It also made me want to kiss him.

And last, it made me want to snap at him because, really, couldn't he just let it go?

I decided speaking was not going well for me so I stopped doing it.

Hop again held my gaze.

Then he looked to the floor while straightening to tower over me, and he did this muttering, "I don't get this from her. Complicated."

He didn't get this from me and I didn't get it from him, either.

Had I mentioned my life stunk?

I held my breath and tipped my head back to look at him. He continued to stare down at me before he shook his head a couple of times, and I watched as he moved to the mess of my clothes he'd thrown on the floor a few hours earlier, after he'd peeled them off me. He kicked some aside with his black motorcycle boot, unearthing his wallet. He bent, nabbed it, shoved it in his back pocket and came back to me.

His hand again wrapped around the back of my neck and then his face was in mine.

"Sleep, lady," he ordered, sounding disgruntled, but still it came out gentle.

It sounded nice, even the disgruntled part.

Damn.

"Okay," I replied but didn't move.

Hop stood there, hand at my neck, and he didn't move either.

Then he prompted, "Like, now, Lanie."

I stared at him a second, nodded, my teeth coming out to graze my bottom lip, something his eyes dropped to watch, that something making me want to kiss him again but I didn't.

I broke from his hold, stretched out and he flipped the covers over me.

Then, God, *God,* I used everything I had left not to process him tucking them tight all around me.

So sweet.

Too sweet.

Damn.

He bent low, kissed the side of my head and said against my hair, "See you tomorrow night, babe."

Tomorrow night. Thank *God.*

I tried not to process that I thought that and mumbled, "Okay, Hop."

I got another kiss and my eyes watched him move to the light. He turned it off, plunging the room into darkness.

I didn't watch, didn't hear his boots on the carpet, but I still felt him leave.

I closed my eyes and took in a deep breath.

I opened my eyes as I let the breath go.

"Complicated," my lips mouthed without sound.

After a few more seconds, I heard a Harley roar.

I listened and I did it hard until I could hear the roar no more.

Only then did I close my eyes.

But I did not sleep.

*　　*　　*

Hop

"Repeat it," Dog clipped, and Hop watched as the junkie Dog had pinned against the brick wall with his hand in his chest and the barrel of Dog's gun to the flesh under his chin, swallowed.

Then the junkie stammered, "I...I won't...won't ever make a buy on...on Chaos again."

"Right now, I'm a little put out," Dog informed the junkie, shoving the gun deeper into his flesh, making him squeak in terror. "I see you on Chaos doin' anything but helpin' an old lady cross the street, I'll be unhappy. Heads up, you don't want to make me unhappy."

The junkie, eyes enormous, gulped and nodded.

Dog let him go, saying, "Outta my sight."

The junkie took off.

Hop looked to the dealer he had shoved face-first to the wall with his forearm against the man's shoulders. Hop had disarmed him and currently had the dealer's as well as his own firearm shoved in the back waistband of his jeans under his cut.

Hop's turn.

"Empty your pockets," Hop growled.

"Fuck, man," the dealer whined, and Hop pressed him deeper into the wall, making his face scrape against the rough brick.

"Empty your goddamned pockets," Hop bit out.

With difficulty, the dealer put his hands in his pockets, pulling out small packets of ice and dropping them to the ground. As he did this, Dog moved them aside with the toe of his boot, then he brought the heel down, crushing the methamphetamine into dust as the dealer whimpered.

After this, Dog moved to their bikes, and Hop moved closer to the dealer.

"You know, five miles," he reminded the dealer. "Five miles around Ride is Chaos. You don't sell here. What the fuck?"

"Benito's claimin' this block," the dealer told him.

"Benito doesn't get to claim this block. He knows it, you know it. So again, what the fuck?" Hop asked.

"I go where Benito says," the dealer replied.

Dog was back with a bottle of water, pouring it over the meth dust on the sidewalk and the dealer groaned.

Hundreds, maybe thousands of dollars washed away.

Benito would be pissed and not just at the dealer.

Hop didn't care.

"You stay off this block. You do not come back. Benito sends you back, you find a way to explain to him; you're here, his product is in the sewer. You got this one warning. Chaos doesn't have patience with this shit. You see me, you're fucked, and I don't mean you goin' back empty-handed to that dickhead. I mean, you'll find it difficult to go anywhere 'cause you'll find it difficult to move. You get me?" Hop asked.

"I don't go where Benito sends me, I'll find it difficult to do *anything* seein' as I won't be *breathin'*," the dealer returned.

"Not my problem. You picked the wrong profession, motherfucker," Hop pointed out, pushing him farther into the wall, his arm sliding up to the back of the dealer's neck, extending it unnaturally. "I gotta teach you this lesson now?" Hop asked.

The dealer, hoping for mercy, decided to get generous and shared, "Benito wants Chaos territory."

"No shit?" Hop shot back.

"No, I mean he *really* wants it," the dealer clarified.

Dog entered the conversation. "I think we get that, dealin' with motherfuckers like you."

"He's kinda determined," the dealer went on.

"Again, man, you think we're not in on this fuckin' information?" Hop asked, shoving him hard against the wall before he twisted him around and then slammed him back into the wall with a hand wrapped around his neck. "What Benito has got to get is that Chaos is *more* determined. You feel helpful, you share that with him and try to be convincing. But don't matter if you are. We're happy to put in the work to convince him. What you gotta take with you when we let you walk away right now is, he sends you out of the trenches, we see your head pop up, we're aimin' at *you*. We gotta get our message across to him, we'll use any means necessary and that means takin' out every soldier he sends our way until we drive it back to him."

"Chaos isn't ready for this fight," the dealer replied, and Hop moved so he was in the dealer's face.

"My brothers bled to keep this pavement, fuckwad," he ground out. "You got a brother's blood in the sidewalks, it never goes away, you never let it out of your control, you keep what you fought and bled for. Benito needs to get that. You can't convince him, the other dealers and whores we send back to him can't, *we will*."

The dealer pulled breath in through his nose, stared at Hop before his eyes shifted to the side and he took in Dog then he came back to Hop. What he saw on their faces must have convinced him because he nodded.

"Again, one warning. Next time, you don't walk away," Hop stated.

The dealer nodded again.

Hop jerked his hand up to the dealer's jaw, yanked him away from the wall then slammed his head into it. The dealer cried out before Hop let go and stepped back.

The dealer crumpled to his knees, one hand to his throat, the other one to the back of his head. He tipped his head back, looked at Hop and Dog, got to his feet, and took off.

Hop and his brother watched until the dealer was out of sight.

Then Hop asked, "You callin' this into Tack or you want me to do it?"

"I got it," Dog grunted, pulling out his phone.

"Brother," Hop called, and Dog looked from his phone to Hop. "We patrol every night. Used to be, few and far between, we find this shit. This is the second night this week."

"Escalating," Dog agreed.

Hop turned his head to look down the sidewalk where the dealer had taken off.

Benito Valenzuela had been a minor player years ago but one Tack had heard about and intuitively kept his eye on.

Tack's intuition, as usual, was right.

When things shifted in the underworld of Denver—big players like Darius Tucker opting out of the drug trade,

Marcus Sloan downsizing operations, the Russian Mob losing its leader and reorganizing, amongst other things—Valenzuela saw his opportunity and didn't waste time. He quickly amassed territory however he needed to do it, negotiating for it or going to war for it.

But Benito didn't bother approaching Chaos for a piece of their island.

For over a decade it was known the five square miles around the auto supply store and custom car and bike shop the Chaos MC owned and ran was clean of drugs and whores. The brothers fought for it to be that way and went out every night to keep it that way.

Benito knew better than to ask.

So he was going to take.

Everyone who tried before Benito, and they were very few, left with a Chaos warning.

But the battle to free Chaos, inside and out, of all that shit had been fought so long ago, new players like Valenzuela didn't know or didn't remember how brutal it was. He didn't know how far Chaos would go to keep their patch clean.

Hop remembered how brutal it was. That memory was burned in his brain and inked into his skin, the last just like every Chaos brother.

They didn't need this shit.

Dog started talking and Hop turned his eyes to him.

They didn't need Benito's shit but they were ankle deep in it.

And it was rising.

Hop turned his eyes back to the night, listened to Dog reporting in, and he did this thinking...*fuck*.

After patrol, he wanted to go to Lanie's, take off his clothes, lie his body down in her soft sheets, curl her warmth into his and fall asleep smelling her perfume.

He couldn't do that, for a variety of reasons.

Instead, he did what he had to do. When Dog finished his call with Tack, they moved to their bikes, threw their legs over and resumed patrol.

And when they were done, Hopper went home and laid his body down in his empty bed.

CHAPTER TWO

We've Got Tonight

I WAS ON an upward glide when I heard Hop's voice, low and growly, order, "Enough, lady, come here."

I didn't go there. I kept working his cock, lips, tongue, suction, *and* hand, bobbing and stroking, giving it my all.

His hands, both cupping my head, moved, his fingers sifting into my hair, and he repeated on a half groan, half grunt, "Lanie, enough. Come here."

I ignored him and kept going. Pushing it. Wanting to give it to him. Wanting to drive him wild.

It worked. I knew this when his hips drove up, his hands in my hair pressing down, filling my mouth with his cock. I moaned against it even as he groaned, "*Fuck.*"

I pulled out all the stops and gave him more.

"Goddamn it," he snarled, his hands moving from my hair to under my arms, and I lost purchase on his cock because Hop hauled me up his body and rolled both of us so I was on my back. He was on top of me and he kept snarling but this time in my face even as he thrust inside, plunging deep, filling me, making me whole, "Come here."

I was there, *he* was there and, incidentally, I was coming.

My eyes closed and my head shot back, pressing into the

pillows but only for an instant because his hand drove into my hair, fisting hard.

"Look at me," he growled, thrusting deep, so deep I knew tomorrow I was going to ache. Ache in a good way. Ache like I'd ached every day for thirteen days. An ache I savored. An ache, when it started to fade, I craved having back.

"*Look at me, goddamn it,*" he bit out and, even still coming, getting my fix, feeling the drug that was him course through my veins, I opened my eyes and looked at him.

The minute I did, his neck twisted, his hand in my hair yanked my head back, he buried his face in my throat and groaned deep against my skin as he buried himself to the hilt inside me and gave back what I gave him.

My arms were already around him, but as he felt it, I wrapped my legs around him too and tightened both, holding him close as I came down. Holding him close as he came down. Waiting for it. The aftermath, the sweet crash I savored after the high.

I blinked at the ceiling when it didn't come. When I didn't feel the tickle of his mustache against my skin. The nourishment of his lips moving there. The nectar seeping in of his tongue on me.

I would know why when he lifted his head, looked down at me and I saw, regardless of the fact he just had an orgasm, Hopper Kincaid was *pissed.*

"Who has to clean up now?" he clipped and I blinked again.

Oh God, he didn't use a condom.

Damn! He didn't use a condom!

His hips pressed into mine and he kept talking, his words curt and angry. "I tell you to come here, Lanie, you fucking," he dipped his face closer to mine, "come *here.*"

He'd never been pissed at me and, looking into his face darkened with anger, not hunger, it scared the pants off me—though, obviously, I wasn't wearing pants.

Still.

"Hop—" I began, but he interrupted me.

"I wanna come in your mouth, Lanie, I'll come in your mouth. The big clue you got that I don't is when I tell you to," he paused and his face got darker and scarier, "*come here*."

"I was—" I began again only to get interrupted again.

"Not listening."

"I know, but the thing is—" I tried again only to fail again.

"The thing is, you gotta listen. You don't, you drive me there, you get what you want but maybe not where you want it. I come *in you*, Lanie. You know that. You got two weeks of knowin' that shit."

He was not wrong.

Before I could say a word, he did.

"I also don't come on my gut. I give it, somewhere in you, you're gonna take it. That said, I think we established the other night you don't like it in your mouth so what the fuck?"

He was not wrong about that either.

My voice was small when I told him, "I wanted to make you wild."

"Well, you got that, babe," he shot back then bit out with no small amount of sarcasm, "excellent work."

As I felt the uncomfortable throb of his sarcasm hit me straight in the belly, he pulled out, rolled off me *and* my bed.

I rolled to my side, pulled the sheets up my front, and got up on an elbow.

"Hop—" I called as he immediately bent and nabbed his jeans.

He twisted to me even as he began to get dressed. "You on the pill?"

Scared to speak in the face of his anger and the not insignificant fact it looked like he was preparing to leave, I nodded.

"Thank Christ for that," he muttered as he yanked his jeans to his hips and, not bothering to button them, he bent to tag his tee.

Okay, I didn't know why but that kind of hurt.

I stopped trying to speak and watched him dress.

Night two of thirteen that he would leave me before dawn.

He snatched up his socks and boots, prowled to the bed, sat on the side but down toward the end where I wasn't close and he pulled them on while speaking.

"Sharin' info I'd rather not and wouldn't have to if you didn't pull that shit. Since it began with you, it's only been you." He yanked on a boot but twisted his neck, still bent toward his feet, and pinned me with his eyes. "Before you, babe, I was not abstaining. I use protection but shit happens."

I pressed my lips together.

"Like tonight," he went on.

My teeth came out to skim my lower lip. His eyes dropped to them like they always did when I did that, but this time his face didn't get soft and gentle or hard and hungry. He looked angry(er).

Then his eyes came back to mine. "Though not as good, which sucks 'cause I liked it even if I'm pissed as all fuck about it," he finished, turned back to his boot, and tugged it on.

All right, maybe that was good news. He liked it.

He straightened from the bed, turned and glared down at me.

"Later, Lanie," he grunted.

He was leaving.

As usual, without a word, he stalked out of my room, but not as usual, he didn't pull the covers around me, tuck me in, turn out the light or kiss me.

He was just ... *gone*.

I looked over my shoulder toward the door and I stared at it.

I did this a long time.

Hop didn't come back.

I kept staring.

Hop still didn't come back.

As I stared, I refused to process how much I didn't want him gone. I refused to process how disturbed I was by that scene. I refused to process how upsetting I found it that I made him angry. I refused to process how troubling I found it that he was angry but he didn't let me speak and then he stormed out still not letting me speak.

Instead, in order to keep successfully not processing all that, I shifted off the bed and moved to the bathroom to clean up. Making light work of that, I moved out of the bathroom, grabbed a clean pair of panties, pulled them on and grabbed a short, pale pink, satin nightie with thick black lace at the bodice and hem and tugged that on.

Still forcing myself to think nothing, I moved to the bed, got in, pulled up my own damned covers, tucked in my own damned self, and turned out the light.

I settled in and stared into the darkness.

Hop was pissed.

Hop was gone.

Hop was the kind of man who didn't let you get a word in edgewise when you were somewhat arguing, but you were also somewhat *not* arguing because he wouldn't let you get a stinking, stupid word in edgewise.

Hop was the kind of man who got mad at you because you gave head *too good*. Then he stormed out because you gave fantastic blowjobs that made him so wild, he buried himself inside you and forgot to put on a condom.

Therefore it was good Hop was gone because if Hop was there, I would have kicked him out.

"So that's it. You got nothing?"

My body jerked in the bed as his voice came from the door and something occurred to me.

I was so busy trying not to think, I didn't hear his Harley roar.

I switched on the light, got up to my booty in the bed, shoulders to the headboard, and saw him casually leaning against my doorjamb. There was nothing casual about the look on his face.

Still pissed but now, *more*.

"Two weeks, you got nothing?" he asked.

"What?" I asked back.

"So that's it," he said again and I stared at him, perplexed.

"What's it?" I queried.

He pushed from the doorjamb, took one step into the room, stopped and planted his hands on his hips.

Unfortunately, all his hotness heated up significantly, hands on slim hips and handsome face angry.

Fortunately, I was not only perplexed, I was getting angry, so this didn't affect me as it normally would.

"Lanie, you throw a shit fit when your soda fizzes over. The man you're fuckin' gets pissed and takes off, you got nothin'? You just put on a nightie, turn out the light and go to sleep?"

I felt my eyes get wide as I pointed out, "Hopper, you didn't give me the chance to *give* anything."

"You didn't take your chance," he shot back.

"Are you serious?" I asked, hoping he wasn't.

"Do I look serious?" he asked back and I studied him.

He did. In fact, he *seriously* looked serious.

Something else hit me and I felt my brows shoot together. "Was that a test?"

He shook his head as he took his hands from his hips and crossed his arms on his chest, which was unfortunate because that pose assumed by a badass biker with kickass tattoos of flames on his sinewy forearms was even hotter. By...*a lot.*

"No. Don't play games," he announced. "Don't wanna know what kind of men you've had in your bed before me outside of the one I *do* know so, since I know about him, you gotta know, I get it. No offense to the dead, but unless he had Superman under all that geek, babe, I know whatever you got from him you liked, but it wasn't what you get from me."

He was not wrong about that.

Hop kept going.

"But the way I like it, you've had night after night of comin' to know. So you knew what you were doin' and you also knew, I said, 'come here,' you come there. You know you'll get your times to play, but you also know *I'll* fuckin' give them to you. That's the way I roll, the *only* way I roll. And last, you know you get off on that so do not try to bullshit that you don't. So, no games. You pulled that shit anyway, knowin' I wouldn't be down with it so I was pissed. Then I sat on my bike, thinkin' I shouldn't haul ass but come back and work it out, and as I was decidin', I saw your light go out. You didn't phone me. You didn't text me. You didn't even call my fuckin' name as I walked out. I'm here, I'm gone, all the same to you. So, again, I'll ask, that's it?"

I wasn't entirely certain I understood his question, but at the same time, scarily, I thought I did.

I went with what I thought but did it gently, "Honey, you know we don't have that."

I found I was right when his mouth got tight right before it opened to say, "And you know, two weeks, no cool down, fuck, if anything, our fire is blazing brighter; that's bullshit."

Oh God.

"Hop—"

"Or I thought so until your fuckin' light went out."

He stared at me.

I stared at him.

Neither of us spoke.

This time, Hop didn't break it and it went on so long, it felt like the silence had become a weight and it started getting heavy on me. Heavy in a way I couldn't breathe.

I had to breathe. I had to let something out. Therefore, I had to share.

Just a little bit.

"I don't have anything to give, Hop."

His response was immediate. "That's bullshit, too."

I shook my head.

He shook his, dropped his arms from his chest and came farther into the room, stopping at the foot of the bed.

"Tyra will get it," he declared then added, "eventually, and if she doesn't, who gives a fuck? We do."

I felt my breath catch.

We do.

He got it.

I got it.

We got it.

We absolutely did.

It was a drug for him like it was for me. He was my crack. I was his.

He'd just admitted it but I already knew it.

Thirteen nights, dark until dawn.

Feeling the hollowing of my belly whenever he left.

Counting the minutes until he came back.

I liked that he got it. I did. God, I did.

But I couldn't let myself like it.

I also could absolutely not let myself have it.

"It isn't Tyra," I told him.

"You told her about us?" he asked instantly.

I shook my head again.

"It's Tyra," he stated, and he was right but only sort of.

"It's more, Hop," I informed him.

"Share," he ordered on a clip, leaning in slightly and visibly losing patience.

"You don't get that," I said softly and carefully.

"Fuck me, babe, seriously?" he ground out then threw a hand toward the bed. "You knocked yourself out to make me wild. You told me your fuckin' self. Why, Lanie? Why the fuck would you pull out all the fuckin' stops to make a man already drunk on you *drunker*?"

Oh God.

He was drunk on me.

Drunk.

On.

Me.

I knew it but it felt good that he said it, right out, no lies, no hiding, no games.

My mind screamed, *Do not process that, Lanie!*

"I was just—" I started, scrambling to hold myself together.

Hold myself back.

"Don't deny it, babe. Remember *you* came to *me*."

"For one night," I reminded him.

His hands went back to his hips as he bit out, "Jesus, that's bullshit too."

"It isn't, Hop. I told you then exactly how it was," I returned.

"You lied then and you're lyin' now."

"I'm not."

"You are."

"I'm not," I snapped but it didn't sound angry. Stupidly, I didn't control it and it came out sounding desperate.

His head jerked. He heard it.

Then he gave it to me.

"You're searchin' for it, same as me. If you haven't found it, fuck, babe, same as *anybody*."

No, no I wasn't searching for it. I was, years ago. Then I thought I'd found it. Then I lost it.

And I wouldn't even allow myself to think he was searching.

"I'm not," I denied.

"Serious as shit, Lanie, that's bullshit too, worse than the rest 'cause you're not only tryin' to feed me that shit, you're forcin' it down your own fuckin' throat."

This had to stop.

I shook my head. "What you asked earlier—I'm sorry, honey, but the truth is, yes, that's it." I shrugged, hoping for nonchalant. "You're gone, lights out."

His eyes narrowed in that scary, sexy way, and suddenly he moved and he did it *fast*. He was no longer at the foot of the bed but up it, knee in the mattress, arm around my waist, other hand behind my neck, both hauling me up with such power and speed my body slammed into his.

I made an *oof* noise, but that was all I got out before his hand at my neck moved, went between us, and my nightgown was yanked up my belly.

I felt myself instantly get wet as my body stilled.

I stared into his eyes trying to breathe as his hand at my midriff slid back down, slow, light. I shivered but he wasn't starting something, something fabulous, like angry fighting sex that might lead, hopefully much later, to non-angry make-up sex.

He was saying something.

My still body turned to stone when his fingers stopped.

No, not when.

Where.

"You can't hide it," he whispered, and I felt them, tears crawling up to choke me, biting the backs of my eyes, but I wouldn't shed them.

No way.

I couldn't give that to him.

I didn't have it left to give.

"From the very first time, baby, I saw them. I saw them all. You can't hide them," he went on.

I stared at him, unmoving, not speaking.

"Here," he ran his fingers lightly across the ridge on my belly. My scar. One of three. Opened up by a bullet, opened bigger by a scalpel. "Here." He moved his hand to the pucker that ran along the top of my left thigh then his hand lifted. "And here," he finished, his finger lifting to the mark that marred the skin just under my right breast.

I kept staring at him, unmoving, not speaking.

He held my eyes as his hand moved again, sliding down my arm, his fingers curling around my hand. He lifted our hands, pushed them between our bodies and pressed mine, palm flat, against my chest.

Against my beating heart.

"That's you alive, Lanie," he kept whispering, then his head moved, coming my way, his lips hit the side of mine, his mustache tingling against my skin as his mouth slid along my cheek to my jaw and down, to my neck where he stopped and murmured against my pulse. "Feel you alive here, too, lady."

I closed my eyes, my hand against my chest closing in a fist, my other hand lifting and curling into the fabric of the sleeve of his tee.

His lips and whiskers slid up to the skin just under my ear where he stated, "I'm right. You know it. You're hiding. Right out in the open, Lanie, you're trying to hide. Hide from me. Hide from everybody. I don't know about everybody, lady, but you gotta know, you're not hiding from me."

I dropped my head, my forehead hitting his shoulder, and I admitted, "I can't do this."

"You won't," he returned.

"I can't," I parried.

"You won't," he repeated.

I pulled in breath then did what I had to do.

For me.

For my protection.

For my sanity.

I stated, "Okay then, Hopper, I won't."

I felt his whiskers prickle against my neck harder than normal as he shoved his face deep before he lifted his head and looked in my eyes.

"Okay, lady, so you won't. But we got tonight."

We had tonight.

Tonight.

Just tonight.

I could do that.

I could give myself tonight.

One more night of not being alone. One more night of not being lonely.

One more night of the drug that was Hop.

"We've got tonight," I agreed.

His head dipped forward, his forehead coming to rest on mine as he closed his eyes, and I felt it coming from him, the same thing I felt deep inside me, and my stomach hollowed out again in a way I knew it would never, ever feel full.

And it was then I realized I'd felt hollow a really fucking long time.

It was just that I really didn't need to know that Hop felt the same way.

I had this realization for about a second before his mouth moved to mine and he kissed me—not hard, but deep, wet, long and unbearably, excruciatingly *sweet*.

Hop pressed his torso to mine, taking me to my back, kissing me sweetly the entire time, his hands moving on me, under my nightie, whisper-soft against my skin, making me shiver, making my skin tingle, and then he did to me what he'd never done to me. He took his time. He was thorough. It lasted forever and it was beautiful. The most beautiful thing I'd ever experienced.

Beyond the best I'd ever had. It was the best I'd ever have.

And what it was was Hopper Kincaid making love to me.

After, when my mind was shut down, my body languorous, my limbs wound around the sheets, the pillow he'd tucked under me held tight, I watched him walk to the bathroom and then I watched him walk back.

He didn't grab his jeans.

He didn't grab me for another go.

He switched off the light, and I felt the sheets tugged gently away, the pillow pulled out and thrown to the head of the bed, his warm, long, lean, strong body sliding into bed beside mine, the sheets and comforter pulled up and, finally, he tugged me close and held tight.

"Hop—" I whispered the start of my objection into his chest where my cheek lay.

His arm tight around my back gave me a squeeze. "We've got tonight."

I shut up.

Hop's hand found mine, curled around it, and pulled it up his chest where he rested it, and I could feel his heart beating, strong and true, against the back of my hand.

I closed my eyes tight.

"One more thing I want from you, Lanie," he said into the dark, and I closed my eyes tighter.

I'd give him one thing. I'd give him a million things. I'd give him anything.

I knew that in my bones.

That wasn't about great sex.

That was about him tucking the covers around me before he turned out the lights.

I didn't tell him that.

I didn't say anything.

Hop didn't need me to.

His arm again squeezed and, this time, stayed tight. "Those bullets tore through you, baby," he said gently, and I felt my body tense. His other hand let mine go, came up, and slid into the side of my hair, holding my head to his chest as he kept talking. "But you didn't leak out. You're still here. You lost blood, Lanie, and someone you loved. But you're still here. Give me one more thing before this is over and promise me you'll try to find it in you to remember that."

So he would stop talking, I gave him what he wanted even if it was a lie.

"I promise, Hop."

"Good," he muttered, his hand pressing lightly against my head then sliding out of my hair, his palm gliding against my cheek before it fell away and he finished, "Sleep, lady."

Sleep, lady.

I memorized his deep voice wrapping around those soft words as I replied, "Okay."

My cheek rose as his chest rose to take in a deep breath.

My body relaxed as his chest fell when he let it out.

I paid attention and I kept doing it until I fell asleep and I knew I fell asleep before Hopper did.

But I slept deeply.

I knew this because, hours later, when I woke up, he was gone.

*   *   *

That night, I sat on the couch, heels to the edge, knees to my chest, arms around my calves, chin to my knees, staring at it.

Staring hard.

I didn't ever look at it. I didn't even know why I'd put it there. I didn't know why I didn't hide it away. Pack it up in a box and shove it into the back of a closet so when I moved or when I died and someone went through my stuff, they'd find it and wonder. Wonder what it was. Who it was. And if they knew, they'd wonder why I kept it.

I stared hard.

Then my feet came out from under me, hitting the floor as I straightened out off the couch, walked to it, and snatched it off the shelf.

I brought it to my face.

Elliott and me. Arms around each other, my head on his shoulder.

Smiling.

Happy.

I stared at the picture.

I brought it closer, my eyes moving over his face in the only place it could ever be anymore, contained in a frame, and I found my lips whispering, "You got yourself killed, nearly got me the same way, got Tyra stabbed for... fucking...*flowers.*"

Elliott had no reply.

"You fucking *asshole,*" I hissed.

Elliott made no response.

My body twisted, my arm going with it, and the frame flew across the room, slamming against the wall, the glass shattering before the frame fell and the shards tinkled to the ground.

I glared at it for long moments before I stomped to my purse, yanked out my iPod, and stomped to my stereo. I shoved the little thingie on the cord that led to my stereo into the little thingie on the top of the iPod, turned on the stereo, bent my head and moved my thumb on the pad until I found it.

Bob Seger & the Silver Bullet Band: *Nine Tonight (Live).*

I scrolled to the track, hit play, and walked to the couch, resuming my position, staring at my stereo as the crowd cheered then went silent as the piano started up and Bob started singing "We've Got Tonight."

I listened to the words.

When the song ended, I got up, hit back, and played it again.

I listened to the words.

When it ended, repeat.

And repeat.

Again.

And again.

I did not cry.

I would not cry.

Not ever again.

I didn't have it in me.

I had nothing left to give.

I not only had nothing left to give, I just had nothing.

And I was going to keep it that way.

If you had nothing, you couldn't feel more pain because you had nothing left to lose.

CHAPTER THREE

My Eye on You

Three weeks later...

"Uh...Lanie, honey, where's the frame?"

I was smiling at Tack, who was standing in my doorway waiting for Tyra to pull the lead out and follow him to his bike, but at my best friend's words I felt my smile freeze on my face.

Tack didn't miss it.

Tack, the single-most decent man I'd ever met (regardless of how much he swore, which was maybe more than Hop did), was also the smartest.

He didn't miss anything.

So when my smile froze, his sapphire-blue eyes dropped to my mouth and his dark brows snapped together.

I pulled in breath and looked to Ty-Ty.

"What frame?" I asked. It was a lie and, worse, I knew Tack would know it.

Tyra did, too.

This wasn't a surprise. She knew me well. We'd been friends a long time.

Kane "Tack" Allen was tall, dark, handsome, and rough.

He was also very smart, very loyal, very funny, and very in love with my best friend.

Tyra Allen was curvy, redheaded, green-eyed, and not rough in the slightest. She was also far from dumb, very loyal, very funny, very in love with her husband, and very true to me.

She and I had been through a lot even before we'd been kidnapped together years ago because of Elliott's problems with the Russian Mob. Although she'd been tied up and kept in a dark room while I was interrogated by the Mob, and we'd been rescued separately, when you've shared something like being kidnapped, bonds formed, even if the bonds already there were strong.

Sometime later, the day I'd been shot and Elliot had been killed, Tyra had been kidnapped, tied to a chair, and stabbed repeatedly.

Tack pulled out all the stops and paid a fortune to have a plastic surgeon erase her scars.

Mine still marred my skin. A reminder, a strong one, never to forget.

Tyra also came and got me from Connecticut, rescuing me from the dysfunction I'd moved to Denver to escape in the first place. She thought she was rescuing me from something else, and I let her think that. I don't know how convincing I was. I just knew Ty-Ty was letting it lie. She had me in Denver, under her watchful eye and close enough to feel her comforting hand. When that hand needed to form a velvet-gloved iron fist was anyone's guess.

I just knew by the look on her face it would not be now.

Even so, Tyra had looked askance at that frame of Elliott and me tons of times. I even once caught her giving Tack eyes about it, jerking her head toward it, whereupon he shook his head. She bugged out her eyes. He rolled his to the ceiling. She crossed her arms on her chest and glared at him. As for me, I pretended I missed all this when I didn't.

Suffice it to say, Elliott wasn't her favorite person. He got me kidnapped. He got her kidnapped, twice. He got me shot, repeatedly. He got her stabbed, repeatedly.

So Elliott, even dead, was *persona non grata*.

As he should be.

For years, Ty-Ty had simply looked askance at the photo but ignored it and didn't mention Elliott. I knew this was partially because, even though he was dead, she was pissed at him for getting me hurt, not to mention getting her hurt. This was also because her husband was loyal and he adored her, and Elliott got her hurt. If Elliott were still breathing, it was pretty clear that Tack would make sure he wasn't doing that for much longer. The breathing part, that was.

As for me, I didn't mention Elliott. Not ever. My fiancé nearly got my best friend dead. Once we found out about his dealings with the Mob, Tyra advised me strongly to break it off with him. I stuck by his side. She was right. I was wrong. But we both paid for me being wrong, and I didn't go there. I didn't go there because all I had in me was the ability to rejoice that she didn't turn her back on me after I nearly got her killed. I held onto that like the lifeline it was. Like I was never going to let it go, and no way I was going to bring him up, my decision to stay with him, and rock that boat.

So, obviously, it being an unspoken bone of contention, she wouldn't miss the photo being gone.

And equally obviously, I was not going to share that I'd thrown it against a wall, shattering the glass. I also was not going to share that I then obsessively listened to Bob Seger singing "We've Got Tonight" because every word in that song was true, even as I wouldn't allow myself to admit that it was. I was further not going to share that I'd had my "night."

That night was with Hop (as were the thirteen before—and I was not going to share that either) and, at the time, it hadn't even been a day, but I was already jonesing for a drug I had to get off cold turkey.

No rehab to help me deal with losing my high.

I had to get through it on my own.

And I damned well would.

So the frame and glass and the stupid picture of me and my dead fiancé had long since been taken away by the garbage man. As had all the other pictures I had in albums upstairs. As had my wedding gown that I didn't get to wear, that I kept for some ridiculous reason, that cost a mint, but I didn't even give it to Goodwill or anything.

No one needed that bad juju.

So the garbage man took it to where it belonged. The dump.

At my fake-innocent question as to what frame they were referring to, Ty-Ty's eyes slid to Tack. Mine did too.

He was looking at his boots.

In the years I'd known Tack Allen, I'd learned all the meanings of him looking at his boots. These were threefold.

One, he didn't want Ty-Ty to see he found her amusing, and this was solely when she was ticked at him, which she would not find amusing that he found it amusing, but he mostly always did.

Two, he was ticked at one of his kids—the older two, Rush and Tabby, that he'd had with another woman—not Cutter and Rider, the boys he had with Tyra. As an older dad on his second time around, he had all the patience in the world with Cut and Rider. This was good, seeing as they were still little boys, but they were also total hooligans (and thus why they weren't with us right then, ruining a relaxing dinner, but with Big Petey, a vintage member of the MC, likely destroying his house). Tack being ticked at Rush and Tab came rarer now, as they were older, and he looked at his boots when he was trying to stop himself from shouting or, maybe, strangling them.

Three, he was with Tyra and me and—for whatever reason we were squabbling, gossiping, or giggling—he was not going to get involved.

Luckily, my eyes went back to Tyra before hers came to me.

I tried to come up with an answer to anything she might say.

Surprisingly, she didn't say anything. Not about the frame or my lie.

Instead, she said, "Nothing, honey," as she walked to me, wrapped her arms around me, tighter than usual, and gave me a long hug. "Thanks for dinner," she said in my ear.

"Yeah, babe, good food," Tack called to me from his place at the door, and my eyes moved over Tyra's shoulder to him.

I smiled.

Tack did not.

He tipped up his chin, but his gaze stayed glued to mine, intense. Somewhat like how Hop looked at me, minus the admiration and, obviously, the sex or foreplay, but adding open contemplation I had a really bad feeling about.

Tyra let me go, and I tore my eyes from Tack to smile into hers.

"Thanks for coming," I said to her and I chanced looking back at her husband.

"Don't have to thank me for sittin' down at a table with two beautiful women and good, bona fide, Southern cooking," Tack replied and, finally, I smiled a genuine smile.

One thing my mom didn't try to leave behind in

Tennessee was her cooking. She did it all the time, and she taught me and Elissa how to do it like her momma did with her, and Mamaw's mom did with her, and so on.

She did this because she often tried to be a good mom. She also did this because it was tradition. But it stunk because I knew she did this mostly because Dad loved her cooking. Or, more aptly, he loved that whenever they had dinner parties, people would shower him (yes, *him*) with glowing compliments about how he was smart enough to marry a woman who knew how to make honest-to-good-ness, down-home meals.

Needless to say, learning to cook in the Southern tradition, I grew up in Connecticut, but I didn't know you could steam vegetables until I moved to Denver. As far as I knew, they were either fried in an iron skillet with butter or breaded or battered and dropped in hot fat.

Luckily, I had the metabolism of a sixteen-year-old high school point guard.

Also luckily, my cooking was good enough for Tack to mention it (again) and get everyone's mind off the frame.

"Anytime, anything you want, Tack. Just call and your wish is my command," I offered, as Tyra and I walked to him at the door.

"Don't offer that. He does most of the cooking. He'll be over three times a week to get a break," Tyra told me, a smile in her voice.

I kept my mouth shut mostly because having them come over three times a week would be fine by me, and I didn't want them to know that. It would expose too much. But the truth was, I'd run an advertising agency and I'd rush home and fry chicken and make a pecan pie from scratch all the way down to the crust if it meant three nights of not being alone, watching TV or worse, what I'd been doing lately:

listening to Bob Seger's slow songs with candles burning and doing everything to ignore the gaping void in my belly, which meant I did nothing but think of the gaping void in my belly.

"Next time, my turn," Tack rumbled, bending to touch his lips to my cheek.

His goatee tickled my skin.

At the feel of it, the memories it invoked, that gaping void I could never stop thinking about widened, consuming vast areas of my body, making me feel empty from throat to toes.

I hid this as his head came up and I smiled into his eyes.

He stared into mine even as his hand came out, and his fingers curled around mine tight before, just as quickly, they disappeared.

Tack Allen never missed anything.

Not anything.

Ever.

Damn.

I gave Tyra another hug and then stood on my front porch, lights on, another Southern tradition my mom taught me, and waved at them until they were out of sight.

This bugged Tack. I knew it because Tyra told me he wanted me to stop doing it. He wanted me in the house, door closed and locked before they rolled away.

That was sweet and I tried but I couldn't do it. Years of training ingrained in me forbid it. I shared this with Tack; he roared with laughter and shut up about it.

I went into the house, turned off the porch light, closed the door, and locked it.

Then I went to the windows, opened the plantation shutters, and peeked out.

Long moments elapsed before I heard the roar of his bike then I saw them slide by.

Yes, Tack shut up about it.

He also rounded the block and came back to check all was quiet at Lanie's house before he and Tyra headed up the mountain.

I watched them disappear and smiled at the street, happy I had good friends, and happy my best friend had found a good man.

Then I slid the shutters closed and headed to the bottle of wine.

Minutes later, glass of wine in hand, candles lit, I moved to the stereo.

*　　*　　*

I lay there bleeding, the phone I used to dial 911 several feet away.

Too far to reach. I could hear the voice of the 911 operator calling from the phone, but I was too weak to reach for it.

All I could do was lie on the carpet and feel the warm, sickening rush of blood pooling around my body.

And all I could see was Elliott, five feet in front of me, on his back, his head turned to the side, his eyes open wide and lifeless.

He was dead but he still looked surprised.

I put myself in front of bullets for him.

He didn't put himself in front of me. I put myself in front of him.

I knew this was not why he was surprised.

I knew he was surprised I didn't save him.

*　　*　　*

I came awake with a jerk, my torso swinging up, breaths coming in gasps, heart beating a mile a minute, the dream still having a hold of me.

No, not a dream.

A nightmare.

A memory.

I sucked in breaths. They came shallow so I forced them deep and I listened hard.

They weren't out there. They were never out there. It was memory coming through as a dream. Just as it often did.

Tack had taken care of Gregori Lescheva. The Russian Mob was no longer interested in me. They had their revenge. It was lying in a grave fifteen miles away from my house.

I was safe.

I didn't feel that way.

I jerked my head around and looked at the clock.

Twelve-oh-two. I'd been asleep about an hour.

I pulled in one last breath then threw the covers off me. I got up and went to the walk-in closet. I flipped the switch on the outside and walked in, looking around at the rails stuffed full of clothes.

Mom and Dad got me gift certificates for everything. If I took a breath, one would wing its way from Connecticut and land in my mailbox as a celebration.

Guilt money. Guilt for Dad being a jerk and Mom being weak. Just like my car. They knew I left Connecticut to escape their lunacy, the heartbreak that lived and breathed and festered all around. So, in true Dad fashion, he'd bought me a car that cost hundreds of thousands of dollars to try to wash away the feel of living amongst love gone bad.

I accepted it. I accepted everything. It was too much hassle not to—Mom's pouting, Dad's disappointment.

Elissa didn't buy into the lie. My sister didn't go home for Christmas. She didn't call on Thanksgiving. She didn't put up with their shit. She'd drawn that line years ago and lived without parents.

"Why do I need them when I've got you?" she'd asked me.

Sweet, loving, loyal. Then again, that was my Lis. All of that in spades.

By the way, Lis hated Elliott too. She'd loved him, probably for the reasons I loved him, before he died. After he died and how he did, nearly taking me with him, not so much.

I carefully selected an outfit and shoes. Grabbing them I dashed to my bed and laid them out. At the dresser, I carefully selected underwear. I had a lot to choose from. I didn't pay attention to just how much lingerie was shoved into my drawer or to my room, with its cream walls, which held a hint of pink, the tall, huge king-sized bed with its colossal, sweeping, padded headboard and matching footboard. The expensive sheets and shams. The wide, round, antique white nightstands with their curved, elegant legs. The smooth, shining, crystal-based lamps.

All the trappings of home.

Thinking of it, suddenly feeling suffocated, I rushed to the bathroom, bent under the vanity, and pulled out my basket of makeup. Leaning over the basin, I applied it, *all* of it, and there was a lot.

On to my hair, spritzing and squirting and spraying and teasing until it was out *to there*. I pulled just the top back in pins an inch from my forehead then teased and sprayed the hair at my crown so it was taller.

Sluttier.

Out to the bedroom I went and pulled on the scanty, sexy, lacy black demi-bra and teeny-weeny panties. The short jeans skirt. The tight, nearly see-through white blouse with its wide collar, close sleeves, long cuffs with a dozen small pearl buttons each; the buttons down the front didn't start until mid-cleavage.

On to the jewelry box. Big hoops. A wide silver choker. Lots of silver rings.

Spritz of perfume. Another one. More.

High-heeled platform sandals with sassy ankle straps.

I turned out the lights, teetered downstairs, grabbed my purse and keys, and headed to my car.

I'd never done this before, not in my life.

But I was alive, breathing.

Alive.

Hop told me so.

Time to start living.

I walked through the courtyard, opened the back door to the garage, hit the garage door opener, swung into my car, pulled out, and headed into the night.

* * *

I was alive, breathing.

Living.

And I'd fucked everything up.

I knew this because I was in the dark parking lot of a biker bar, lured there because I was more than a hint drunk, far more than a hint stupid, and thus an easy mark.

The guy said he had big tires on his truck, huge, taller than me.

That was something I had to see.

The girl came with us. She was there to set me up. What she thought would happen to me after she backed away and disappeared into the night, I didn't know. I just knew she didn't care, which made her, officially, the number-one biggest bitch in history.

Setting up a sister?

She should be stripped of membership.

Of course, if I made it through this alive and breathing

and hopefully not violated, I would approach the Council of the Sisterhood and ask them to see to this immediately.

Unfortunately, there wasn't a Sisterhood Council to report bitches to.

Alas.

Also unfortunately—much more so—it didn't look like I would make it through this not violated.

The alive and breathing part was up for grabs.

"Seriously, I want to go back inside," I told him, pushing against his big, doughy body, smelling beer on his breath.

He had me pinned up against the tire of his truck and, bad news, it *was* taller than me. So was he.

"Baby," he ran his hand up the outside of my hip, "don't play this game. You were all over me."

"We danced," I reminded him, trying logic first. Just in case a miracle happened, he'd see it and back off without an ugly scene. At the same time, pushing harder, wishing my purse, which he'd pulled off my arm and thrown to the ground, was closer since my phone was in it, and wondering if anyone would hear me scream. "That's hardly all over you."

His head dipped and his mouth went to my neck. I felt his tongue, damp and sloppy there.

At that, I also felt bile slide up my throat and pushed harder, definitely deciding to scream.

"You danced close," he muttered against my neck, pushing me further into the tire, which didn't feel real great.

"I did not." And I hadn't. We were line dancing, for goodness' sakes!

His hand was gliding up my side and getting close to my breast.

Okay. Time to scream.

And, possibly, engage my fingernails.

I opened my mouth to do just that, heaving at the same time when, suddenly, his face was not in my neck and his body was not pressing me into the tire.

No, I watched with some fascination, some awe, and some queasiness as his head snapped back unnaturally and his body went with it. The former did this because Hop had his fist in the guy's hair and the latter did this because Hop had his arm around the guy's chest.

Although I was thrilled beyond belief that I was no longer against the tire and someone was there to save me (although I wouldn't have picked Hopper for obvious reasons, at that point, I was also not going to quibble), I wasn't sure this was good. The guy was a jerk. Not to mention, he was huge. He had to have three inches and fifty pounds on Hop.

It was then I watched with some fascination, a lot more awe, and no queasiness—because there was so much awe there wasn't room for queasiness—as Hop beat the absolute *crap* out of the guy.

He did this swiftly, methodically, effortlessly, viciously, and with what appeared a good deal of practice.

It took him, maybe, three minutes.

I watched the whole thing, frozen, with my mouth open.

When the bloodied, unconscious mountain of beefy jerk dropped to the pavement of the dark parking lot, I stared at him lying there, not moving.

"You. Bike. Now."

The queasiness came back but it was different. This time it came in the form of fear. Fear caused simply by the low, lethal, enraged tone of Hopper's voice.

Slowly, my eyes rose to his.

Yes, enraged.

And lethal.

Oh dear.

"Hop—"

"Lanie, swear to God, swear to *God...*" he trailed off, lifted a hand in my direction, palm up, and scowled at me. Then he dropped his hand and bit off, "You. Bike. Fucking *now.*"

I decided it might be prudent to go with him to his bike even though my car was right here in the parking lot.

The problem was, I didn't know which one was his bike. There were around seven thousand of them lined up outside the bar.

"Uh..." I mumbled. He lunged toward me and I found myself back against the tire again, but this time I'd pressed myself there.

I wasn't there long.

Hop clamped his hand around mine. He yanked me away from the tire, pulled me three steps, stopped only to bend and snatch up my purse, twist around and toss it at me. Luckily, I caught it. Then I and my platform sandals teetered unsteadily but very quickly behind Hop as his ground-eating strides took us to a black Harley.

He let me go and threw a leg over.

As he did this, still being prudent (belatedly), I studied his movements.

Big Petey, a member of Chaos, a *founding* member, thus not a spring chicken, had taken me out on his Harley Trike, and he'd done this numerous times.

Big Petey was in his sixties, and a Harley Trike was not even close to what this sleek, kickass machine was in front of me.

Big Petey was nice and he cared about me.

He was not lean, mean Hopper Kincaid, who might not want to kill me but was definitely furious enough to do it.

I had never ridden on a Harley that had only two wheels. I'd never ridden on any motorcycle that had only two wheels.

Necessity, the mother of invention and the savior of stupid women in biker bar parking lots, came to my rescue. I found the foothold, told myself it was good no one was around to catch a glimpse of me not being a lady as I swung my leg over to get my short jeans skirt–clad booty on the seat behind Hop, and I settled in, hands on his waist.

The instant I settled, bike already growling, he backed it out. Then his hands came to my wrists, yanked them roughly around his middle so my front slammed into his back, and I had no time to say or do anything, just hold on, as we shot from the parking lot.

The wind in my hair, a monkey on my back, I didn't enjoy the ride.

I fretted the entire way from the bar to Ride Auto Supply Store, otherwise known to those in the know simply as "Chaos." The store, the big-bayed garage behind it where they built custom cars and bikes, the massive forecourt of tarmac in front of it, the large building beside it—known as the Compound—was all Chaos. The boys owned Chaos collectively. The boys *were* Chaos.

And, according to Big Petey, five square miles around it was known as Chaos territory.

But we weren't just in Chaos territory.

We were *on* Chaos, an island of land in the city of Denver that was biker-controlled.

This was not good.

You could get lost on Chaos. It was theirs. They owned it. They ruled it. They didn't let in anyone they didn't want there. They also didn't let *out* anyone they didn't want to go.

Tug, another one of the members, told me even cops knew that unless they *had* to turn into the forecourt and onto Chaos, they didn't. It was sacrosanct. It was its own little mini-nation, ruled by Tack. The knights at his rectangular table wore leather cuts with Chaos patches sewn on the back.

Therefore, riding back there with a knight in his cut with the Chaos patch stitched on the back, who also happened to be very angry, I knew I could get lost.

Which meant I was in trouble.

Although slightly inebriated but mostly, literally, scared straight, I was able, through the drunkenness and fear, to form a plan. And my plan was to go with the only option I had. That was, try to talk my way through this. However, I would need to pick my moment.

This plan kept me silent as Hop parked next to two other bikes in front of the Compound. It kept me silent when he twisted his neck and scowled at me, which I accurately took as my cue to get off the bike. I stayed silent as I swung off. Hop swung off, grabbed my hand, and dragged me and my platform sandals to the Compound. I remained silent as he dragged me through the door, through the beer-sign-decorated common room, which was filled with pool tables, beat-up couches and a rounded bar, to the back hall, down it and into his personal room at the Compound.

He tugged me in, and I took the four steps the momentum of his pull forced me to take before I stopped and turned to him.

He slammed the door, walked three steps but stopped to the side of me, keeping a distance, at the same time shrugging off his leather cut. Tossing it to an easy chair in the corner, he turned to me and stopped.

Okay, now, I decided, it was time to talk.

I opened my mouth.

His hand sliced up, palm out toward me, and he shook his head. "Don't, Lanie. Don't say a fuckin' word."

I closed my mouth.

It was at this juncture that I thought maybe I should have formed a different plan, one that involved running and not talking.

He dropped his hand and glowered at me.

I pressed my lips together and waited.

His eyes slid from hair to platforms to hair again, then down to my breasts then to my face.

I knew what he saw.

What he saw wasn't me.

I pulled my lips between my teeth.

Finally, he shook his head before he dropped it, lifting a hand to wrap around the back of his neck, and he stared at his boots.

I had been around Chaos for a goodly amount of time. Nearly eight years. And I'd been paying attention to Hop for a lot of the time I'd been around.

Still, unlike Tack, I didn't know what it meant when Hop stared at his boots.

When he did this for a very long time, so long I was inwardly squirming, I couldn't stop myself.

I broke the silence.

"Do you, uh . . . go to that bar often?"

His head snapped up, his hand dropped, his eyes narrowed on me, and he asked, "Are you shitting me?"

It seemed like it was maybe time for more silence so I went with that.

Hop, unfortunately, didn't feel it was time for more silence.

He declared, "Babe, you are so fucked up you're the fuckin' *definition* of fucked up. You think, you bein' fucked up and me knowin' just how much, I haven't kept my eye on you?"

My breath froze in my lungs.

He'd kept an eye on me?

Hop wasn't done.

"I see you take off after midnight, go to the fuckin' lousiest joint in all of goddamned Denver. A place, except for where bangers hang out, that's also the fuckin' riskiest. Then you pick a lunatic to fuckin' *line dance* with. You're talkin' to his girl, I take a chance and go to the can, come out, you've disappeared. I look every-fucking-where for you and I find you pressed against a monster truck tire with an asshole's mouth on your neck and his hand nearly on your goddamned tit."

This was a regrettably accurate recount of the evening.

"So no," he continued. "To answer your question, Lanie, I do not go to that bar often. I go to that bar when a beautiful woman I care about decides to get a wild hare up her ass, take off in the middle of the night, and put her life in jeopardy."

My breath unfroze only to start burning in my lungs.

A beautiful woman I care about...

"You know," he stated conversationally before he socked it to me, "your mind mighta been shut down, babe, but your body wasn't and it fought to keep breathin', keep you alive. Story I heard, story that holds true with the marks you carry—gut shot, lung shot—it was a miracle you survived. The story I *know* is true is that your goddamned ass was in Critical Care for six goddamned days, and you were in a coma most of that time. Your body goes all out to heal and pull you through and you repay it with that fuckin' garbage?" He swung a hand to the door.

A beautiful woman I care about...

"Lanie, what did you think you'd find there?" he asked when I said not one word.

I pulled in breath, opened my mouth and closed it.

Hop's mouth got tight, then it loosened so he could declare, "Babe, you wanna find me, you want more of me, you know where I am. You do not go lookin' for rough trade in hopes of getting back what you gave up. I'll tell you now, I do not have a replacement. There's only one me. You want it, you find," he jerked his thumb at his chest, leaning toward me and concluded, "*me*."

I blinked. My lungs stopped burning as my eyes started flaming, not in despair but in fury as I stared at him.

Then I asked, "You think I was out looking for your replacement?"

"You ever been to that bar before?" he asked back.

"No," I answered. "But I was *most certainly not* out looking for your replacement."

"What were you lookin' for then, babe?"

This was, alas, an interesting question.

"Not your replacement," I snapped, my tone sharp to hide my sudden uncertainty.

"Christ, we're back to your bullshit," he clipped, scowling at me.

"You're very arrogant, Hopper Kincaid," I told him, my tone now so sharp it was cutting, and there was no hidden uncertainty.

"Yeah, well, man gets that way when a woman that looks like you comes as hard as I can make you come and, when you lose my dick, you go out searchin' for more of what you lost. Stupid shit is that you looked in the wrong place when you know exactly where to find me."

He could not be serious.

"Okay, tell me you didn't say that," I invited.

"You heard what I said, Lanie, and, gotta tell you, not a word of it I'd take back, because you and I both know every word is true," he returned.

"Okay, don't take it back. Instead, take me back to my car," I demanded.

"Five beers, three shots of vodka says you are not gettin' behind a wheel tonight," he shot back.

Oh dear. He'd been paying a good deal of attention.

Time for a new tactic.

I pulled my purse off my arm, starting to dig through it, declaring, "Right, then I'll get a taxi."

Suddenly my purse was yanked out of my hand and I was staring at Hop digging through it. He pulled out my phone, shoved it in his pocket, then tossed my bag across the room where it landed with a bounce on the ratty easy chair that was mostly covered in dirty clothes as well as his leather cut.

I stared at my purse then I stared at his face, then I looked at his jeans pocket before I looked back at him, lifting my hand, palm up.

"Give me my phone," I ordered.

"You want it, go for it," he goaded.

I crossed my arms on my chest, murmuring, "Oh, I see."

"You don't see shit," he ground out.

My brows lifted. "I don't?"

"No, babe, so goddamned blind, purposefully, you're stumblin', bumpin' into shit, but barrelin' ahead anyway, bound for a world of hurt."

That was way too close to the bone so I ignored it, uncrossed my arms and lifted my hand his way again.

"Hopper, give me my phone."

"You're sleepin' here tonight."

I planted my hands on my hips, leaned in and hissed, "Told you, *I see*. I know what you're doing."

"You don't know shit either."

"I know this is bullshit," I fired at him.

"Well, you got one thing right," he fired back.

Gah! He had an answer for everything. He was *so* annoying!

I took a calming breath, which didn't calm me, before I snapped. "Give me my phone."

"No."

"Hop, *give me my damn phone!*"

He ignored me. "You sleep in one of my tees. The ones here are all dirty but don't matter. Even dirty, they're better than what you're wearin'," he stated as he flipped a hand out and up, indicating me.

Backed into a corner, I decided to get nasty.

"I've been around you a lot, Hop. I've seen you. I've seen what you like. This," I swept a hand down my front, "is the way you like it."

Nasty was not—and I knew it, I'd learned that lesson before—the way to go.

I learned it again then when, one second, he was three feet away. The next, he was right on me, hand in the back of my hair, arm wrapped around my back, his face in my face, lips nearly on mine.

"Yeah, I liked skank," he bit off. "Liked the taste. Wild, free, and easy. Went back for more. Repeatedly. But that was before I had my mouth between the legs of a lady. You get that, you don't go back."

Oh no. The area between the legs where he'd had his mouth got wet at his words, and it didn't help he was so close; my breaths were mingling with his, my breasts were brushing his chest, and my mind was centering on the fact that I knew what it felt like, my breasts bared, his chest the same, and my nipples brushing against his chest hair.

At the memory, my breaths got shallow but faster and those nipples swelled.

He either felt or sensed my reaction, and I knew this

because his hand in my hair fisted, his lips moved so they grazed mine, and the mood of the room shifted so immensely it was a wonder we didn't rock with it.

In response to all that, my breaths got shallower and my legs started trembling so much I had to lift a hand and curl my fingers in the side of his tee.

"Three weeks," he growled. "I go to bed, lie there and think of you. Wake up, you're the first thing on my mind."

Oh God.

I liked that.

Oh God.

I *couldn't* like it.

I tried to wipe his words from my brain but he went on, "Tell me you don't feel that."

I shook my head, short, sharp, and his fist in my hair tightened.

No pain.

Control.

Possession.

I liked that, too.

Yes, when we hit Chaos, I hit trouble.

My knees started to get weak, and I lifted my other hand to curl into the other side of his tee.

"You feel it," he whispered against my lips. "You do the same, lady. You go to bed thinkin' of me, wake up with me on your mind. You do the exact, fuckin' same."

I closed my eyes.

"Look at me," he ordered.

I opened my eyes.

"Tell me," he demanded. "You do the same."

"No," I breathed.

He held my eyes.

Then I felt the tip of his tongue sweep my lower lip.

Without my permission, my body swayed into his, pressing deep, and my eyes closed again.

"Liar," he whispered.

He was right. I was lying.

I felt the same. I did the same. I went to bed thinking of him. I woke up, he was the first thing on my mind. Further, throughout the day, he slid into my brain constantly to torment me.

I had to end this.

I had to shut him up.

In order to do that, for some insane reason, I kissed him.

Not surprisingly, he kissed me back.

His kiss was better and my whole body thought so, especially my mouth, which moaned into his and my arms, which wrapped around his neck.

Seconds later I was on my back in the bed, Hop's mouth still on mine, his tongue in my mouth.

Needing his taste, craving it for weeks, not having it, my tongue forced its way into his mouth.

Just as I remembered, he tasted great.

Spicy.

Manly.

Intoxicating.

Then his mouth and tongue were on my neck, and my shirt was torn open, flimsy little pearl buttons giving up the fight easily, the ones that didn't popped right off. Hop's head moved as his fingers curled into the cup of my bra and yanked it down.

I gasped.

His mouth closed on my nipple.

My back arched, forcing it deeper.

Hop accepted the invitation and sucked hard.

My fingers slid into his long hair, my head went back, and a low moan escaped the back of my throat.

This was good, so, so good to have back, what I needed, the only thing that filled the void in me.

He paid delicious and long-lasting attention to one nipple, then yanked the cup at the other side of my bra down and paid the same attention to that nipple.

Panting, moaning, and squirming, even as I held his head to me, I begged, "My turn, honey."

Hop lifted his head then his torso and he was on his knees in the bed, straddling me.

I knifed up as he yanked off his tee. Hands and mouth moving on him, his belly, his sides, his pecs, his nipples, my tongue sliding up that dense line of hair to the valley at his pecs and then it veered off to the side and my lips closed over his nipple.

Hop cupped the back of my head with his hand as his hips moved forward and he pressed his crotch against my breasts.

With his hardness against me, understandably, I lost interest in his nipple and went for his belt buckle. Scrambling to get my knees under me for better balance and maneuverability, I barely got them where I wanted them before Hop's fingers curled into the hem of my skirt and yanked it up. Then his fingers went in and slid down, right into my panties.

I dropped my head to his pec and slid my hands up to curl around the side of his neck as his finger hit the spot and swirled.

God, *God*.

The best.

He pressed his face in my neck and muttered, "You're wet. Ready. Not your mouth, baby, your pussy. Get your panties off."

I nodded, my forehead rolling on his chest, and moved back. I pulled my skirt up at the sides, feeling his eyes on me but I was concentrating. I yanked my panties down, dropped to a hip and peeled them along my legs, over my ankles, and tossed them away.

Back to my knees I went and saw he had his jeans tugged just to his hips, and he was rolling on a condom.

God.

Hot.

"Climb up, Lanie."

My eyes went to his. I wet my lip with my tongue, his face got hungry, and I wrapped an arm around his shoulders. Then the other one. Then a leg around his hip. I used his shoulders for leverage, did a knee hop to get the other one up and around. He bent into me to catch me at my ass at the same time he dropped me to my back in the bed and then he was inside me.

Yes.

Yes.

Injected, the drug that was Hop coursed through my veins. I had it back in a way I couldn't believe I'd ever managed to live without it.

"Fuck me, your pussy," he groaned into my neck, his hips moving, slow, steady, sweet. His head came up and his eyes captured mine. "So tight, baby. Wet, sleek glove. Nothin' like you, lady. Nothin' like that beauty."

I lifted my head, pulling him to me with one arm, pressing my chest to his as my other hand slid over the skin of his back and I urged, "Faster, honey."

"Takin' my time, Lanie."

"Faster, baby." This time it was a plea.

"You take me as I give it and I'm takin' my time."

I moaned my disappointment against his mouth.

Hop kissed me.

That was better.

He took his time but he did it while kissing me.

Then he went faster.

That was also better.

Then harder.

That was even better.

Then his hand slid over my belly, down, and his thumb found me.

That was the best, and I knew it because I came. Hard. The explosion excruciating in its beautiful intensity.

"Look at me, Lanie."

With effort, as what he gave me swept through me, I righted my head and slowly opened my eyes.

He stared into mine as he moved inside me.

"Most beautiful eyes I've ever fuckin' seen," he part muttered, part growled, going faster, deeper, his thumb pressing in and swirling, and my hips jerked.

"Hop," I breathed, not quite done coming when the impossible happened and it started building again.

"Missed your eyes, baby," he whispered, his hips powering fast, his thumb pressing deep.

"Hop," I panted, my limbs around him tensing.

"Missed *you*, lady."

Oh *God*.

I pressed my mouth to his. He drove hard with his hips and pressed his thumb tight then circled.

The best.

I just had the best and, God, God, he made it better.

"Missed you too, honey."

That was me, sharing what I shouldn't, doing what I shouldn't, holding tight, lifting my hips to get as much of him as I could, seeking his thumb, pressing against his body, my lips moving against his.

"I know you did, baby," he groaned before his tongue slid into my mouth, his thumb executing a maneuver that should be patented. My second orgasm seared through me so deep, it had to have left an internal scar, and I whimpered down his throat.

He planted himself to the root, and his grunt turned into a groan that drove down mine.

We kissed through our orgasms and heavy breathing, miraculous and beautiful, and only when it slid away did his mouth and his 'tache glide down my cheek to my neck where he gave me the sweet crash after the mind-blowing high.

I held on, felt it, memorized it, every inch, his cock buried deep, his weight on me, the smell of him, his warmth, his mouth, the tickle of his whiskers, his everything.

Before I could accomplish this feat, he spoke.

"You're sleepin' here."

I closed my eyes and my limbs convulsed before they loosened so I could prepare to push him away.

His hips pressed into mine. That felt really good, which was really bad, and I was dealing with that when his head came up.

"You're sleepin' here. When I let you sleep, you're doin' it not in your slut clothes but in my tee, and tomorrow, when we wake up, we're talkin'."

"Hop—"

"Shut it."

I shut it but my confused, scared, post-orgasmic haze lifted so I shut it on a glare.

Before I could take him to task for telling me to shut it, he began talking again.

"Tonight, you got drunk and you nearly got yourself raped. Tomorrow, we talk about what's in your head, what's in our future, and how we're gonna play it. You are not closin' down on me. You are not shuttin' me out. I tried to give you that, you nearly got raped. I'm done givin' you that."

"We don't have a future," I informed him.

"We have a future," Hop informed me.

"We don't."

"Lady, we do."

My eyes narrowed and I snapped loudly, "Don't!"

He grinned and pointed out, "Seated deep, babe. I get rid of this condom, gonna eat you until you come 'cause I miss you on my tongue. Then I'm gonna fuck you again and maybe let you go down on me before I fuck you again. You wanna keep arguing, we'll do it tomorrow when...we..." his grin didn't leave as his face dipped closer, "*talk*. Now, I gotta go get rid of this condom. You gonna do somethin' stupid so I have to cuff you to the bed?"

His last words made me blink in surprise, and such was my surprise that I forgot how much his first words turned me on and how his words before that ticked me off.

Therefore, it was with curiosity as well as stupidity that I asked, "You have handcuffs?"

Hop moved, swiftly and unexpectedly. He pulled out. I gasped. He kissed my throat then my body was hauled around so I was righted in the bed. Before I knew it, one arm was up and one bracelet from a set of handcuffs was on my wrist, the other around a slat in his headboard.

My head tilted way back. I stared at my wrist cuffed to the bed.

"Yeah, Lanie, I got handcuffs." Hop stated the obvious.

My eyes went to him.

He grinned.

I growled.

Yes, actually *growled*.

He smiled.

"Uncuff me!" I cried.

"Maybe, when I'm back from the can."

"Hop, do not move before you uncuff me," I demanded.

He bent and kissed my chest, then he did precisely what I told him not to and rolled off the bed, yanking his jeans up his hips.

"Hopper Kincaid, *uncuff me!*" I shrieked.

He stopped on his way to the bathroom and turned to me. "Don't know, honey. It's a crapshoot. They're here often so Tyra and Tack could be just down the hall."

My mouth snapped shut.

Hop burst out laughing.

This miffed me because he looked good doing it.

He always looked good laughing but somehow, even infuriated, cuffed to his bed, it hit me that he looked better doing it in his room, shirtless, jeans undone, after just having bedded me.

Damn!

I glared at him and watched as he and his great ass sauntered into the bathroom.

I flopped on the bed and jerked my cuffed hand around to see if the slat might be loose.

It wasn't.

I stopped doing that, stared at the ceiling and seethed.

Mostly I seethed about Hop cuffing me to the bed, grinning and looking good laughing when I was angry, and I did this so I wouldn't seethe at me getting out of bed at midnight, inexplicably finding trouble that could have been life-altering in a *bad* way, and ending the night somewhat naked, cuffed to Hop's bed on Chaos.

I felt Hop come back into the room, but I was concentrating so deeply on seething, I didn't look at him. This got harder when the bed moved as he got in it. It got even harder when his hands wrapped around my ankles, pulled them apart and up, cocking my legs at the knees and planting my feet on the bed.

"You gonna stay pissed as I go down on you?" he asked. I tipped my chin down and saw him up on his forearms between my legs and something about that was exceptionally sexy.

Maybe it was because he was hot and he looked amused and...

Damn.

Happy.

I spoke no words. I just glared.

"I'll take that as a yes," he muttered.

"Take whatever you want, you're going to anyway," I snapped.

"Damn straight," he stated, dropped his head, kissed my belly then moved down to grasp my ankles.

He threw them over his shoulders.

I closed my eyes and, against my will, my body braced for bliss. It did this from experience. Hop liked the taste of me. He didn't hide it and he also didn't hide he liked me wrapped around him when he buried his face between my legs. When he ate me, he did it with my legs over his shoulders so he could eat with me all around, feel my excitement when I dug my heels in his back, scoop me up with his hands at my ass, suck hard and bury his tongue deep.

He lowered his mouth to me.

At just a touch, the heels of my platforms dug in and my neck arched in ecstasy.

Just a note: it was impossible to stay pissed at a handsome man when he had his mouth between your legs.

Especially if he really, *really* knew how to use that mouth.

So I didn't.

Our night progressed just as Hop said it would.

Exhausted, I fell asleep against him.

Wearing his dirty tee.

CHAPTER FOUR

Take a Chance on Me

THE BED SHIFTED.

Or, more accurately, Hop shifted in the bed and I woke.

Keeping my eyes closed, I noted we were spooning. I could feel Hop's chest against my back; his arm was heavy on my waist and he had one knee cocked into both my bent legs.

All of this felt nice but his knee felt the nicest. It was forced between my legs so his thigh was resting, warm and hard, against the heat of me.

My first thought was to rub myself against his thigh.

My second thought was, I'd forgotten how fabulous it was to wake up next to a warm body cuddling me.

My third, far saner thought was how the hell I was going to get out of there.

This thought flew from my head when he shifted again, and I felt his lips at my shoulder where he kissed me then I felt his body slide gently away.

Gently and carefully, going slow, his hand copped a feel of the skin on my hip, exposed by his tee, which had ridden up. Other than that, it was clear he thought I was asleep and he was doing everything he could not to wake me.

This was, unfortunately, what I was coming to realize was Hop. He tucked me in bed. He kissed my hair, forehead, temple, or shoulder soft and sweet whenever he left me. And he moved carefully in order not to wake me.

Making matters worse, he obviously thought I was asleep.

Still, before he left me, he kissed me.

The gesture didn't even count for brownie points since he thought I was asleep and he still did it.

I didn't want more confirmation of knowledge I was trying not to process and I wished I didn't have it.

So I shoved it into the back of my head.

Then, as I lay there alone in his bed feigning sleep, the events of the evening before crashed over me. This forced me to exert not a small amount of sleepy effort in order not to process the fact that the evening before, I found out a badass biker cared about me and thus kept an eye on me, saved me from being raped, gave me honesty I refused to acknowledge, and then gave me four orgasms before he let me fall asleep in his tee.

This took a lot of effort, which was near on impossible without coffee. Therefore I heard the toilet flush before I realized that I should have taken the opportunity while Hop was in the bathroom to get dressed and get the heck out of there.

This was a moot point because I felt his presence in the room right before I heard a knock on the door.

I tensed.

I didn't want anyone to know I was there.

I loved Ty-Ty. She'd been my family for a long time—true family, real family, the kind you choose, not the kind fate chooses for you. Tack and the boys had all welcomed me when they welcomed Tyra. They'd gone all out to protect

Elliott and me, Tack especially. When I returned to Denver, they folded me in Chaos arms. Growing up close to a country club with a banker father and a wealthy, Southern farmer princess mother, I would not have expected I would feel comfortable in the bosom of that particular family. But if Chaos adopted you, the way they did it, it was impossible not to feel comfortable.

So I didn't want whatever might come of someone finding out Hop and I hooked up. Even if it was over (something I would share with him again when we talked), it was not anyone's business. I had an agency to run. I had employees and clients who depended on me. I had something happening to me that I didn't quite get and didn't have the energy to find a way to understand. I didn't need to deal with whatever reaction anyone would have, most especially Tyra and Tack, if they found out about me and Hop.

No, I *couldn't* deal.

So I didn't want to be in the position of having to.

"Brother," I heard Hop greet whoever it was quietly. "Not a good time. We'll talk later."

A knowing smile in his voice, I heard the reply, "Got gash in there?"

This voice I knew. High, one of the brothers. I liked High even if he was less approachable and good humored than some of the other guys. He'd always been nice to me.

But at his words, my body tensed. "Gash" was one of the not-so-nice words the guys used to refer to women, not so nice in a way that I hated it, as any woman would.

"You like your nose like it is?" Hop growled, and my eyes opened so they could blink.

He had been talking quietly, thinking I was sleeping.

Now he was unmistakably *ticked* in a way it was clear he didn't care if he woke me.

"Come again?" High asked. His tone no longer smiling. He sounded surprised.

No, shocked.

"You like your nose like it is, brother, you shut your fuckin' mouth," Hop warned.

This was met with silence.

Hop broke the silence. "You not leavin' tells me you got somethin' to say. Say it. Got shit to do."

"Tug and Roscoe were on patrol last night," High declared.

Patrol?

"And?" Hop prompted.

"Three of them on the corner of Broadway and Mississippi."

I stared at the pillow uneasily and with some confusion, since I didn't know what these words meant, but I could feel a hostile wave rolling through the room.

"Benito put three bitches on a four-lane road that leads into the heart of the city?" Hop asked, his voice dripping with disbelief that was less incredulity and more hope that High would tell him he was joking.

"Dick has balls," High answered, which I took as affirmative.

"Christ," Hop muttered.

"Tug says they ousted them, but those bitches know we got no beef with them so they got no danger from us. This means they ain't scared of us. They're scared of Benito. And you know that means Benito sends them to a corner on Chaos, they'll go back," High stated. "Tack's up the mountain, comin' down. Roscoe reported in to him, Tack called me. You and me are up for patrol tonight. We find gash, he needs us to make a stronger statement than Tug and Roscoe can make."

Oh dear.

What did *that* mean?

"Talk to Dog or Brick. Got somethin' on tonight," Hop told him, and I closed my eyes.

"Tack wants you. You got a way with gash," High replied, and I didn't like the sound of that at all so I closed my eyes tighter.

"Talk to Dog or Brick, High. I got somethin' on tonight," Hop repeated, his voice low and impatient.

This was met with another long silence. Then, "I'll talk with Dog or Brick."

"Obliged," Hop muttered, and I heard the door click.

Moments later, the bed moved as Hop got back in it.

His body shifted right to mine, curving in, his hand finding the bunched-up end of his tee and moving in, up my skin, toward my breast.

My body tensed.

His fingers curved around my breast, warm, claiming.

Sweet.

I pressed my lips together.

I felt him shift again before I felt his 'tache at my ear.

"Babe, know you're not sleeping,"

I said nothing and continued to feign sleep.

Hop pressed closer. "Lady, you sleep loose and you're wound up tight. I know you aren't sleeping."

I kept my eyes closed but asked, "Who's Benito?"

His fingers around my breast curled tighter before they relaxed and his hand moved up to my chest. His body moved away from mine, and I found myself on my back because his hand on my chest pressed me there.

Then his hand moved out of his tee as he rolled over me. I opened my eyes just as his fingers slid into the side of my hair and his thumb stroked lightly at my temple.

He looked good in the morning, his stubble around his

mustache thick and dark, his eyes still holding a hint of sleep.

Not to mention, the thumb at my temple thing felt nice.

Gah!

"First," he began softly, "good morning."

"Good morning," I replied, then asked again, "Who's Benito?"

He grinned before his head dipped closer and his lips brushed mine.

That felt nice, too.

Then again, it always did.

He lifted his head and caught my eyes as he muttered, "She starts right up, not even waitin' for coffee."

"Who's Benito?" I repeated.

He studied me.

Then he said, "You want it, baby, you got it."

His hand moved to cup my jaw and I waited but not long.

"Depending on the brother, old ladies can be in the know or not. If they are, they don't talk. Not to other brothers, not to each other. As for you, what you heard was unfortunate. I opened the door to get rid of who was behind it and I did it buck naked so I couldn't move into the hall. That shit won't happen again. Beyond what you heard, you aren't gonna know."

There were not many sentences there but, regardless, there was a good deal to go over.

"I'm not your old lady," I declared.

He grinned and asked, "You aren't?"

"No," I stated firmly.

"In my tee, in my bed, after a night where my condom stash got lighter by three, lady. Beg to differ," he replied.

"So that's what it takes? A tee and sex?" I queried, my brows going up.

"No," he answered, his voice going deeper, his thumb stroking sweetly along my jaw. "Now, honey, since it's time you got to know me, you're gonna get to know me."

Oh dear.

Before I could protest, he kept going.

"Got rules for the women I take to my bed. No sleep. Don't ever wake up to a woman. It sends the wrong message. *Really* no fuckin' tee. Bitches claim tees. I don't need to be clothing half of Denver."

"Is that how many," I hesitated before saying with emphasis, "*bitches* you've had? Half of Denver?"

"Do you care?" he fired back instantly.

"No," I lied.

"Liar." He called me on it.

I shut my mouth.

He grinned but opened his. "You, babe, can have my tee."

I rolled my eyes.

When I rolled them back he wasn't grinning. He was smiling.

"You, it's about bedroom eyes. Fuckin' great hair. Long legs. A tight, sweet pussy that gets so fuckin' wet, swear to Christ, every time I have it, don't know whether to bury my face or my dick in it. Your perfume on my sheets. The way you look at me when I tuck you in bed, like I gave you diamonds, something precious, something you wanna keep safe, something you want forever. Woman like you could get diamonds just crookin' her finger, so a woman like you shouldn't find a man tuckin' you in bed precious. But you do. It's also about you tellin' me you won't take it there with me but, I kiss you, you ignite. Some men like a game. Others like a challenge." His smile got wider. "You found a man who likes a challenge."

"Great," I muttered, and his grin didn't waver.

He also wasn't done.

"It's also about you tellin' me you miss me and, lady," he said swiftly when I opened my mouth to speak, "don't deny it. You said it. You meant it. You'll learn you can't bullshit me, but, I'll just say in case it sinks in early, you can't bullshit me. All that might not be enough for another brother, but babe," he gave a light shrug, "it's enough for me."

"That's insane," I told him.

"Lanie, I'm a member of a motorcycle club. Used to people out there in the other world thinkin' I got a screw loose. Also don't give a shit they think that way."

He gave it to me, my opening, so I jumped on it. "So you don't give a shit I think that way?"

He grinned again. "Honestly? No. Not now. You aren't thinkin' straight so you think that way with your head as messed up as it is?" He shook his head. "I don't give a shit you think that way."

"My head isn't messed up," I announced, and his grin got bigger and, that close, in the morning, sexier.

Gah!

"Babe."

That was all he said.

Time to move on.

"It's my understanding that old ladies hold a slightly elevated role in your world. Not that high, since your structure includes the brotherhood up top, bikes under that, living and riding free under that and, possibly, old ladies, if one was lucky, under that," I stated. "Women in your world have to work to that position, something I haven't done nor do I intend to do. You and I are fuck buddies. Or we *were*."

His brows went up. "Were?"

"This ends this morning," I declared, to which, immediately, he threw his handsome, stubble-jawed head back and burst out laughing so hard it shook me *and* the bed.

"Do you find something amusing?" I asked irately through his laughter.

Also through his laughter he focused on me and spoke. "Yeah, honey. The clue is me laughing."

I glared and decided I was done with our talk. Therefore I lifted my hands to his shoulders and shoved.

This had no effect except that he dropped his head, buried his face in my neck and kept laughing there.

I glared at the ceiling, trying not to process how nice that felt.

His hilarity muted to chuckling so I decided it was time to speak again.

"Get off me, Hopper. I'm getting a taxi to my car and going home."

He lifted his head, smiled down at me, then shook that head. "No you aren't. We're gonna talk, get things straight, then we're gonna fuck, then I'm taking you out for breakfast."

"Those may be your plans for this morning but they aren't mine."

"They're yours."

I didn't say anything mostly because the back and forth of me saying something and Hop disagreeing was both frustrating and irritating and I wasn't doing it again.

The problem with that was, unable to contradict him, I couldn't do what I wanted to do since I also couldn't shift him off me.

"Hopper, get off," I ordered.

"No."

"Off."

"Babe, no."

There we were again, the back and forth.

Frustrating *and* annoying.

I shoved hard at his shoulders and grunted, *"Off!"*

He pressed into me, his face got close and I stilled because suddenly he looked serious.

"You're Cherry's so you've been let in, babe, but do not think for one fuckin' *second* observing the Club lets you in the know about what goes on in a brother's head, his home, or his bed. Any of us," he started.

The way he said this made me hold my breath.

"That said," he went on, "that shit you spouted about what you understand about a brother's woman is more proof your head is totally fucked up, because part of that is selective and the rest of it is twisted and you know it."

I hated to admit it but he had a point.

He went on to force his point home.

"You cannot lie under me after watching Tack with Cherry for eight goddamned years and tell me his brothers, his bike, and livin' free means more to him than his wife and, I'll add, his fuckin' kids. That, you know completely, you witness it, you feel it. That's your girl. You know what she's got. Seen you cacklin' with Sheila, who's sweet as sugar, but that don't mean she'd take shit from any man. She gets it good from Dog, you know it, so you know that bullshit that came outta your mouth doesn't hold true with Dog, either. Seen you also sit close with Brick, seein' to him when one of his bitches cuts him, so you know he's got shit taste, but when he lets them in, he opens up so they can dig deep."

All of this was true too.

Very true.

Hop continued, "Other Clubs might be about the brothers, the bikes, the carousing. You look at our leader, you know *exactly* what this Club is about. So do not lie there and tell me you know differently."

Obviously, I'd struck a nerve and, unfortunately, he was right, I was wrong, *very* wrong, and worse, I felt terrible about it.

So terrible, I couldn't let it stand. It was only fair that I admit I was wrong.

"I shouldn't have said that."

"No, you shouldn't have," he replied.

"Well, I'm sorry I said that since you're right. I know it's not true," I told him. "Not with Chaos."

"Was gonna let it lie, seein' as your head's fucked up, but you keep fightin' me, had to point it out," Hop returned.

Okay, I was beginning to feel less terrible and more annoyed.

"I'd like to request that you stop telling me my head's fucked up."

"Let me help you get it straight, I'll quit tellin' you that shit," he retorted.

I clenched my teeth.

Then I unclenched them to say, "Hop, I keep telling you that isn't going to happen."

"And Lanie, clue in, I'm not *not* gonna let it happen."

My heart started beating hard and I brought us full circle.

"Who's Benito?" I asked.

"Told you, you know as much as you're gonna know about Benito."

"Who's Benito?" I repeated.

"Babe—"

"Who's Benito?"

"Lanie—"

"Who's Benito?"

His brows drew together. "Goddamn it, lady—"

All of a sudden loud and shrill, I shrieked in his face, *"Who's Benito?"*

Hop went perfectly still on top of me, but his eyes grew intent, watchful, concerned as his fingers flexed into my jaw.

"Who's Benito, Hop?" I asked.

"Baby, please, breathe deep, calm down and let's be quiet a few seconds. You calm down, I'll get us some coffee and we'll talk."

"Answer my question," I demanded.

"Lanie—"

"God!" I shouted. Unable to roll him off, I scooched up, shoved out and, miracle of miracles, found myself free so I scrambled across the bed.

Hop reached for me but stopped when I did, on my knees in his bed a few feet away from him. Without hesitation, my hands went to his tee and yanked up. I tossed it aside so in his bed he saw nothing but me in a pair of teeny-weeny, black lace panties.

I didn't hesitate to reach out and grab his wrist, pulling it to me and flattening his hand to the scar under my breast.

I leaned in and reminded him, "I had a man, Hop, who did dangerous stuff and didn't tell me."

Realization dawned clear in his features. He adjusted, coming to his knees, his eyes glued to me. They were pained, troubled, *disturbed*, and I noted this as he whispered, "Lady."

I jerked his hand down to the mutilated skin on my belly.

"Wanna guess how big I am on letting *any* man in my life and then wanna guess again how big I am on letting in a man who lives dangerously?" I shook my head and didn't give him a chance to speak. "Don't bother. I'll tell you." I pressed his hand into my flesh. "It is *not* gonna happen."

He shifted closer, his free hand moving to my hip and around. I felt his body heat as he gently pulled my chest toward his and his chin dipped down to keep hold of my eyes.

"I don't live dangerously, Lanie," he said softly.

"Who's Benito?" I repeated yet again.

His mouth shut and his jaw clenched.

I closed my eyes and turned my head away.

He forced his hand out of my hold and brought it up to wrap around my jaw, forcing me to face him so he could again capture my eyes.

When he accomplished this task, he said quietly, "I would never let anything hurt you."

My reply was not quiet. "I don't believe you."

"Give me the chance to prove it to you," he requested.

"No," I answered. His hand slid from my jaw, up and back so his fingers sifted in my hair even as his face dipped super close, his eyes scanning my features before locking to mine.

"Lanie, baby, I can see what you can't. This shit is eating you alive."

"Good. At least that shit is company," I snapped and watched him wince.

He recovered and stated, "You gotta get rid of it. Let me in. Let me help you get rid of it."

"Not a chance."

His hand slid back into my hair, fisting gently, and I knew what that meant.

He was not going to let me move. He was not going to release my eyes.

I would understand why when he admitted, "Last night, you didn't hear me."

This came out of the blue, surprising me, so I asked, "What?"

"I know the story. Fuck, babe, everyone does."

"What are you talking about?"

"You put yourself in front of him. Boy that drilled holes in you, that the cops found, thought he could lessen his sentence by sayin' you weren't the target. He didn't go there to hurt you. Wasn't gonna touch you. Certainly not pump rounds into you. Says, first, you threw yourself in front of Belova and then, second, Belova used you as a shield."

At his words, I jerked violently in his arms.

This got me on my back with him on me, his hand still in my hair, his eyes still imprisoning mine.

"Not that that shit is ever fuckin' gonna go down again, but luck turns sour. If it does, no way, babe. No way would you be my shield."

"Get off me," I hissed.

"No way would I let you put yourself in the path of a bullet for me."

"Get off me!" I snapped.

"No way I'd let you put yourself in the path of *anything* for me."

"Get... *off!*"

He didn't get off.

He kept right on talking.

"That's the point I'm tryin' to make. If you don't know shit, you don't feel shit. You breathe easy if you take a chance on me. What I do, I do. What the Club does, it does. You'll learn to trust me, the brothers, Tack. I don't use you as a shield. I *am* the goddamn shield, and I'm not talkin' about bullets because shit like that does not touch old ladies. *Ever.* I'm talkin' about assholes with monster trucks. I'm talkin' about Club business, life, every second you live, every breath you take. You take a chance on me, your biggest worry is your 7Up fizzing over."

"You can't promise that," I told him.

"Yes, I can," he told me.

"You think Tack promised that to Tyra before they took her and stuck her until she almost bled to death?"

His face got soft and his voice was cautious but tender when he returned, "I think you don't wanna go there since it wasn't Tack who got Tyra stuck."

It was my turn to clench my jaw and, unable to turn my head away, I closed my eyes tight.

He was right, it was Elliott who did that and, through Elliott, me.

"Lady, look at me," Hop ordered gently.

I opened my eyes.

"Take a chance on me," he whispered.

"No," I whispered back.

"Take a chance on me," he repeated.

"No," I repeated too.

"Baby," his lips dropped to mine but his eyes didn't let mine go, "Christ, I'm beggin' you, let me in. Let me help. Let me in so I can untie that shit you got wound up inside you."

I held his eyes.

Then I pushed my head in the pillows. He got my message, lifted his lips from mine, and I announced, "I stepped in front of those bullets."

I felt his body jerk then still.

I wasn't done.

"He let me," I shared.

He closed his eyes and murmured, "Fuck me, Lanie."

"Look at me, Hopper."

He opened his eyes and God, *God*, they were so intense it was a wonder they didn't burn two holes straight through me.

"I'm not taking a chance on you," I declared. "I am not taking a chance on anybody."

His eyes started burning a different way.

"He was alive, I'd fuckin' kill him," he clipped.

"Well then, it's good he's dead. Now get off me," I returned.

"Seven years, Lanie, you've held that monster inside and, I'll repeat, it's eatin' you alive."

"I know that monster, Hop, I understand it," I sort of lied. I knew it before. Since I propositioned Hop at a hog roast, it was acting unpredictably. "It's the world outside I don't understand," I finished, and that was the honest to goodness truth.

"Then come full into Chaos, Lanie. Our world is simple. You got nothin' to understand but family."

God! He had an answer for *everything*.

"Please listen to me. That's not going to *happen*," I stressed.

He went quiet.

So did I.

He ended the silence.

"I'll wear you down," he proclaimed.

"No, you won't," I denied.

"You won't let me in, I'll break in, sneak in, blast in," he promised.

"You won't *get* in," I contradicted.

He shut up again and stared at me.

After long moments, I watched as suddenly, weirdly and, most of all, scarily, he saw something in me that made his face clear.

I didn't think that was good.

I would find out I was right.

"Let you in on a secret, babe, and you think on this," he told me.

I was not going to think on *anything*.

"Hop . . . get . . . *off* . . . me," I snapped.

His body pressed into mine so he could lift his hands up and frame my face.

"I'm *already* in. Just gotta wait for you to realize it."

This, unfortunately, was a scary statement because, more unfortunately, I suspected he was not wrong. Furthering my misfortune, he'd read that in my face, which meant he knew or was learning how to read me.

This was not good.

At all.

Hiding my discomfiture, I advised, "Don't hold your breath."

He dropped his head, touched his lips to mine then lifted, shifting to plant his forearms in the bed at my sides. "You want me to take you back to your car?"

"Not on your life," I answered.

His mouth twitched.

Then he asked, "Want me to ask one of the boys to do it?"

"Absolutely not," I answered.

His mouth curved.

"Wanna fuck real quick before you go?"

I didn't "wanna fuck real quick." I actually wanted to fuck real slow.

I didn't tell him that.

I demanded, "Get off me."

He rolled off me.

I tried not to feel disappointment and rolled the other way.

As I hastily dressed, I informed him, "I'm stealing your tee since you messed up my blouse."

"I'll buy you a new one," he said from the bed.

"Don't bother," I muttered, then felt it important to note, "And I'm not stealing your tee because it's yours."

It was his turn to mutter and when he did, he muttered, "Right."

"I'm not," I declared, zipping up my skirt.

"I believe you, lady," he stated like he absolutely did not.

I decided to let that go and get out of there.

Sandals in hand, I moved to his jeans on the floor and yanked out my phone before I moved to my purse in his easy chair. I grabbed it and walked to the door barefoot.

I did this intent on leaving, intent on not looking at him. Just as, when he left me, he didn't look at me.

So intent, I didn't think when he called my name when I was at the door, and I looked at him.

He was lying naked across the bed, up on an elbow, head in his hand, eyes on me, looking so amazing I had absolutely no idea how I didn't throw my stuff aside, rush across the room, take a flying leap and join him.

"See you tonight," he stated. My head jerked because I was focused on my thoughts, so his words came as a surprise.

"What?" I asked.

"See you tonight," he repeated.

I finally got it together and therefore was able to lie. "I'm busy tonight."

He didn't say anything.

"So I won't see you," I went on.

"You'll see me," he declared, and my eyes narrowed on him.

"Hop—"

"Tack's comin' down the mountain, lady. You wanna be gone before he gets here or any boys around get up, you better haul ass," he advised.

Damn!

"Careful of High," Hop went on. "He's curious so he's gonna be lurking."

Double damn!

"You sure you don't want me to take you to your car?" he asked.

"I don't want anything from you," I answered.

He grinned.

I glared.

This went on for some time before he prompted, "Babe, you don't want anything from me, why are you standing in my room staring at me?"

Gah!

"I'm not staring, I'm glaring," I countered.

"What you're doin' is hangin' on to an argument that's long since over 'cause you don't wanna leave me," he shot back.

God.

I gave him one last glare, opened the door and shot through it.

I didn't slam it.

I walked as quietly as I could through the Compound, calling a taxi service while I made my way to the door. I then walked as quickly as I could through the forecourt of Ride while I ordered my taxi. Last, I sat on the bench of a bus stop a block away to wait for my taxi and, while I waited, I put my sandals on my now filthy feet.

And I did all this not thinking that I was looking forward to seeing Hop that night.

No, I wasn't thinking that.

Definitely not thinking that.

Absolutely not.

Even though I was.

Damn.

CHAPTER FIVE

Whatever

I WAS IN my office at work.

I had taken the morning to fight back the overwhelming craving the promise of seeing Hop that night caused, created a plan to avoid him and put it in action.

Therefore, I had not hung at home or at Tyra's, went out to get a pedicure, or done anything I normally did on a Saturday.

I had bought a big sub, a bag of chips, a six pack of diet cherry 7Up, and a huge chocolate chip cookie, and went to my office in downtown Denver. I picked my office as shelter from the storm because I had a strict rule that I didn't work weekends. My weeknights might end at nine, ten, even ten thirty, but my weekends were my own, so no one would think I'd be there. I also picked my office because it had a good security system, the kind where you could arm the door but move around the offices without tripping it.

In other words, no one could breach my sanctuary without me knowing it.

I had also packed a bag and made a reservation at Hotel Monaco for two nights. I'd always wanted to stay there even though it was located in the same city where I lived. I often thought of booking a weekend, getting away, doing nothing but being in a cool hotel in the heart of a beautiful city and just vegging. I'd just never found the time.

To escape Hop, I decided now was the time.

So my overnight bag was on the floor beside the couch in my office, and I was seeing the silver lining of the situation.

I was getting my shot at Hotel Monaco and I'd been at the office for five hours. Five hours without the phone ringing, emails coming through, or any of my ten employees walking into my office. This meant I got to do things I never did, like clean up my email inbox, tidy my desk, organize my files, and concentrate on work without distractions. This also meant I did ten hours of work in that five hours, and not only would I hit my organized desk on Monday, I'd do it ahead of the game.

I thought this was fabulous. The first hint of fabulousness I'd had in *weeks*.

No, months.

No, *years*.

And this was the thought I was having when I heard the warning beep of the security system that said the door was opened and you had a minute to put in the code or the call was going to dispatch.

My body jerked, my eyes went to the wall of windows that looked into the interior office, and my mouth dropped open.

Hop, in deliciously faded jeans, his black motorcycle boots, his black leather cut with his hair falling appealingly in his face, and his jaw not shaved since that morning, was just inside my office. He was carrying a white plastic bag that looked like it held Chinese food containers.

He was also with a Native American man who had his gorgeous, glossy black hair pulled back in a ponytail at his nape. The guy was standing at my beeping security console.

Without me telling them to do so, my feet pushed back my chair, my body straightened from it and, woodenly, I walked across my office to come to a halt just inside the door.

Hop watched me do this. When I stopped, he called casually, "Hey, babe."

I stared at him, then my eyes drifted to the Native American guy who was working at the wires he'd pulled out of my console. The beeping stopped. He twisted his neck and took me in then aimed a slow, shit-eating, unbelievably sexy grin at me.

A shiver shook me from top-to-toe; his grin was that good. Not to mention, he was shockingly handsome. He also had a very wide, gleaming gold wedding band on his finger, beaming so bright against his luscious brown skin, I could see it from across the interior office.

"Yo," he called.

"Uh…" I mumbled.

His shit-eating grin got bigger and sexier.

A tremor shook me.

"This is Vance Crowe," Hop introduced, jerking a thumb at Vance and telling me something I already knew.

Vance Crowe worked for Lee Nightingale of Nightingale Investigations. He was famous. All the Nightingale men were famous. This was because newspaper articles and books were written about them. And newspaper articles and books were written about them because they were all talented private investigators who had a knack for the business and a way of finding trouble. Bad trouble. And that trouble usually had to do with a fantastically beautiful damsel in distress who would, in the end, find herself married to one of the Nightingale men.

I looked back at Vance to see my console again looked normal with no wires hanging out and he was turned to me.

"Manual override," he stated. "*Very* manual," he went on. "It's good now. When you leave, just set it like normal."

I blinked.

Vance turned to Hop. "Later, man."

Hop stuck out a hand and they did a complicated, jerky, manly, completely cool and weirdly hot handshake as Hop stated, "Marker."

"You got it," Vance replied as they broke contact. "I need you, I'll call."

"Right," Hop said, jerking up his chin.

Vance jerked up his, turned to me, and gave me another grin. I got a chin jerk then he turned and disappeared through my door.

Hop moved to it, locked it and then turned to me.

He started talking as he walked toward me.

"Took some work, had to ask around and be cool about it but got it from Big Petey. Kung pao shrimp."

I blinked again.

Hop made it to me, shifted slightly sideways and, either by necessity or design, his hard body brushed mine as he moved by me and into my office.

Again woodenly, I pivoted to see Hop looking around as he walked to my desk and dumped the bag on it.

He turned to look back at me. "Cush; babe."

I didn't look at my button-backed white leather couch against the wall. The high-backed white leather executive chair behind my sleek, modern but feminine glass-and-chrome desk. My all-in-one, huge-screened computer. The white leather chairs in front of my desk. The thick rug on the floor with its stark graphic design in white, black, hot pink, and tangerine. Or the fabulous art deco prints on the wall.

I stared at him.

He looked back to the bag and started to unearth white

containers with red Asian designs on their sides, muttering, "Expected nothin' less."

"What just happened?" I asked.

He twisted his neck to look at me, his hand wrapped around paper-bound chopsticks. "Crowe's good at bypassing security systems."

"What just happened?" I repeated.

Hop straightened to full height and turned to me, whereupon he explained more fully, "Lookin' for you so I could bring you dinner, saw your car in the underground garage. Came up. Saw the security console through your door, you at your desk. Console stated security was engaged. Called Crowe. Did some snooping. Found out you liked kung pao shrimp. Ordered it. Got it. Met Crowe here. I picked the lock. Crowe bypassed your system. Now we're eatin' while you finish up and shut down then we're goin' to my place to watch some TV and spend the night."

There was a lot there so I started at the top.

"I didn't see you come up." I motioned to the wall of windows beside me that had a straight view to the front doors, which were also a wall of windows.

"I didn't want to be seen," he informed me.

I went back to staring at him, forgetting about the rest of what we needed to go over.

He went back to the food. Placing my container in front of my chair, he took his, sat in one of my sleek white leather chairs, shifted low, leaned back, and lifted his motorcycle boots to my desk, ankles crossed.

He then commenced eating.

At this point, I remembered what we needed to go over, prioritized quickly and announced, "I'm not eating dinner with you."

"It's Imperial," he replied.

Damn.

Imperial kung pao shrimp was the best and I was hungry. I'd had a big lunch but that was five hours ago.

And anyway, what would he do with that food if I didn't eat it? Would it go to waste?

Sacrilege.

Okay, maybe I was going to eat.

Moving on.

"I'm not going to your place to watch TV and definitely I'm not spending the night," I declared.

"Okay, we'll go to yours," he returned.

"We're not doing that either."

His eyes hit my overnight bag then came back to me while I tried to ignore the smell of delicious Chinese food filling the air.

"Where we goin'?" Hop asked.

"Where *I'm* going is none of your business," I answered.

He grinned, clamped his chopsticks around some noodles and shoved them in his mouth, eyes on me, the grin never leaving his face.

I watched this thinking it stunk that even watching him eat was somehow sexy. Then I moved to thinking it stunk that seeing him slouched in my sleek white leather chair with his feet on my desk was also sexy. He was all hot biker in leather and faded denim, stubble, unruly hair. My office was all pristine, clean edges, glass, chrome, and splashes of bright colors. He didn't fit. His presence there, regardless of his casual pose, was an invasion, and I'd discovered weeks ago I liked all the ways Hop could invade.

Just then, I discovered this kind of invasion was included.

He was not of my life, my work, my home. He came from a life that was wild and free. Where it was okay not to shave or get regular haircuts. Where you didn't throw away supremely faded jeans; you wore them because they were fabulous. Where you casually broke in somewhere you wanted to be, bringing along your buddy who could adeptly, if feloniously, disarm security systems.

Where rules didn't apply, only feelings did.

You went with your gut, you led with your heart, you did what you wanted and you didn't think of consequences.

You lived.

You were free.

Yes, Hop invading my office bringing Chinese food brought all this to me.

And I liked it.

I shook these thoughts off and realized he hadn't replied.

"Hop—" I started, but he swallowed and interrupted me.

"Sit down, Lanie, and eat. It's getting cold."

I took two steps into the room, stopped and said quietly but firmly, "I don't have the energy to spar with you tonight. I've been working for five hours and although not physically taxing, it's been mentally draining. I just want a quiet night." I shook my head and amended, "No, I *need* a quiet night."

"Then it's good we're just gonna watch TV. And when I fuck you later, you're golden. I'll do all the work."

That got me another shiver even as I felt my palms start to itch.

God! He had an answer for everything.

I didn't know what to do. I had not one idea how to get him to leave me be. What I did have an idea about was that I refused to consider the fact that I didn't want him to let me be.

It was then I decided I should eat. Brain food. If I had Imperial kung pao shrimp, I was certain my mental juices would start flowing and something would come to me.

Putting this plan into action, but deciding to do it with

extreme ill-grace, I stomped around my desk in order to get to my food.

Unfortunately, Hop felt like providing a commentary as I did this and, equally unfortunately, I liked what he said or, more accurately, muttered.

"Christ, a Saturday, alone in an office for hours. Still she looks fuckin' spectacular."

I drew in a deep breath, sat in my chair, successfully ignored how his words affected me and glared at him.

Another thing my mother ingrained in me, which was incidentally one of the few things, like knowing how to cook, that she taught me that I liked, was that I never should look bad.

Even if I was dinking around at home, I didn't do it in ratty sweats and old t-shirts. I might not do full-on makeup, perfume, and overly styled hair, but I was never, not ever, a slob. I had knockabout clothes but they were fashionable loungewear like comfortable yoga pants, hoodies, wraps, and stylishly cut tees.

If I was going to step foot out of my house, although on occasion my loungewear worked, normally I ratcheted up the effort.

Like today. I had on a pair of bootcut jeans that I knew did miracles for my ass, which wasn't, like Ty-Ty's, something to write home about. Purple leather platform, spike-heeled booties that skimmed the bottom of my ankle and had a saucy, silver zip at the side (these also did miracles for my ass). And a thin weave, soft wool, silvery sweater that was slightly see-through, showing my lilac cami underneath, and it had an intriguing, drapey neckline that was close to my neck on one side but went wide on the other, exposing goodly amounts of shoulder and half my collarbone.

I was reconsidering this life rule and making plans

to troll Goodwill stores for stained, used sweatpants and
sweatshirts, trying to contain the queasiness this thought
was giving me as I opened up my food and the scent of sub-
lime Imperial kung pao shrimp hit my nostrils.

Heaven in a Chinese food container.

I totally forgot about my Goodwill plans and snatched
up the chopsticks. When my cell on my desk rang, I was so
distracted by my watering mouth and a mind way too filled
with garbage that I stupidly picked it up, hit the button, and
put it to my ear. I did this, one, without reading the display
and two, without thinking about the fact that Hop was sitting
right across from me.

"Hello," I greeted.

"Lanie, darling! Guess what?"

Mom.

Mom sounding excited, which was never good. You'd
think it would be but it never, ever was.

Mom on my phone with me in my office with Imperial
kung pao shrimp, one of my drugs of choice, and Hopper
Kincaid, another one, Hop being the drug that was harder
to beat.

Why me?

My eyes went to Hop to find his eyes curious and warm
on me.

He had great eyes.

Gah!

Everything that was happening crashing over me, my
forehead went to the edge of my desk, where I pounded it
repeatedly.

"Lanie?" Mom called into my ear.

"Babe, Jesus, stop doin' that," Hop called across my
desk.

Silence from Mom but as for me, my entire body went

still, which fortunately meant I quit banging my head on my desk.

"Lanie, baby girl, are you with a man?" Mom asked, sounding breathy, which meant even more excited.

Damn!

I started banging my forehead on my desk again.

"Lanie, seriously, stop fuckin' doin' that," Hop ordered, closer, like he was leaning across my desk, and also sharper, kind of like a gentle bark.

"Oh my goodness, Lanie! Are you there? What's going on? Why aren't you speaking? Are you out on a date?" Mom asked, and I shot up to sitting in my chair.

When I did, I saw Hop did not have his feet on my desk. He was out of his chair, leaned across the desk toward me. His food container was set aside, one of his rough, callused, beautiful, strong, intensely masculine hands planted in the middle of my desk. His eyes were intent on me.

"Lanie! Are you there?" Mom called, beginning to sound panicked.

"I'm here, Mom, and I'm not out on a date," I finally replied.

Hop held my eyes.

Mom said nothing for a few moments, then, "All right, then who's that man I hear?"

"No one," I told her.

Quiet from Mom again until, "Uh, whoever that no one is, he has a nice voice."

He did. It was deep, slightly rough, mostly smooth, and this might sound impossible but it absolutely wasn't. It could get rougher or smoother, depending. For instance, it got smoother when he was doing something to me. It got rougher when I was doing something to him.

"Though," she continued, luckily breaking me out of

these heated thoughts, "it's rude to use the f-word. If he's an acquaintance of yours, you should find a quiet moment to tell him that."

Argh.

I pulled in breath, tearing my eyes from Hop's, I turned slightly in my chair and said, "Listen, Mom, I'm at work, getting a few things sorted. My mind was occupied when I picked up. Sorry. What's up?"

"Oh, okay, darling," she murmured then, back to excitement, "Guess what?"

I didn't want to guess, because I knew whatever "what" was was not going to be good for me.

With no choice I asked, "What?"

Mom didn't make me work for it. She never did. She didn't have patience for that kind of thing. If she was hepped up about something, she let it rip.

Something else, alas, she'd given to me.

"Your dad and I are coming out next weekend!" she cried with glee.

Oh God.

Oh no.

Oh hell.

Damn!

This was not happening!

Thinking quickly and thus stupidly, I rushed out, "You can't do that. I'm having my house fumigated next weekend."

"Oh my Lord!" Mom exclaimed in horror. "Do you have an infestation?"

No, I did not. In fact, I wasn't even certain what fumigation was since I'd never had to have it done so, in desperation, I turned to my computer, grabbed the mouse and hit the icon to load Explorer in order to look it up.

"Uh . . ." I mumbled, stalling for time, trying to ignore the feel of Hop's eyes on me. I knew he'd moved away and sat back down but I refused to look at him as I tapped frantically on my keyboard.

"That's terrible, darling," Mom's voice came in my ear. "Hold on, let me talk to your father. We'll come up with something."

That was what I was afraid of as I quickly read that yes, indeed, fumigation was a means of controlling pests.

Ugh.

Well, the good news was, this wasn't a total lie considering, if Hop didn't leave me alone by next weekend, I would need a fumigation. But I didn't think there were companies that had chemicals that could keep handsome badass bikers at bay.

I sat back in defeat in my chair, avoiding Hop's gaze by turning mine to the ceiling.

Not long after I began my contemplation of the ceiling tiles, Dad's voice sounded in my ear. "Lanie, honey, what's this about an infestation?"

I moved my eyes to my shrimp. "It isn't as bad as it sounds, Dad. I just can't have visitors next weekend."

"That's outrageous," he declared pompously. "That brownstone is in an excellent neighborhood, sound construction, premier carpentry. How on earth did this happen?"

He would know all that. He'd insisted I accept the healthy down payment that made my mortgage affordable on a home I would never have been able to afford on my own.

No way *his* daughter was residing in anything but the absolute best.

With bad timing, this brought to mind the fact that I had also allowed Elliott to take the unprecedented stand that *we* were going to pay for our wedding. He knew how I felt about Dad's guilty generosity so he put his foot down that we were going to have the wedding we wanted and we were going to pay for it.

This had a variety of disastrous results. The first being Dad, who had no respect for Elliott, getting some.

"Didn't know the boy had it in him," Dad had mumbled with surprised admiration.

It also meant that when Elliott made a bad investment and lost everything, he had to turn to the Russian Mob to give me the wedding of my dreams.

On me.

That was on me.

Everything was fucking *on me*.

"Well, it's good we're coming out then," Dad stated, and I blinked. With my mind jumping all over the place, I was not keeping up and I·was also wondering how *anything* was good. "I'll talk to the Roths. They have a condo in Vail. I'll see if it's open this weekend."

"Dad—" I began, but it was like I didn't speak.

"We'll arrange a limo to come get you, bring you to the airport. I'll rent an SUV and we'll drive up. That way the Lexus can stay safe in your garage."

"Dad—" I tried again.

"We get in Friday afternoon and leave Sunday evening, last flight out. A nice long visit."

"Dad—"

"I'll have my secretary email you the details."

"Dad!" I called.

Again, he did not hear me or chose not to.

"Now, your mother says you're at work so we'll leave you be. You'll get an email Monday. See you next weekend, honey."

"Dad, I can't—"

"I'll tell your mother you said good-bye. Love you, Lanie."

Then he was gone.

As you can see, this was *precisely* how I never managed to manage my parents.

I stared at my phone screen, which announced the call had ended.

I put it down and stared at Hop.

Then I asked accusatorily, "Why didn't you *do* something?"

His brows shot up as he asked back, "Come again?"

"Throw my computer through the window. Trip the fire alarm. *Something!*"

My voice was rising and, yes, it was with hysteria, but *my parents were coming for the weekend.*

He studied me and his lips curved up. "I'm sensing you're not close with your parents."

"Wrong!" I snapped. "I am. I just don't *want* to be."

His lip curve faded and he continued studying me, but now with his warm intensity and he also ordered, "Talk to me."

In the throes of a drama, I didn't hesitate.

In the throes of a drama, I *never* hesitated.

This was one thing, amongst many, that I really needed to work on.

I just had no intention of doing it right then.

"I'm spending next weekend with my mom and dad in Vail while my house is not getting fumigated."

"And this is bad because...?" he prompted when I said no more.

I held his eyes.

Then I socked it to him.

"This is bad because my mother is an alcoholic."

His warm, intent eyes got soft as he drew in a quiet breath.

Then he let it out, murmuring, "Lady."

"It'll be okay. Totally fine. She'll drink wine with dinner. More than Dad and me but she won't get hammered. No, she'll say she's going to bed with a book, having sneaked a bottle or two or four up to their room. Dad will stay with me and we'll both ignore the fact she's up there reading at the same time getting sloshed, and I'll go to bed knowing Dad is staying up later, waiting for her to finish up by passing out. This means the entire weekend will be a lie. This means all of us will spend it dancing around the dysfunction, something we always do, something I find seriously un-fun at the same time emotionally exhausting. They'll leave. I'll call my sister Elissa to vent. She'll lecture me on how I should cut them out of my life like she has because this is insanity. Even though she is absolutely right, I won't listen to her like I never do, and then it starts up all over again because now they only have one daughter and thus only one daughter's life to make a misery."

To that, instantly, Hop decreed, "Me and the kids are coming up to Vail next weekend."

I felt my eyes bug out as my lungs seized.

Was he crazy?

I knew he had two kids and I knew his kids. They came to the Compound all the time.

Molly, his eleven-year-old daughter, was the female epitome of her dad. Black hair. Gray eyes. Long, lean body. Easy, bright smile. She was a good kid. Funny, sweet. A little weirdly watchful, though very loving, of her dad, but I figured kids from broken homes could be that way.

Cody, his nine-year-old son, was not the epitome of his dad, and I always found that strange. Hop had clearly dominant traits that not only personality-wise but scientifically should naturally come out on top hereditarily. But Cody was sandy-haired, blue-eyed, and although he was tall and lean, his body somehow didn't fit the shape of his dad's. He was gangly in a way you knew he'd never stop being gangly. Hop was not at all gangly.

He was also a good kid, funny and sweet and loving of his dad.

They were all tight and, if I would admit it to myself (which I wouldn't), I'd always loved watching him with his kids. They were loving of him and he returned it in spades.

But Cody, maybe being younger, maybe being a boy and not as sensitive, didn't seem watchful of his dad like Molly was.

Cody also didn't look like Mitzi, Hop's ex. Or maybe he did since she had platinum hair that was not handed to her by God, but she also had green eyes, a tough demeanor that didn't invite approach, and she was buxom but petite.

I had paid attention to Hop over the years, and although I was not around when they were together or when they fell apart, there was always talk amongst family. Chaos was family, so I heard this talk. Further, since they shared kids, I'd seen her at the Compound. She didn't come to party or hang out but she sometimes came there to pick up her kids.

I knew she was not well-liked by the brothers. I also knew that their break was ugly, as in extremely ugly, though I didn't know the details. I just knew she didn't get a lot of love when she showed. Even Sheila, who was really sweet, didn't have anything good to say about her. The murmurings were there, the detail wasn't, and if I pressed for it I feared it would expose my interest in Hop so I hadn't.

Hop declaring he and his kids would meet me in Vail when I was with my parents could not happen for so many reasons that it was impossible to relay them all.

It just couldn't happen.

"That isn't going to happen," I told him.

"It is," he told me.

Here we go again.

I leaned toward him. "Hop, that *isn't* going to happen."

He leaned toward me. "Lanie, it *is*." I opened my mouth to say something but he beat me to it. "I'm not talkin' about showin' and broadcasting to my kids or your folks how we tear each other up. I'm talkin' about givin' my kids a good weekend in the mountains. They love the mountains. They know you. They like you. And us bein' there and wrangling a meet gives you a break from that shit with your parents."

Under normal circumstances, this would be nice and I'd latch onto it like a sucker fish to the side of an aquarium.

Obviously, in these abnormal circumstances, it wasn't.

"Hop, no offense and you know I don't share these sentiments, but my father's the president of a bank that has forty branches. My mother is a banker's wife. They live in Connecticut. They belong to a country club. They own a fabulous condominium on the beach in Florida. They vote Republican. My dad has pictures of himself shaking hands with senators and congressmen on the wall in his den. My mother owns nothing that contains even a hint of synthetic fibers. She also has seventeen pearl necklaces and two drawers filled with scarves. In other words, they are not biker friendly."

"Lady, to live the life I chose, I can't spend it giving a fuck who is and who is not biker friendly," Hop returned immediately. "They got a problem with my lifestyle, it's theirs. Not mine."

"I understand that," I shot back. "But can you understand, you show up, how that would be *my* problem?"

"You're with me, you gotta learn to make it not yours, either."

God! Seriously?

I threw up my hands. "Hop, I'm not *with* you!" I cried.

"I broke into your office fifteen minutes ago, baby. Did you call the cops?" he asked.

"Of course not, you're Chaos. You're family," I snapped. It just came out and it was true but it was stupid and I knew that when his eyes warmed on me again.

"You kissed me last night. You remember that?" he asked, his voice quieter and gentler.

I sighed.

I remembered.

I did it to shut him up but I chose kissing him, not pushing him away, not screaming bloody murder, not kicking him in the shin.

I kissed him and even I couldn't deny or shove in the back of my head why I did.

"Cody, Molly, and me'll be up in Vail next weekend," Hop concluded our discussion.

His words were still gentle but also very firm.

Too firm.

I didn't have it in me to butt up against his firm.

So I gave up.

"Whatever," I muttered, rolling toward my desk and, more importantly, my food.

"Now, babe, where we spendin' the night tonight?"

I ripped the paper off my chopsticks, eyes on my food, mouth stupidly moving. "Hotel Monaco."

"Class," he murmured, and I lifted my eyes to him. "Nice," he finished.

I looked back at my food and shoved the chopsticks in, repeating on a mutter, "Whatever."

I successfully clamped down on a big, juicy, butterflied shrimp and brought it to my mouth.

Miraculously, it was still warm and, as usual, delicious.

"Lady." Automatically, my eyes moved to Hop at his soft call. "Next weekend, it starts."

I didn't want to know.

My mouth did. I knew this when it swallowed and then asked, "What?"

"You gettin' to know your shield."

My breath caught, my throat closed, and my heart started beating hard.

Hop wasn't done.

"Nothin' fucks with you, even your parents. You take a chance on me, you'll learn, starting next weekend, you breathe easy."

"You don't know them," I told him softly.

"I don't care about them. I care about you."

At that, my heart accelerated so much I felt it beat in my neck.

"Hop—" I whispered.

"Eat," he ordered, dipping his head to my food. "Do it closin' down your machine and gettin' ready to leave. My lady's tired. Gotta get her somewhere she can relax."

I felt the pulse pounding in my neck and it took the rest of the minimal amount of energy I had left to beat back tears.

I won the fight and bent back to my food.

Tomorrow, I'd fight again. Tomorrow, I'd form a plan.

I swallowed delicious kung pao shrimp, my favorite, my favorite that Hop had made an effort to discover was my favorite, buy, and bring to me.

I shoved those thoughts into the back of my head and snatched up another shrimp thinking, tonight...

Whatever.

*   *   *

I was doing all the work.

My choice, I climbed on top.

But I was doing it slowly, taking my time, gliding up, sliding down, my head tipped to his, my eyes locked to his, not him making me, me taking him in every way I knew how.

My hands were at his head, pulling back his hair, my thumbs sliding along the sides of his mustache, bending slightly to touch my mouth to his or the tip of my tongue to his.

Taking him in.

"Faster, baby," he murmured against my lips.

I ignored him and kept my rhythm slow, steady, taking him in, letting him feed me.

His hands gripped my hips. "Faster, Lanie."

I dipped my head at a slant, ran my tongue along the side of his 'tache, feeling the bristle of stubble, loving the feel, continuing to ride him the way I wanted to take him inside of me.

When it was time, he would take over. I knew it. When he was done with me taking, he'd take over and give it to me.

I was right and I knew it was coming when he slid a hand up my spine, into my hair and he brought my mouth to his.

"Sorry, lady. Can't take more," he whispered then flipped me to my back, shoved his face in my neck and rode me, fast, his hips pounding, his hands gliding up the outside of my thighs. Fingers hooking behind my knees, he jerked them high and drove in deep.

A moan tore up my throat, and his head came up, his eyes searing into mine.

"You want my thumb?" he asked.

I gave a slight shake of my head. "Just your cock."

"You got it, baby," he growled, thrusting hard, deep.

"Hop," I breathed. It was building, burning high, feeding the need.

I pressed my legs to his sides, one of his hands moved to the side of my neck, curving around, gripping then down, curling around my breast. His thumb and forefinger closed on my nipple, squeezed then pulled and that was it. He filled me to bursting as I exploded.

My hips came up, my lips parted and Hop's came to them, his eyes holding mine, his tongue gliding in my mouth as my orgasm burned through me.

The burn continued as his thumb and finger released my nipple, but his hand stayed curled warm and claiming on my breast and his tongue moved out of my mouth to trace my lower lip.

"I love that," I gasped.

"I know you do, baby. I do too," he murmured against my mouth.

My hands slid up his back into his hair and, coming down, controlled by the beauty, I repeated, "Love that."

"Me too, baby," he grunted, powering in, powering deep, continuing to fill me, feed me, give me what I needed. "I'm there. Tighten, Lanie," he growled his order, and I gave him what he wanted, flexing around his cock. He shoved his face in my neck, buried himself deep and groaned against my skin.

I loved that too.

I kept my legs tight to his sides, sifted my fingers through his thick waves and waited.

Hop, not one to disappoint, *ever,* gave it to me. Back to front, he gave me the burn then the crash as his whiskers tickled me and his mouth moved on me.

I loved that too.

I closed my eyes, turned my head slightly, and rested my lips against his ear, doing nothing but that, smelling him, feeling him, connected to him.

Still feeding the need. Like a junkie, powerless against the pull.

His lips trailed up to mine, his mouth took mine in a soft, long, wet kiss, then he slanted his head, kissed my jaw and slowly slid out. He rolled off, I rolled to my side, and he pulled the covers over me, shoving a pillow under my head, shifting my hair off my neck.

"Be back," he muttered.

I slid my eyeballs up to him sitting on the side of the bed and nodded, then watched him walk to the bathroom.

He disappeared. I studied the fabulous décor of Hotel Monaco, which was just like all the pictures on their website said it was cracked up to be.

I did not think about relaxing with Hop in a hotel room that was supposed to be mine but he made ours.

I did not think about ending up making love with him in the bed in that room.

I didn't think of anything.

He came out of the bathroom, turned out the lights, and slid in bed beside me.

Only after he arranged me pressed tight to his side and partially draped on his front, his arm tight around me, his other arm crossing his chest to sift through the side of my hair and along the length of my back, did I think about something.

"Hop, will you listen to me?" I whispered to his chest, a chest I was cuddling.

"Yeah, lady."

"This has to end," I told him honestly but insanely, considering I was cuddling him after having sex with him. "For me."

His hand in my hair stilled before his body turned into mine, his hand going to the back of my head, cupping me there and pressing my face to his throat as his other arm held me close.

"This has to keep goin'," he replied, both his hand and arm giving me a squeeze. "For you, lady."

I closed my eyes tight and felt Hop's lips come to the top of my hair.

"Got a monster to beat," he murmured there.

I opened my eyes and admitted, "It lives in *me*, Hopper. I know it. It can't be beat."

His hand moved as his body shifted slightly and I found my cheek pressed to his chest.

In this position, held close to his long, hard, warm frame, I heard him whisper, "We'll see."

I closed my eyes again.

Kung pao shrimp.

I sighed.

Tomorrow, I'd plan.

My body, powerless against Hop's pull, pressed closer.

Tonight...

Whatever.

CHAPTER SIX

Getting to Me

Six days later...

I STOOD AT the end of my bed staring at my packed suitcase that was ready for my trip to Vail. Except for closing it, I was all packed.

Sorted.

I looked to the clock on the nightstand.

I had thirty minutes until the limo arrived.

My parents were up in the air, fast approaching Denver International Airport. Soon, we'd be driving up to Vail, with Mom chattering at the same time fretting about getting to a liquor store.

And me...

Me...

I was screwed.

Suffice it to say that in the last six days, I had not formed a plan.

No, I had not.

Not even close.

*   *   *

Last Sunday, waking up at Hotel Monaco tangled with my fix, I partook of the high immediately. Or, more accurately, Hop woke up in the mood and wasted no time bringing the mood over me.

First thing in the morning sex led to cuddling, ordering room service, having a shower, watching TV, having more sex, ordering more room service, dozing, watching more TV, ordering more room service, having more sex, and then falling asleep.

All with Hop.

I didn't even protest.

I just went with the flow and essentially gorged myself on the drug that was Hop.

It was fantastic.

Monday morning we woke early, checked out, and Hop drove my car and me home. He kissed me at my front door and walked out, and I watched through the plantation shutters as he swung into the passenger seat of a black van driven by High.

They drove away.

I didn't allow myself to think of anything but getting to work and taking advantage of being ahead of the game for once.

Mid-afternoon, Hop called me.

"Like I told you, babe, got the kids this week. Thought they had a gig tonight that meant they'd be home later so we could have dinner and do a little business. Their gig's cancelled so they'll be home after school. Can't do dinner or business."

This, I told myself, was a relief, but even as I told myself this I didn't believe myself.

"Okay, Hop," I said.

"I'll come tomorrow, take you to lunch."

Oh dear.

I had to come up with a plan to end things. Or, more accurately, buy time to create an elaborate plan that might actually work against the onslaught of all things Hopper Kincaid.

"I can't," I told him. "I have a lunch appointment tomorrow."

This, fortunately, was true.

"Wednesday," Hop immediately replied.

Damn. I didn't have a lunch appointment on Wednesday and I needed a lot more time to create a plan that was so elaborate it might actually work.

"I work through lunch," I informed him. It was lame but it was all I had.

"My old lady doesn't work through lunch. She gets food in her belly and she does it eating with her old man. See you at noon."

This was Hop's response right before he hung up on me.

I stared at my phone for long moments before dialing him back.

Smartly, probably knowing why I was calling, Hop didn't answer.

Gah!

Half an hour later, I received a call from a huge potential client. They were having some issues with the creativity of their current agency drying up and they were shopping around for fresh ideas. They were giving a number of agencies a try including my agency as well as my old agency, which had half-heartedly made efforts to undercut me at the same time making overtures for us to merge, something that was not going to happen. I liked being my own boss. I liked the freedom to create without someone breathing down my neck. And anyway, my offices were *way* cooler than their offices.

The potential client was a heavy hitter and had a massive advertising budget. It could mean big things that didn't only include more money but possibly more clients. This approach was good. No, *fabulous*.

I wanted that action.

That was the good news. The bad news was, they wanted a pitch on Thursday, which was nigh on impossible with the current workload even if I had come to work ahead of the game.

This meant that by Tuesday afternoon, when Hop called again, I'd worked until ten the night before and had my mind on our pitch, not on my plan to end things with Hop.

"How you doin', lady?" he asked when I answered.

"Crazed, Hop. We have a potential new client and to build the pitch, keep up with other stuff, and be able to take off Friday afternoon to meet my folks, I can't do lunch tomorrow." After I delivered this, I lowered my voice to finish, "I'm sorry." And I did it actually being sorry.

Even though I didn't want to, I had to admit, I missed my fix.

"That's cool. I'll bring sandwiches to your office."

I stared at my desk blotter.

Why did I think I might get away with a valid excuse?

"Hop, seriously. It's nuts around here."

"Lanie, seriously, with your work, my kids, and your parents here this weekend, my time seein' you is curtailed in a way I don't like a whole fuckin' lot, so I'll bring sandwiches, you work, I'll see you and it'll all be good."

"You're distracting," I snapped, and this was met with silence. When that lengthened, I called, "Hop?"

"Nicest thing you've said to me," he answered, a smile in his voice I felt in the region of my heart. "When I'm not fuckin' you, that is," he amended. "And outside you askin' me if I wanted to fuck you and all the shit you said with that the first time you asked me to fuck you," he went on.

I rolled my eyes to the ceiling.

"Right. Leavin' you to get back to work after you tell me what kind of sandwich you like," he stated.

I rolled my eyes to my computer. "This conversation could go on for four hours and you'd still be here with sandwiches at noon tomorrow, wouldn't you?"

"Yep," he replied, another smile in his voice.

Ty-Ty was not wrong. These boys rolled right on through even if you didn't want them to. How I found this both irritating and attractive, I had no idea. I didn't process that, either, except the irritating part.

"You do realize that's kind of a jerky thing to do when you know I don't have time to fight with you," I pointed out.

"Yep," he replied, still with a smile in his voice, which also meant no remorse.

"You don't care, do you?" I asked to confirm his lack of remorse.

"Means I have lunch with you, look in your eyes, hear your voice, check you're okay." He paused then, "Nope."

I sighed, liking that he wanted to look in my eyes, hear my voice, check I was okay.

God.

There it was. The reason I found his macho stubborn streak attractive.

"I like pastrami," I told him.

"Got it," he replied.

"And turkey. Or roast beef but only if it's rare and only with swiss on it. Provolone if it's pastrami. I also like Reubens, but you need to tell them to go light on the sauerkraut if you take that route. I don't like meatballs or anything that could be messy and get on my clothes, except for a Reuben, that is. No onions. My staff would be forced to smell them all day and that's not nice. Chips, plain, nothing that could stain my fingers—like cheese puffs—or flamin' hot. And a cookie or brownie wouldn't go amiss."

I stopped talking and was met with silence.

"Hop?" I called again.

"Anything else, beautiful?"

No smile in his voice. It was vibrating with suppressed laughter.

It sounded really nice.

So nice, I didn't have it in me to do more than whisper, "No. I think that's it."

"All right, see you at noon tomorrow."

"Right, Hop. Have fun with your kids tonight."

"Always do," he muttered. "Later, baby."

"Bye, Hop."

He disconnected and I put my phone on my desk at the same time it occurred to me my staff was going to see a rough, badass, albeit hot, biker walk in and have lunch with me in my office.

With ease, I shoved this from my mind.

This, I didn't care about. Everyone had wondered why I was with Elliott, too, and I hadn't cared about that either. I had my way of doing things. I had my baggage. I had my issues. I had my demons. But I had few pet peeves, though one of them was anyone judging a book by its cover or judging anything at all, including anyone who might judge me or my decisions.

No, I had enough head space taken up by judging myself and my decisions. I didn't need to give more over to what anyone else thought of me.

So I didn't.

Wednesday rolled around and the pitch was in disarray. I knew I was facing another ten o'clock night, but when I felt the vibe of the office change—this wafting through my wall of windows—my eyes went there.

I saw Hop striding toward me, smiling, carrying a white paper bag held in the crook of one arm, bags of chips visible out of the top, and a six-pack of diet cherry 7Up in his other hand.

At the sight, the pitch, the client, my staff, and everything else flew from my mind.

I had lost myself in work for two and a half days so it was easy (sort of) not to think of Hop except when I was in bed, trying to fall asleep and missing doing it with him and waking up in his arms.

Him there in my office—walking toward me, bringing me lunch, being hot, smiling a smile that was sexy and all for me—he was the only thing on my mind.

He was the only thing in the universe.

He hit my open door and, eyes never leaving me, greeted, "Hey, babe."

He kicked the glass door with his boot. As it swung closed I replied unconsciously, "Hey, honey."

His eyes and smile got warmer. He walked through the office and dumped the stuff on my desk.

"I have a stash of 7Up," I informed him.

"Now you have a bigger stash," he informed me.

Okay, damn.

I had to admit it.

He was getting to me.

Hop unpacked the sandwiches, handing me mine and a bag of plain Ruffles, yanking a cold 7Up off the plastic and setting it on my black desk blotter. Then he sat with his food as he had with his Chinese, feet up on the desk, open bag of Doritos in his lap, sandwich held close to his face, a 7Up at the edge of my desk.

"Pastrami," he muttered. "Provolone. Had them grill it
and hold the mustard. Nothin' should mar that blouse, lady."
He dipped his head to my blouse, his lips curved up with
appreciation. "There's packets in the bag if you wanna go
wild."

I reached for the bag thinking, yes, he was getting to me.

I mean, everyone knew you had mustard on pastrami, but
very few would think to hold it in case you were willing to
make the sacrifice because you were wearing a nice blouse.

Thoughtful.

Sweet.

I also was thinking we never had this, sitting, eating,
everything normal, no fighting, Hop not saving me from the
unwanted advances of a monster truck owner, us not having
sex or about to have sex or in the aftermath of sex.

I claimed some mustard packets, opened up my sandwich and was squirting mustard on, looking for topics of
conversation.

Eventually, I found one.

"How are the kids?"

"Good," he said through a mouth full of sandwich. He
chewed, swallowed, and smiled at me. "Lookin' forward to
Vail this weekend. Found a rental. They're psyched."

"Right," I muttered, closing my sandwich, picking it up,
and taking a bite.

Delicious. I didn't know where he got it but I was going
to find out.

"You prepared?" he asked, and his tone of voice made me
look to him.

I chewed, swallowed, and asked, "Prepared for what?"

"The weekend," he answered.

"I'm never prepared, Hop," I told him honestly and took
another bite.

"Got two days, Lanie," he said softly. "Train your mind to think you're gonna be in God's country, at the foot of mountains in a spot that's one of the most beautiful places in the world. Away from this." He threw out a hand to indicate the office. "What you're facing sucks. Where you're gonna face it doesn't. Try to think of that."

This was actually a good strategy, and I couldn't stop myself from giving him a small smile.

"I'll train my mind, Hopper."

"Good, baby," he muttered, his face soft and, God, *God*.

He was definitely getting to me.

I looked back to my sandwich, took a bite and chewed while I put it down and reached for my chips.

I swallowed my bite.

"So, what's the deal with their mom?"

Yes, this came out of my mouth.

"Say again?"

That came out of Hop's.

My eyes went to him and my mouth backtracked. "Sorry, not my business."

"I asked," Hop stated slowly. "Say again?"

"I really—"

"Babe, if you mean Mitzi, it is your business. You mean Mitzi?"

I stared at him.

Was he seriously, openly, without hesitation, going to talk about his ex?

"Well, yeah. I meant Mitzi, but I shouldn't have asked. It *isn't* my business."

"Fuckin' you, intend to keep fuckin' you, want to know more about you, pleased as fuck you asked about me, so it *is* your business. To answer your question, the deal with Mitzi is, she's a fuckin' bitch."

I blinked.

"No, a cunt," he amended casually and my chest depressed.

"That isn't very nice," I told him.

"Nope. But it's true," he told me.

"Women don't like that word, Hop," I educated.

"Then women shouldn't act like cunts," he returned.

I didn't like that.

Maybe he wasn't getting to me.

"That's unbelievably harsh," I said softly.

He took his boots off my desk, dumped his bag of chips and sandwich on the desk, and leaned toward me, wrists to the desk, giving me all his attention.

"She is not a good woman, Lanie. Always on my ass when we were together, tough as hide, hard as nails. Don't speak to her and, if I can help it, don't look at her. I hate her."

"That's harsh..." I hesitated, then finished with emphasis, "*er.*"

"Yep, but it's also true."

"Wow, Hop. I don't know what to say," I replied.

"Nothin' to say. I do not *not* like her. I hate her. Can't stand the sight of her."

This was not good.

"How does that, um...affect your kids?" I asked cautiously.

"They feel it, I know it, and it sucks. Kids feel everything. Even if you're careful, you can't hide shit from kids. They suck stuff up like a sponge. Struggled with that, did what I could, burned in my gut every time I had to pretend to be nice to her, realized I wasn't teachin' them a good lesson by not bein' true to me. I'm not a dick to her. I don't get up in her face. I just avoid her. This has the added bonus of not givin' her the opportunity to get up in mine."

I had a feeling I knew what that meant.

"So she's not a big fan of yours either?"

"She wasn't. She's learned. Took a while but she figured out what she had and lost. Tried to be friends. Way she fucked me, I wasn't down with that. She wasn't stupid enough to try to get back together. She knew that was a no fuckin' go in a big fuckin' way. Now, she just avoids me like I do her 'cause she doesn't like to be faced with what she created."

"What did she have and, erm . . . lose?"

His head cocked to the side. "Babe. *Me.*"

I studied him, thinking I knew what that meant too.

"So, you loved her?" I asked.

"Made a family with her," was his answer, which I thought was an answer but it also was not.

I let that go.

"How did it go wrong?" I asked, and he leaned farther toward me.

"You don't have enough time for me to explain all the ways it went wrong, that's how wrong it went. Honest to God, spent a lot of time thinkin' about it and I do not have any fuckin' clue what I was thinkin' about, starting shit up with her. She was never sweet. She looked good. She was great in bed. She doesn't hold a candle to you but, until you, she was the best I had. But told you, I like a challenge and that was Mitzi. Her parents were assholes, both of them, hated their daughter, hated the life I led, made sure we both knew it. Freaked me out because it was like Mitzi fed on that, got off on it. Figured it out too late that one of the reasons she was with me was because she hated them right back, maybe more, and she got a kick out of shoving me right up their asses."

That was not good, either, and it did make Mitzi sound like a bitch in a way that leaned toward the c-word.

I felt my brows rise on my query of, "Seriously?"

"Serious as shit. She was a rebel in her fuckin' thirties.

Hadn't found her way. Hadn't found herself. Still stickin' it to her parents like she was a teenager throwin' a shit fit because they didn't like the posters of the bands she had on her walls and, I'll repeat, doin' this in her fuckin' thirties. Bitches that hang around bikers, babe, you gotta be careful. I wasn't."

"What does that mean?" I asked carefully, seeing as I was sort of a "bitch" who hung around bikers.

"You got to have sat with Brick after he was fucked over enough times to know," he answered.

I had, indeed, sat sipping a beer while Brick did shots after a woman broke his heart, and I did it more than enough times.

"Well, yes," I admitted.

"They take advantage of a tough guy with a soft heart. That's what he picks. Strung out, needing to be fixed, unfixable; he gets fucked in the end. Then there are the ones who have an idea about bikers and they got problems. They think they're gonna get worked over, torn down, dominated. They want that shit, and I know you're gonna think that's all kinds of whacked, but it's also the goddamned truth. Had a woman in my bed, honest to Christ, babe, she asked me to punch her. *Punch* her. Not spank her, not even smack her, which I wouldn't do, but fuckin' hit her. Begged me for it. That shit got her ass kicked out of my bed."

"Oh my God," I breathed, staring at him, unable to take this information in.

"Not fuckin' with you," he told me, going back to his sandwich.

"I...that's...that's crazy," I told him.

He took a bite and his eyes came to me as he muttered, "Yep."

He finished chewing, swallowed, and continued his tales of lunacy.

"That stuff you said the other night about where old ladies fit in the life of a biker, club then bike and all that shit, women are drawn to that. They don't think enough of themselves to find a man who thinks the world of them so they look for a man who'll fit them in kinda close to the top and they're down with that. They think that's makin' out good. Others are so weak all they wanna do is party, get high, get laid, and lay everything on their old man's shoulders, so they can keep partying, getting high, and getting laid. Shit's whacked. They're all over. Next hog roast, honey, I'll point them out. They come back again and again hopin' one of the brothers is not gonna read them and know what they're buyin' if they go there. Fuckin' crazy."

"Was Mitzi like that?" I asked, digging into my chips.

"No, Mitzi was just a bitch on a mission 'cause her head was messed up, and I didn't spot that either. Didn't like her folks because they didn't like me but, outside of being judgmental pains in the ass who hated a daughter who hated them back, they're decent enough folk who I think genuinely wondered where they went wrong with their girl. And not sayin' Mitzi pulled the wool over my eyes bein' sugar sweet. Just didn't know what was under all that hard, but I did know I wanted to find out. What I found was, I'd hit spots of soft that felt good, warm, lasted awhile, and I thought I'd struck true. Then the hard would close around again and I couldn't breathe. In the end, there weren't any soft spots left to find."

"That sounds awful, Hop," I whispered.

"It wasn't a fuckuva lot of fun, Lanie." He did not whisper.

I licked my lower lip and gave it time before I told him honestly and quietly, "You know, people talk."

He held my eyes. "I know."

"They don't talk much," I shared.

"I know that, too."

"But they said it was ugly."

He drew in breath then stated, "Yeah, it was and what this is, over sandwiches in your office, is not even half of it. I'll tell you because you're with me, you gotta know. But I'll say, lady, I'll tell you when the time is right for you and this is not it. I'm not keepin' shit from you. But things you gotta know for the now, my kids are good. I'd rather their lives be steadier, but I went back to her more than once to give them that and got nothin' but a rough ride when I did. They didn't need to see their dad go through that. But in the end, she fucked me, babe. It was not pretty and you do not fuck me. You can be a bitch. You can bust my balls. I'm not gonna lie down for it, but there's a lot a man will do for his children. But never, ever fuck me. She fucked me. We cope by limiting our time in each other's space to near to nothing. It works. For you, that's the end for now."

When he stopped speaking, I held his eyes.

Then, hesitantly, I asked, "Are you…looking for soft spots with me?"

It was then he held my eyes for one beat…two…three.

Then he threw his head back and roared with laughter.

I felt my eyes narrow.

"Hop," I called.

He kept laughing, his head now bowed, hand up, waving at me to give him a moment.

Yes. Apparently what I'd asked was that funny.

"Hop!" I snapped. His head came up and his eyes caught mine. "I was actually being serious," I informed him.

"I know," he choked out.

"Stop laughing!" I clipped, short and angry, and he abruptly stopped.

Just as abruptly, he pushed out of his chair and rounded my

desk, and before I knew what he was doing he was bent into me, hands on either side of my head, his face all I could see.

"You put yourself in front of bullets for your fiancé," he whispered, and my breath stopped. "Baby, you don't have any hard spots."

"I—"

His hands on my head pressed in gently just as his forehead came to rest on mine.

"You don't, and just so you know, that is not why I'm with you or why I want you, the fact that you're the kind of woman who did that for him. What you did was beautiful, the ultimate, but it's *who you are* that interests me."

He had to stop.

"Hop, you need to take your hands off me and step back."

"Worried what your staff will think?"

"I don't care what they think," I retorted. "But you're being sweet again, saying nice things *again* and getting to me, and I need a break and I want to finish my sandwich."

"I'm getting to you?"

"Step back."

His eyes held mine a moment before he muttered, "I'm getting to you."

I rolled my eyes.

"Babe," he called.

I rolled my eyes back.

"Wanna know part of who you are that interests me?"

"Are you going to say something nice?"

"Yes."

"Then no."

I watched his eyes smile.

Then he started to speak and, per usual, he did it against my wishes.

"Part of who you are that interests me is that you don't

care what they think. I walk into your cush offices, you say 'hey, honey' and don't even fuckin' blink. Wearin' motorcycle boots or a suit, it's all the same to you. And a woman like you, so knockout gorgeous, most movie stars would give their left nut just for you to walk up a red carpet on their arm, a banker's daughter who sleeps in unbelievably soft sheets and drives a sweet ride ninety-nine percent of the population can't afford acts like that. Now *that* interests me."

Okay, I was back to him getting to me.

"I've decided to be un-biker-friendly," I announced, and watched his eyes smile again.

"Too late."

"Figures," I mumbled.

"Right. I'm here, kiss me, we'll finish our sandwiches and then I'll let you get back to work."

"Hop, I've got pastrami breath."

"So?"

"It might be gross."

Another smile. "It won't be gross."

"It'll be gross."

"Kiss me."

"No."

"Kiss me."

"No!"

Hop slanted his head and kissed me.

I kissed him back.

He let me go, we finished our sandwiches, and he kissed me again before he let me get back to work.

I got looks all afternoon and I didn't care because I wouldn't normally care, but also because all I could think about was Hop getting to me.

And that I sort of wanted him to bring me lunch the next day.

And that I not so sort of wished he'd be in my bed that night.

Alas, Thursday, I got nothing but a phone call. I was busy with work. Hop was busy with Chaos business and his kids.

But Friday morning, about two and a half seconds after I got the call, I turned to my cell, snatched it up, and called Hop.

"Lady," he answered.

"We got the account!" I shrieked.

I could actually tell the smile in his voice was huge when he replied, "Good news, baby."

"Great news. *Fabulous* news. Christmas bonuses for the staff news," I corrected.

Hop was silent.

When this silence spread, I called, "Hop? Did I lose you?"

"You absolutely did not lose me."

No smile in his voice but the rough tone of it that communicated colossal things made my body go completely still.

"You work your tail off for that account, your first thought is Christmas bonuses for your staff," he stated.

I said nothing, just concentrated on breathing and ignoring the warmth shrouding my heart.

"No hard, Lanie. All soft," he whispered like that meant everything to him.

Everything.

I again said nothing.

"And fuck, but I like it," he finished.

It meant everything.

"Hop," I whispered.

"Wish we could celebrate. We'll do it next week. Yeah?"

I closed my eyes.

Then I opened them and said, "Yeah."

I did this because I wanted to celebrate, I wanted to know how Hop celebrated, and because he was getting to me.

"Lettin' you go," he replied.

I didn't want him to let me go. I wanted his voice in my ear. I wanted that warmth he gave me to stay close around my heart.

I didn't say this.

I said, "Okay, Hop."

"Later, lady."

"Bye, honey."

We disconnected and, without a big new client to concentrate on, I was unable to keep him off my mind.

Also unwilling.

And my thoughts didn't go to planning how to end things.

They went to how Hopper Kincaid would celebrate his old lady getting a big new client.

Now, I was standing in my bedroom, staring at my bag and facing a weekend with my parents and trying to train my thoughts on Vail, God's country, which was gorgeous.

Suddenly I sensed movement that shouldn't be there since I was alone in my house and I jumped, whipping my head around to see Hop walking into my room.

"What are you doing here?" I asked as he moved to me.

He made it to me, his hand lifting, fingers curling around the side of my neck, thumb extended, which he used at my jaw to push my head back as his dipped down and his lips and 'tache brushed my lips.

When he lifted his head, he answered, "Wanted to see you, check you're okay, and someone has to haul your suitcase down the stairs."

That warmth hit my heart again.

He wanted to see me, check I was okay and, he didn't live

in Siberia and take a flight to do the deed, but he *did* go out of his way just to carry my suitcase down the stairs.

"I can carry a suitcase, Hop," I told him.

"Babe, you were at Hotel Monaco for two nights and your bag weighed half a ton."

I felt my lips quirk as I said, "It didn't weigh half a ton."

He grinned at me. "Close."

I grinned back.

His hand at my neck gave me a squeeze as his eyes got serious. "You good?"

"God's country," I replied, and his grin came back.

"Yeah," he muttered, looked at the bed then at me. "This good?"

I nodded.

He pulled me slightly to him and then pushed me gently back, swaying me with his hand at my neck before he let me go and bent to the bed. Flipping the case closed, he zipped it and hauled it off the bed.

I took one last look around, checking for lights left on or anything that I might have forgotten, and followed him downstairs.

He dropped the bag by my front door and turned to me. "Half a ton."

I smiled up at him. "Hardly."

His hand snaked out, grabbed me around the neck and pulled me to him. My head tipped back. His came down. My arms wrapped around his shoulders. His free arm wrapped tight around my waist. His lips hit mine. Mine opened.

And we kissed, wet and deep, for a long time.

Hop broke it, moving away an inch. "Leavin' now, gettin' the kids, headin' up. Text you in the morning where we're gonna be for breakfast so you can get your folks there."

I nodded. "Drive safe."

"Got kids, always do."

I smiled again, and his eyes dropped to my mouth before coming back to mine.

"Still gettin' to you?" His question was whisper soft.

No.

The honest answer to that was, he'd already gotten to me.

I dipped my chin and pressed my face to his throat.

His hand at the back of my neck slid up into my hair as I felt his lips against the top of my head.

"Like that answer, lady."

My arms around his shoulders got tight.

"God's country, Lanie," he said against my hair.

I nodded against his throat. "God's country."

I felt his lips leave my hair as his hand at my head gave me a squeeze. I got the message, pulled back and looked up at him.

Hop touched his mouth to mine then lifted up and touched his lips to my forehead. He moved back, his eyes caught mine, he gave me a sexy smile that engaged the lines at the sides of his eyes then he let me go, turned to the door and disappeared behind it.

I went to the plantation shutters, slid them slightly open and looked out, watching him saunter to his bike, throw a leg over, and roar away.

He'd come all the way to my house to carry one suitcase down one flight of stairs.

And to check on me.

I slapped the shutters closed, leaned my forehead against them, and smiled.

CHAPTER SEVEN

One Way or Another

MY CELL ON the nightstand clattered, waking me.

Sleepily, I reached out, looked at the display, touched it with my thumb and put it to my ear, a smile curving my lips.

"Hey," I greeted quietly.

"How'd it go last night?" Hop asked.

He'd been worried about me.

God, *God* . . . I liked that.

"It went," I answered.

"My mouth is between your legs."

I blinked at the pillows. "What?"

"Fuck, you taste like honey," he growled.

My legs shifted under the sheets.

I knew what this was. It was an excellent way to take my mind off things and I wanted it.

"Hop—"

"Touch yourself, lady," he whispered.

Without delay, I slid my hand in my panties.

I must have made some noise because Hop was growling again in my ear. "My tongue's right there."

Oh God, this was good.

"No," he stated. "I'm sucking."

Oh *God,* this was *good.*

"Baby," I breathed.

"Quiet, lady, and listen to me."

I did as he said and miraculously, because usually when I did this my fingers didn't work, I needed a toy, Hop achieved spectacular results with taking my mind off things.

After I came down, I heard silence.

"Do you want me to keep going? Give the same to you?" I offered, my voice sated, husky.

"Don't come on my gut, babe."

He had noted this before but, in these circumstances, I found this was interesting and surprising.

"You don't, uh ... ?" I trailed off.

"I do but not with a woman."

"Um, just pointing out, honey, I'm not with you."

"You on the phone?"

I smiled and answered, "Yeah."

"Then you're with me," he stated.

Even on the phone, I was with him.

Nice.

"I gave you that, you make it up to me Monday night," he finished.

"I can do that," I replied.

"I know you can," he told me. I could hear the grin in his voice as he went on to say where he'd be with the kids for breakfast and when. "You think you can get your folks there?"

We were going to "bump into each other," friends coincidentally on the same mountain at the same time, all so Hop could have my back without my parents knowing he did.

"I'll do my best."

"Do that, babe. See you in a few."

"Okay, and ... Hop?"

"Right here."

"Uh, thanks for the orgasm."

He didn't hide the laughter in his voice when he replied, "Anything you need, lady, I'm there for you one way or another."

Yes, it seemed he was.

"Thanks, honey."

"Later, babe."

"Bye, Hop."

We disconnected. I looked at my phone a moment before putting it back on the nightstand. I stared at it resting there while stretching a bit and smiling a whole lot more.

Then I curved my arms around a pillow, holding it close.

Anything you need, babe, I'm there for you one way or another.

Yes.

It seemed he was.

My smile got bigger.

*　　*　　*

"Miss Lanie!"

This was screeched the moment I walked into the restaurant behind my mother but ahead of my father, who was holding the door, and it was shrieked by Molly Kincaid.

Obviously Hopper hadn't told his kids I'd be there. I knew this because Molly was screeching, and Cody was sitting on a bench at the side of the entry of the restaurant and considering me with some surprise. Hop was standing by him looking his usual amazing in faded jeans and boots. He had a black thermal henley under his cut, and his hair was falling in his face.

All him, just him, no pretense.

However, he had shaved but he'd left a new patch of whiskers under his lip as he'd said he'd do.

It was a good addition.

I only had seconds to take all this in because Molly was racing to me with her usual Molly exuberance.

She skidded to a halt, her head tipped back, her long, gorgeous, wavy black hair wild and free, her gray eyes shining with little kid excitement.

"I can't believe you're here!" she cried then twisted toward her dad. "Dad, look! Miss Lanie's here!"

"I see," Hop murmured, moving toward us, and it crashed over me this sucked because I couldn't touch him, kiss him, even smile at him like I wanted to smile.

Instead, I caught his eyes and greeted, "Hey, Hop." I looked down to Molly. "How are you, sweetie?"

"Great!" she cried.

I grinned at her and looked to Cody. "Hey, Cody."

"Yo!" he called, all mini-biker badass.

I smiled at him, my eyes slid to Hop and I thought, to hell with it.

I moved into him, wrapped my hand around the leather over his bicep and leaned in.

Brushing my lips against his cheek close to his ear, quick and low, I whispered a much different, "Hey."

"Hey." His return whisper was also quick, low, and *rough*.

I pulled back, caught his eyes, saw they were intent, warm, and pleased, gave him a small smile then turned toward my parents.

"Mom, Dad, isn't this fabulous?" I asked even though they were taking all this in, especially Hop, the blank masks on their faces didn't quite hide their aversion to our present company. "This is a really good friend of mine, Hopper Kincaid." I motioned to Hop. "And his kids, Molly and Cody." I motioned to the kids.

"Hey!" Molly chirped, grinning big at Mom and Dad.

"How do you do," Mom replied and, at her formal words uttered to an eleven-year-old, my head quickly turned to Hop whereupon I rolled my eyes before I turned back to Mom and Dad.

I did this hearing Cody's repeated, "Yo!"

Dad's mouth got tight before he forced it to smile at Molly then he looked to Hop.

Hop stuck out his hand. "Mr. Heron."

"Yes," Dad mumbled. "Good to meet you, erm... Hopper."

Hop gripped Dad's hand tight and let it go. "Hop."

"I'm sorry?" Dad asked, taking a step he didn't need to take away from Hop.

"Hop," Hop repeated. "Friends call me Hop. Lanie's a good friend, means her family are friends." He smiled at Dad. "So call me Hop."

"Right," Dad murmured, then obviously forced out a mumbled, "Hop."

Hopper ignored that, leaned into Mom and took her hand, saying, "Mizz Heron."

"Well, um... of course, uh... pleased to meet you," Mom stammered, uncomfortable and also moving back quickly after Hop released her.

We all stood there and I waited.

It didn't happen.

This ticked me off so I did something about it.

"Just FYI," I began. "Mom and Dad aren't Mr. and Mrs. Heron. They're Joellyn and Edward."

Mom's face was so hard I thought it would crack when she pushed her lips up into a smile. Dad jerked up his chin.

Ugh.

My eyes went back to Hop and I watched his eyelids go

soft, a barely there movement but it eloquently stated he was good; he didn't care my parents were how they were and I shouldn't either.

So I decided not to.

"Hey!" I exclaimed, clapping my hands. "I know!" I looked to Hop. "Have you put your name in already?"

"Yeah, Lanie," Hop replied, his lips twitching.

"Well, we'll go to the hostess station and change it." I looked to Mom and Dad. "Table for six!"

Dad's face looked as if it had become carved in stone, and Mom made a strangled noise but I just looked down at Molly.

"Would you like that?" I asked.

"Yeah!" she cried, jumping toward me, grabbing my hand and tugging me to the hostess station.

I went but turned my head as I did so, asking Cody, "What about you, kiddo?"

"Cool," he stated nonchalantly.

I threw him a smile, went to the hostess station and changed Hop's table request to a six top. I got the bad news a bigger table was going to take ten minutes and headed back to the crew. Mom and Dad were clearly uncomfortable, but Hop was just Hop, hot and casual. Cody was swinging his legs, oblivious to everything.

"We're in," I announced. "But it'll take ten minutes or so."

"Bummer, I'm starved," Cody muttered.

"You'll live," Hop rumbled, looking down at his son and smiling.

"I'll do it starving," Cody returned.

"But you'll do it," Hop retorted.

I grinned at them.

"So, how do you know our daughter?" Dad asked a question he was being purposefully obtuse in asking because he knew the answer, and Hop's eyes went to him.

"She's Chaos," he answered, and that warmth gathered around my heart again.

"I'm sorry?" Dad queried.

"Chaos. She's Chaos. Her girl, Tyra, is married to a brother of mine," Hop explained. "Known Tyra years, known Lanie years. Both of them are Chaos."

"Right. Of course," Dad said, sounding like he didn't think it was right at all. "I had heard that Tyra had..." He trailed off then to me, "I haven't asked yet. How are Tyra and her boys?"

He pointedly did not ask after Tack.

I ignored this. "She's great. Over the moon happy. Tack's good, too. The boys are good kids even though they're hooligans."

"They aren't hooligans," Cody contradicted, and I looked down at him. "They're awesome." He looked at my dad. "They're younger than me but I hang with them because they got good ideas." He lifted his hand and tapped his fingertips to his head. "Genius."

"Genius at getting in trouble," I put in, and Cody looked at me.

"Mister Tack doesn't mind."

"Miss Tyra does," Hop stated, and his son looked up to him.

"Girls do that, not likin' the way boys act," Cody retorted.

"They do that when boys act like idiots," Hop returned.

Apparently Cody couldn't argue with this, because he shut up.

I started laughing.

Molly leaned into me and she laughed too.

I slid my arm around her and pulled her closer. Hop trained eyes to his daughter then to me and the warmth in them, the soft around his mouth, made the snug feeling around my heart gather closer.

"What are you doin' today, Miss Lanie?" Molly asked, and I looked down at her.

"Don't know yet, honey. My parents are here from Connecticut so just visiting, I guess," I answered.

"You can't *just visit* in Vail!" she objected and looked from Dad to Mom. "You should hang with us. We got all sorts of fun things planned."

I decided in that moment I loved Molly Kincaid.

"I don't think—" Dad started, but I was faster than him and jumped at Molly's innocent offer.

"What a fantastic idea!" I cried and looked to Mom and Dad. "Isn't that a fantastic idea?"

"Darling, we don't even know their plans," Mom noted logically but slightly desperately.

We didn't but I knew whatever it was would be a lot more fun than visiting with Mom and Dad.

"Kids make everything fun," I declared.

"Can't argue with that," Hop put in, then looked between the elder Herons. "You'd be welcome, and my kids would love it. They think the world of your daughter."

That was well played, an out-and-out invitation no one could politely refuse coupled with a compliment to their daughter that was clearly genuine, making it additionally impossible to refuse.

It was so well played, it took a mammoth amount of effort not to smile huge at Hop or, say, throw my arms around him and kiss him hard. Instead, I just caught his eyes and hoped he read what was in mine.

He did, and I knew it when his eyes flashed and a wave of goodness surged from him and crashed into me.

Hop's remark was met with silence. Through the wave of goodness I noted this and I looked to my mom and dad.

Mom rallied first, too Southern not to.

"We'd be delighted, of course. Any friends of Lanie's, and obviously, children do make everything fun."

She apparently decided to ignore all the things she didn't like about Hop and smiled with real warmth at his kids.

"Awesome!" Molly cried, jumping away from my arm but grabbing my hand again.

"Sucks there's no snow," Cody declared. "But there's like, a *gazillion* candy shops in the village, and Dad says we can hit them all."

Molly let my hand go to lift both of hers in the air and yell, "Sugar high!"

"Right on," Cody mumbled, grinning up at his sister.

I grinned at him then I turned to find Hop grinning at me.

All good. It was all good.

Because Hop made it that way.

And, well, Molly, but Molly was Hop's so I decided to give him the credit.

"Kincaid? Party of six?" We all turned to the hostess and she smiled. "We had a table open up early."

"Well, isn't this an all-around lucky day?" I declared, curving an arm around Molly and turning us both to the hostess.

No one answered. I didn't care.

It *was* a lucky day, and I was hanging onto that.

The hostess took us to the table.

Hop smoothly engineered a seating situation where he sat by me, which meant he could press his thigh against mine and steal touches to my leg and, outwardly casually but anything but, hook his arm around the back of my chair when we were talking and not eating.

Dad didn't miss it and wasn't happy about it, casual or not.

Mom pretended to ignore it.

Molly and Cody didn't catch any meaning to it.

I loved it.

*　　*　　*

"Will they be okay for fifteen minutes?"

I whispered this in Hop's ear.

It was late August. There was no snow, but the golden leaves of the aspens seemed to glitter in the sun, and the mountain air was a shade nippy. Waning summer was on the mountain, which meant daytrippers and weekenders were abundant, and someone had organized kids' games on the base of a slope.

Therefore, Molly and Cody were currently engaged in a three-legged race with a gaggle of other kids. My guess was they'd win seeing as Hop had given them what he promised, and they were both currently burning through the sugar high to end all sugar highs.

Mom and Dad had murmured that they needed a sit-down with a cup of coffee so they were in a coffee shop down the main drag of Lionshead Village.

This meant Hop and I were alone.

He turned his head and looked at me with warm curiosity. "You good?"

"I will be," I told him. His head cocked in question, and I moved, walking away from the slope to the side of a building where there were public restrooms.

One of them was a single for handicapped people.

I had to admit, I felt some guilt about occupying a handicap bathroom as I walked to it, but when I looked back at Hop, I liked the curiosity I saw in his features.

But the need was on me.

I slid through, holding the door open for him.

He slid in behind me.

I let the door close and locked it.

"Lady, what the fuck?" he asked, and I turned to him.

Then I walked right to him, pressing my chest against his and cupping his crotch in my hand.

His head instantly bent to mine, his hand driving into the back of my hair and fisting as he growled unintelligibly against my mouth.

Then he asked, his voice rough, "You seriously down with this?"

"Absolutely," I whispered. "Hurry."

"Fuck," he groaned, slanted his head and kissed me, backing me up until I hit wall.

That was all I needed. Hop's mouth. Hop's body.

Hop.

I was ready.

Then again, I was ready before I walked in just knowing Hop was following me.

His hand in my hair, his other one tugged forcefully at my belt buckle, undoing it, then the button of my jeans, then the zip went down and his hand went in.

God, that felt good.

I moaned into his mouth.

"Get these off," he ordered. "Now."

Heretofore unknown illicit excitement bolting through me, I moved immediately to do what I was told. It wasn't easy, because Hop didn't move, his chest pressing into mine, which pressed me into the wall. His hand went to the back of his jeans to get his wallet.

I yanked down my jeans as best I could then shifted my legs to tug them off over my boots, kicking them aside, repeat with my panties.

Hop was free, hard, and gloved by the time I did this and he growled, "Hop up."

I wrapped my arms around his shoulders and hopped up.

He caught me at my ass, pressed me into the wall. My legs curved around his hips and he thrust in, hard and deep.

I shoved my face in his neck, held on tight with arms and legs and whimpered.

"Fuck me, goddamn *hot*," he grunted into my neck, pounding between my legs.

"Harder, baby," I urged breathlessly.

He thrust harder.

"Tip for me, Lanie," he rumbled into my neck, and I tipped my hips toward him. He drove deeper and my breath hitched loudly.

"Love that," I panted.

"Me too, honey."

"Love it, Hop," I gasped, suddenly close and it was going to be mammoth.

"Hold on, lady."

I held on harder than I already was holding, and he moved a hand from my ass to the back of my head half a second before I came, my head shooting back, slamming his hand into the wall.

"Look at me," he ordered roughly.

I trembled in his arms, holding tight, unable to do anything but feel the beauty of the high.

His hand fisted in my hair. "Lanie, fuckin' look at me."

With effort, I struggled through the haze, dipped my chin and looked at him.

He kept pounding, stopped, ground in, and I whimpered.

"All soft, every inch. Got my dick buried in beauty," he grunted.

I loved that too.

A lot.

I put my lips to his. "Keep fucking me, honey."

He began thrusting again, harder, faster, pounding me into the wall.

"Yes, beauty," I breathed. His hand twisted in my hair, crushed my mouth down on his, and he groaned his orgasm down my throat.

I took it in. Happily.

Coming down from his climax, he started kissing me then broke the kiss to slide his lips and mustache down my cheek to my neck where his mouth stopped to work.

I pressed my lips to his neck, took a taste then moved them to his ear.

Closing my eyes tight, smelling him, feeling him holding me, filling me, I knew it was time.

He'd given so much, I could no longer stop myself from giving back.

"I'm thinking I like my shield," I whispered, and his body went solid in my limbs.

But I wasn't done.

"Thank you, Hopper Kincaid. Suitcases. Sandwiches. Chinese. God's country. Sweet kids. I didn't go to sleep last night buried under emotional exhaustion. I went to sleep looking forward to seeing you. That's a miracle, honey, and you have to know I appreciate you making that miracle happen for me."

He didn't move, didn't speak; his mouth stayed at my neck but it didn't glide, taste, lick. His cock stayed planted, but his hips didn't so much as twitch.

I didn't know what to do with that. I thought he'd like what I said, and his inactivity didn't say he didn't but it also didn't say he did.

I shifted my head, trying to pull back, but his hand pressed forward, keeping me where I was.

"Hop?" I called uncertainly.

"I'm in there," he murmured into my neck.

Yes. Oh yes.

He was in there.

I sighed, moved so my nose tweaked his earlobe and gave him more.

"Uh...yeah. Presently in more ways than one."

His head went back, he let mine up and he caught my eyes.

I caught my breath at what I saw in his.

"Then don't thank me, lady. You give me that, it was all worth it." My teeth came out to graze my lip, his eyes dropped to them and stayed there as he ordered. "Kiss me hard while I'm still inside you then we gotta get back to the kids."

"Okay, honey," I agreed, pressed my lips to his, kissed him hard as he pushed me into the wall and ground his hips into mine, which made me give a soft whimper against his tongue before he ended the kiss, eased me back, eased out of me, and eased me to my feet.

I held on as my trembling legs recovered.

So did Hop.

"Steady?" he asked. My eyes caught his and I nodded.

I was.

Steady.

Maybe.

Finally.

I pulled in breath. He bent in to kiss my temple then he slowly let me go.

I went to my panties and jeans.

Hop went to the toilet.

I was leaning against the wall and, with no small amount of difficulty, tugging my jeans over my boots when Hop crouched at my feet, his hands out to help me.

My jeans successfully pulled over my boots, I straightened. He did too and slid an arm loosely around my waist as I tugged them up, zipped, buttoned, and belted them.

"Um...not big on putting these back on after they've been on the floor of a public bathroom," I murmured, giving my panties in my fingers a little twirl. "And I don't have a purse."

Hop's eyes got dark but he said not a word, grabbed my panties and shoved them in his front pocket.

Knowing my panties were in Hop's jeans pocket, my thighs quivered.

"Just so you know," I started, feeling suddenly nervous, "I've never had public handicapped bathroom sex before."

"Just so you know," Hop returned, grinning, "I haven't either."

"Uh...okay," I muttered, finding it difficult to hold his smiling eyes and wanting to look at his shoulder. Instead, I lifted my hands to rest them there.

"Stall sex with a skank, yeah," he went on, and my head jerked. "Twice," he continued, and I felt my lips part. "Though, a private handicapped restroom is definitely the way to go with a lady. I'd never do you in a stall."

He was teasing so I relaxed.

Slightly.

"I don't think I could do a stall," I shared.

"Like I said, wouldn't do you in a stall."

My lips curved up. "It's good we agree on that."

"Yeah," he replied and tipped his head to the side, asking quietly, "You good?"

I did a mental assessment.

I was.

Shockingly, I not only was good. I was *very* good, and in more ways than one.

"Yeah," I answered. It was his turn for his lips to curve up, and then they came to mine for a touch.

When he finished with that, he led me to the door while I asked, "So, is that true? Twice?"

"Yeah, it's true."

Wow.

"Bikers don't have boundaries," he imparted, unlocking the door, but he didn't open it, so I looked up to him. "Pleased as fuck to learn my woman doesn't either, babe. I think you clued in when I started fuckin' you against a wall about a minute after you got me in here that I thought that was hot, but just in case you missed any of that...that was *hot*."

I stared into his eyes.

Hop stared into mine, not done. "You keep getting better and better."

He did too.

"Well, good to know," I started softly, "that I'm returning the favor."

His face went dark, his eyes went hot and he growled, "Fuck, don't do that shit."

"What shit?" I asked, perplexed at his expression and tone.

"Did you against a wall in a bathroom and you bein' sweet makes me want it again."

"I think the kids and my parents will wonder where we are."

"That's why you can't do that shit."

"Okay, I'll stop being sweet." I gave in.

"Be obliged."

I grinned.

Hop looked at my mouth.

I swayed into him.

Hop looked into my eyes.

"You go out first, lady. I'll follow in a few."

I nodded.

He dipped his head and gave me another lip touch.

When he lifted his head, I got on my toes and gave it back.

He gave me a squeeze.

Then he let me go and I went out first.

He followed in a few.

Thankfully, the kids were engaged in a sack race by the time we returned so they had no clue we'd been gone, and my parents didn't rejoin us until fifteen minutes after we got back.

As for me, I stood in the Colorado sun at the base of a magnificent mountain in the heart of God's country feeling good. Feeling steady. Feeling fabulous.

Finally.

*   *   *

"I'm going out to take a walk," I called from the door of the spacious, well-appointed, six-bedroom "condo" owned by my parents' friends. It was currently occupied by me at the door in my coat, Dad in front of the TV, and Mom already in bed with her crutch even though it was only eight thirty. "The night feels great. I'll probably be a while."

"Lanie!" Dad called back, and his voice was closer than I expected it to be.

He was coming my way.

"Later!" I cried, slipped out, closed the door, and hustled my booty on its way toward the village.

I pulled my cell from my pocket, found the text Hopper sent me and scrolled through it. Then I followed his directions out of the posh area where I was staying with my parents, through the village, and into the denser area of attractive condos where Hop and the kids were staying.

I found his, walked up the open flight of steps at the side, and knocked on the door.

Seconds later, it was thrown open.

Molly looked up at me then turned to shout into the condo, "Finally! Miss Lanie's here! Now we can play Pictionary!"

She raced into the condo, leaving the door open and me outside.

"We aren't playing Pictionary!" I heard Cody yell.

"We so are!" Molly yelled back.

"We aren't. It's gay!" Cody shouted.

"Games can't be gay, boy. People are gay, games aren't, and it isn't a bad thing to be." I heard Hop's rumble but it was coming my way so I stepped in and closed the door.

"Dad!" Cody cried.

"Shut it," Hop warned then appeared in the entryway.

I pulled off my jacket.

Hop's head, looking back into the condo, turned to me.

My heart warmed and my lips smiled.

His eyes dropped to my mouth and his teeth caught his lower lip.

I'd never seen him do that. It was a good look, so my legs trembled, but I managed to stay standing as Hop made it to me.

"I'm getting Pictionary," Molly yelled as Hop rounded me and took my jacket but did it close.

His lips came to my ear. "Wish I could kiss you."

I wished that too.

I twisted my neck and caught his eyes.

At the look in his, my legs nearly buckled.

"We should play Wii. They have a Wii, we should play it." I heard Cody declare.

"We have a Wii at home, Cody," Molly told him.

"So?" Cody asked.

"Though, this shit is killin' the mood," Hop muttered, and I grinned as I moved into their condo.

It was spacious too but warmly, not architecturally.

"Hey, Cody," I called.

"You like Wii?" he called back.

"You wanna say hello?" Hop suggested from behind me in a way that was not entirely a suggestion.

"Yo, Miss Lanie," Cody mumbled, wisely taking up his dad's thinly veiled order.

I smiled at him.

Molly materialized at my side. "Do you like Pictionary?"

I looked down at her. "I do, but we can't play."

Her face fell. "Why not?"

"Because it's a moral imperative to play boys against girls and we'd whup their butts. I'm sort of creative, do it for a living. This means I never lose at Pictionary," I announced.

"Dad and me'll kill you," Cody declared.

I looked at him and threw out the challenge, "Impossible."

He hurled himself over the back of the couch, racing away, shouting, "I'm getting Pictionary!"

My work done, I moved to the couch and sat down.

Already this was better than TV with Dad.

"Nice work, lady."

This was murmured in my ear by Hop. I turned my neck. He was behind the couch but bent toward me. I caught Hop's smile and gave him one back.

He straightened and moved away while Cody raced back with the game and got on his knees beside the coffee table. Molly moved in to help him set up.

I took in a deep breath and let it out right before I felt cold on my arm. I looked down, saw a bottle of beer pressed there, and lifted a hand to take it even as I tipped my head back to smile my gratitude at Hop.

He smiled his acceptance.

Definitely better than TV with Dad.

Pads and pencils disbursed, timer at the ready, we settled in and I played Pictionary with badass biker Hopper Kincaid and his two kids.

The best.

The best I'd ever had.

And, incidentally, Molly and I whupped their butts.

Three times.

*   *   *

Hop and I were standing outside his condo door making out, me in my jacket, him in his thermal henley.

This was lasting awhile, and I was going with it, hoping Hop knew the drill inside where his kids were getting ready for bed, so he'd know how much time we had to enjoy what we were doing.

I was also going with it because we'd never just made out, it leading nowhere but to the goodness of taste and touch, bodies pressed together in the cold.

It was fabulous.

Eventually and regrettably, he broke the connection of our mouths but not our embrace.

"Gotta make sure they're good," he muttered.

"Yeah," I muttered back.

"Also gotta let you know, before you got here, got a call from an old buddy of mine. He's gonna be close. In Denver for the first time in a while. I don't wanna miss seein' him. We were tight back in the day. It'll be good seein' him, but my only shot is Monday night."

This was a disappointment, but still I said, "Okay."

"Want you to come with me."

I held his eyes in the outside lights.

I'd made a decision. It wasn't conscious, it was intuitive. Going with my gut, leading with my heart, I was moving forward not thinking about the consequences.

I'd let Hop in.

That day, I'd eaten breakfast, spent the day and played Pictionary with his kids.

Was I ready to meet an old buddy?

"I'd like that," I stated before my brain could catch up and do something other than go with my gut and lead with my heart.

"Good," he replied on a grin, then his arms tightened and his grin faded. "Check in in the morning. Wanna take your pulse."

Afraid for a long time where my gut and heart might lead, I hadn't listened to them for years. It was good to know, from Hop's concern, I could trust them again.

"I'll call."

"Do that," he murmured.

I grinned.

He touched his mouth to mine.

When he lifted his head, I whispered, "I better let you go."

"Don't ever do that."

His words flowed through me in a way I couldn't help but press close, angle my head and push my face in his neck.

"Are you real?" I asked his skin.

"Baby, you're standing in my arms," he answered.

"Please be real," I whispered.

"Feel this." He gave me a squeeze. "I'm real, Lanie."

I drew in breath, drawing him in, then I pulled back and looked at him.

"Okay, then I won't let you go but I will say good night."

"That, I'll accept," he replied, his lips curving up.

I moved in to touch mine to his. He let me then shifted to kiss my forehead.

He let me go, and I moved to the stairs. Hand on the railing, I looked back to where Hop stood in the doorway.

Hop was watching me and, for my troubles, he gave me a grin and a chin lift.

I returned the grin and raised it with a wave.

His grin turned into a smile.

I let his smile feed me as I skipped down the last few stairs and headed to the village.

It was late and, I hoped, late enough my mom would be passed out so my dad would have joined her.

I felt guilt that I'd left them to play Pictionary with Hop and his kids. But Mom was down for the night, and Dad wasn't a brilliant conversationalist, preferring to stare at a television set and let the screen mute the guilt he should feel at what his deception and disloyalty had manifested upstairs in his bed.

He didn't need me around for that.

I slid inside the door to our condo, closing it quietly, feeling the house at rest and letting the tension that had grown during my walk ebb, knowing that I'd timed things right. I could just go to bed, look forward to checking in with Hop tomorrow, and endure the best part of my parents' visit. The end of it.

Hand on the banister and foot lifted to walk up the stairs to my room, I stilled when my dad's voice hit me.

"I know what he is to you."

I turned at the foot of the stairs to see him standing there, his fingers curled around a cut-crystal glass of Scotch. He rarely drank. He let Mom do the drinking. His addiction was betrayal and he indulged in that liberally.

"Hey, Dad," I said quietly, my mind reeling to find the right way to play this.

"You think you two are being clever but you didn't hide

it. Maybe your mother missed it, and his kids are too young to understand, but I didn't miss it," Dad declared, and I looked at him.

He was angry.

But I was thirty-nine and I didn't need my father's approval in regards to who I spent time with.

So I straightened my shoulders and declared, "Hop and I have known each other for a long time. Recently, we got together. His kids don't know yet."

He shook his head and took two steps toward me before he stopped and asked, "Lanie? Seriously?"

"Seriously what?" I asked back.

"Seriously, you didn't learn a lesson that it was impossible to miss when your *last* choice got you in Critical Care for six days?"

That was a blow he meant to land viciously, and he succeeded brilliantly.

"Dad—"

"And this one, this…this…*man* is *worse*. By far. My God, when was the last time he cut his hair?"

"I'm not sure when Hop does or does not cut his hair is the measure of a man, Dad," I replied.

"You would be very wrong, Lanie, and I'll point out again, not for the first time," Dad shot back.

Blow two. Direct hit.

"You don't know him," I returned.

"I don't need to know him. One look at him and I know the kind of man he is."

God, I hated that from anyone, but especially my father.

"Sorry, but unless you have clairvoyance, something like that is impossible," I bit out.

"I don't need clairvoyance when I have age and wisdom, Elaine Heron. The first of those is creeping up on you without you seeming to realize it, your life wasting away, and the second seems to have escaped you."

"I've known Hopper for eight years and you've known him less than a day and you think you can stand there and tell me you know him better than me?" I asked.

"We can start with that. What kind of name is Hopper for what kind of man?"

I had to admit, unlike all the other guys, Hop didn't have a nickname that the brothers used almost exclusively to refer to him, and I'd always been curious about that. One of the many inconsequential (but I found fascinating) facts I'd learned about Hop before I was with him was that his name actually was Hopper Kincaid. Seeing as he already had a name that fit, the boys didn't bother giving him another one.

And I liked it.

But I wondered at it.

"I don't know," I answered Dad. "The name his parents gave him?"

"That's ridiculous," he bit out.

"I like his name," I returned sharply. "I like pretty much everything about him."

Dad took two more steps toward me, stopped again and hissed, "Lanie, *wake up*. Do it now before you waste your life. No children, no decent man to look after you, no future. Before you're dragged into yet *another* world that is not good for you in any way, by a weak man who takes the easy path of life, and you find yourself paying for *his* choices."

His words, each one...

No.

Each *syllable* slammed into me, breaking something I was holding together by a miracle.

And when it broke, there was no way to hold back what it was keeping at bay.

So I let it rip.

"Would that Papaw took the time before he died to warn Mom of that very thing," I clipped, and Dad's head jerked. "You gave her children but you took away everything else, being a weak man who chose his own selfish needs over his family. You cannot stand there and say Hop is not decent, at the same time sinking in the mud you stepped in your own damned self. All that while Mom's passed out cold upstairs, losing herself in a bottle because she can't cope with the fact she lost her husband three decades ago. But he didn't have the courage to cut ties and walk away so he tortures her with his selfishness every single day."

His face turned to stone before he made an attempt to do something he couldn't do. That was, putting the lid back on his boiling over pot of deceptions.

"I don't know what you're talking about."

"Yes, you," I leaned toward him, "*fucking* do."

"Remember who you're speaking to and who you are, Elaine. That language—"

"Go fuck yourself, Dad," I snapped, and his head jerked again.

"I cannot believe you would dare—"

I took a step toward him and hissed, "Believe it!" I leaned back and threw out both my hands. "You know, when you go to her, you don't just fuck over Mom. You fuck over Lis and me. Every time. Every time you go to her, it says, straight up, you do not give one single," I leaned into him again, "*shit* about any of us."

"This, this right here is the effect of spending time with that Tyra friend of yours and the kind of people her husband and your friend *Hopper* are."

"Yes," I agreed, nodding my head. "Yes, Dad. This right here is the effect of being around people who are loyal, decent, and *honest*. This right here is the effect of being around people who do not let other people mess with their heads or screw them over. This right here is the effect of exactly that. And, in about five seconds, there'll be another effect. The effect of me walking upstairs and packing my bag. After that, the effect will be me walking out of here. After that, the effect will be you having to explain to Mom tomorrow where I've gone. And after that will be the effect of me explaining to Mom that I'll speak to her if she doesn't call me drunk off her ass but I am never again speaking to *you*."

"You play that game, just like your sister, you'll be cut off," he warned.

"Newsflash, Dad. Just like Elissa, I wanted a father who was loyal and true to my mother and, if he couldn't be that, he could at least let her go so she could find happiness in herself or someone else. Money and cars and houses, nothing holds a candle to that, so you can't buy my love and loyalty and you can't hurt me by taking things away I never wanted in the first place."

"You say that now but—"

"Save it," I bit off, lifting my hand and throwing it out at the same time turning on my boot and stomping to the stairs.

"Lanie, you leave, you do this, your mother will be devastated," he called to my back. Four steps up, I turned back to him.

"You're right. She will. And that sucks. But you know what? She's lived with devastation a really long time. She knows the drill."

On that, I turned again and stomped up the steps.

I yanked out my suitcase while pressing buttons on my phone.

"Lady," Hop greeted after one ring.

"I...uh, Hop..." I trailed off mostly because my throat closed and I couldn't force words out of my mouth.

He heard it, sensed it by Hop Magic or both.

I knew this when he ordered low, "Talk to me."

I forced down a swallow and tossed my suitcase on the bed. "There was a, um...some unpleasantness...when I got back. Actually I would say it was more like...*extreme* unpleasantness."

He didn't ask.

He didn't hesitate.

He just clipped out, "Pack. Text your address. I'll be there as soon as I can."

My body stopped dead and my eyes closed tight.

"Lanie? You hear me?" Hop called.

"Yes," I whispered.

His voice was gentle when he replied, "Pack, baby."

"Okay."

"Text me first. I want to be waiting at the door when you're done."

"Okay."

"See you soon."

"Okay."

"Bye, lady."

"Bye, Hop."

We disconnected and I moved, flying through the room, packing with haste.

I was nearly finished when Dad appeared in my doorway.

"Don't say another word," I warned, not looking at him.

He didn't heed my warning.

"Please understand. I started that downstairs because I'm worried about you, Lanie. Your mother and I are both worried. Very worried, and we have been for years. You've been alone for a long time and a beautiful girl like you, a girl with your heart...honey, that's just not natural."

I made no reply, just kept packing.

"I love her," he whispered, and pain seared through me.

"Not another word, Dad."

"I love both of them."

Oh God!

I stopped and whirled on him. "Not another word, Dad."

"Can you imagine, living years, loving two women, knowing what you're doing to both of them?"

"No, I can't and I don't want to and furthermore, what is the *matter with you* that you'd even ask me that shit? I'm *your daughter.*"

He winced.

I went back to packing.

"I love you too, Lanie," he said quietly as I zipped up my case.

I yanked it off the bed, stomped to him and stopped.

"Then prove it. Pick one or the other. If it's Mom, get her in a program. But do *something*, Dad, because this is going to end in tragedy one way or another. You've had a good run but you lost one daughter to this, and you're losing another right now. Two tragedies. Don't court more."

With that, I shoved by him, hauling my case with me. I struggled down the stairs (it *did* weigh half a ton) grabbed my purse off the side table by the front door and took off through it.

Hop in his shiny, black, twin-cab Dodge Ram was idling outside my parents' condo.

He leaned across the cab and pushed open the door the minute he saw me, the interior light coming on.

With a heave, I failed to toss my bag in the truck bed. On the second heave, it was caught in Hop's hands, pulled from mine and tossed over like it weighed as much as a pillow. Without hesitation, I turned to the car door and, with another heave, I hauled my body into the passenger seat.

Seconds later, Hop hauled his in on the driver's side.

"Babe—"

"Go," I whispered to the seatbelt I was wrapping around me.

"Lanie—"

I twisted to him and cried, "Go, go, *go!*"

Eyes glued to me, he put the truck in gear. He only looked to the road when we were moving.

"You gonna talk to me?" he asked.

"No."

"Didn't like leavin' the kids, babe. Gotta take you back there."

"Okay."

"You sleep with me. We'll get up early."

"Okay."

"Lanie—"

"Please," I whispered and got silence.

We were closing in on his condo when he broke it.

"Your eyes are haunted, honey. This is more than your mom bein' an alcoholic and your family livin' in denial, and that's already fuckin' bad enough."

"Yes."

More silence while he waited for me to share.

I didn't.

Hop didn't push. He parked, came around to my side, hauled my suitcase out of the back, and grabbed my hand. His condo was quiet when we got in. I hadn't been gone long, but clearly his kids had crashed after an active day.

And clearly Hop read my mood because he took me and my bag straight to his room and ordered, "Get ready for bed. I'm closin' down and lockin' up. Be back."

I nodded, did as ordered and wandered from the master bathroom into his room while he was pulling off his tee.

I went directly to the bed.

Hop went to the bathroom and met me in bed after he turned off the lights.

He didn't turn me into his arms.

I burrowed there.

"Thank God you came up here. Thank God. Thank God. Thank God," I chanted quietly into his chest.

He gathered my hair away, and I felt his lips at the top of my head where he whispered, "Lanie, talk to me."

I shook my head.

"Later?" he asked.

"Later," I answered, relieved I didn't have to get into it then. I didn't have it in me.

"Promise?" he asked.

"I promise," I answered.

His hands left my hair and he closed his arms around me.

I let his warmth and strength seep into me, feeling the tension and pain dull. It did not go away, but I'd take it dulling for now.

"It's his."

Hop said this into the dark.

"What?" I asked.

"Knew it the minute I saw the arrogant, stick-up-his-ass fucker."

I lifted my head and looked at him in the dark. "What, honey?"

"That monster in you. It might have fed on other shit along the way, got strong and took control, but it was your father who planted the egg that hatched."

I dropped my face to his chest. This was my way of answering in the affirmative.

He cupped his hand to the back of my head.

"Enough. I'm done. You sleep," he ordered.

"Okay."

His hand sifted through my hair.

I turned my cheek to his chest and held onto his warm, strong body.

His fingers kept sifting through my hair.

My body had melted into his, my eyes drooping, I was close to sleep when I whispered, "Please be real."

His hand in my hair stilled, curled around my head, and Hop whispered back, "Lady, I'm as real as it gets."

I burrowed closer and fell asleep hoping he was telling the truth.

No.

Counting on it.

CHAPTER EIGHT

"You'll Accomp'ny Me"

Hop and I were sitting at a table in a biker bar that was so much better than the one where I'd met Monster Truck Man, it wasn't funny. That said, it was still rough but rough in a cool, kickass way, not a scary, precursor to being violated way.

Two mornings before, Hop had woken me early at his condo in Vail with a kiss that led to some cuddling and groping, but he didn't take it anywhere. Still, it felt nice and it was better than phone sex even if it didn't lead to fruition. This was because it involved Hop, his hands, his mouth, his rough, sleepy voice right in my ear and his body right there for me to put my hands and my mouth on. It was fantastic.

We were up and out of bed before the kids woke. I was in the kitchen making pancakes when they cutely and sleepily made their way downstairs.

As an aside, Hop got gold stars because he had buttermilk available for pancakes. These stars started shining when he told me pancakes weren't worth making without buttermilk and, since this was the God's honest truth, I took it as happy indication that Hopper Kincaid and I might just be soul mates.

As they were waiting for pancakes. Hop gave the kids a vague explanation of why I was there, saying my parents had to go home early, and he was helping out by giving me another day in Vail. The kids took this in, but they did it in a way where I knew explanations were unnecessary. They liked pancakes. They liked being in Vail with their dad. They liked me. So it didn't matter to them why I was there. They were just happy to go with the flow.

We did pancakes, we went into the village, we had lunch then we headed home. Riding the high that was being with Hop and his kids, not to mention Hop coming to my rescue in a Dodge Ram the night before, I asked if they wanted to stick around when they dropped me off at my place and I'd make them dinner.

To this offer, I got two enthusiastic replies from the back of the cab and one eye slide complete with sexy, warm grin from the driver's seat. I took this as a ringing endorsement for my idea. I also didn't try to stop myself from processing how nice that felt.

I didn't have food so we stopped by the grocery store before we went to my house. Hop dragged my suitcase upstairs while the kids alternately explored and chattered to me, and I made chicken fried steak, mashed potatoes, thick white gravy with loads of pepper, and green beans. Since I didn't have time, I cheated on the key lime pie and made the pie my grandmother taught me how to make, "When you're in a pinch, sugar plum." That was, frozen lime juice concentrate mixed with Cool Whip, tossed into a premade graham cracker crust and chilled. It didn't hold a candle to the real thing but, like Mamaw said, it did in a pinch, or at least the way Hop, Molly, and Cody wolfed it down, it seemed to.

Dinner was another revelation of all things Hop.

After taking my suitcase upstairs, he, like his kids, explored my house.

But there was something sweet and strangely profound in the way he did it. So much so, I found my eyes wandering to him, and I found that warmth around my heart growing.

This was because I caught sight of him holding the framed picture of me and Lis. We were in profile, our foreheads pressed together, looking in each other's eyes, smiling huge, clearly close and loving. When Hop was looking at it, his lips were curved up in a sexy smile, his eyes were soft, his expression something I felt like a physical touch. The same with the picture of Ty-Ty and me, both in little black dresses, both sitting at a swank bar, both holding a martini glass, both laughing so hard our heads were thrown back. The same when he ran one of his long fingers down the fake fur of the stuffed black panther I had on my couch. It was my aunt's. She'd died young, but before she died she gave Lis and me a lot of loving. When she died, that panther was the only thing of hers I wanted. I got it and I kept it right on my couch so I could see it every day.

I could tell, because he didn't hide it, that Hop liked having the opportunity to get to know me better by taking in the things I kept around me.

And I liked it that Hop liked it.

Another revelation was Hop and his kids eating my cooking. The kids just liked it, were polite enough to say so, but their enthusiasm while eating said it better.

For Hop, if there was a test to pass with him, the way he ate my food, I knew I'd passed it. But it was the way he looked at me after he took his third bite, the expression on his face taking all of my attention, his lips muttering, "Good food, babe," that I knew it was less a compliment and more a revelation about me that *he* liked.

A whole lot.

And I liked that too.

Because of the kids, we didn't get to make out when they left. We did get to have phone sex later because of Hop.

He called late. I answered on the first ring.

He opened with, "Not gonna push, lady. Not a good time to share over the phone and I want you to share when you're ready to do it, but just wanna know, you good?"

I liked knowing he wasn't going to push but still wanted to make sure I was okay.

"I'm good, and thanks for coming to my rescue and giving me a good day so it would take my mind off things."

"One way or another, babe, got your back," he replied, then he moved us out of the heavy and into the fantastic when he told me to cup my breast.

He gave me an orgasm and then gave me a warning before he rang off. "Now you owe me again. Tomorrow night, lady."

This meant I went to sleep relaxed, happy, and looking forward to the next day.

I woke up refreshed.

After a weekend with my parents that included a blowout with my dad, this was a miracle.

And I owed it all to Hopper Kincaid.

Therefore, letting him in further, I called him that day at work.

He answered in one ring. "Lady."

"Hey. Things good?" I asked.

"Kids are gone, which is not good. Took 'em to school so they'll do the switchover without me havin' to see their mom, which *is* good. And got plans with my woman tonight and that's definitely good."

This was an excellent answer.

I didn't tell him that. I told him, "I need to know the dress code tonight."

"The dress code is, you wear what you want. You work anything you put on," he told me.

This was also an excellent answer.

"But, if you gotta plan," he went on, "we're goin' to a bar to watch a band, and they probably don't have martini glasses."

I smiled into the phone and confirmed, "Message relayed." Then I asked, "A band?"

"My buddy's the lead singer, lead guitarist of a band. Been at it for decades. They're good. He and me'll connect during their breaks. You and me'll connect before they play and after we get home."

Now *that* was an *excellent* answer.

Therefore, I gave him my understatement. "Sounds fun, honey."

"The first part will be fun. The second part will be wow."

I remembered Hop's brand of "wow."

Definitely something to look forward to.

I was smiling into the phone again when I said, "Gotta get back to work."

"Pick you up at seven," he replied.

"See you then, Hop."

"Later, baby."

"Later, honey."

We disconnected and I smiled through the day. I did this even with the knowing looks I got from my staff. I also miraculously did this even after calling my sister to give her the lowdown of the weekend.

Elissa was ticked because it happened, livid at what Dad said to me, but happy I finally found the backbone to lay down the law.

"Now stick to it, Lanie," she advised. "The thing that business with Elliott should have taught you is not what Dad says it should have taught you, but that life is way too short to put up with dysfunction like that. If Dad didn't get the wakeup call from that whole scene then there's nothing more you can do. Now, I know you have to work but I want sister time, ironclad, in your calendar, at least an hour so you can tell me all about this Hopper Kincaid guy. And you've got forty-eight hours to fit me into your schedule, girl. If you don't, I'm flying to Denver and I'll find out about this guy myself. It isn't like the Chaos MC and Ride Custom Bikes and Cars are located in secret bunkers, so don't force me to do anything dramatic."

Obviously, I'd had to tell my sister about Hop to give her the whole scoop about Dad. Also obviously, the drama gene had been inherited from Mom by both of us.

"I'll call you tomorrow at lunch," I assured her.

"Holding you to that," she returned. "Now, you get back to work."

We rang off and I got back to work. I knew she got back to work, too, but this consisted of doing laundry, cleaning house, doing school runs, and cooking for a family of four, thus she was probably a lot busier than I was.

Later, Hop picked me up and took me to the bar and Hop did all this again without pushing me to share what had happened with Dad.

For some reason, we weren't on his bike. We were in the Ram, so there were opportunities to talk on the way to the bar, as well as when we shared a Lanie-approved evening meal of bar food including hot wings, fried mushrooms, and stuffed potato skins. He just didn't force me to talk. Not about that.

We ate. We drank beer. We chatted. We laughed.

Hop, without my drama, his kids, or sex, was mellow and amusing. I knew this since I'd known him for years, but having all that to myself, his body close, our knees brushing, his attention solely on me, felt so good it was hard to process. Not because I wasn't letting myself do it, just because I'd never had anything so simple and good.

And right.

I'd dated a lot. I'd had more than my fair share of male attention. I'd been treated to posh restaurants, the finest champagne, and effusive compliments. Elliott, in his geeky, sweet Elliott way, gave me all of that in spades.

Hop gave none of that to me.

But that date was the best I'd ever had.

Bar none.

Feeling very good about all of this, the remains of our grease fest laying in front of us, new beers having recently been added, I turned to Hop. We were sitting side-by-side at a round table facing a now empty stage so when I turned and leaned in, my breast brushed Hop's arm and he immediately gave me his attention.

"Can I ask you something?"

"You can ask me anything," he replied.

Another excellent answer.

I smiled and leaned farther in, something Hop liked, and I knew it when he twisted to me, lifting his arm to lay it on the back of my chair as he moved closer.

"You know the Club talks," I started and watched his face change. His expression wasn't guarded, but it was clear he was bracing for what I'd say next.

"Yeah," he prompted when I said no more.

"Well, all the boys have nicknames," I told him something he knew. "But you don't. Your name is Hopper, which is kind of...unusual."

His expression cleared and he moved closer to me as he grinned. "You wanna know how I got my name."

"I've always been curious," I shared.

His grin got bigger and his eyebrows inched up. "Always?"

I took a breath.

Then I let him in farther.

"Yeah. Since I found out that was your real name. Always," I confirmed.

He took his arm from the back of my chair, slid his fingers through the hair at the side of my head, then rested it back on my chair, all this while grinning, this time with approval.

Only after that did he begin.

"My dad, if given the choice, which he wasn't, would have been in an MC. No doubt."

There was not much there and yet, there *so* was.

"Uh…" I mumbled in an effort to communicate this to him. Hop's grin became a smile, and his arm gave my chair a jerk so our thighs were plastered together and I was super close.

"My younger brothers are named Jimmy and Teddy," he told me. "Jimmy's a high school gym teacher and basketball coach. He's got an ex-wife who married a man who makes a lot more than Jimmy does and she doesn't hesitate to rub his nose in it. They have two boys. Now he's got a new woman who is the shit. She treats him like a king, loves his kids. So his ex can be as big a bitch as she wants. He's got it good so he doesn't give a fuck."

I nodded and Hop went on.

"Teddy apprenticed to be a cabinetmaker, made journeyman and about two days later, decided he wanted to be an electrician. He went all the way with that and now he's apprenticing as a plumber. His whole life, he's been restless. The fact that he's had three professions and five ex-wives and he's in his early thirties lays testimony to that bullshit."

Although this was all fascinating, most especially how it was even possible to have five ex-wives and be in your early thirties, it didn't explain Hopper's name.

"Well…" I started, and Hop kept smiling at me.

"What I'm sayin' is, Dad got in there before Mom could do shit about it and he named me a name he liked. The name he thought sounded like the name for a biker. Hopper, James, and Theodore don't go together, so you can take it as Mom learnin' her lesson and layin' down the law after me. Mom was good at layin' down the law. Dad was good at gettin' his balls busted. Lookin' back, I get this. She was a knockout and still is. Beautiful. But hard. Tough. Bossy. And sometimes mean. He took it as long as he could, and when I say that I mean he ate that shit every day of his life until he couldn't eat it anymore. He left her and the next day bought his first Harley. Now he has three. I reckon it was part born in me, part given to me by my old man, since he took me, not Jimmy or Teddy, to the bike shops all the time. He talked to the salesmen, the customers, practically fuckin' salivatin', wishin' he was livin' his dreams. Now he lives the life he always wanted but he doesn't live it how he wanted because she's not in it."

Oh dear.

"So, you're saying, he still loves her?" I asked carefully.

"Yeah. I'm sayin' that and I'm sayin' the apple doesn't fall far from the tree. I'm a lot like my dad, includin' the fact I found a hard, bossy, tough-as-nails woman I thought I could fix and make happy. Unlike my dad, when I could take no more, I moved on. He didn't. Like me and Mitzi, my parents don't get along. This is because Mom still wants to control Dad and he's not down with that, but Dad still loves Mom so he's always strugglin' with the idea that maybe he should be. It's not cool and it's hell on the kids. Dad comes out two or three times a year but he only does it anytime he hears word Mom's thinkin' of comin' out. So he makes his plans, and she gets shitty and backs off. Kids see their granddad but they haven't seen their grandma in three years. He plays that shit with her all the time just to dick with her 'cause he's pissed she isn't what he needs her to be. Drives her nuts and she gives that anger to me, and while he's here I have to listen to his shit when he crows about stickin' it to her. It's insane and a pain in my ass."

It sounded like a pain in the ass.

"That isn't very nice," I noted, again carefully.

"Nope," Hop agreed. "But I can't find it in me to say she doesn't deserve it. The best day of my life up to then was the day he left her. She busted his balls and he took it, but that didn't mean he didn't go down without a fight. They fought all the fuckin' time. Morning, noon, and night. Loud. Vicious. Told you kids suck shit up like a sponge. With that, Jimmy, Teddy, and me didn't have to suck it up. It was shoved down our throats. She was still a bitch after he left, but at least we didn't have to listen to our mother and father tearing into each other all the fuckin' time. It was a relief."

I wrapped my fingers around his thigh and said quietly, "That doesn't sound like a fun upbringing."

"It wasn't," Hop confirmed. "Dad's a good guy, but eventually boys grow up and look at their old man and they can do one of two things. Have somethin' they wanna emulate or get scared shitless that they'll grow up just like him. Jim, Ted, and me, we got the last. Jim, like me, fucked up and moved on. Teddy's so busy movin' on, he hasn't settled so he fucks up constantly. Not a great legacy for either of my folks to give their boys. Honest to Christ, babe, if they weren't such good grandparents, I'd be done with the whole fuckin' thing. But they love Molly and Cody. My kids and Jimmy's kids do not get any of the shit we were treated to, and I want my kids to have that. So even though they bite at each other and that reminds me of unhappy times, I put up with it because the kids have to have one set of grandparents who love them unconditionally, and not with the haze of hatin' their mom and dad hangin' over every damned thing."

"That makes me sad not only for you but for Molly and Cody," I admitted, and after the words left my mouth, his hand curled around the back of my neck and he leaned in so he was all I could see.

"That's why you make buttermilk pancakes and, when the opportunity for a weekend in the mountains comes up, you jump on it. Why, when a beautiful woman offers to make dinner, you take her up on it immediately 'cause you wanna be with that woman but you also want your kids to be around beauty and the goodness of a home-cooked meal. Why, when the last thing you wanna do is play fuckin' Pictionary, you do it 'cause you don't remember one single good time in your life that involved both of your parents that didn't end in ugly words or an out-and-out fight. Why, they laugh and you hear it's carefree, you feed on that shit because you know they know you hate their mother but they still got it in them to laugh real, deep, from their fuckin' gut. So even though that shit is all shit, and they know it as much as you do, it didn't seep into their blood like you were scared as fuck it would and you rejoice in that."

When Hop was done talking, I was staring at him and I wasn't breathing.

All I could do was take him in and let each of his words, the depth of love he had for his kids, settle straight into my soul.

I must have done this for a while because I felt his fingers tense at my neck and he called, "Lanie?"

I pulled in a breath and then told him straight. "You're a good man, Hopper Kincaid."

His expression changed again, surprise sifting through then warmth settling in.

"That beats out you telling me I'm distracting for the nicest thing you've ever said to me," he replied.

I closed my eyes.

"Babe," he called.

I opened my eyes and his hand sifted up into my hair.

"I liked you asked. I liked you were curious. I liked gettin' to share. I want you to know my history but what I want you to take from what I told you is, I didn't learn my lesson from my dad goin' through that. I learned it by goin' through it. But I learned it, Lanie. That monster in you I gotta beat, that isn't me pickin' through hard ice hopin' to find a warm core. Women twist shit in their heads, even innocent shit you say. Don't twist any of that. You know a lot of the reasons I'm sittin' here with you right now. I'll tell you another one and that is, you've been around. I've watched you. I know you. And I know you're the kind of woman who can sit in a bar, eat shit food, drink beer, laugh and enjoy herself without any games or bullshit. A good night. An easy night." He grinned. "It took a while for me to get to it, but now that I got it, it's what I expected. Somethin' I knew I'd like a fuckuva lot." His hand slid back to my neck before he whispered, "And I do."

I had no idea what to say to that, so I just said a breathy, "Okay."

His repeated, "Okay," was not breathy but I got breathier, and this was because his hand at my neck was putting pressure on, his eyes dropped to my mouth, and I knew he was going to kiss me.

I wasn't wrong.

In a rough but cool bar, with the delicious mix of beer and Hop on his tongue, Hopper Kincaid kissed me like he always kissed me, thoroughly and beautifully.

I kissed him back like I always kissed him, happily and dazedly.

He pulled back but even as he did, his hand slid from my neck to my jaw and his thumb swept out and he did what he sometimes did after we had sex (or before or, it could happen, during). His thumb moved over my lips, putting pressure on, dragging my lower lip with it as he watched my mouth intently.

There was something about this crude but intimate gesture I didn't quite get but I liked. It was claiming. It was like he was taking me in, through touch and sight.

No, not taking me in, branding me. My lips were his. No one else's. Hopper Kincaid's. And doing that, beyond my lips, everything that was me, staking his claim at a place so intimate as my mouth, was his too.

Me.

All of me.

His.

I felt that warmth settle around my heart at the same time I felt a tickle up my spine and the tip of my tongue slid out slightly, tasting the salt of his thumb.

His eyes watched my tongue before they cut to mine. His thumb swept away and the pads of his fingers dug in as he yanked me to him, this time forcefully. His mouth slamming on mine, again Hop kissed me like he often kissed me, thoroughly, beautifully but also deep, wet, rough, and *long*.

And I kissed him back like I always kissed him. Happily and dazedly but, this time, more of both.

The kiss only ended when we heard the sounds of a live

(loud) rock band suddenly crashing our way. At the sound of cheers from the crowd, Hop's lips left mine and we both turned to the stage.

Five men, all Hop and my age, all around (but not quite) Hop's gorgeousness (except the drummer who was, alas, not all that good-looking, but his manic smile and his clear talent with a backbeat made up for it in a huge way), were on the stage rocking right the heck out.

Within the first few notes, the crowd went wild, especially the women—whose ages ranged from too young to be in a bar to women who either had ten decades on me or needed more moisturizer—that were dancing up front.

During the first two songs I realized I'd been so into Hop I hadn't noticed that this wasn't a live-band-at-the-local-biker-bar crowd, but that the vastness of bodies taking up the soon heaving space in front of the stage meant this band was a big draw.

There was a reason why.

The band wasn't good. They were fantastic.

So fantastic, I wondered why they were playing a local biker bar. The only reason I could come up with was that the music they played with ease and sheer, swelling rock goodness, were all covers.

Luckily, the stage was up high so the mass of bodies out front didn't limit our view. Although every muscle in my body was screaming at me to get up and move to the beat, sing out loud and enjoy the vibe, Hop's arm around my chair kept me anchored, slouched into him, tapping the beat with my toe.

But I did it smiling.

It was after song five when the lead singer stopped the music in order to speak into his microphone.

"Those of you who been with us for years, you'll know,

sixteen years ago, we lost the best front man in the business. Tonight, you give him a yell, he might come up here and show you how we used to do it. Caid! Why don't you get your ass up here?"

I found this confusing—not only the wall of sound from the crowd that concluded this announcement, but also the fact that the lead singer seemed to be looking directly at Hop.

It hit me that "Caid" was Hop when I heard him mutter, "Fuckin' shit."

Part of the older contingent of groupies started to chant, "Caid, Caid, Caid!"

Still, I was stunned when Hop leaned into me and murmured in my ear, "Be back, babe," before he straightened from his chair and headed around the table.

"Oh my God," I whispered to no one as I watched Hop wind his way through the crowd to pats on his back, applause, and come-hither eyes.

He took a big step up to the stage, and I watched him do a man hug with the lead singer before moving to shake hands with the bassist and give a chin lift to pianist, keyboard guy, and drummer. A guy who appeared to be a roadie ran on stage with a guitar.

"Oh my God," I repeated as Hop looked at the guitar, then wrapped a hand around its neck and lifted the strap over his head.

Hop played guitar.

Hop had been in a rock band.

Oh my God!

He was looking down, strumming the instrument like he was getting used to it, when the roadie handed him an amp plug and he shoved it into the guitar.

Another cheer rose from the crowd.

He was going to sing.

And play.

Hopper Kincaid, badass biker and hot guy, was going to *sing* and *play* with a *rock band*.

I wasn't surprised when I immediately felt my panties get wet (or wetter, considering his last kiss started that action).

I watched Hop do a lips-to-ear brief chat with the lead singer. The lead nodded enthusiastically, grinning like a lunatic, then he turned to his band and shouted something I couldn't hear.

Hop went to the microphone that was front and center.

I again stopped breathing.

"Gotta do this shit again, gonna make it count," he growled into the microphone, his voice coming through the speakers rougher and sexier than ever, and the crowd again went wild. He started strumming and my heart stopped beating when he finished, "This is for Lanie."

When the bassist kicked in, my hand darted out to wrap around the edge of the table, to hold on even though I was sitting, eyes glued to Hop as he started singing about gypsy wind and scarlet skies in that growly, sexy voice of his, his eyes locked to mine.

Then Hopper Kincaid, badass biker and hot guy, sang Bob Seger's "You'll Accomp'ny Me" straight to me.

Straight.

To.

Me.

Words I'd heard time and again (and innumerable times recently) came from his beautiful lips and pummeled right into me.

Exquisite pain.

The kind you wanted to feel every day for the rest of your life.

It was the pain of finally having something you wanted. Something you'd longed for. Longed for since you had memories. Something life taught you to believe you'd never have. Something, if you lived without it, it left a void in your soul you knew would never be filled. Something, without it, you knew you'd never be whole.

It was something you needed.

It was as necessary as breath.

It was what was required to complete you.

And, I found in those four minutes as Hopper sang to me, when you got it, it filled you so full you thought you'd rupture, but it was so precious, you would do anything to hold it all in and not lose a drop.

Not one drop.

That was what Hop gave to me by telling me through Bob Seger's words exactly how he felt about me.

And what he intended to do about it.

By the time he was done, every inch of my skin was tingling, my eyes were burning from holding back tears, and my fingers hurt from gripping the table.

And when he was done, I had no idea what to do. How to communicate what I was feeling. How to tell him what he needed to know.

But I was Lanie Heron, and even if my mind was scrambled by the beauty of all Hop had just given me, my body knew exactly what to do.

So I straightened from my chair. I put one high-heeled boot into the seat, pulled myself up and turned to Hop. Then I lifted the fingers of both hands to my lips and threw them out toward a good man, a handsome man...

My man.

Then I shrieked like a groupie, *"You are the shit, Hopper Kincaid!"*

It was the right thing to do. It got me a sexy smile that I was pretty sure melted my panties clean away (and those of most of the women in the audience) before he followed the *Nine Tonight (Live)* playlist. He turned to his friend, his mouth moved, and they went right into "Hollywood Nights."

I danced on my chair until a bouncer told me I had to get down.

Hop finished the first set with his boys and then the entire band joined us for a drink at both their breaks.

Hop held me so close while he was talking to his buddies I was practically in his lap.

Later, looking back, I had no idea if I even spoke a word.

But I do remember smiling so big and for so long, the next morning, my face hurt.

Like I said.

Exquisite pain.

CHAPTER NINE

No Regrets

"So, you were a rock star?"

I grinned as I watched Hop press his handsome head into the pillow and burst out laughing.

It was Tuesday night.

I was in Hop's bed at Hop's house. It was the first time I'd been there.

I found, after following his directions, that Hopper Kincaid lived in a nondescript split-level on a cul-de-sac in a regular neighborhood, not a clandestine biker bunker I had to be led to blindfolded.

This was a surprise but not a disappointment.

The house was nice, although it was clear he could spend more time on the yard. The moment after I had this thought, my mind purged it. Hopper Kincaid and yard work didn't go together. What did go together was, if his neighbors didn't like it, since he was a badass biker, they probably didn't complain and just put up with it.

The minute I walked in (after Hop laid a hot and heavy one on me in the open doorway), I was assaulted by décor that shouted, *"A man lives here!"*

The prevailing colors were black and brown. *Dark*

brown. The feel wasn't "sit and stay a while," but "kick back and lounge for however long you want, preferably with a beer."

It was not the way I would decorate but I had to say, I liked it.

It was pure Hop.

There was framed rock memorabilia everywhere. Signed pictures of Springsteen, Seger, Clapton, Page, these intermingled with framed tickets, rock concert posters, and posters from motorcycle rallies.

Unfortunately, I didn't have much time to peruse this Museum of Rock (and Motorcycle Rallies) because dinner was ready and I got surprise number two of the night.

Hop could cook.

He made a meatloaf that had been basted in a sweetened tomato sauce that was out of this world. It was so good Mamaw would approve, and that was saying something.

When I shared this information, he grinned at me and stated, "Don't get excited, lady. I can kick ass with ground beef and I can broil the fuck out of a pork chop, but outside that, my cooking is not much to write home about."

I was looking forward to him "broiling the fuck out of a pork chop" for me, but I didn't share that mainly because I was shoveling meatloaf in my mouth.

Now, the dirty dishes were in the sink and we were in Hop's bed. This was because he didn't waste time after dinner in starting the tour of his house. This included a lot more man stuff, the not-surprising knowledge that Hop wasn't exactly tidy, and the equally not-surprising knowledge that Cody was a Hop Mini-Me (seeing as his room was filled with motorcycle and rock stuff).

The revelation was Molly's room, which was painted a pastel yellow and decorated effusively in every shade of purple under the sun, with a liberal sprinkling of daisies in the form of daisy lamps, a daisy motif to the bedclothes, daisy prints on the walls, and a daisy nightlight.

Glancing into Molly's room was more proof badass biker Hopper Kincaid loved his daughter. It didn't belong in this rambling, split-level man cave.

And yet, getting to know Hop, it absolutely did.

The end of the tour was Hop's room, and I was again surprised when confronted with a mammoth, black leather–padded waterbed. Although it looked incredibly cool, I'd slept on a waterbed twice in my life and, albeit an adventure, being tossed on the waves every time you twitched wasn't my idea of a restful night.

I didn't have a chance to think much on this because Hop wasted no time ending the house tour and beginning another one.

The new tour lasted two hours.

During it, it took Hop thirty whole minutes to take all my clothes off me. It took ten more for me to get all his off him.

In other words, it was about taking our time. It was about exploration, rediscovery, and memorization, of touch, taste, sound, and sensation.

Two hours.

Two hours of making love.

It was phenomenal and, by the time Hopper slowly slid inside of me, his eyes holding mine, I was so primed, I came instantly. I did it hard and it lasted a long time.

And it was the best I ever had.

Every time with Hop seemed like new.

And every time with Hop was a new best.

So now I was lying on top of him, his dark sheets pulled up over my booty, his chest hair rough against my breasts, his fingers curved around the cheeks of my ass, pads digging in, and I was doing something I knew in that instant I could do for a lifetime.

Watching him laugh.

When his laughter died down to chuckling, he dipped his chin and focused on me to say, "I was never a rock star, babe."

"You seemed pretty comfortable up there," I noted.

"Yeah, guess it's like ridin' a bike," he mumbled, and I pressed closer, sliding my hands up his chest to wrap my fingers around the sides of his neck.

"Tell me," I urged softly, and he bit his lip, his strong white teeth sinking into the flesh of his full lower lip, and I had to beat back a shiver, it was so sexy.

He stopped biting his lip and started, "Right."

I tore my eyes from his mouth to look into his.

He went on, "After a fight, Dad bought a guitar. Pissed Mom off, which was his intention. She went fuckin' ballistic. When he came home with that guitar, it was the worst fight up until then, but she was dedicated to upping the game so it wasn't their worst fight ever. Still, she was off on one. Dad, for once, didn't back down and return the guitar. He was out in the garage all the time, plucking at it. The whole point was him bein' shit at doin' it, and since it was electric and he also got an amp, him makin' nothin' but noise and that noise bein' loud sent her over the edge time and again."

"I'm beginning to think your childhood was worse than mine," I shared and watched Hop's face get warm and intent.

"How long's she been at the bottle?" he asked quietly.

"One year, she tripped and spilled a glass of red wine on my fabulous gypsy Halloween costume," I answered instantly. "Since it wouldn't do for me to go out in a wine-stained gypsy costume, no matter how fabulous it was, Dad had to cut holes out of a sheet from the guest bedroom so I went as a blue paisley ghost. The sheet was so huge I tripped on it and chipped my front tooth on the sidewalk outside our neighbor's house. My tooth is capped. I was nine."

"Babe," he murmured, his voice low and gruff, filled with feeling.

Feeling for me.

That feeling coming from Hop felt nice, but the reason he was giving it to me didn't, so I shrugged. "Something life has taught me over and over, it can suck."

"That it can, lady," he agreed.

"So anyway," I moved to change the subject. "I take it you confiscated your dad's guitar."

Hop thankfully, but not surprisingly, went with me but he did it while both of his hands drifted up my back, gathered my hair away from my face and one hand held it bunched at the back of my head while the other one moved to stroke my spine.

This felt nice too.

Or, *nicer.*

"Yeah," he confirmed. "Dad got sick of drivin' Mom 'round the bend and I was curious. Picked it up. To this day, don't know how it happened but I just took to it. No lessons, nothing. Just started strumming and made music. Dad was fuckin' thrilled. Thought it was the shit. Mom was pissed. Thought it'd give me ideas of bein' a jukebox hero. I didn't care what either of them thought. Two things took me out of the shit that was my life with them, and that was bein' at a bike shop with my dad or sittin' in the garage, fuckin' around with that guitar."

"How old were you?" I asked.

"Twelve," he answered.

"Wow, that's young," I remarked, and it was Hop's turn to shrug. "That's also really cool," I continued.

That was when Hop grinned. "I thought so too. When I was fourteen, met Danny from last night. He took lessons, his parents wanted him to play classical guitar, but it was all about the rock riff with him. They were disappointed, but he didn't give a shit. That bug bites you, no cure for it."

"Obviously there was a cure for you," I said, and his hand stopped stroking my spine as he wrapped his arm tight around me.

"For me, it wasn't about the same thing as it was for Danny," Hop shared. "He feeds off what you saw last night, standin' in front of a mic, makin' music, women pressed to the front of the stage, shouting, dancing. He gets high off that vibe and he works through that high in a hotel room later with a couple of bottles of bourbon, some grass, and as many warm, soft bodies as he can get. When we recruited the guys and formed a band, if he turned up for rehearsals, it was a miracle. But he never missed a show."

"What was it about for you?" I asked.

"The poetry," Hop answered, and I was so surprised by this answer, I blinked.

"What?"

"Music is poetry, babe. Each note is a word that's uniquely crafted to go with the next note. For me, the only way it gets better is if you put that to lyrics. You take them apart, any good song tells a story separately, through the music and through the lyrics. What makes it grab you by the balls is when you put them together. I didn't have a lot of beauty in my life. Found it in that."

This was deep, another revelation about Hop that didn't surprise me, but I felt my brows draw together.

"So why did you quit?"

"I quit because I had a way with notes. Bog, the bassist we had back then who now lives in LA and produces records with some pretty big fuckin' names, had a way with words, and Danny didn't want to move from covers. He didn't think we could compete with the likes of Seger and Springsteen. He didn't think, the bars we were playing, we'd draw crowds with original music. He said people wanted to hear what they knew."

I thought this kind of made sense but I didn't share that because Hop continued.

"Under all that, he was shit scared. We started to play gigs in high school, which, by the way, did not make my mother happy. We were good, even better back then. Didn't have the practice but we had the passion. We had a good thing and people felt it. We got more gigs. We made money. We did some traveling. Saw a lot of bars, a lot of road and laid a lot of women. He didn't want to fuck that up. Didn't have it in him to take a risk. He didn't get it wasn't about besting the rock gods. Seger, Clapton, the greats laid down such fantastic tracks, nothing, no one, no matter how talented they are, would outshine that. Music isn't about competition. It's about communication. There are countless stories to be told, lady, and even if your story isn't so fantastic it will live for eternity, that doesn't mean it shouldn't be told."

I had to admit, he was right about that and that also was deep.

And cool.

Hop kept talking.

"Bog got frustrated then pissed, took off, formed his own band. That didn't work but at least he tried. I figure he'd prefer to be makin' his own music now but he isn't complaining since he lives his life *in* the life. And Bog takin' off pissed me off. I couldn't do much with words but I could with music, and without a lyricist, I was stuck. Loved music. Loved playing. Didn't like that it was the same thing every night. Danny and I were tight, us playin' together since we were kids were some of the only good times I had. I figured, I kept goin' with that and my world being so narrow, I'd begin to resent it and I'd lose what I had with Danny. So to preserve that, I took off too."

"Did you join another band?"

Hop shook his head. "Auditioned for a couple of them, but that band with Danny was my band, *our* band and," he grinned, "I'm not a man who follows, who likes to be told what to play, what to do, so I knew it wouldn't work for me and I gave it up."

"That's kind of sad," I told him. "If last night is any indication, you're really, *really* good."

He gave me a soft smile in appreciation of the compliment but did it shaking his head again.

"Not sad," he returned. "Danny's livin' the same life, babe. No growth. Nothin' to show for it. They got a loyal following that's a fuckuva lot bigger than what we had back then, which means they have a decent manager who keeps them in gigs and they can pay two roadies so they don't have to lug equipment. But every night it's a different bar, a different body in his bed, a different hotel. Every day it's back in the RV, on the road, headin' to more of the same. His life is still narrow. I think he digs it, and if he's down with that, cool. But he and me are both forty. In ten years, fifteen if he's lucky, those broads up front are gonna look as tired as he is. It won't matter how great he can sell "Feel Like a Number," fresh pussy is gonna dry up, and the gigs are gonna be fewer and farther between and, I guarantee you, lady, he's gonna find himself at a time where he'll look back and reflect and he'll have regrets."

I nodded because this was likely true.

Hop carried on.

"I gave it up and found Chaos. I got kids. I got brothers. I got a home. I got work I like doin' at the garage, the store, with my Club. I got family." His arm gave me a squeeze and his lips tipped up. "I got a beautiful woman in my bed and I've had her enough times, I know what to do to make her moan for me. If I don't fuck that up with her, I keep that and no matter what women think, a real man wants to know how to make his woman moan and takes up the challenge of keepin' that up and makin' it better. Not starting that shit up time and again with another bitch. What I'm sayin' is, I landed in a good place, baby, and I never looked back. I got no regrets."

His words about me, how he knew how to make me moan, how a real man wants to keep that up and make it better, meant everything to me.

Everything.

If I could give him words to say to make me know my heart and gut led me straight to where I should be, naked in Hop's waterbed, they might not have been exactly the same since I wasn't a badass biker.

But they'd have the same meaning.

Therefore, I found myself whispering, "I love the song you sang for me."

His face got soft but his smiling mouth said, "I think I got that when you stood on a chair and screamed I was the shit then jumped me the minute we got in your front door. Seriously, babe, I think I got carpet burns on my ass and shoulder blades, you rode me so hard."

I smiled back but still gave his shoulder a puny slap and returned, "You don't have carpet burns."

He kept smiling through his muttered, "Feels like it." I kept smiling too, and Hop went on, "Good you got a rug inside your front door, lady. You rode me like that with my back on your tile, I wouldn't be able to walk, but that would be the least of my worries seein' as I'd probably have a concussion."

"Shut up," I mumbled, still smiling and his smile got bigger. "Dad knows about us."

Yes, that was what I blurted. I knew it actually came out when Hop's eyebrows shot up.

"Come again?" he asked.

I pulled in a breath.

I said it. I said it in Hop's bed. I said it after making the unconscious but undeniable decision to let him in, so I decided it was time to give him more.

"That was what that thing was about in Vail," I admitted.

"Fuck," he muttered.

"Yeah," I muttered back, and his hand slid out of my hair to wrap around the back of my neck.

"Can't say that's too surprising, baby," he said gently. "We were shit at hiding it."

"Yeah," I repeated.

"He'd have to be stupid *and* blind, and your old man is neither. Caught your mom givin' us looks too and, I don't know, not gonna go there with her until you and me decide it's time, but I don't think it escaped Molly either," he told me and my stomach lurched.

"Really? Molly?" I asked.

"She loves her dad. She pays attention. She's a girl. Even at her age, she swoons over boy band crap and guys on TV she thinks are cute. Romantic fantasy is ingrained in chicks. It might come out slow but it'll always come out. You look great. You dress great. You smile at her like she's the only girl in the world and you make her old man happy. She's gonna get ideas. In this instance, they just happen to be the right ones."

"This is true," I murmured, and he grinned then his grin faded.

"So he said shit to you about me?"

"Yeah," I replied.

"And you packed your shit and walked out."

It wasn't a question, since he didn't have to question seeing as he rode to my rescue, but there was something in his tone. Something that made my heart seize. Something important.

"Well, yeah," I stated. "You rode to my rescue, remember?"

"Your dad said shit about me and you packed your shit and walked out."

Again with the tone. Heavy.

No, *weighty*.

Meaningful.

Something was happening here.

"Hop—" I started but stopped when he rolled us so he was on top, and his hand came up to cup my jaw and I noted he was no longer just looking at me.

His eyes were burning into mine.

"All that shit you no doubt had to live through with your mom, you ever do anything like that before?" he asked.

"No," I whispered.

"But your dad trash talked me, you threw a drama and walked out."

"Yeah," I replied, although I wouldn't refer to it as "throwing a drama." I couldn't debate that I didn't since, technically, I did.

And anyway, Hop was still being intense so I needed to concentrate and not debate terminology.

"So he trash talked me?"

I squirmed a little but stopped when Hop's fingers dug lightly into my skin.

"He said you were a mistake, like Elliott," I admitted cautiously.

"He's wrong," Hop growled, not cautiously.

"Hop—"

"He's wrong, Lanie," he bit out.

"Okay," I said slowly.

"Do not let him feed that monster in you. Not about me," he ordered.

"Okay," I repeated.

"With women, it's about the slow soak, babe. Assholes pour shit on the surface and women keep goin' not even knowin' that shit is soakin' in. Then one day, out of fuckin' nowhere, that acid has burned deep in a way it leaves a wound that will never heal. Wipe that shit away, Lanie. Don't let it soak in. He doesn't know me. He cannot make that call about me."

"That's what I told him," I shared.

"Good," he clipped.

"Uh, Hop, he's a biker bigot and he's, well...other kinds of bigot besides. I told you that before you met him," I pointed out.

"Yeah, you told me that but that was about how he'd be with me. I don't give a fuck he makes a point and steps away from me after he shakes my hand. I give a fuck about him givin' my woman shit and maybe makin' her question bein' with me. And when I say I give a shit, I mean in a big fuckin' way."

Boy, not much escaped Hop.

"He didn't make me question it, Hopper," I promised, then tried to lighten the mood. "And, just to say, it's a little freaky how well you know women."

"Babe, best wool men ever pulled was lettin' women think we think with our dicks. We pay a fuckuva lot of attention. We know your shit maybe more than you do because we live it right along with you, and some of you try to make us eat it. It's just that some of us choose not to get sucked in the drama and instead focus on getting laid regularly."

I felt my eyes get big right before I wrapped my arms around him and started giggling, but I managed to push through my giggles, "Honey, not sure you should share the brotherhood's secrets."

"You talk, no woman will listen. They prefer to think a man's brain is in his dick. Gives 'em something to bitch about."

"Again, freaking me out how well you know women," I said, still giggling, and finally his face cleared and he smiled at me.

Then his thumb swept my lips right before it drifted away and his head dropped so his mouth could brush them.

When he lifted up again, he wasn't smiling.

"You packed and walked out," he whispered.

I stopped giggling and my teeth came out to graze my lower lip before I confirmed (again), "Yeah."

"Means a lot, baby."

It did. Absolutely.

I was just glad he agreed.

I tightened my arms around him but said nothing.

Hop wasn't done.

"Means a lot you're finally in my bed, too."

My hand slid up his back so my fingertips could play with his hair but I again said nothing.

"It'll be good to wake up with you here."

He was killing me.

It felt exquisite but it had to stop before I melted and became one with his waterbed.

"I have to share that I'm also a bit freaked about the fact you have a waterbed but, even through our various, some-times vigorous activities, the waves didn't toss us off."

He again gave me the subject change. His eyes lit with amusement and his hand moved down to the side of my neck so his thumb could stroke my throat.

It felt really nice.

"It's waveless, Lanie."

"Bodies of water, even small ones, and waveless aren't natural, Hop," I noted.

"Bein' on the moon isn't natural either, but man managed to do that," he returned.

"Being on the moon is about harnessing science and technology. Waveless waterbeds are about harnessing nature and that, by definition, is not natural," I shot back.

"Babe, you're not lyin' on a miracle," he said through a lip twitch.

"No, I'm lying under one."

His lips stopped twitching, his body went completely still, except his chin jerked back and his eyes started burning again.

This all confirmed the fact that those five words actually did come out of my mouth.

Damn.

"Hop—"

He cut me off. "You said it. Don't pollute it."

I closed my mouth and his hand moved up, fingers driving into the hair at the side of my head, his thumb moving out to sweep my cheek, his face getting close, his body pressing into mine and his lips whispering, "You givin' me this?"

I knew what he meant. I was becoming fluent in Hop Speak but had already become fluent in Chaos Speak so I didn't miss his question.

I understood it completely.

"This" meant me.

"Hop—" I began.

"Easy question, Lanie."

"No, it isn't," I argued because, well, it wasn't!

"Right, I'll amend. You givin' me a shot at havin' this?"

"Well..." I paused then thought, being naked in his bed, sharing stories and laughter, that it was safe to say, "Yeah."

"No, lady," he shook his head. "You don't understand me. Are you giving me a shot at havin' this," his thumb moved back over my cheek, "you. For real. Sharing. Building. Lookin' at a future."

Okay, maybe I wasn't yet fluent in Hop Speak.

I squirmed again. "Hop—"

"I want that," he declared.

It was my turn for my body to go still.

"I'm forty years old, babe, but I don't mind lookin', takin' a test drive. I'm also old enough to know, with you, I like what I see. I like what I feel. I like what I know. I like everything I learn. So I know I'm ready to work at takin' it there with you. Havin' kids, what I gotta know is, if you're ready to work at takin' it there with me."

After Hop came to my house to check on me and carry one suitcase down one flight of stairs (amongst other things), really, there was only one answer to that so I gave it to him.

"I walked out on my mom and dad because of you, honey."

He held my eyes.

Then he muttered, "You're ready to work at takin' it there with me."

"I think, after Dodge Ram Rescue and Bob Seger's 'You'll Accomp'ny Me,' it's been confirmed you're real, so yes. I'm ready to work at taking it there with you."

There. I said it.

God, I said it.

And I meant it.

His hand moved slightly so his thumb could drag along my lower lip as he growled, "Best decision you'll make in your life, baby."

"Well, at least that's firm...if cocky," I joked, but I did it breathlessly.

"No," he said, then his hand moved so his face could disappear in my neck, and he promised, his 'tache tickling my skin, "I'm about to get cocky. I'm already firm."

My nipples tingled as he pressed the proof of his second statement against my thigh.

"Hop," I breathed but said no more because his lips were moving down my chest.

I was wriggling under him, my hands moving on him, but I stilled when his lips bypassed my breasts, moving through the valley between them and gliding across the scar under them, then down to glide along the one on my belly.

I felt his lips move away and he called, "Lady." I lifted my head to look down my body at him. He caught my eyes then he vowed quietly, "No regrets for you either. I'll see to it. You got my word."

My entire chest got warm and I pressed my lips together momentarily before I gave it back.

"I'll do my best so you get the same from me, Hop."

I watched his head drop and then I watched his lips and mustache again trail the scar at my belly and I shivered a shiver that was good for a lot of reasons.

He lifted his head and his eyes found mine.

"Already know I got it, Lanie. Now open your legs, baby. I want that pussy."

I forgot to feel moved by the moment when a tremor rocked through me and all I could think about was opening my legs.

So I did.

Hop threw them over his shoulders, dipped his face to me and got what he wanted.

So did I.

And, if I wasn't wrong, this happened for the both of us in a variety of ways.

CHAPTER TEN

That Works

Two weeks later…

"THAT SHIT HAS got to stop," Hop announced in a growly voice, sounding pissed.

He and I were in my kitchen doing the dishes. I'd made him fried beef cutlets and Mamaw's fluffy mashed potatoes, which were helped along to decadent by nixing the milk and replacing it with a splash of heavy cream.

And I'd just told him about things that were happening at work.

It had been two good weeks with Hop. Our first week together, as in *together*, we spent every night in his bed or my bed, making love and talking after having dinner together.

I discovered his broiled pork chops were the bomb.

His saying, "That body of yours, baby, does not go with the way you cook *and* eat and pleased as fuck it doesn't. Take you any way you come, but if you came with me havin' to eat a lot of salad, gotta admit, that would suck," was even better.

Obviously, when he had his kids last week, I didn't spend

the night. Instead, we had late-night conversations, which included phone sex and, on top of that, either Hop or I would call sometime during the day just to connect.

That said, Hop had told me he'd decided to introduce his kids "slow-like" to the fact that I was going to be in their life.

"We gotta have our time, and you need to feel this is solid. Solid is also what I want communicated to them so gonna ease my kids into this the same way I'm easin' you," he'd said.

They were his kids so it was his call. I didn't debate the solidness of "us" mostly because, even though it felt good and was going great, we'd had a rocky start. I wasn't fooling myself that I didn't have issues to work through, and we hadn't been together for very long, so even though it was his call, I agreed with that call.

More, I liked how he was protecting his kids against getting too deep into something that might harm them if it went bad.

So easing into it would do, for all of us.

Still, Molly had a dance recital last week, and clearly Hop was not going to waste time easing everyone into things because he asked me to show. I liked his kids, I wanted to see Molly dance, I was feeling things solidify with Hop and I was doing this on a daily basis, so I agreed.

We went separately, met there, and after it was over, I told Molly that Hop mentioned it to me, and since I wanted to see her dance, I came. She was tickled pink I did, which was gratifying. During the show, I sat by Hop with our knees brushing, which was more gratifying. And while Molly was dancing, I turned my head to see Hop's smiling, proud profile, which was even *more* gratifying.

What was not gratifying was the fact that Mitzi was there. Hop warned me she would be, so I was somewhat prepared, but you can never be totally prepared for something like that.

But it was worse than just being in the same room for the first time with your man's ex.

This was because I watched as, with an ease born of practice, they selected seats as far away from each other as possible, and they did this without even glancing at each other. Since Hop had the kids, Cody came with his dad, and although he went to say hi to his mom, he sat with Hop and me.

This felt unpleasant because, although it came naturally to Hop and Mitzi, I suspected it wasn't all that fun for Cody. I also suspected both Hop and Mitzi knew it, didn't like it, but had no intention of doing anything about it.

Further, I chanced a glance at Mitzi at a time she was looking our way, her mouth tight, her eyes on Cody. I didn't have much of an opportunity to take in her bleached, teased-out but still attractive biker babe hair or her hard face, which managed to be very pretty, before her gaze shifted to me and I felt the glacial sting. I fought the chill, gave her a small, noncommittal smile, and aimed my eyes back to the stage.

I didn't talk to Hop about this, because there was nothing to be said. It probably wouldn't surprise him his ex gave me an icy look. That was what exes did, and considering Mitzi's reputation and what Hop said about her, it was not out of character so I didn't need to get him riled up by sharing.

However, although nothing nasty happened, the night was underlined with an uncomfortable feeling. It made me sad to think that not only Mitzi and Hop had to perform this avoidance dance every time they were around each other, but the kids had to endure it too.

This, in turn, made me wonder about my father. I wondered if he'd partially made the decision to stay with Mom so Lis and I wouldn't have to choose sides.

If this entered his mind, it didn't excuse what he'd been doing. But it still made me think.

The kids went back to Mitzi after school on Monday and now it was again Hop and me, dinner, chatting, sometimes TV and then bed.

But while Hop rinsed the dishes and put them in the dishwasher and I put away the food, tidied and wiped down the counters, I told him about my old agency making overtures to steal my big new account. I also shared a bit about how they'd repeatedly been trying to undercut me in an effort to drive me into a merger.

I wasn't surprised at Hop's firm, biker badass response. I hadn't been spending time with Chaos and my best friend, who was married to the president of the Club, and not come to know how these men worked.

Therefore, I moved to the sink, threw the sponge in it, turned to my man and said, "Hop, honey, I told you because it's a pain and I needed to vent. I didn't tell you so you'd do something about it."

Hop shoved a plate in the dishwasher, pushed the rack in, and closed the door with his boot before turning to me.

"Lanie, baby, that might be so, but my woman isn't dumb. You may not have been officially folded into the life, but you been around the Club enough to know exactly what tellin' me that shit is gonna lead me to do."

"This stuff with my old company is halfhearted and eventually it'll die down," I explained.

"Don't give a fuck if it's halfhearted, but I do know it's gonna die down," he declared.

Oh dear.

He wasn't backing down. He was intending to intervene. Biker badass against ad agency.

This was not good.

"I meant naturally, Hop," I protested, trying to cut him off at the pass. "Not them backing off because my man and his biker brethren pay them a threatening visit."

"Chaos doesn't make threats, babe."

Gah!

"Hop!" I cried, quickly losing patience as was my wont. "Seriously. I do *not* want you to get involved. I didn't tell you so you'd get involved. And, most importantly, if you *do*," I leaned into him, "it's going to *tick me off.* Like, *bad.*"

He grinned at me like I amused him and asked, "Like, *bad*?"

"Don't make fun of me," I snapped.

"Don't be cute and I won't make fun of you," he returned, still grinning.

"I'm not being amusing, Hopper Kincaid, I'm being very serious," I warned. "This is my career, and I've worked hard to make a name in this business. I've worked hard to build my agency. It *means* something to me," I shared. "I can't have a bunch of badass bikers stomping around in their motorcycle boots and leather cuts giving me a reputation I *do not need.*"

The grin faded clean from his face and it got hard before he asked, "A reputation you don't need?"

Uh-oh.

He took that the wrong way.

"You know that wasn't what I meant," I said.

"Then, babe, it'd be good you tell me what you did mean and do it real fuckin' quick," Hop shot back, and I stared at him as an unpleasant burn hit my belly.

Then I said softly, "That isn't cool."

"Damn straight it isn't," he retorted, and I shook my head. "No. You don't understand me. That isn't cool, not even close to cool, Hop, that you'd think for *one second* that's what I meant."

"Again, lady, you need to *tell me* what you meant."

"Not once," I pulled in a calming breath before going on, "not once, Hopper, not since that very first moment when Brick walked into my house with Tyra, when she told me Elliott was making whacked decisions, and then you showed later to put me on the back of your bike and take me to Ty-Ty's, have I ever, *ever*," I leaned in again, "done one *stinking thing* to indicate I was a biker bigot."

"Yeah, until you just told me you'd get a reputation I get involved in your life," he returned, not letting it go.

"No, I didn't say that. I said I'd get a reputation if you got involved in *my business*," I amended sharply. "And it wouldn't matter if you were a biker or a businessman, Hop. I'm a businesswoman, and we've come a long way, but it's still a man's world, and *any* man sticking his nose into my business makes it look like *I* can't see to my business. I've worked too damned hard to prove I'm good at what I do, to demand credit for my work when some ass was taking it from me, to prove I can manage accounts, staff, an entire agency, to compete for business and best the competition, to have another man, no matter he's my man, I care about him and he thinks he's looking out for me, make me look like I'm not strong enough to do it."

I was glaring at him and breathing heavy when I was done with my speech, so it took a few moments for me to see the hard had gone out of his face and his eyes had warmed.

He understood me.

I didn't care.

What he said was bad, and I was still ticked.

He made a move to take a step toward me, but since I was still ticked, I stepped back. He stopped and his eyes locked on mine.

"Not lost on me the way you live," he said low, his hand

swinging out to indicate my house. "Your office. Your clothes. The sweet ride you drive. Your parents. That fuckin' condo that was three times the size of the one I gave my kids."

"And?" I prompted acidly.

"Eventually we were gonna have this conversation," he explained, but it didn't explain a thing.

"Why?" I asked.

"Babe, you are not of my world," he informed me.

"Really?" I retorted. "So do I have a Biker Babe Lanie Clone I don't know about who's been going to hog roasts and shooting the breeze in the Compound the last seven years?" I asked sarcastically.

He rested his weight in a hand on the edge of the sink and said in warning voice, "Tone it down, Lanie. We gotta talk this out, but we don't have to do it ugly."

"Okay, so, when I infer you're a bigot or something equally distasteful, I can rest in the knowledge you'll be cool in the face of me being an asshole?"

His jaw tensed hard before he replied, "No, babe, I get where your anger is comin' from, but you gotta rein in the drama and see where I'm comin' from."

"Your turn to tell me what *you* mean," I snapped.

"I've met your parents," he began. "I know how you grew up, who you grew up with, and how they think. And you know, babe, they raised you and so it isn't a leap to think there's a possibility that at least some of that shit is in you."

He could not be serious!

"First, Hop, it is since you've known me years and you've been *getting to know me* for weeks and you know that's not right. Second, I thought you didn't care what people thought of your lifestyle."

"I don't but you aren't people, Lanie. You're mine and I

care a fuckuva lot what you think about me, about the way I live my life, about how you feel you'll fit in it, about fuckin' *everything* when it comes to you."

Okay, that was nice, very nice, but I was still ticked.

Too ticked.

And too Lanie Heron to fight back the drama.

Therefore I fired back, "Right now, I'm rethinking that life option," and I felt him lose it.

I didn't see it. I didn't hear it.

I *felt* it.

Then I heard it.

"Everything," he said in a sinister whisper, "everything about you, I like. Including the drama. I'll stop likin' it if you blow shit like this out of proportion and you say shit you can't take back."

"So far, I haven't said anything I'd like to take back," I replied, and his eyebrows shot up.

"So you're good with threatenin' to take you away from me, *you,* somethin' you know I want and I want it bad, bad enough to work at it, bad enough to twist myself in fuckin' knots for it because you're justifiably pissed but unjustifiably not opening your mind to where I was comin' from and therefore not seein' I'm explaining myself or givin' me a shot at apologizing?"

That shut me up because, unfortunately, he was right. I was mad. I wasn't listening. And I'd threatened to take me away from him when he was definitely working on us and doing it by twisting himself into knots.

I didn't speak. Hop didn't either.

This lasted a very long time. So long, I was inwardly squirming and it was so uncomfortable, I was about to say something to smooth things over, get us back on track.

Unfortunately, I waited one second too long to do this.

"Fuck me, I can add fuckin' stubborn to high maintenance and a drama queen. Not good, babe," he bit off.

My temper, which was cooling, flared again.

"I'm not high maintenance!" I exclaimed, and he pushed away from the sink.

"Seriously?" he asked incredulously. "Been in your bed when you get up at fuckin' five thirty in the fuckin' mornin' to do your gig in the bathroom before you go to work and I've hauled your shit up to my bedroom so you can do it at my place. Lanie, you live fifteen minutes away from your office and you get there at eight. Over two hours every day just to do your hair and makeup. Diana fuckin' Ross in her heyday probably took less time to get ready for a show. Babe, if that isn't high maintenance, I do not know what is."

The Diana Ross comment was funny but I didn't laugh.

"I eat breakfast in that time too, Hopper," I reminded him.

"You swallow down some yogurt and suck back coffee, lady. You don't bake a quiche and eat it at your dining room table with cloth napkins and mimosas," he fired back.

It was unfortunate he was amusing when he was angry. Hop even saying the word "quiche" was hilarious.

I wanted to laugh. I really did.

I didn't.

He wasn't done.

"Fuck, you stand in your closet for a full fifteen minutes every fuckin' time I've been at your house in the morning like you're makin' your wardrobe selection of the day to announce your candidacy for president."

"Stop being funny, Hopper," I hissed, leaning toward him, and he leaned toward me.

"Baby, I am *not* bein' funny."

I took in his expression.

He wasn't being funny. Definitely not. He *was* funny but he wasn't being funny.

He was angry and this was serious.

"You cushioned my fall."

That came out of my mouth and I knew Hop didn't get it when he blinked.

"Say again?" he asked.

"Chaos. You. Tyra. Tack. Big Petey. Brick. Dog." I threw a hand out toward him. "You all cushioned my fall, Hop. You all knew how far I fell, and landing after a fall like that could destroy you. It didn't destroy me because Chaos cushioned my fall."

The anger slid out of his face as his lips muttered, "Baby."

I shook my head and kept talking.

"You all mean something to me. You're family and you intimating that I might think I'm better than you or think badly about you…" I drew in breath before I admitted, "I went over the top when I got ticked because you all mean something to me and I don't want any of you, because of my clothes or house or job or car, thinking I'd *ever* think bad things about you. And, for obvious reasons, I especially don't want *you* to think that way."

After I finished speaking, Hop held my eyes, and I let him because I was soaking in the look he was giving me.

It was a look I'd never seen from him or anyone.

Not aimed at me.

But I'd seen it. I'd seen it hundreds of times.

I saw it when Tack was watching Ty-Ty with their sons. Or when she was giggling with his daughter, Tabby. Or when she was goofing around with the guys and he was distanced but watching and liking what he saw.

Or, my favorite times, when he just caught sight of her walking into a room.

It was a look filled with warmth. A look filled with intimacy. A look of harmony.

The look of love.

Yes, right then, Hopper Kincaid was giving that look to me.

"Come here, lady," he ordered gently, and when I stayed frozen, stuck in the glow of his look and didn't move immediately, he leaned toward me, hooked a finger in the belt loop of my jeans and he brought me there.

When I was close, he wrapped his arms around my waist and, automatically, I lifted my hands and rested them on his chest. But I was careful not to lose contact with that look in Hop's eyes.

Hop didn't seem to notice I was mesmerized, because he started talking.

"I fucked up, jumped to conclusions, said somethin' stupid, and you were right to get pissed," he told me, and I stared up at him, stunned, pleased, warm…

Happy.

Hop wasn't done.

"I hear you about your work, and I won't get involved."

My body gave a slight, surprised jerk, taking me out of basking in the glow of his look, and I felt my eyes get wide.

"Are you serious?" I asked breathily.

"Yeah," he answered. "But I reserve the right, that shit ever turns ugly, to have another conversation about it. And if I feel you need me, that conversation might have a different ending."

Oh my God.

It just kept getting better.

Compromise.

Hopper Kincaid, member of Chaos Motorcycle Club,

badass biker who could beat unconscious a mountain of a man who owned a monster truck and do it in three minutes, was willing to compromise.

"Wow," I whispered, and my whisper encompassed a lot of things and even more feeling, and I watched Hop grin.

But his face got serious and his arms got tight when he continued, "You need to take two things from that. What you obviously took and that you do not bury shit because you're worried about my reaction to it. You need to get it off your chest, lady, I'm here. It starts messin' with your head, your sleep, your enjoyment of the work you do, *that's* when I'll expect to have our conversation. You down with that?"

It was my turn to grin but I suspected it was less of a grin and more a beaming smile.

"I'm down with that, Hop," I agreed.

His eyes moved over my face and his grin came back. "Good. Now the dishes are done. You wanna watch TV or you wanna go upstairs and fuck?"

Fight over and the way Hop ended it, a way I liked, liked in a way I knew I could like for a lifetime, I melted into him and asked, "Do we have to go upstairs to fuck?"

He dipped his face closer and answered, "In the mood to dominate, babe, and not big on givin' my old lady carpet burns."

He was in the mood to dominate.

Yes.

It just kept getting better.

I smiled at him and slid my hands up so my arms could round his neck before I suggested, "How about we break in the couch?"

His eyes flared and his lips hit mine.

"That works."

An hour later, I found Hop was right.
It worked.
We worked.
We *so* worked.
In a lot of ways.

CHAPTER ELEVEN

Safely Locked Inside

A week and two days later…

I WAS IN my office and running late.

I had to go home, change, and then meet Hop and the kids at Beau Joe's for pizza.

This wasn't big but this was bigger than my "surprise" showing up at a dance recital.

I was meeting them there. This meant even at their ages, the kids would soon get that seeing me occasionally at Chaos family events then suddenly seeing me everywhere meant something.

I wasn't nervous, as such. I knew they liked me.

But liking me as Lanie, some woman their dad knew, and liking me as Lanie, their dad's woman, were two different things.

So even though I wasn't nervous, I still kind of was.

To get home and change, I should have left ten minutes ago. But the new client was taking a lot of time, my day had gotten away from me (in all fairness, this had happened before the new client and it happened frequently), and I was considering coming in on Saturday and getting caught up since Hop had his kids for the weekend.

This wouldn't exactly be breaking my rule of not working weekends since I was already breaking my habit of working late into the evenings.

I had Hop to go home to, eat dinner with, and go to bed with. With that to look forward to, staying late at the office had lost its allure.

I was closing down programs on my computer, at the same time shoving stuff in my purse when I sensed movement so I looked out my wall of windows.

At what I saw, my breath froze in my lungs.

Tack was walking my way, his eyes on me, his face serious.

Tack had been to my office on several occasions, usually when I had plans with him and Tyra to go out to dinner after work, which meant he always drove so Ty-Ty and I could tie one on if we felt in the mood. Therefore Tyra always came with him.

He'd never been here alone and unannounced.

He knew about Hop and me.

Oh God, *he knew about Hop and me!*

I sat immobile, staring at him walking my way, my insides inexplicably seized with panic.

His gaze never left me as he walked through the open door, but once he got inside, he greeted, "Hey, Lanie."

"Uh, hey, Tack," I replied. "Is everything okay?"

He stopped in front of my desk and answered, "You tell me."

I blinked.

"I'm sorry?" I asked.

"You tell me, Lanie. Is everything okay?"

Oh God, he knew. Damn! He knew!

"I, uh…"

God!

What did I say?

Tack moved to one of my chairs, sat in it, and again looked at me.

His voice was soft when he said, "Gave it time, babe. A fuckuva lot of time. After dinner at your place a while back, thought on it and decided I can't give it more."

Okay, now I was confused. That didn't sound like he knew about Hop and me.

"Gave what time?" I asked.

"You," he answered.

Right, now I was *really* confused.

"Me, what?" I queried and he leaned toward me, his eyes intense, searching but kind.

"You and Belova," he replied, and I felt my insides seize again. "You were not movin' on. Years passed, you didn't move on. Tyra, she was not good about this, babe. She might get pissed at me sharin', seein' as my woman doesn't know I'm makin' this stop, but you gotta know. She's been worried, and when I say that I mean *worried*. She just didn't know what to do. She didn't wanna say somethin' and set you off. She didn't wanna not say somethin' and watch you waste your life away. Now she's even more worried, that photo's gone, what that might mean. And you haven't said shit about it."

Oh.

This was about the photo.

"Tack—" I started, and he shook his head.

"That path, Lanie, that path that leads to healing, you can get blinded, think there's only one path to choose but there isn't. There are lots of different paths but some of them don't lead to healing. They lead to other shit that is not good and, darlin', you've been on the wrong one." He leaned into me and his voice dipped quieter, rougher, "Trust me on this, I know, watchin' you go through it and watchin' my daughter go through it."

I swallowed.

About a year ago Tack's girl, Tabby, had lost her fiancé suddenly in a car crash only three weeks before their wedding. It was tragic and Tabby put on a brave face, but everyone knew she was suffering. How could she not? But with that brave face, it was hard to know what path she was on.

Unless you were as observant as Tack.

He leaned back and kept talking, "Shit you endured, Red, me, all of us had to put on kid gloves with you. I don't wanna freak you but, that frame gone, means you made a decision, a decision you aren't communicating about, so those gloves gotta come off."

"Tack—"

"You gotta move on...the right way."

"Well—"

"You gotta find a life outside this office," he threw out a hand then pinned his eyes on me. "You gotta find a man."

My back snapped straight. "Tack, really—"

He didn't miss my response. He just misinterpreted it.

"Don't go woman on me and tell me you don't need a man to complete you. It's bullshit. Woman looks like you, goddamn waste. But a woman who has the love you got to give, that's not a waste. That's a crying shame."

I closed my mouth because that was sweet.

Then I opened it to remind him, "Uh, FYI, I can't go woman on you since I *am* a woman, so going woman is redundant."

He grinned. "Just sayin', got a good one but that don't mean I don't notice other good ones, darlin'. You're a good one and a man would be lucky, he got you."

Wow, that was *really* sweet.

I held his eyes then I leaned toward him. "Thank you for coming, saying what you've said and caring, Tack, but I promise you, everything is good."

"Bullshit."

I blinked at his reply.

"You've thrown away that frame and locked yourself in," he declared.

"Locked myself in what?" I asked, again confused.

"Days here, nights here, your life...*here*..." He lifted a hand and pointed to the floor. "In this office. Buried in your work. Sure, you go out with your girl. You do yourself up. You spoil our sons. You show on Chaos and laugh with the brothers. But the majority of your life is this job, Lanie, and that shit can't go on."

Oh dear.

How did I play this?

"Tack, really, I promise you, I'm fine."

"A life that's work is not fine. It isn't even half a life. I dig you enjoy what you do and that's cool. You bein' so good at it is cooler. But the world is full, darlin'. You're only eatin' off half the plate, you're missin' the meat and, worse, you're missin' dessert." He paused a moment before he said quietly, "You need to live your life, Lanie."

"I promise you, Tack, I am."

"Then why is it after six and you're still at the office?" he returned.

I couldn't tell him I was heading out to meet Hop and his kids and thus I couldn't tell him I was late doing that and should have left fifteen minutes ago. I also couldn't tell him that my life was very much not all work. Not anymore. It was dance recitals. It was broiled pork chops. It was listening to Hop tell me the story of taking one of his "bitches" to a Seger concert. She got high before they went, lost herself in the vibe and threw her T-shirt toward the stage. I laughed through this because Hopper also told me she wasn't wearing a bra, and they were nowhere near the stage so neither Bob nor any of the Silver Bullet Band could appreciate her gesture.

However, I had to tell him something. I just didn't get the chance.

"Talked with Mitch and Lucas, they got a buddy, say he's a good man," Tack started.

Oh my God. Was he talking about setting me up?

Tack continued, "Don't know him. Don't wanna lose one of my girls to a guy on the force, but they say he's a good man, I believe them. They're gonna set you up."

Oh my God!

Tack was setting me up!

It was nice he thought of me as one of his girls, but this was a disaster.

Truth be told, I knew Mitch Lawson and Brock Lucas and I liked them. They were both good cops. They were both good guys. They were both friends of Tack's. They, and their wives, Mara and Tess, and their kids would often come to Chaos functions. This was incongruous, cops and bikers, but there was history, serious history, that made it not only understandable but imperative. So, knowing Mitch and Brock and knowing they were good guys, I knew they wouldn't set me up with a jerk or a loser.

That didn't make this any less of a disaster.

"Tack—" I began, but he again talked over me and he did it while standing.

"Goin' home, talkin' to Red about this. She'll hook up with Mara and Tess and they'll sort it. You just gotta look beautiful and show up. The first part comes natural. The second part will be where I'll trust you not to fall down."

I stared at him as he stood before my desk, and when he stopped talking, I asked, "Do you do this to Ty-Ty?"

"What?" he asked.

"Not let her get a word in edgewise," I answered, and he burst out laughing.

I waited patiently for him to stop, thinking not for the first time that Tyra was lucky. Tack laughed deep and rich, it came from the gut and he looked good doing it. He also did it a lot.

When Tack stopped laughing, he looked back at me and replied simply, "Yes." I opened my mouth to say something and again failed in this endeavor. "Though, only when it's important and she's bein' a pain in my ass."

"Are you implying I'm a pain in your ass?" I enquired.

"Nope," he shook his head, grinning. "But, you give me lip on this, I won't imply it. I'll just say it straight out."

"Tack—"

"Go on the date, Lanie."

"Tack!" I snapped, and he bent over my desk, putting his hand on it and pinning me again with his blue eyes.

"Do it for Tyra," he said softly, and I shut my mouth.

How the heck was I going to get out of this?

"She's worried," Tack went on. "Heal yourself, help my woman stop worrying. Go on the date."

I closed my eyes then opened them and nodded.

I mean, what else could I do?

Tack smiled.

Damn.

"Good, glad we had this talk," he declared. "And Red's gonna be glad you're takin' a shot at life again and I hope, it works out or it doesn't but it whets your appetite to have back what you're missin', *you'll* be glad."

It really stunk that he was such a good guy and he was

here doing this for me and I couldn't tell him this was all unnecessary and they could stop worrying.

"Okay well, thanks again, Tack," I said.

He straightened away from my desk. "Go home. Do somethin' fun. Whatever. Just get the fuck out of here," he ordered, throwing out an arm to indicate my office.

"I was just leaving," I informed him and got another grin before he moved to my door.

He stopped in it and turned back.

I should have lifted up my mental shield and braced.

I didn't.

So when he shot his arrows, they tore straight through my flesh.

"Don't regret what you did. Don't regret the decisions you made. You did right. You followed your heart and that is never wrong, darlin'. But shit went down and it was extreme. That's over, Lanie. Long over. Move on."

I didn't do right.

He knew that. I knew that. Tyra knew it.

He was just being nice.

Forgiveness is beautiful, and it feels good when someone gives that gift to you.

But it's one thing for someone you wronged to forgive you.

It was another to forgive yourself.

Too much was lost. Rivers of it. Rivers of Ty-Ty's blood on the floor of a house I'd never been to and she'd only been there once. That blood flowed because of me.

It could have meant we lost everything, Tack and me.

But, the way he loved her, mostly Tack.

He forgave me.

I just didn't forgive myself.

I didn't tell him any of this.

I just said, "Okay."

He nodded. "Okay, darlin'. Have a good night."

"You too. Tell Ty-Ty I said hi."

"Will do. Later."

"Later, Tack."

He lifted a hand to flick it out and then I watched him walk out of my office, thinking yet again my best friend was very lucky.

Then again, so was Tack.

I looked at the clock on my computer and realized to be in time for pizza, I wasn't going to be able to get home and change.

I shut it down, pulled out my phone and called Hop to tell him I might be a bit late.

Then I got out of my office to live my life.

*   *   *

I heard a Harley. Lying on my couch, reading and drinking a glass of wine after a fun dinner with Hop and his kids, conditioned to that roar meaning good things, I listened absentmindedly but contentedly thinking about that night's dinner.

I thought about how Molly's exuberance was catching. About how nice it felt when a little girl told you she liked your outfit. About how Cody might not look like his dad but he acted exactly like him. About how Hop deftly negotiated Molly's severe dislike for all things sausage, "The juice leaks across the side, Dad!", and Cody's demand that we get a meat lover's since, "Pizza doesn't matter if it don't got meat," by buying two Beau Joe's pizzas and muttering, "Leftovers for a week."

He was not wrong, though he was understating it. One Beau Joe's pizza could feed half a battalion.

So that Harley roar outside not only reminded me of all good things Hop and a great night with his kids that, after it was over, told me I had nothing to be nervous about, but it made me smile.

I kept listening, not absentmindedly, when the roar stopped at the back of my house.

I aimed my eyes over my couch to the sliding glass doors and was shocked to see Hopper's tall body materialize through the dark there.

"Open up, babe," he called through the glass, and I set my Kindle aside and got up, quickly moving to the door, unlocking and opening it.

"What are you doing here?" I asked, shifting back as he slid through and shut the door. "Where are the kids? Is everything all right?"

He turned to me. "I don't know. You tell me."

Great.

I'd had this beginning conversational gambit once already from a biker that night when Tack visited me, and from the look of concern and inquisitiveness on Hop's face, I was thinking I wouldn't like this one much better.

"What are you talking about and where are the kids?" I asked.

"Kids are asleep and Sheila's with 'em. You showed at dinner, still wearin' your work gear, acting funny, not meeting my eyes so I called her, she came over, I hopped on my bike and hauled my ass over here. What's up?"

"Nothing I couldn't tell you over the phone," I explained. "You didn't have to drag Sheila over to your house."

"You don't meet my eyes during dinner, it's somethin' that you don't get into over the phone. Now, Lanie, one more time. What's up?"

Usually, I rejoiced that Hop was a man who paid attention. This meant he did things and said things and, it's important to repeat, *did* things, *good* things, because he paid attention.

Sometimes, like now, it was annoying.

I decided this discussion would go better with wine, so I walked to my wineglass.

Once I'd grabbed it and taken a sip, I looked back at Hop to see he hadn't moved except to cross his arms on his chest.

Leather jackets, especially a beat-up, black biker one with a patch on the back, were not my thing when it came to guys.

Hopper worked that cut like no other.

"Lanie," he prompted, his voice a warning low, and I stopped appreciating Hop in his cut.

"Tack talked to Mitch and Brock. They're setting me up on a date with a cop," I announced.

I did this because I thought it best just to get it out there and over with.

Anyway, it was no big deal. Hop had to know I was into him. We both knew we were working on something important. I'd just had dinner with him and his kids so that was plain.

Therefore, I'd decided on my way to Beau Joe's just to go on the date then explain to the guy, Tack, and Tyra that we didn't click, and I'd explain my plan beforehand to Hop (but not during dinner with his kids) so he wouldn't worry. This meant I'd do my duty to Ty-Ty and Tack then I'd start doing other things that made them quit worrying about me. Like take a creative writing class with the explanation I might meet someone there when I had no intention of doing that. And, anyway, a creative writing class would be fun and I'd always wanted to do it.

Whatever. Bottom line: in the end, all would be well.

Looking at Hop, I realized he would not be at one with my plan.

"Come again?" he asked, and his tone was scary.

I threw out my hand with the wineglass in it, thankful it was low so the wine didn't slosh out. "They're worried I'm not healing, moving on appropriately after Elliott, burying myself in work, so they're setting me up."

"They're setting you up," he repeated, his voice still scary.

"Hop, it isn't a big deal," I told him and watched his head jerk.

"Are you going?" Now he didn't sound scary. He sounded disbelieving and more than a little bit angry.

"It isn't a big deal. I'll go and, after, explain I wasn't attracted to him. They'll think I'm moving on and all will be good."

"You'll go," Hop stated.

"Just one date," I assured him.

"Just one date," Hop again repeated after me.

"Hop—"

I stopped abruptly when he leaned into me and roared, *"Are you outta your fuckin' mind?"*

Yes, definitely not at one with my plan.

I lifted both hands placatingly and started, "Hop—"

He took two steps toward me, his body shuddered to a halt like he was controlling his movements, but just barely, and he clipped, "Tell me *exactly* what went down."

I held his eyes and explained exactly what went down.

Hop held mine when I was done and asked, "And your solution to this problem is to go out with this fuckin' guy?"

"It's the easiest solution I can think of." I told him something I thought was obvious.

"I don't know, Lanie. I can think of an easier one," he retorted, and his sarcasm wasn't lost on me.

"Hop, honestly, you don't—"

He interrupted me, "You wanna know my solution?"

I figured I knew it, I didn't want him to verbalize it, but I nodded anyway.

"Maybe, I don't know, but it might be easier, babe, just to fuckin' *tell them* you got a life and that life is movin' on *with me*." He planted his hands on his hips. "Fuck, I don't even know why you didn't tell Tack that shit straight out when he proposed that ludicrous fuckin' idea."

As he spoke, his mood deteriorated. This was reflected in the way he rapped out his words.

But at his words my lungs seized, so I had to force out my cry of, "We can't do that!"

He threw his hands up in the air. "Why the fuck not?"

I knew he was ticked. I knew why he was ticked.

But something was happening. Something I was trying to ignore. Something that was building inside me so huge it was impossible to ignore.

Panic.

Sheer, unadulterated *panic*.

"We can't do that," I repeated.

"And why the fuck not, Lanie?"

"We just can't," I told him.

"Are you shitting me?" he asked.

"No, I'm not," I answered, that feeling growing, eating away huge, gluttonous bites of me.

Hop studied me a moment, his expression shifting, and he was talking quieter when he asked, "Ever?"

"Ever what?" I asked back.

"You don't wanna tell them now. Are you ever gonna wanna tell them?"

Oh God.

How could I be standing there at the same time being eaten alive?

"Lanie?" Hop called, but I just stood immobile, losing entire chunks of myself to my monster. "Lanie!" Hop clipped, before he strode toward me, pulled the glass out of my hand, set it aside, and wrapped his fingers around my upper arms. "Jesus, babe, what the fuck?"

"No, not ever. We can't ever tell them about us," I whispered, staring into his eyes.

He moved his hands to either side of my head and dipped his face close.

His eyes roamed my features before he murmured, "It's got you. Fuck, Jesus, I'm standin' here watchin' that monster tear you apart."

"We can't tell them," I stated.

"Why?" he asked.

"We can't ever tell them," I declared, my voice getting loud.

"Why, baby?" he asked, his voice going gentle.

"I don't want them to know," I told him.

"Why don't you want them to know, honey?" he pushed.

"They can't know."

"Lanie, get this shit out."

I stared into his eyes, feeling his warm hands on either side of my head, his body close, and the monster shoved its arm down my throat and dredged up, "She told me."

"Keep goin'," Hop encouraged.

"To break it off with him."

Hop closed his eyes.

"I didn't."

Hop opened his eyes.

"Tyra told me to break it off with Elliott after we got kidnapped by the Russian Mob that first time."

"Okay, Lanie, baby, that's good, it's enough. Shut this shit down now."

I didn't shut it down. The monster was dragging it out.

"I didn't listen. I told her through better or worse."

"Fuck," he murmured, shifting so he could curl me in his arms.

I wrapped my arms around him and pressed my cheek into his shoulder.

"It got worse," I whispered.

Hop didn't answer. He just stood there holding me tight.

I held him back the same way.

After this went on for a while, Hop gave me a squeeze and asked, "You with me?"

"Yeah," I answered.

"Breakin' that shit down and, lady, stop me if I got this wrong, but you made a decision about your man, it got your girl hurt and you're carryin' that shit around, transferrin' it on your new man."

I hadn't thought about it that way. In fact, I hadn't thought about it at all.

"Maybe," I told his shoulder.

"You wanna end this?" he asked.

"End what?"

"End us."

I felt my entire body wind so tight, I feared it would snap, hurtling me across the room like a broken rubber band. I pulled my head back to look at him.

"Do you?" My voice trembled on those two words.

"Fuck no," he replied instantly and I felt my brow furrow.

"Then why did you ask?"

"Because, babe, neither of us wants to end this, she's your girl, Tack's my brother. How the fuck are we gonna go on hidin' what we have from them?"

He had a point.

"We have to."

My mouth said it before my brain caught up, and I watched his head jerk to the side.

"Lady—"

"For a while," I finished, and he stared at me.

"You wanna know it's solid," he guessed.

"I want this monster out of me," I confessed, pressing closer. "I want...I wanna be able to face them both and know. Know I believe. Know I'm right this time. After what happened last time, how bad it was, how we nearly lost Ty-Ty, I *have* to know this time. It *has* to be solid. For you. For me. So Tyra can believe."

His face changed, unease washing through his expression, and he told me, "You were right the last time, baby. He did wrong but you did right."

I shook my head and Hop watched me do it.

Hop let me go, shifted us both into the couch, tucking me tight to his side. I lifted up my legs and curled them on the couch beside me as I snaked an arm across his stomach and pressed my forehead into his neck.

"For a while, babe, we'll keep this between you and me," he gave in. "But you gotta remember that I'm easin' you into my kids' lives and I'm not gonna ask them to lie. Kids say shit and they are not strangers to Chaos. You also gotta be aware that High picked me up here so he knows, and I asked him not to talk, but I am not gonna get in his face if he does. So if you keep this from your girl, you're walkin' a tightrope, baby, and the longer this carries on, if she finds out before we share, the more you're gonna have to explain."

I nodded.

I'd worry about that later.

A lot later.

"Right," he muttered, and I pressed closer.

We fell silent and neither of us broke it for a good long while.

Finally, Hop did.

"Don't know who won this one, the monster or us," he mused.

I didn't either.

I just knew it was an entirely different experience, battling that monster with Hop at my back.

"You sensed something was up, called Sheila to stay with the kids, and drove all the way here to talk with me," I reminded him.

"Yeah," he agreed, and I lifted up to look at him.

"That monster always bests me, honey, but I'm thinking you did great."

Another expression washed through his features, this one better. Surprise and satisfaction.

I got to enjoy it for half a second before he kissed me.

When he broke the kiss, I noted, "I hate to bring this up but we have to figure out what to do about this setup."

"Don't worry about it, I'll deal with it."

I stared at him. "How are you going to deal with it?"

"I'll think of something."

After Hopper Kincaid said those four words, there was one thing I knew with a surety that was astonishing.

He would.

One way or another, Hop would think of something and make my troubles go away.

I liked this so much, to communicate just how much, I pressed my forehead back into his neck and burrowed close.

Letting go of that scene, a thought came to me.

"So, uh...I'm taking it from this conversation that you want us to be exclusive?" I asked and felt his body tense before it shook slightly with laughter.

"Uh, yeah, babe. I want us to be exclusive," he confirmed, his words also shaking with laughter.

Good to know.

No. *Great* to know.

I burrowed closer before I told him, "If we're exclusive, you should know, I have the birth control thing covered."

There was no laughter in his voice. He sounded surprised when he asked, "You good with me ungloved?"

I pulled my face out of his neck and again looked at him. "I don't know. What did you mean when you said, 'shit happens' that night you got angry with me?"

"It means, for your peace of mind, I'm visiting a clinic."

Hop, for me, was visiting a clinic.

Yes, oh yes, it just kept getting better.

I smiled at him. He smiled back before his hand sifted in my hair and he pressed my forehead against his neck. He held me for a while before he told he had to get back to his kids.

He kissed me again, and I walked him out to his bike, where I kissed him.

Then he told me he wasn't leaving until he saw my outside light go on and off, indicating I was safely locked inside.

That was sweet and protective so I kissed him again.

Ten minutes later, I flicked my light on and off, indicating to Hopper I was safely locked inside.

But I stood inside feeling something I hadn't felt in a very long time.

Safe.

CHAPTER TWELVE

Knife in My Gut

One week and three days later…

"So, HOW DID it happen for you?"

"How'd what happen for me?"

I moved my face out of Hop's throat and looked down at him. "How did you find Chaos?"

It was Sunday morning and we were in his bed in the Compound. Considering we were still keeping our relationship a secret, this was a risk. However, last night, I'd joined Tyra and our friends Gwen and Elvira at the Compound for drinks prior to going out. This was at Tyra's invitation, and even though I would have preferred to spend my Saturday evening with Hop, in order to hide what we had, I'd agreed.

Tack, Brick, Shy, Tug, and Big Petey were all there, so we ended up not going out and, instead, we all got plastered in the common room.

Later in the evening, after some clandestine texting to let Hop know where I was, he showed.

This was fun, too fun. Then again, times with Ty-Ty always were. Throw Elvira and Gwen in the mix, it went off the charts.

Elvira was a black woman who was totally crazy (but in good ways). Gwen was a white woman who was only slightly less crazy than Elvira, but I figured this had to do with the fact that she was married to Hawk Delgado. I wasn't sure, since Gwen didn't talk about it, but considering he always wore cargo pants, skintight shirts, sturdy boots, a forbidding expression, and a gun belt, I figured Hawk was a commando.

An actual commando.

My guess was, being married to a commando curtailed your level of craziness because no one wanted to call home to a hubby who was a commando and explain the trouble they'd got themselves into. I didn't know but I figured commandos had enough trouble professionally. They didn't need their wives buying them more.

Gwen being Gwen, even though she was a mom married to a commando, she still knew how to have herself a good time.

Elvira, on the other hand, was seeing a very good-looking, African American cop. Unlike Hawk, Elvira's man, Malik, thought her craziness was hysterical and cute. I knew this because I'd been around them and he'd said it. A lot. Because she was crazy. A lot. And it was good he thought this because it meant the drama she liberally injected into their relationship was something he enjoyed, rather than something that set him running for the hills.

Needless to say, we got plastered, and men like it when women get plastered. Therefore, Tack took off with Ty-Ty in tow so they could enjoy her being drunk in their house in the mountains. Hawk showed and guided his tipsy wife and Elvira to his SUV while Elvira talked on the phone with Malik, which meant Malik was going to catch the hint his woman was blotto, and I figured he'd meet her at her house in order to take advantage.

As for me, I kept drinking and enjoying my time with the guys until High showed. Although I was inebriated, it looked to me like Hop gave him a signal, and High somehow managed to talk the other boys away from the bar and off on some Chaos errand.

Alone in the Compound with Hop, he wasted no time leading me to his room, where we had wild, crazy, drunken sex (okay, that last bit was just me) and it...was...*fabulous*. More fabulous now since Hop's visit to the clinic brought good news. He could go "ungloved," which meant it was just him and me with nothing in between.

I promptly passed out, only to be awoken by my man forty-five minutes ago, whereupon he made sweet, slow love to me.

It was debatable, but that might have been more fabulous.

I was slightly hungover.

I was also not-so-slightly happy.

"How did I find Chaos?" Hop asked, and I grinned at him.

"Yeah."

"Tack came to a show."

I tipped my head to the side. "What?"

"When I was still with the band, Tack came to a show. My family's from Nevada. Mom and Dad still live there, but Bog put out feelers everywhere so we got gigs in Denver. After a show, Tack came up to me and told me he dug what we did. Liked him, he seemed solid, and it was cool he went out of his way to say that shit to me. When I quit the band, I thought about where I wanted to land, and by that time, even though I was only twenty-four, I had a lot of miles in. Place I liked best was Denver. Came here, remembered Tack. Not hard to miss, seein' as he was wearin' his cut, that he was in a club, and I rode into town on a bike. Seemed a fit. Sought him out, told him I left the band, he told me about

Chaos. Invited me to a bash. I went." He smiled. "The rest
is history."

"So you've been in the Club since you were twenty-
four?" I asked.

"By the time I got here, made the decision, finished my
time as a grunt, full membership at twenty-seven."

"And you never looked back," I noted.

The ease of our post–making love morning drifted from
his face when he replied, "Never looked back."

"What's that?" I queried.

"What?"

"That look on your face," I explained, and he hesitated
before he rolled us. I had been lying on him. Hop situated us
so I was on my back and he'd pressed his front to my side,
his hand splayed on my belly.

"Tack didn't invite me to join so much as recruited me,"
he stated in a way that sounded weirdly like a confession, and
I felt my eyebrows draw together.

"I don't get it. I mean, aren't all the guys recruited?"

"Not for what Tack recruited me."

I knew from his tone and the look on his face, our happy
morning seemed to have gone south somehow.

I just didn't get it.

"What are you saying?" I asked hesitantly, not wanting our morning to go south and not really sure I wanted to
know what he was saying.

"What I'm sayin' is, the Club was different back then.
You and me, we stay solid, you're brought officially into the
fold as an old lady when we let out the news about us, you'll
hear talk." He studied me a moment before finishing, "You
might have already heard it."

"I haven't already heard it," I shared. "How was the Club
different?"

"They were into some serious bad shit then."

Oh dear.

I was right. I didn't want to know.

Still, I had to.

So I pushed. "What kind of serious bad shit?"

"Seriously serious bad shit," Hop evaded.

"Hop—"

"Lanie." He lifted a hand and cupped my cheek. "It was not good. What it is, is over."

"I think maybe I need to understand this," I told him, though I didn't think I needed that. But I knew if we went the distance I'd have to know.

"I think maybe you need to trust me that you don't."

"So what if I hear talk?" I pressed.

"You'll know it's over."

"Hop—" I began, and his face suddenly got closer.

"Drugs," he bit out, the word sharp but almost strangled, like he had his own monster who'd dragged it out of him and he had no control, no way to hold it back.

I gasped and he continued. "And girls. Seriously bad shit, lady. Seriously bad shit that Tack wanted nothin' to do with. He wasn't president back then, but that didn't mean he didn't have an exit plan for the Club on all that shit. He also had patience. A lot of it. And part of his plan was not only workin' behind the scenes to turn brothers to his mission but also to recruit brothers who would fight his side. I was one of the brothers he recruited. Dog and Brick, too. It took time, and the takeover was hostile. It was a dark time for the Club but Tack planned for that, too. He led us to the light and that's where we are now, Lanie. Swear to Christ. We're in the light."

"Drugs and girls?" I asked breathlessly.

"It's over."

"Girls?" My voice was pitching higher.

"Baby," his hand pressed into my face, "it's *over*."

"So, if it's over, what about Benito?" I asked.

"I already told you, not talkin' about Benito, and you gotta trust me on that, too."

"Hop—"

He interrupted me this time by rolling full on top of me and framing my head in both hands.

"This shit…*fuck*," he ground out, paused, and his face betrayed an inner battle before he continued, "you gotta know. You asked, this is part of me, but this shit, I didn't wanna tell you until later. But you asked so here it is. When I got in the Club, we were into that shit. You became a brother, you did your duty to the Club, and part of my duties was that shit."

Suddenly, something High said weeks before penetrated.

"Exactly what part of that shit did you do?" I asked.

He held my eyes and answered straight out. "Lots of it, but mostly looked after the girls."

My body jerked under his like it was trying to get away, but his weight pinned me to the bed and his thumb swept down to press into my lips.

Even with his thumb hindering my words, I said, "You have a way with gash."

His eyes flashed at my words. "Lanie, hear me, I did not like doin' that shit and I wouldn't have done it if I didn't know that it was a means to an end. Tack made promises, promises he kept, that it was temporary."

"So you were a pimp?" I whispered in horror, and his thumb swept away.

"Chaos pimped. I just took care of the girls."

"I'm not seeing the nuance of difference, Hop," I told him, my hands now at his shoulders, putting on pressure, and his jaw clenched.

"Hard to see since that nuance is just that. Chaos is me, I'm Chaos. But I wasn't a pimp, woman. Another brother had that job. I was an enforcer. A girl got worked over, she came to me and I dealt with it. I wasn't just an enforcer for the girls, I was one for the Club. I'm good with my fists. You learn that shit when you spend most of your life in bars, you have a guitar in your hands or not. When we were starting out, some of those bars were rough and shit happens. The president of the Club back then, he noticed I had talent in that area and he was a man who used that kinda talent. I took their backs. The girls just trusted me. I don't have a way with gash, Lanie. But a john works you over, and a man goes out and makes him bleed for that mistake, that bitch is gonna be grateful. It came natural, and those women would have given it to any brother who took their backs like that."

He was angry at my comment. I knew it because I felt it, but I also knew it because he called me "woman" and he'd never done that.

It was also interesting to understand how he felled Monster Truck Man so easily.

I didn't share this with him.

I told him honestly if cautiously, "I'm not sure that's much better."

"You would be right," he retorted. "I'm not gonna lie to you. I did what I did but it wasn't my choice and it wasn't my decision. But it *was* my decision to join the Club, take Tack's back, help him maneuver himself to the gavel and be a soldier in the war that would get us out of that shit. In order to do it, I had to do what I had to do."

"Did you sleep with those girls?" I asked.

"Fuck no."

"Give them drugs?"

Hop went silent and bile crawled up my throat.

I pushed through the sick. "You gave them drugs?"

"No, but Chaos had access, and brothers, brothers that are gone now, did."

I closed my eyes and turned my head to the side.

Hop moved it back into position, and I opened my eyes to glare at him, because I did not like this, *any* of it, only to see him scowling at me.

"Two years, Lanie, two fuckin' years I worked those girls, keepin' them together, tryin' to get them straight, helpin' them plan for when Tack executed his takeover and we cut them loose. That life, not a good one, and you're hooked on shit, you'll do pretty much anything to keep yourself supplied with it. I tried to do it smart, keep them quiet and move them out of the life, and two of those bitches talked. We lost a brother because of that, Lanie. They opened their mouths, shit got out to the wrong people, and Tack had to move to shut it down, and we lost a brother. Takin' us out of that life into the one where we are now was not easy, everyone's hands got dirty. Blood flowed but, where we are now, what we can give to our kids, it was worth it."

"You lost a brother?" I asked, and he unexpectedly knifed away, lifted an arm and pointed at the tattoo on his bicep.

I'd seen it before, time and again, not only on Hopper but all the brothers had it. It was a set of unbalanced scales. The top scale had the word "Red" inked in it, rivers of red blood dripping over the sides. I knew, without anyone telling me, that this indicated Tyra and what happened to her because of Elliott. The bottom scale had the word "Black" with a hooded, skull-faced reaper that had creepy blue eyes and a scythe in his skeleton's hand. The support of the scales was fashioned out of the words, "Never Forget."

"Black. A brother. Dead because of gash. Gash and greed, Lanie."

He sat in bed staring down at me and kept talking.

"I get this is a shock and I get why. Trust me, babe, I like it a lot fuckin' less than you do I got that shit in my history. I like it less knowin' Black is no longer breathin' on this earth. He was a good man. He wanted good things for the Club and his family. So much, he died for it."

This wasn't easy for Hop, I knew, I could see it, but I was too shocked about all he was telling me to do anything about it.

Hop continued.

"You would like him because he was likeable, loyal, smart, solid. I am not a soldier in the normal sense, but I know by experience, you fight a war for something you believe in, you gotta be prepared to do some serious, sick, crazy, messed up shit to win. I came into this Club knowin' where Tack wanted to lead it, what he wanted to give to his brothers so they could give it to their families, and I came into it goin' all in. I never had a good family, and anyone who spends five seconds with Tack Allen knows the kind of man he is. He promised me he could deliver me to something I wanted. I believed in him and I was right. I enlisted to fight that war, Lanie, and I'm not proud of what I did to help win it, but I'm proud that I did my part to get what we won."

I stared up at him not knowing how to process his words, the hard, determined look on his face, or the information he'd just given me.

I also didn't have the considerable time I was certain it would take to process this before there was a knock on the door.

Our discussion and that knock, what it might mean, who might be behind that door, sent a wave of panic through me, and before I told my body to move, it did.

In a flurry, I threw back the covers, rolled out of bed, and snatched up Hop's T-shirt, chanting, "I'm not here, I'm not here, I'm not here," as I pulled it on and ran to the bathroom.

I shut the door and deep breathed.

I knew Tack's eldest son Rush having the boys for a sleepover meant no way Tack or Ty-Ty were coming back down the mountain. Both of them were older than me, and I was far from the days where my biggest hope was making the high school cheerleading squad, but that didn't mean they didn't go at each other like jackrabbits. Until I had Hopper, I didn't know men with the kind of libido Kane "Tack" Allen had existed. I thought he was an anomaly, a happy one for Tyra, but one all the same.

Feeling somewhat safe from detection, I had allowed myself a lazy, happy morning (that unfortunately turned whacked) in Hopper's bed.

But that didn't mean whoever was behind that door wouldn't talk, and it was one thing for my car to be outside the Compound in the morning (I'd crashed, on occasion, in one of the boys' beds after tying one on) and another for me to be found naked in Hop's bed.

"Brother, serious as fuck, you got bad fuckin' timing," I heard Hopper growl.

"Know she's here, got back last night, saw her ride. She left her purse on the bar. I tagged her keys and moved her car," High replied. If I wasn't in Hop's T-shirt and nothing else, I would have gone out and kissed him. "Here's her purse but, brother, Benito made some moves last night, not good. Tack's been informed and he's callin' a meeting. Boys'll be descending soon. You gotta get your woman's ass outta here."

Oh no.

Tack was coming down.

And oh no *again*.

Benito.

I had not forgotten about Benito. I just had not thought about him, seeing as there was a lot of other stuff I had to think about, and my head just didn't have the space for more.

Now, knowing what Hop just told me, Benito again entering the picture, it felt like my head was going to explode.

"Thanks, brother," Hop replied to High.

"Not sure I get why this shit's a secret, but you two bein' just a hookup is not where that's at. Unless you're goin' for the all-time record of longest hookup, and, just a heads up, brother, there's another way people refer to that shit and it's called a relationship. Tack won't care but respect to Cherry, you two better sort this out. Only so many times I'm gonna hightail my ass to her ride and hide it, Hop. Lanie's the shit and far from hard to look at, so not one brother will have a problem seein' where you're comin' from. But secrets like this amongst family can tear brothers apart. They can do worse to sisters. You hear me?"

Okay, High had never been a favorite. I liked him but, I had to admit, him being surly and all, he wasn't a favorite. Even if his words made me feel guilt, they also now made him a favorite.

"Lanie's workin' through some shit," Hop responded vaguely.

"Help her work through it faster," High shot back, and I heard a door close.

I gave it a moment before I opened the door and took one step out. I limited it to one when I saw the look on Hop's face.

"Now my brothers are bustin' their asses to cover our shit, and you race to the bathroom like you're fifteen, we're in your bedroom, I just popped your cherry, and your dad's at the door. Babe, I get you got issues but on top of all our other shit, we gotta spend some time sortin' those out."

This was an unfortunate opening, mostly because it ticked me off.

"Are you saying it's more important to talk about that right now rather than our earlier conversation?" I asked.

"I'm sayin' we got a lot to work through, and your other shit bein' in the way is not gonna make this current shit any easier."

I held his eyes for long moments before I queried carefully, "Did you honestly think I'd be down with all that?"

"No, because I wasn't down with it," he answered. "What I honestly thought was that you know me. I'm no different now that you know my history than the man you made love with an hour ago, babe. I wasn't hankerin' for the time I shared that history with you but I honestly thought, you bein' Cherry's girl, Cherry knowin' about all this shit, Cherry gettin' it, *you* would get that that man was never me. That man was the man he had to be to get this Club to the point it could be a family that would cushion a woman's fall."

A blow and a dirty one.

"That's not fair," I said quietly.

"It's not only fair, it's real and you know it," he returned. "My brothers fought, bled, and died for you to have this family, lady. You can't get in my face weeks ago about bein' non-judgmental and then stand here in my room and my tee and force your judgment on me. Even if that shit *was* me and I found redemption, it's not anymore, and you're the woman I thought you were, you'd be down with that, but, like I've explained, it never fuckin' was."

It stunk but he had a point.

"Since we're letting it all hang out," I started to suggest, "perhaps we should revisit Benito."

"Said all I'm gonna say about that motherfucker," Hop replied.

"Is that old life over?" I asked.

"Told you it was," he answered.

"Then who's Benito?"

"Scum that wants a slice of Chaos territory. Problem with that, he eats that slice, he'll want more. So you hold him back."

"And how do you do that?"

"For you, babe, I said more about that motherfucker, but now I've said all I'm gonna say."

Again, we stood there staring at each other in silence until I broke it.

"I need time to process all I learned today."

"You got two seconds," he returned instantly. "You take more than two seconds to walk your ass over here and put your arms around me, accepting me for who I am despite what I used to do, we got problems."

Oh God.

"What kind of problems?"

"The kind of problems that come from me knowin' you lied. Me knowin' you judge. And I don't want that shit in my life or around my kids."

Was he crazy?

"Hop!" I snapped. "You just told me you were an enforcer and Chaos dealt drugs and prostituted women."

"Never said Chaos dealt drugs," he shot back.

"Were drugs involved in your operations?" I retorted.

"Yes," he clipped.

I leaned toward him. "Then we're arguing about me saying tomatoes and you saying toe-mah-toes."

"No, babe, we're arguing about me laying the honesty on you, letting it all hang out, somethin' you missed wasn't real easy to do, just as it wasn't real easy to do the shit I used to do, and I told you that too, and you passing judgment on me."

"I just asked for time," I reminded him.

"And I just told you, if you know what we got between us is real and you're in it all the way with me, you don't need that time."

"I'm a fledgling old lady, Hopper. Give me a break," I returned.

"You won't be an old lady, Lanie, if you don't give me one."

My mouth dropped open.

That was it, my breaking point. I'd had enough, and honestly, who could blame me?

I mean, really?

To communicate this, I shouted, *"Fuck you!"* and stomped to my clothes.

"Lanie—" Hop started.

"No, oh no!" I yelled, yanking on my jeans. "You do not get to throw my words in my face and then threaten to take away," I jerked to standing and jabbed a finger at him, "*you*, which is the same *exact* fucking thing you lost it about when I did it."

I went right back to dressing and was stalled in this effort when Hop gently pulled on my arm. I not gently yanked it out of his grip and kept dressing.

"It wasn't easy sharing that," he stated, his voice more calm.

I sat on the bed to pull on my boots but cut my eyes to him. "And it wasn't easy having my man lie on top of me and share it, having no fucking *idea*," I shouted the last word, "he had that in his history. It wasn't easy learning it. And you wanna know something, Hopper Kincaid?" I asked as I stood and snatched my purse from the bed where Hop obviously tossed it after High gave it to him.

I paused but not long enough for him to answer.

I gave it to him.

"It wasn't easy to learn that a man, *my* man, the man I thought was a *good* man, doesn't have it in him to understand I need," I lifted up a hand, thumb and finger half an inch apart, "a wee bit of time to come to terms with some significant information about his past before we move on. That was the worst. So, newsflash, Hopper. Your old lady would have come to terms with it. But you not giving the woman who wants to be your old lady the opportunity to come to terms with it and prove her salt as an old lady means you aren't going to *have* an old lady."

And on that, I rushed to the chair, snatched up my jacket, and stormed out.

Unfortunately, Hop was on my heels.

Equally unfortunately, Shy was in the back hallway looking at us in a way that I knew he didn't miss me shouting. But, I noted with distracted surprise, even in the morning (or maybe especially in the morning), Shy was not with a girl. This was a surprise since it seemed he was *always* with a girl. He was young, he was hot, he was a badass, and he used all that, frequently, to get laid. In fact, he was known for it and nicknamed "Shy" as a joke since he absolutely was not shy.

Even though these thoughts came to me, I ignored them and Shy.

"Lanie, goddamn it, slow down," Hop growled.

"Fuck off," I shot back, came to a halt in the common room and looked at High, who was behind the bar. "My car?"

"Block north, turn right, two blocks up," High answered, his eyeballs shooting from Hop to me.

"Thank you. I'd kiss you if I wasn't so ticked off, so you'll have to take a rain check," I told him.

"Lookin' forward to that," High told me.

"Fuckin' shit," Hop snarled from behind me, and I whirled on him.

"Have a good life, Hopper Kincaid," I hissed then turned on my boot and dashed out.

I got halfway through the forecourt when I was swung around with a firm grip on my arm. I stopped by crashing into Hop's body, whereupon both his arms clamped around me.

"You get this drama, babe, you got until the end of Tack's meeting to burn it out, but mark this, Lanie. After that meeting, I don't give a fuck if you're strapped into a rocket to go to the goddamned moon, I'm findin' you, we're sortin' this shit out and we're movin' on," he warned.

"I just made a mental note to find a plastic surgeon who does emergency face alterations so you won't know who to look for," I shot back.

"Jesus, I'm pissed as all fuck and still she's cute," he groused like he wasn't talking to me but actually complaining to the Son of God.

"Jesus works on Sunday, Hop. You want a direct line, time to haul your biker ass to church," I shared.

"You want me to let you go so you can burn this out, you better stop bein' cute, lady. You keep bein' cute, I'll kiss you in the goddamn forecourt and I won't give a fuck who sees."

I snapped my mouth shut.

"That's what I thought," he muttered.

"Are you going to let me go so I can burn this out?" I prompted.

"You gonna hide from me?" he asked.

"I haven't decided," I returned.

"This may help you make your decision. You hide, Lanie, you waste my time havin' to look for you, you'll be providing payback for that time. I'll get payback and, in the end, you'll like it, I promise you, but before that, I'll make you beg to give it to me and you beggin', baby, is gonna last a long fuckin' time."

Oh my God.

How could I be *that* angry and still have a mini-orgasm in the forecourt of a garage?

"You aren't letting me go," I pointed out.

"You gonna be at your house when this meet's done?"

I glared at him then bit off, "Yes."

His eyes dropped to my mouth and he murmured, "Fuck, I wanna kiss you."

Another mini-orgasm.

God, he was killing me.

"Hop—"

His eyes came back to mine. "You mean the world to me, Lanie. No one but my brothers knows the shit I did for the Club. No one. I didn't trust a goddamn soul with that and that includes Mitzi. I trusted you because I care about you and I wanted you to have that part of me because I want you to have *all* of me. So while you're burnin' out your drama, think about that and also think about the fact that I feel it like a fuckin' knife in my gut right now havin' to let you go and walk away without bein' free to take your mouth to say good-bye."

I stopped breathing.

Hop let me go.

"Think about all that, baby," he said gently and finished, "I'll be at your place in a couple of hours."

Then he walked away and I watched him go.

He disappeared behind the door to the Compound, and it took a while before I remembered where I was and that I had to get out of there.

So I turned and walked fast to my car.

*   *   *

Three hours later...

I was working in the kitchen when I heard the Harley pipes. They stopped behind my house.

I washed my hands to clean off the dough for the homemade rolls I was making but stood behind the island and faced the sliding glass doors.

Hop's eyes locked on me when he was in the courtyard, and he didn't tear them away as he walked in and slid the door closed.

When he came to a stop and crossed his arms on his chest, I was the first one to speak.

"You mean the world to me, too."

The room infused instantly with sheer beauty.

"Get over here," he growled.

I felt those three words in three very good places but I didn't move.

"I'm dramatic," I reminded him.

"Get over here, Lanie."

"I go over the top."

"Over. Here."

"I create scenes."

"Lanie. Now."

"You have to get used to that. It's part of who I am."

Hop didn't speak.

"I don't like that you did what you did, but I do like that you're a man who'd fight for what he believes in in order to make it real."

His eyes closed and his head dropped as his arms uncrossed and he rested his hands on his hips.

"Honey," I called, and his head came up. "You have a monster too."

"I did. My woman just slayed it."

It was my turn to close my eyes and drop my head because that felt so good, I couldn't let anything in but the feeling.

"Lady," he called, and I lifted my head.

"I'm worried about Benito," I announced.

"I know you are," he replied.

"We disagree with how to deal with that."

"Give it time, babe, you'll trust me, understand my brand of protection, and that will not be an issue."

We both fell silent.

Then I gave in, "Okay."

I watched how my capitulation affected him as he let the emotions wash over his face. Softness, warmth, then the darkness of passion.

He stopped at the passion and ordered, "Now get over here."

"Are you going to give me a rug burn?" I asked.

"No. But you're gonna become acquainted with the seat of your couch and not because your ass is gonna be in it but because your face is gonna be in it. Your ass is gonna be over the back of it, which is how you're gonna take me."

Another mini-orgasm.

"I think you just gave me a mini-orgasm," I shared.

"If you get your ass over here, I'll give you one that is *not* mini."

Oh wow.

There it was again.

"That's four," I admitted then stupidly went on, "I had two in the forecourt, FYI."

"Lanie, you bein' cute is only makin' me want to fuck you harder."

"Is that bad?"

Hop lost patience.

"Lady. Get. *Over. Here.*"

I got over there.

The minute I was in reaching distance, Hop crushed me in his arms and slammed his mouth down on mine.

Not long after, I got acquainted with the seat of my couch in a way I never expected I would.

It was fabulous.

CHAPTER THIRTEEN

Perfect

One week, two days later…

I HAD MY head in the fridge, trying to figure out what to have for dinner and thinking maybe we should do takeout, when I heard the sliding glass door open.

"Hey honey, you want a beer?" I asked as I heard the door slide shut.

"Bourbon," Hop answered.

I pulled my head out of the fridge and turned to him to see he had a face like thunder. He was also opening the doors over my pantry where I kept my hard liquor.

"Is everything okay?" I asked, moving to the island.

Hop uncapped my Jack Daniels then threw back a healthy slug straight from the bottle.

I made a mental note to buy another for company and leave that one all to Hop.

He dropped the bottle and sliced his eyes to me. "Get this shit, Shy is doin' Tabby."

My mouth dropped open, my heart swelled, and the look on his face was the only thing stopping me from doing a girlie jump in the air, arms overhead, shouting, "Hurrah!"

Tabitha Allen was Tack's only daughter. She was in her early twenties, but when she was in her teens, she had a screaming crush on Shy.

I had no idea why Hop looked like he wanted to kill someone, but maybe he didn't know that Tab used to have a huge crush on Shy. Regardless, I thought it was cool. This meant she was healing from her loss. She had sunk so deep in her grief, we all feared for a while that she would drown in it. But she'd come back to her old self.

I wondered if Shy had anything to do with that and I hoped he did.

"Uh, is it Shy you want to kill and if so, why?" I asked, and Hop just scowled at me so I gave him another option. "Or are you generally just pissed at the world because you had a bad day?"

"Did you hear me?" he asked.

"Yes, you said Shy and Tabby have gotten together."

"Shy is Shy, babe. That means he's doin' her."

"Well, yes, she's past the age of consent and Shy is Shy. He's hot and maybe it's good she's getting some."

"From a *brother*?" he spat with disgust.

I decided to try silence for a bit to see if he'd share more so I'd know what the big deal was.

This didn't work, Hop stopped talking and slugged back more Jack.

When he again dropped the bottle, I told him, "Hop, this is one of those times you need to remember your old lady is a fledgling old lady and you need to explain."

"She's Tack's daughter," he reminded me of something I knew.

I nodded.

"Off-limits, babe," he declared.

"Well—"

"And he knows it."

I moved to him, got close, and lifted a hand to rest it on his chest before I said, "The heart sometimes doesn't care about limits."

Something in his eyes changed, and I knew him well enough to know that change didn't bode well for me.

This knowledge was confirmed when he stated, "They been at it a while, better at hidin' it than you and me, which, FYI, Shy knows about us. High you already knew, Hound was in the kitchen when we had our go 'round and Hound's got a big fuckin' mouth, so Boz, Tug, Brick, Dog, Snapper, and Bat also know."

Oh dear.

"And Big Petey took me aside and counseled me," Hop went on. "No one told him jack but the old man's got nothin' to do but hang around and observe. Not much is lost on him."

"Who does that leave?" I asked, not having a good feeling about this.

"Arlo, Roscoe, Speck . . . and Tack."

He was making a point. I just didn't feel like taking his point so I changed the subject. "Are you done slugging bourbon? Do you want a beer?"

He lifted a hand to curl it around the side of my neck. "Babe, Shy and Tab kept that shit from Tack and he's seriously fuckin' pissed. He's got reason and, I'll admit, it's different, what we're doin', but not by much. Tab's his daughter. Shy knows better but they lied. They hid. Tack wants him out."

My lungs convulsed. "Seriously?"

"He says he loves her but this is Shy, and she's fuckin' Tabby."

I stared at him, my lungs easing and my heart swelling.

"He says he loves her?"

"Babe, this is not Cinderella and Prince Charming."

"Yes, it is."

He blinked before he asked, "Come again?"

"She used to crush on him huge."

"Lanie—"

I cut him off. "A girl, Hop, any girl who crushes on a boy like that, well...you aren't a girl and thank God for me you aren't. Still, that means you'll never know. To have a crush like that and then have that boy fall in love with you, Hop, that's a dream come true. Tabby lost so much, honey, she deserves to have a dream come true."

His jaw clenched and he looked to the side, which was something else that didn't give me a good feeling.

"What?" I asked.

He looked back at me.

"We had a showdown today, or Shy did with Tack, and the Club backed Tack. Tabby came tearin' in and it went from really fuckin' bad to cataclysmic. Shy says he's willin' to give up his cut for her."

Give up his cut?

That was insane. No brother willingly gave up their cut.

Unless they were *really* in love.

"Oh my God," I whispered.

"Yeah," Hop said. "That rocked our shit, as any declaration of lettin' go of the brotherhood would do. Then her mom strolled in, and you were gone, lady, you never met her, but Naomi, Tack's ex, is one serious bitch. Made an art out of bein' one, and her masterpieces were bustin' Tack's balls and tearin' Tab down 'til she felt like nothin'."

I knew this. I'd heard about Naomi from Ty-Ty. And from what I heard, Hop was not wrong. She was one serious bitch.

Hop went on, "Most of the boys know Naomi went at Tack and Tabby with equal venom, so she is not our favorite person, so much so, she'd been warned off Chaos. But Shy, swear to Christ, that woman walked in, thought Shy was gonna rip her head off. No hesitation, he had her out the door and was in her face, so harsh, the bitch didn't say a fuckin' word, and Naomi's got an arsenal of words and she uses 'em as weapons. Not a peep. Got in her car and went. Knew Shy was a good brother, outside this shit with Tab, more than pulls his weight, he's smart, got no fear, that's why I backed him to recruit, but I had no idea he had that in him."

I smiled. "Love makes you able to do a lot of things you didn't think you had in you."

His fingers dug into my skin as his eyes went intense. I realized what I said and felt my smile die away.

"Baby," he murmured.

Really not wanting to be on this one, I quickly changed the subject again. "I think this all sounds good, Hopper. I know it's a shock. You all have known Tabby since she was a little girl, so it'll take time for you to adjust to the fact that she isn't a little girl anymore. But nothing you said is bad. Everything you said, honey, if you listen to your words, isn't good either. It's *great*. Willing to give up his cut, dealing with her mom. That's beautiful."

"You're missing my point," he said gently.

"I know," I whispered.

He pulled in a breath through his nose.

Then he stated, "That scene we had where I watched that monster tear into you, lady, you gotta know I don't wanna take you back there but this shit is goin' on too long."

Oh no.

This wasn't happening. Not now. Maybe in a week. Or three. Or one hundred and fifty.

"I'm not ready," I stated hurriedly.

"My job to make you ready."

I clenched my teeth and looked away.

"Lanie, baby, look at me."

I looked back and he dipped his face close.

"You need to talk to Tyra and not about us."

That feeling swelled inside me, growing, taking over. "Hop—"

"She does not blame you."

"Please stop talking."

He shut his mouth. Then he shifted to put the bottle of bourbon on the counter and came back to me, lifting his other hand to curl it around my neck, and his face again came close.

"Hold it back, hold it at bay, for now, control it like you got to, lady, but do all that letting this in," he started, and I didn't think that was a good start so I braced.

It was good I did.

"I have never been shot. I have never watched someone I love die. But I have carried the burden of feelin' I fucked up and someone got hurt because of it."

"Hop—" I tried.

"Listen, lady," he whispered.

I shut my mouth.

Hop kept going.

"Black got whacked because my girls talked. I struggled with that for a long time. He left two boys and an old lady, the Club takes care of them but that's not enough. That'll never be enough. She hasn't moved on. She loved him so goddamned much, she unraveled and she never wound herself back together. That weighed heavy on me, baby, until Tack noticed and we talked it out. He made me get that I didn't drill rounds into our brother and I didn't yap to the wrong people, puttin' him in danger. I did my job, carrying out the orders he gave me. He told me he also carried the same weight because he gave the orders that led to Black being brought down. But the bottom line for both of us was we didn't do the deed. You did what you thought was right, Lanie. But you never stuck your girl with a knife. You gotta let that shit go."

"Will you stop talking now?" I asked, my voice small.

I understood logically what he was saying, but for some, malevolent reason, that monster in me fed on the guilt and it was growing out of control.

I knew Hop saw this when he replied, "I will but I'm givin' you fair warning, you've had time. That time is runnin' out. You mean somethin' to me in a way, for a man, he wants the world to know it. I'm proud you're on my arm and in my bed and I want to share that with my family. Don't keep takin' that away from me."

I stared into his eyes as the monster deflated inside me.

Poof!

Then I tucked my chin and planted my forehead in his chest.

Oh God.

I was in love.

God. I'd fallen in love with Hopper Kincaid.

"You gonna find it in you to help me slay that monster?" he asked, his arms moving around me.

No, I probably wasn't.

I just knew right then Hop had it in him to do it.

Still, I answered, "Yes, Hop. But give me a few more days. Okay?"

"You got it, baby."

You got it, baby.

I had it.

I love you, I thought, but the words didn't come out.

Instead, I wrapped my arms around him and held tight.

"What're we doin' for dinner?" he asked.

I closed my eyes and held tighter.

He was letting it be.

I so totally loved him.

I opened my eyes and dropped my head back. "Takeout?"

"Works for me."

I gave him a shaky smile.

His return smile wasn't shaky.

"Hop?"

"Right here, lady."

"Find it in you to give Shy and Tab a chance."

"You already talked me to that conclusion, babe."

Yes. I was in love with Hopper Kincaid.

"Good," I whispered.

"Chinese, pizza, or Mexican?" he asked.

"You pick."

"Mexican," he decided.

"Perfect," I agreed.

He dropped his lips and brushed them against mine, his 'tache tickling me.

Then he let me go and went to the fridge to get a beer.

I watched him, thinking, a badass biker in faded jeans, a faded black henley, and beat-up motorcycle boots. He needed a haircut and a shave. He used profanity way too often. And there were shadowy things in his life he had to protect me from.

But, yes.

All that was perfect.

Absolutely.

CHAPTER FOURTEEN

Get Him Back

Three days later…

I STOOD AT the sink in Hop's bathroom, wearing nothing but my underwear, looking at myself in the mirror, so I didn't miss it when Hop, in a pair of cutoff black sweats, slid in behind me.

I watched with some fascination as he wrapped his flame-tattooed arms around me and dropped his head to touch his lips to my shoulder.

His mustache tickled and I felt that thrill on my shoulder and down my spine.

He needed a shave, like four days ago.

I didn't tell him this because, although he needed one, I liked it that he was a man who didn't care.

He lifted his head and caught my eyes in the mirror.

"You good?" he asked.

I nodded.

"Sure?" he pushed.

"No," I whispered.

Today was the day.

I'd told him the night before that I was ready. I was going

to take off work a bit early the next day, hit Ride and talk to Tyra.

I'd had several conversations with Tyra since the Tabby and Shy drama went down to make certain all was well and because she shared that prior to the faceoff in the Compound, she and Tabby had had a scene. Ty-Ty felt bad she jumped to conclusions about Shy and she'd hurt Tabby, who she adored.

Further, we'd learned that Tabby's mother had shown on Chaos when she was not wanted (and when the boys told you that you weren't wanted, any sane person would stay away) to share the news that Tabby's grandmother had died. So I also wanted to see if Tabby was okay without bothering Tabby, who'd had a rough couple of days, in order to ask.

So I was going to Ride to take my friend's pulse.

I was also going to Ride to talk to her about how I felt about what befell her because of Elliott and the decision I made and...*God*...to find out how she felt about it.

Last, I was going to tell her that Hop and I were together, I was in love with him, and I hoped we'd be together for, well...ever.

And I was terrified.

"She loves you," Hop told my reflection, pressing his front deeper into my back. "She doesn't blame you. But she worries about you. This will make her feel better and, however that monster is twisting it inside you, lady, I swear to fuck, it'll make you feel better too."

I hoped he was right.

Hop watched the anxiety move through my features and his arms got tighter.

"Baby, seriously, it's been fuckin' years. You think she'd drink with you, let you spend time with her boys, make you a part of her family, if she held a grudge?"

"This feeling isn't logical, Hop."

"This feeling, honey, isn't about Tyra."

I blinked.

"What?"

He held my eyes in the mirror then he kissed my shoulder again before looking back at me. "You get this step done, we'll get into the rest of it later."

My hands moved quickly to his arms when he made a move to let me go, so he stopped.

"What are you talking about?" I asked.

"Proud of you," he replied, and that was nice but it didn't answer my question, so I opened my mouth to speak but he kept going before I could start. "This is a big step. I see it's takin' a lot out of you. But you know in your gut she doesn't blame you. You blame yourself. That's somethin' else to get over. But, baby, this is about that and it's more. No one, man or woman, lies bleedin' on a floor with someone they love lyin' dead feet away and comes away from that unmarked. Your issues don't end here, lady. My guess, you're focusin' on this so you won't focus on that. So we'll focus on this, get past it, then I'll help you focus on that. But bottom line, step by step, we'll beat this shit."

"I'm not sure that makes me feel better, Hop," I confessed.

"And you aren't gonna feel better for a while, Lanie," he told me flat out. "You go into battle, it fucks you up. Then you come out a winner, you're just that, a winner."

"Okay, that's nice and all but, I have to admit, now I *really* don't feel better. I'm not big on being fucked up," I told him and he grinned.

Then he asked, "Where am I?"

I didn't understand the question so I asked back, "What?"

"Where am I?" he repeated, and when I still looked

confused, he went on, "Right now, Lanie, where am I standing?"

It sifted through me what he meant and left warmth in its wake.

"At my back," I answered softly.

"At your back, baby, now and always," he replied, kissed my shoulder again, gave me a squeeze, and another sexy grin. Then he let me go and walked away.

I looked at myself in the mirror.

And I felt better.

* * *

I wasn't feeling better as I walked up the concrete stairs that led to Tyra's office at Ride.

That feeling had worn off now that the time had come.

Tyra was the office manager at Ride and had been since before she and Tack got married. They'd met because she got hired there. That was, the weekend before she started work, she'd gone to what she thought was a company party but was really a Chaos hog roast blowout. Tack plied her with tequila and shrouded her with his hot-guy, badass aura, and she'd fallen in his bed and in love with him in one night.

Unfortunately, at the time, Tack just thought she was a piece of ass and made that clear to Ty-Ty. He also didn't know she was his new office manager. When he found out, he tried to fire her, but she lost her mind. He woke up when she served up the Ty-Ty attitude and from that point on went balls to the wall to win her.

He succeeded.

The rest was history.

I was thinking this instead of re-rehearsing (for the seven thousandth time) what I was going to say when I opened the door and moved into Tyra's office.

I got two big smiles.

Elvira was there.

This was good. Elvira might be crazy but she was also honest and loyal. Further, the woman was pathologically social but it wasn't about not being alone or collecting all the friends she could get. It was just that she had a lot of goodness to give and she gave it without hesitation. I'd seen her make BFFs in a bar with a woman on the stool beside her that she'd never met, and she broke the land speed record doing this. She was so infectious with her personality and so obviously someone you'd want to know.

Hop—right then I knew since he promised he would be—was in the Compound waiting for me to come to him after this was over. He figuratively had my back from afar.

Elvira being there meant she'd have it from up close.

"Hey," I called as I closed the door behind me.

"Hey honey," Ty-Ty called back.

"Get this," Elvira announced in greeting. "After the big to-do with Tabby, now we've learned Hop's got some bitch he's nailin' on the sly, and the boys won't say who she is."

I stopped dead and blinked.

Oh God!

"What I want to know is, why it's a secret," Tyra said to Elvira. "I mean, I understand why Tab and Shy kept their secret, but why Hop? He isn't a secretive guy." She grinned. "I'm guessing she's a librarian."

Elvira threw her head back and laughed at the very idea of Hopper Kincaid and a librarian.

"Maybe a female cop," Ty-Ty went on, her voice trembling with amusement. "The boys would *freak* if he was doing the nasty with a cop."

Elvira, clearly finding this the height of amusement, which I did not, kept laughing.

"What we know is," Tyra carried on, "she isn't a stripper at Smithie's, a cocktail waitress, again at Smithie's, or one of those women who wears their tank tops cut off so it shows the bottom of their boobs while they stand on a podium with a new bike at shows and does the old, 'you buy this bike, you might be able to lay a biker babe like me,' gig." Tyra's dancing eyes came to me. "Hop's usual biker babe of choice."

My breath caught in my throat.

Elvira kept right on laughing.

"Though that's good," Ty-Ty unfortunately continued blabbing. "Biker babes like that get it when it comes to bikers like Hop."

My stomach clenched.

What did that mean?

"Bikers like Hop?" Elvira, always one for juicy gossip, immediately quit laughing in order to hone in on this snippet and do what she always did. Draw it out.

"Yeah," Tyra said. "He's a good guy, I like him. Seriously, and I know it's going to sound crazy because, well, I somehow feel like I shouldn't but I just do. Maybe it's because Tack likes him and respects him. Maybe it's because I know he's down with the brotherhood in a big way and he'd do anything for Tack, me, my boys. Maybe it's just because he's mellow and good to be around. Still, unlike the other guys, with Hop it's a struggle."

"That all sounds good," Elvira noted. "Why is it a struggle?"

"Chaos stuff, biker stuff, stuff you have to get used to," Ty-Ty lifted her hands and did air quotations, "in the life."

"Like what?" Elvira pressed.

"Like stuff I'm not going to share with you, because you have a big mouth," Tyra replied, and Elvira leaned back in affront.

"I do not!" she snapped, and that was a total lie, but since I was freaking out, I didn't make the scoffing noise I would normally make.

Tyra, however, wasn't freaking out so she called her on it. "Girl, you totally do."

Elvira leaned in. "Yeah, okay, I do but I keep it all in the family. I don't run my mouth to people I shouldn't run my mouth to and you know it, Tyra Allen. So, give."

"Elvira—" Tyra started.

"Give, girl. You know, one, you're gonna do it because you got a big mouth, too, and don't you deny it, and two, I'm not gonna let it go until you do and you know that, too, so . . . *give*."

Tyra studied her, and it seemed neither of them noticed I was not moving and had not even come fully into the room.

"You have to promise to keep this tight," Tyra warned, giving in as I knew she'd do because she did kind of have a big mouth.

"I work for a commando. I know how to keep shit tight," Elvira shot back.

There it was. Confirmed. I knew it. Hawk was an actual commando.

I didn't really register that because Tyra clearly took the "commando tight" declaration as indication she could share and spoke again.

And what she said tore me apart.

"Hop and I had a rocky beginning seeing as when he was with Mitzi I saw him in his bed in the Compound with a biker groupie bitch extraordinaire by the name of BeeBee."

My vision went blurry.

"Holy crap," Elvira breathed. "I always liked him. He's a cool guy. And, never thought I would say this in my *whole* life, but that badass biker 'tache of his does things to my girl parts. I can't believe this. He's a cheater?"

Tyra nodded and the room started swaying.

"Tack says it's none of his business or mine. Boys do what they do. Some of them are true to their old ladies, some of them are, well..." she shrugged, "not. It's uncool but it's part of the life. Actually, part of life since cheating isn't limited to bikers, and Tack's right, it really isn't my business."

I had the weird sensation of feeling I was going to pass out at the same time I was hyper-alert and concentrating on every word Ty-Ty said.

"Honestly," she continued, "no offense to the sisterhood, but after all that went down and things got super ugly with Mitzi, Tack didn't share any specifics but she came around and was totally a bitch, like, a Naomi bitch, so I have to admit, it was the one time in my life I kinda got it. Though he should have cut her loose before he nailed a biker groupie, especially one like BeeBee."

"This is what I don't get," Elvira grumbled. "They wanna go lookin', they want fresh meat, why don't they cut us loose first? Why they gotta keep us on a string? I mean, haven't these dudes seen *Fatal Attraction? Hope Floats*? That shit destroys a woman, both women involved, for God's sake, and it isn't like men don't know it."

"Is Tabby okay?" I blurted, and both their heads swung my way.

"Pardon?" Tyra asked.

"I, well, sorry girls, but I don't have a lot of time. I need to meet a client. Last-minute meeting. But I wanted to stop by, Ty-Ty," I looked at her and held all I was feeling in by the skin of my teeth. "See if Tab was okay with her Grandma and, you know, everything."

"She's good. They're heading down for the funeral this weekend. The rest, well, the Club has drama then the Club smoothes out drama, and they tend not to screw around so that's all good," Tyra answered. Her eyes narrowed on me and I nodded. "Are you good?" she asked.

"Yeah, just, I have this client on my mind and, you know, blowout on Chaos, the whole thing with Tabby," I lied. "But it's good things are good."

"Girl, you sure you're good?" Elvira asked, and I looked at her to see her eyes were also narrowed on me.

"I just, just..."

God, I had to get out of there.

I looked back to Tyra.

"You know Tack visited me?"

I saw my best friend's body go still before she replied, "I know."

"I, well, I've been thinking about that and I thought I was ready to, um...discuss things with you. So I kinda came here to do that, as well as, of course, check on Tab. But, being here, I think I need a little more time. Just, I don't know, a week or, uh...two."

Her face changed, went soft, sweet, and last, immensely relieved.

She loved me.

She was worried about me.

She was happy I was there to talk things out.

So Ty-Ty.

At least that was a relief, a massive one I unfortunately couldn't fully feel seeing as my heart was bleeding.

"You take all the time you need, honey. I'm always here," she replied.

She always was. Why hadn't I remembered that?

I nodded.

"Always," she repeated, and I nodded again.

"Me too, girl," Elvira put in.

I looked at her. Her face was soft, sweet, and concerned. She'd been worried about me too.

So Elvira.

I nodded at her too.

"I have to go," I said hurriedly.

Both of them smiled at me.

My smile was shaky and I knew it, I knew they saw it but I didn't have much strength left to hold back all I was feeling so I had to move on before I lost it.

I did this by turning and going out the door on a vague wave. My pumps clicked on the forecourt as I practically ran toward the Compound. I threw open the door, went through and saw Hop sitting on a stool at the curve of the bar. His eyes came right to me. He caught my expression and worry suffused his features.

He got off his chair and when I made it to him, he grabbed my hand and murmured, "My room."

I nodded.

He led me to his room. I pulled my hand free and walked in three paces.

After he closed the door, he turned to me and took a step toward me.

I took a step back.

His brows shot together and his eyes studied my face.

"Jesus, fuck, it didn't go good with Cherry?" he asked with disbelief.

"I know about BeeBee."

I watched his body freeze.

There it was.

He'd done it.

He'd cheated on Mitzi with a woman named BeeBee.

God!

"We're over," I declared. "Over," I repeated. "I do not fuck cheaters. I do not look at cheaters. I do not even breathe the same air," I leaned into him and finished on a hiss, "*as cheaters*. I never want to see you again, Hop. I never want you to touch me again. As of now, you've ceased to exist."

After I delivered that speech, I ran.

I ran out of his room, through the Compound, and to my car.

The problem with this was that I knew he came after me.

He didn't say a word but when I started up my car, I heard a Harley roar and I knew it was his. And when I drove, I saw him on his bike right behind me. And when I parked in my garage, he pulled into my back drive.

So when I hustled through my courtyard, opened the sliding glass door, I couldn't close it because his hand was on it and I could feel the heat of his body at my back.

I gave up, rushed in and whirled on him, feeling, actually *feeling* myself coming apart at the seams.

He had *to go*.

"You don't get to be here, Hop. You *never* get to be here again," I clipped.

"Cody isn't mine."

My body swayed from an unexpected blow landed so accurately, I had to put a foot back to catch myself so I wouldn't fall.

"Yeah," he growled, not missing my reaction.

"Oh my God," I breathed.

"Yeah," he growled again. "I didn't know that fucked up shit when I fucked BeeBee and yeah, woman, I fucked BeeBee, but Tyra sharin' that shit is *uncool*. She doesn't know why I did it, she doesn't know where I was at in my head when I did it, she doesn't know shit, and she isn't entitled to know shit because it's none of her goddamned business."

"Hop—" I tried to break in but failed.

He was angry, furious. His rage filled the room, making it hard to breathe.

And he was on a roll.

"But before I'm done with you, you're gonna know it all."

Before he was done with me?

"We were on a break, Mitzi and me," he shared. "I didn't know it was a break then. I thought it was over. Before that happened, she got pregnant with Cody and she didn't let me touch her. Barely even fuckin' looked at me. Tried everything, she didn't let me in. She gave me a son, or I thought she gave me a son. Didn't know, at the time, he wasn't mine. Then she had him, I was over the goddamned moon, and she *still* froze me out. Worse than before, far worse. For me, I had a son, he was fuckin' perfect, I was goddamned beside myself, and my woman? She freezes me out? I couldn't take it. Tried. Failed. Packed my shit. Got out. I'd had enough. Years of that shit. Years of tryin' to break through. It wasn't an easy decision. Molly, so fuckin' little, Cody, just a baby, but I couldn't take one more day of her fucked up shit. So I left."

"Honey—"

"Shut it, woman. You bought this, take it."

I snapped my mouth shut.

Hop glowered at me a moment before he continued.

"I was stayin' at the Compound, lookin' for a place. Bee-Bee was available. I hadn't had a lay in nearly a fuckin' year so I took advantage. None of Tyra's business why. Tack's. Yours. Anyone's. I got off. It wasn't good. It didn't suck.

What it was was a onetime gig, a man fuckin' available gash with no strings. I was a free agent so why the fuck not?"

"I don't think Tyra knows that," I said carefully.

"I don't give a fuck she does or doesn't," he returned.

I fell silent.

Hop carried on.

"Not long after that, Mitzi talked me back. I thought she wanted to give it another shot. What she wanted was someone to help her with dirty diapers and a mortgage payment. She pulled the wool, and I wanted a family so bad, to wake up knowin' my kids were under my roof, I let her. Then, one day, I come home and some woman is sittin' on our porch. Never seen this bitch before. I get off my bike, walk up to her, she looks me straight in the eyes and lays it out. Everything. Everything I worked hard to get and Mitzi never gave to me. Everything I learned from a goddamned stranger."

When he stopped speaking and didn't seem like he was going to go on, I prompted, "What did you learn, honey?"

"I learned why Mitzi was such a cunt. A spoiled rotten, worthless piece of shit who I wasted fuckin' *years* with. The piece of shit who was the mother of my children. Or, I found out that day, my daughter. Not my goddamned son."

I was trying not to hyperventilate and had to concentrate so much on this, I only had it in me to nod.

"She was a cheerleader," Hop announced and I blinked.

"What?" I forced out.

"This bitch. Blonde. Blue-eyed. Perfectly honed body. Goddamned ponytail in her hair. She was the kind of cheerleader who was gonna hold onto that shit, the glory days, until she fuckin' died. Or she thought she would until Mitzi blew her life apart."

I didn't get it.

Hop didn't make me ask for an explanation.

"See, back in the day, Mitzi had a thing for the quarterback of her high school football team. She wanted him. Problem was, he was dating the head cheerleader. But Mitzi, Mitzi wanted what she wanted, so she gave it her all to get it. In high school terms, that means she put out. This fuckin' guy took what she gave, kept her on the side and went to homecoming and prom with his good girl. This was the beginning and until that day on the porch, it didn't have an end. Mitzi fixated on this guy. He was all she wanted and, way that bitch told it, she went all out to get him. The shit she said, she was not fuckin' jokin'."

I kept deep breathing.

Hop kept telling his tale of treachery.

"He went to college, his girl went to the same college, but he still kept Mitzi on the side. And she stayed there, givin' him what his cheerleader couldn't or wouldn't. They graduated, got married, he got a job, kept Mitzi and his wife until his work transferred him to another state. That's when Mitzi realized it might not ever be her so she had to have a plan B. He took his wife, said good-bye and didn't look back."

Hop paused, I nodded again and Hop kept going.

"That's when I came into the picture. That's why she never let me in. Pinin' for that guy. Still in touch with him. Holdin' a torch, holdin' onto hope. She led me into a life together knowin', she got a shot, she'd cut me loose and go for him. He got transferred back to Denver after we had Molly and they started up again. Good news for her, she thought, when she found out his wife couldn't have kids. She and me, things not good, I wasn't hankerin' to make another baby with her until I was sure we were solid and it didn't look like that would happen, so I was surprised as fuck she turned up pregnant since she was on the pill. But shit happens. I got my son. I rejoiced even if Mitzi was a bitch. My son's my son, so who wouldn't rejoice?"

"No one," I whispered.

"Damn straight," he bit off. "But, see, this bitch on my porch, she tells me that Mitzi went to her husband and threatened to tell her their history and the fact that Mitzi had his kid if he didn't break it off with her. To cut her off at the pass, this guy told his wife the whole fuckin' thing. Feelin' like spreadin' that joy, the bitch comes and shares it with me. Shit blows sky high, as it fuckin' would, tests are performed, Cody isn't mine."

My heart clutched so hard, the pain excruciating, all I could force out was, "Hop."

"But he fuckin' *is,*" Hop snarled. "That motherfucker didn't hold Mitzi's goddamned hand in the delivery room. That motherfucker wasn't the first human being to wrap his arms around my boy. That motherfucker didn't give him his first bottle, change his first diaper, sit with him in a rocker until he fell asleep. I told all of those assholes, they'd see a courtroom before they took my kid. The guy talked his wife around, got another transfer, happily told me he was good with me raisin' his son and they took off. Mitzi saw that she threw her hail Mary and the guy let it drop. He was done with her, and in her twisted, fucked up head, she blamed me and laid a pile of shit on me so heavy, it's been years and it's a wonder I can breathe after that stench. Then she woke up and saw me with her kids, saw what she had and threw away, tried to sort shit with me. I told her I was so far from inter-ested in that, it wasn't goddamned funny, and further, she pulled any-fuckin'-thing with me or my kids, she wouldn't like my response. And here we are."

There they were and, truthfully, I was surprised Hop had it in him to give that woman the courtesy of ignoring her and finding a chair far away from hers at their daughter's dance recital. I didn't know what he would do besides, not with his kids involved. What I knew was that was a further insight into the character of Hopper Kincaid that he'd breathe her air at all.

For his kids.

For both his kids, even when one of them was his by claim, not blood.

"Does Tyra know any of this?" I asked.

"I don't know. I don't give a fuck. For Cody, I didn't spread that shit around. As far as anyone's concerned, he's mine every way he can be. If someone looked at him and guessed, they kept it to themselves. That isn't what's important right now, Lanie. What's important is, I don't know what shit Tyra spouted or how it came out, you took that shit in, came to me and didn't let me say a goddamned word before you tore us apart and tore outta there."

Unfortunately this was true.

"I actually didn't have a chance to share anything with Tyra and, in her defense, Tyra didn't want to share, but when I walked into the office, she and Elvira were gossiping, you know how Elvira is, and it came out. She doesn't know about us. She didn't share it vindictively, Hop. It just…" I paused and finished lamely, "came out."

"That's good, babe, that ticks one thing off your list. You don't have to share 'cause now, this shit, there is no us she needs to know about."

I felt my eyes get wide and my stomach plummet.

"Hop, I—"

"Save it," he clipped. "I don't wanna hear it. You said what you had to say, you made your fuckin' judgment which, Lanie, you seem to do a lot of judging even gettin' pissed that I'd think you would. You're the master of the backtrack. I

spend a lot of time listenin' to you do it, even gettin' maneuvered into fuckin' *apologizin'* to you about it and I do not
need that shit in my life."

"That isn't fair," I whispered.

"No, what isn't fair is you bein' with me, you knowin'
exactly the man I am, and you walkin' into my room and
layin' that shit on me. You fuckin' know, woman, fuck me,
you *goddamned know* I am not that man. And you got such a
loose hold on your drama, you laid that shit on me. Well, I'm
done with your goddamned drama, Lanie. All day, worried
goddamned sick about you, goin' into battle with that monster, goin' to have words with Cherry, then you lay that on
me? You jump to conclusions, tell me to my face you never
want me to touch you again?" He shook his head. "No. You
don't want my hands on you, woman? You got it."

I stood frozen in fear as he turned to the door and he had
it opened before he turned back.

"You breathe one word about Cody to anyone, so help
me God, you'll deal with me. That's mine to share. Nothin'
about me is yours. Not anymore."

And on that, as every word he said drove home, slicing
through me, he moved through the door, slid it closed, and
prowled away without even a glance back.

I stood, immobile, trying with difficulty to manage the
pain and staring at the door thinking how hard that had to
have been for Hop to share. How difficult it must be for him
to wake up every day and know his woman cheated on him,
gave the son he wanted to another man. How he didn't care
and went to the mat to keep a son who wasn't his but who
was. How lucky it was that even though Cody Kincaid's bio-
logical father was a total dick, God saw fit to insert Hopper
into his life. How I really, *really* needed to learn how to get a
handle on my drama and not blow things out of proportion.

I now knew the definition of a cunt.

I'd just hurt my man, forced him to share something in anger when he wasn't ready.

And last and most importantly, how the hell was I going to get him back.

CHAPTER FIFTEEN

Come Inside

The next day…

"HOP, PLEASE CALL me. I was an idiot. I shouldn't have done what I did. I promise I'll get a hold on the drama. I promise, Hopper. *Swear.*" I took a deep breath. "We need to talk this out, honey. Please call me," I begged into my phone.

I'd given it the night but this was my third voicemail that day.

I put my phone on my desk, ignored the cautious vibe coming from the staff in my office, which I knew was caused by me, and tried to get to work.

But I couldn't stop thinking about Hop. What I'd done, what he'd said, how to make it better. Needless to say, I didn't get anything done.

Hours later, I called him and left another voicemail.

Hours after that, before going to bed, I called him again but since he didn't answer, I hung up.

Tomorrow.

I'd try again tomorrow.

I settled into bed.

I didn't sleep.

* * *

Three days later…

I know you're angry, honey, but please, PLEASE, call me. I need to apologize face to face.

That was text two of the day. It was nine o'clock in the morning.

There would be five more before I laid my head down on my pillow in order not to get a wink of sleep.

* * *

Two days later…

I sat sipping a beer in the Compound. Brick was with me, shooting the shit.

I knew he knew or suspected. All the brothers did. I knew they knew I was hanging there hoping to see Hop.

This was kind of embarrassing.

I did not care.

Hop had his kids so it was a long shot in the evening he'd show but I was willing to take it. I was willing to do anything.

"Gotta hit the head," Brick muttered. I gave him a smile I knew he knew I didn't commit to by the sweet smile he gave back and the squeeze he gave my knee before he took off toward the bathroom.

I felt a hand warm and strong at the back of my neck and I twisted to see Big Petey standing close.

"How you doin', sweetheart?" he asked quietly.

Yes. They all knew.

I stared at Big Petey thinking I had nothing left to lose.

Nothing.

"Do you know where Hop is?" I asked, and his face got soft.

"No, Lanie darlin'. Sorry to say, I don't," he answered.

"Have you seen him?" I asked.

"Seen him around. Haven't had words with him in a while."

"Is he okay?" I went on, needing something, anything, even just the knowledge Hop was in a bad mood would feed the need.

"Don't know, honey."

I pressed my lips together before I went for broke.

"If you see him, can you ask him to call me? It's important. Like *really* important," I stressed.

His hand still at my neck gave me a reassuring squeeze, which didn't reassure me. "Will do."

"Thanks," I whispered, then said, "Can you tell Brick I have to go? I forgot, there's something I need to pick up at the drugstore."

"No problem."

I smiled another smile I didn't commit to. Big Petey let my neck go and I skedaddled.

Hours later, lying in bed, I called Hop.

"You're worrying me, honey," I said into my phone, my voice sounding strange, hoarse.

Scared.

"Call me," I finished then I hung up.

Again, I didn't sleep.

The next day, Hopper didn't call.

*   *   *

Four days later…

I'd been sitting in my car at the curb outside Hop's house for a very long time before he pulled up on his bike. It was Monday, after his kids were gone.

It was also time to know.

He didn't return a single message I left and I left many. He didn't return a single text and I sent loads of those too. And he didn't show at the Compound in the evenings. I knew he didn't because I went there every night and had a drink just in case I'd run into him.

So when Hop had showed at the Compound the day before, walking in, spotting me, turning right on the spot and leaving, even though I made a fool of myself running after him, calling his name, he didn't look at me when he threw a leg over his bike, made it roar, and rode away.

After that, I needed to know.

And as I watched the single headlight approach, watched Hop ride into his front drive, watched him switch off his bike, walk to his front door and then walk through it, all without glancing my way, I knew.

He was done with me, no going back.

So he needed to know.

I took a deep breath, threw open my door, walked up to his house, and hit the doorbell.

No answer.

I hit the bell again then knocked.

He made me wait.

I fought back tears.

He finally opened the door and, with a bottle of beer in his hand, cut me off before I could start.

"This isn't going to happen."

"I was eleven, I was in the city with my class on a fieldtrip, we were there to see a Broadway show when I saw him," I began.

His eyebrows drew together but his lips said, "Lanie, whatever you gotta—"

"My dad in a restaurant, kissing the neck of a woman who was not my mother."

His mouth snapped shut.

I held his eyes and gave it to him as I'd practiced during the two hours I sat in front of his house.

"He saw me, right through the window. I just stood there, staring at him. I didn't get it. I was too young. But I sure grew up fast, standing on that sidewalk staring at my father with another woman."

"Lanie—"

"Our teacher shouted my name because I wasn't moving. That's why he turned his head and looked out the window. He must have heard her shout my name."

"Lanie—"

"You bought this, you take it," I whispered, and his chin jerked back before his face went soft.

I wasn't immune to the beauty of that look. It took a lot, but I didn't give him a single indication I wasn't immune.

"He didn't move, Dad didn't. Didn't get out of his seat and come to me. Didn't even mouth my name. He just sat close to her, holding her hand on the table, staring at me until the teacher pulled me away. Dad never mentioned it. Not a word. He never explained himself. He never even lied to try to make it better. But, I figure, with what happened next, he decided, since the cat was out of the bag, he didn't have to bother with pretending. Hiding. So he didn't."

"Come inside, lady," Hop invited gently.

Lady.

Gutted.

Again.

Like he did after every call he didn't return, every text he didn't reply to, walking away from me the night before as I ran after him, calling his name.

Gutted until I was hollow.

Again.

"I'm good out here."

Hop's jaw clenched but he said nothing more.

I did.

"I don't know if she moved there or he moved her there or what, but they didn't carry on their affair in the safety of the city anymore. He wasn't blatant about it but he didn't give keeping it under wraps a lot of effort. People saw him going to late movies with her. Saw them eating dinner together one town over. Saw them shopping together. My sister, Lis, saw them, too." I paused. "I saw them, too."

"It's cold, baby. Come inside," Hop urged, but I didn't move.

"That's why my mom is an alcoholic. It's an addiction, a weakness; it isn't all his fault but I know that started it. Looking back, I think she knew he was stepping out on her even before he moved his mistress to our town. If she didn't spot them together sometime in all these years, it would be a miracle. But people talk. She'd hear the whispers. She'd catch the looks. Her friends would find their times to tell her. I know. I heard the whispers, I caught the looks but I was too young to drown in a bottle the pain I felt living in a house where love was a lie."

"Lanie, honey, please, come inside."

"That's why I picked him."

Hop closed his eyes, opened them and I saw disquiet in them when he murmured, "Baby—"

"Don't get me wrong," I interrupted him. "I loved Elliott, I really did. I didn't put myself in front of bullets just for a guy I felt safe with, knowing he'd never cheat on me. But, having thought on it for years, as much of a bitch as this might make me sound, I gave him a shot because he wasn't in my league. I gave him a shot because I knew he'd worship the ground I walked on and never treat me like dirt. I'd had guys treat me like garbage for a long time, my father being the first of them, so it wasn't lost on me that having a man that devoted to me was a good thing. So I hooked my star to his. At first, he made it worth it, and not because he treated me like gold but just because he was a good man who loved me. You know how it was in the end."

"You don't come inside, Lanie, I'll carry you inside."

"You touch me, Hop, you'll never see me again."

His body went visibly solid even as he flinched.

"You're right," I continued. "I heard Tyra talking about you and I did what I always do. I flew off the handle. I had no idea about Cody. I knew your breakup with Mitzi was bad but that kind of bad never entered my mind. But you know I'm like that. You know I blow things out of proportion. What you didn't know was, even if I was wrong, thinking for even a second you'd cheat on your woman would hit me somewhere deep, somewhere that's been wounded and bloody since I was eleven. You got angry with me for not giving you a shot at explaining. But you didn't give me that shot either, Hop."

"You've done it, lady, now come inside so we can finish talking this shit out where it's warm."

"That isn't going to happen," I declared, and his head jerked.

"What?"

"I am who I am and I can't be something else for you. For over a week, I've called, texted, and sat in the Compound while your brothers knew I was waiting for you, humiliating myself by sitting there, hoping I'd get the chance to make things right with you. They did their best to be nice, it's their way. But you didn't give me that shot, they all knew it and I knew it too. You didn't return a call. You didn't send back a text. You walked away from me, twice, and just now you saw me and walked into your house without looking at me. You don't need my drama in your life, Hop? Well, I don't need a man who can so easily cut me out of his."

"You didn't know about Cody, babe, I didn't know about your dad."

"You didn't ask."

"I'll remind you, you didn't either."

"Oh, you don't have to remind me, Hopper. I remember. God, I remember," I told him, the words sounding choked in the end so I swallowed as Hop shifted toward me, but I took a step away so he stopped.

"This doesn't work," I declared.

"Yes, it does," he contradicted.

"No," I shook my head. "It doesn't. We fight all the time."

"We also fuck all the time."

He had a point there, just not a good enough one.

"We don't work," I stated.

"Baby, the good we got, how can you say that?" he asked.

"I have a week and a half of knowing it, Hop," I answered. "You *cut me out.*"

"You fucked up then I fucked up, babe. We're gettin' to know each other. That'll happen and, just a heads up, even when we got time and experience in, it'll still happen."

"You cut me out."

"I fucked up."

I leaned in and hissed, *"You cut me out,"* and he blinked at the sudden harshness of my tone. "Do you have any clue, *any fucking clue* how much pain I've been in? A week and a half, knowing I hurt you like that, knowing I forced you to relive that, knowing I did wrong, calling you, texting you, *begging you* to let me talk to you, apologizing and you not giving me *anything?*"

He stepped out on the stoop and I took another step away.

"Lanie, come here," he urged.

"No." I moved back another step.

"Goddamn it, Lanie, you're gonna fall off the fuckin' stoop," he growled, so I stepped down the two steps and stood on his front walk. "Jesus, lady, just come inside the fuckin' house."

"I wanted one night," I reminded him.

"Lanie, baby—"

"That's it. One night. But you pushed in, I let you in and now I remember, Hop. I remember what, for seven years, I've been guarding against."

He stepped down. I stepped back.

"You have something, you have something to lose," I went on, slowly backing up. "You don't have anything, you have nothing to lose. I didn't want any part of it, but you made me want it then you gave me something and you took it away and reminded me how bad it hurts, how it *kills* to have something to lose."

"Please, honey, fuckin' come inside."

"We're done."

"Take a deep breath, calm the drama, think a second, then come the fuck inside."

I stopped dead, he stopped dead, and I pinned him with my eyes.

"This isn't a drama, Hop. Pay attention. I'm not ranting. I'm not in a tizzy. I've given this a lot of thought. Thanks to you, I've had a good amount of time to think about it. And we're done. I don't need this pain. I've had twenty-eight years of living with this kind of pain, watching my mother endure it, and I'm done."

His face went hard.

"I'm not doin' to you what your motherfucker of a father is doin' to your mother," he growled.

"It's not the same but it's still heartbreak," I returned and, just as quickly as it came, the hardness washed out of his features.

"Do not do this, Lanie."

"It's already done. It was done when you got off your bike, walked into your house and broke my heart. Just like my father. You didn't even have it in you to do it up close and personal."

He grabbed my arm, but with a savage twist I pulled away and took two steps back.

"It was good you shielded your kids from what we might have been, Hop. I'll miss them but they won't miss me."

"Jesus, fuck, babe, I'm beggin' you, come inside."

"Good-bye, Hop."

"Baby—"

I turned and ran.

He turned and ran into his house.

He didn't have his keys.

This was good.

This meant I got a head start and when I hit a motel parking lot, Hop had no idea where I was.

It was only when I was sitting cross-legged on the ratty bedspread did I allow myself to burst into tears.

*   *   *

Two days later…

I sat on my couch, twisted toward Tyra to my left, lifting a bent leg just like hers to rest it on the couch, and I sucked back some wine.

Since I gave her the wineglass before I sat down, she'd already had her sip, so when I took my glass from my lips, she was prepared to launch in.

"I don't blame you."

I closed my eyes.

"Lanie, honey, look at me."

I opened my eyes.

She leaned toward me and wrapped her fingers around my thigh. "I don't blame you for me getting stabbed."

"I know," I whispered something I did know but had been denying for insane reasons until that moment I wouldn't allow myself to get. Understandable fear after what happened that led to irrational guilt that no one gave me any indication I should feel. I just fed off it, or more to the point, let my monster feed on it in a vain and crazy attempt to keep myself safe from ever being hurt again.

"I hope so," she told me. "Since I told you way back when that I didn't."

I drew in breath then confided, "I hear it over and over again in my head."

Her head tipped to the side and she scooted closer. "You hear what in your head?"

"Our conversation. You telling me to end it with Elliott. You advising me that his getting us kidnapped was a concrete wall you can't scale when it comes to love. Me telling you—"

"Stop it," she interrupted, squeezing my thigh.

"I think that's it, sweetie. I think that was why I couldn't forgive myself even though you and Tack never blamed me. I think it's because I play that conversation over and over in my head and it reminds me there was something that needed to be forgiven," I admitted.

"Honey, *you* didn't kidnap and stab me and you have to find some way to get that straight. I don't know how to stop you playing that conversation in your head," she stated. "I just know, together, Lanie, we have to find a way to do that."

I took a sip of wine, my way of being noncommittal. I couldn't tell her we could do that, since I hadn't been able to do it for seven years. With this, I'd taken a big step. Who knew how long it would take me to get to the next one.

The day after the break with Hop, I'd called her and told her I was ready to do this. Not surprisingly, she'd told me to tell her when and where and she'd be there.

I gave her the when and where and last night, sleeping at home again, I waited for Hop to show or call.

He didn't.

It was over.

That killed but I'd survived worse (I told myself) so now it was time to move on with my life. Do this. Fight the monster myself without Hop at my back.

And hope I won.

"I think this all might have to do with, uh... well, me getting you hurt, feeling guilt about it since you told me to dump Eli but also, mostly, that whole thing," I waved my hand around, sloshing the wine I held dangerously, so I righted it and finished, "in Kansas City."

"Do you think you need to talk to a professional?" she asked.

I put the wine to my lips, murmuring, "Maybe," before I took a drink.

Her next question was voiced with hesitancy. "Do you want to talk about Kansas City?"

I didn't.

Even so, I looked her straight in the eye and declared, "He used me as a shield."

"I know," she said so low I could barely hear her.

"You know and you knew," I stated and her head gave a slight jerk of confusion.

"I know and I knew?"

"You know what happened and you knew it would happen. That was what you tried to warn me about."

She shook her head. "I didn't know the Mob would find you in—"

"That's not what I mean," I cut her off. "You knew, in that situation or any situation in life, Elliott getting involved with the Mob at all stated it clear to you, he would not protect me."

She sighed before she scooted closer, took another sip of wine, then locked her eyes with mine.

"Yes, I knew. There are some guys, and Elliott was one of them, that just aren't built that way. Luckily, the Mob doesn't normally enter someone's life so they aren't put to that test. I didn't know if it came down to bullets flying he'd use you to take them for him. I just knew that he made a bad decision on how to invest money. Then, when he lost his money, he made a bad decision on how to get it back, and it just went downhill from there. So, yeah, I knew. But I didn't love him, Lanie. Tack is the exact opposite of that. He'd fight, kill, and die before he let anything happen to me, but that doesn't mean he isn't sometimes a pain in my ass. He is. Elliott made it worth it to you in his ways. Tack makes it worth it in his. It's just the way it is."

I couldn't argue with this so I said nothing.

She took another sip of wine before she finished.

"It's easier to see this stuff clearly when emotion isn't involved and, remember Lanie, you didn't want Tack for me in the beginning. You hated him, wanted me to quit and walk away. Pretty much any good girlfriend at that time, before he exposed the man he really is, would say the same thing because they care about their girl, not the guy. They see stuff from the outside, not with emotion coloring everything. Sometimes they're right, like I was with Elliott. And sometimes they're wrong, like you were with Tack. But neither of us had all the information. It's just that you got it all when it was too late."

That was *very* true.

I took a sip of my wine then set the glass on my coffee table, dropped my hands in my lap, and looked at her.

"I dream of Kansas City."

Sorrow suffused her face and she whispered, "Oh, Lanie."

"I see his eyes open and staring at me. He looks surprised. Not just in my dream. When it happened. He was dead but still, he looked surprised."

She grabbed my hand and squeezed.

"I think he was surprised I didn't save him."

I watched the tears start shimmering in her eyes.

"I wanted a man who'd save *me*," I confessed.

"Maybe, if you looked, you can find that man," she suggested.

That wasn't going to happen.

"I think I need to give that more time," I evaded.

"Lanie, honey, I want to be sensitive but don't you think that seven—?" She stopped talking and turned her head just as my eyes shot to the sliding glass doors because we both heard a Harley roar up to the back of my house.

My entire body strung tight.

"Tack knows I have my car and he doesn't have to come and get me. God, do you think something's up with the boys?" she asked, setting her wineglass aside, quickly getting up from the couch and hustling to the door.

She was out the door and in the courtyard when I heard the Harley roar away.

I closed my eyes.

It wasn't Hop.

"How weird was that?" Tyra asked, back in the house, and I looked at her.

"Weird, sweetie," I agreed.

She walked back to me and sat. "Could swear that bike came right up to your garage but it was gone before I got to the back gate."

"Maybe bad sat nav directions," I murmured.

She grabbed her wine. I followed suit.

Again, she got her sip in before I did and thus she could sock it to me.

"Mitch and Brock have a guy they want you to meet."

"Ty-Ty—"

She shook her head. "I know Tack talked about him with you, he was going to call Mitch about it but maybe things with Tabby got him off track. I'm going to call Mara, get things back on track."

"This really is too soon," I told her.

"You wait any longer, honey, it's going to be too late," she replied, her voice sweet but firm.

I closed my mouth because she wasn't wrong. But she also was and I couldn't explain how.

"Right, I want you to do two things for me," she started, and when I nodded, she continued. "One, think about going to counseling. Even if it's short-term counseling, get rid of those dreams. Talk to someone about Kansas City. Try to let that go."

I could do that.

And I *should* do that.

It was time.

"Okay," I agreed, then took a sip of wine.

"Second, go on this date with Mitch's buddy," she stated, and I nearly choked on my wine.

"Ty-Ty!" I cried when I recovered.

"Not tomorrow, not next week, just let Mitch give him

your number. Talk to him on the phone. Get to know him a bit. Then," she grinned, "maybe the week after that, just meet for coffee. No pressure. Just coffee."

I stared at her a moment before I suggested, "How about this? You corral Elvira and maybe Gwen and go on a reconnaissance mission. Find this guy, follow him around, get pictures, go through his trash, stuff like that. And, in a month or so, report back to me and I'll make my decision then."

"I'm not going through trash," she replied.

"Get Elvira to do it."

"Lanie, do you *know* Elvira? I've never seen that woman in jeans. She is not going to wear one of her fabulous dresses and heels and go through trash. Hell, she's just not going to go through some guy's trash."

"Maybe Gwen will," I kept trying.

Her eyebrows shot up. "Okay, now, do you know Gwen?"

That was true. Gwen wouldn't do it, either.

"Maybe we could get Gwen to get Hawk to—"

Ty-Ty broke in. "Let Mitch give him your number."

I ignored her. "Or maybe I could just go and talk to Hawk and Gwen won't have to—"

"Lanie!" she exclaimed on a laugh. "It's just giving a guy your number. If you don't like the sound of his voice or he's a terrible conversationalist, you don't even have to have coffee. But let Mitch give him your number."

She thought I was being crazy mostly because I was but that was my way.

She also didn't know about Hop. She would. It was just that I figured I'd tell her that later, after we got the tough stuff we were currently processing out of the way.

This all meant that I had no choice.

"All right, tell Mitch to give this guy my number."

She grinned huge.

I sucked back more wine.

"I'm so glad we did this."

I stopped sucking back wine at the tone of her voice. It wasn't smiling. It was thick.

"Ty-Ty, sweetie," I said softly.

"You don't cry anymore," she told me and I blinked.

"What?"

"You used to cry at the drop of a hat. You don't cry anymore."

I swallowed before I shared, "I fight it. I... don't want to be that woman anymore."

"Nothing wrong with that woman, honey."

"Crying is weak," I declared.

"Crying is a release, and if you let yourself feel the feelings your mind is telling you to feel rather than fighting them, maybe you could let some of this stuff go."

This idea held merit so I gave her a small smile

"I've been so worried about my girl," she admitted, and I felt the guilt hit me again like a moving brick wall going at the speed of sound.

"I'm a terrible friend," I announced.

"You're a woman who went on the lam with her fiancé, watched him die and got shot in the process. That's big shit to deal with. I let it go on too long. *I'm* a terrible friend."

"You didn't know what to do," I defended her. "Tack told me you were torn and didn't want to set me off."

"Well, that's true," she agreed.

"So I should have noticed you were worried, come to you sooner and ended it," I stated and she smiled.

"I'm thinking we could talk about who was the worse friend until we're old and gray," she said.

"Maybe, but I suggest we don't since I don't think this bottle of wine will last that long," I returned.

She made a choking noise then burst out laughing.

I grabbed her hand, held tight and smiled.

When she stopped laughing, we sipped more wine, then I squeezed her hand until she looked at me.

"I'm going to be okay," I shared, and strangely, the words came out resolved.

I meant it.

I would.

And I knew that because, throughout the conversation, my monster hadn't made an appearance.

Not once.

I didn't fool myself it was over. It was just that the first step was easy so maybe the next ones wouldn't be so hard.

It was bittersweet to admit that Hop had been right. We talked and Ty-Ty felt better.

So did I.

"I know," she replied.

She believed in me.

Yes, maybe the next steps wouldn't be so hard.

"Mostly, I'll be okay because I've got you," I whispered.

She pressed her lips together.

I lunged toward her and hugged her.

Ty-Ty, my best girl, hugged me back.

*　　*　　*

Tyra had been gone for five minutes when I heard the Harley pipes pulling up my back alley.

I was standing at the sink, rinsing out the wineglasses and I went still. My eyes slowly moved to the back doors when those pipes stopped in my back drive.

Oh God.

Had it been Hop who came earlier? Did he see Tyra's car in my drive and ride away?

The answer to these questions came clear when I saw him walk through the gate and into my courtyard.

Oh God!

Damn.

I watched him, eyes on me, walk through my courtyard.

Right. This was okay. I'd locked the door. I always locked the doors. I would ignore him, finish rinsing the wineglasses, turn out the lights, go upstairs, and fall apart up there where he couldn't see.

I turned off the water, set the glass aside and did all of this with my eyes on Hop, who came right to the glass door but didn't knock. He didn't call. He crouched, pulling something out of the back pocket of his jeans. Then he worked at the lock.

My mouth dropped open.

I heard the lock click.

My breath caught in my throat.

Wow.

He picked my lock.

He straightened and walked in, sliding the door closed behind him.

I stood staring at him, statue-still.

He took three steps in, stopped and asked, "You talk to Tyra?"

"Yes," I answered.

"No, babe, did you *talk* to Tyra?"

"Yes," I whispered.

"Good," he whispered back and, God, that whisper, full of pride and relief.

It killed.

I straightened my shoulders. "Hop—"

"Now *we* gotta talk," he declared.

I shook my head. "That isn't happening."

"Lanie, I gave you some time. Now we gotta sort this shit out."

Oh. He didn't show last night because he was giving me time.

That was nice.

And supremely unfortunate because it was too late.

"There's nothing to sort. It's over," I announced.

"Babe," he leaned toward me, "it isn't."

"Hopper," I leaned toward him, "it *is*."

He leaned back and studied me.

Then he said, "What we got, you know, it's worth gettin' past this."

"I know what we have and it isn't worth that work," I retorted, and his body twitched.

"Come again?"

I threw out a hand. "I know how this goes, Hopper. I've been here before. I fall for a guy and he makes stuff about me he doesn't like clear, and I knock myself out to stop doing that stuff, and I'm not *me* anymore."

"You fell for me?"

I clamped my mouth shut.

Hop's face got soft and he took another step toward me. "We'll let that go for now and start with the other. What is it you think I don't like about you?"

"The drama," I answered.

He grinned. "Babe, I like the drama."

"You throw it in my face all the time when we're fighting."

"And lady, I fuckin' love it when we fight because I love how we make up and don't bullshit me, you love it too."

He wasn't wrong about that.

"Anyway, I never said I didn't like it," he went on.

"You're always bringing it up."

"That doesn't mean I don't like it."

"Well, I'll give you some insight. Insight, I'll note, that you already know with your speech about stuff soaking into women, burning a wound that will never heal. If you mention something, it's going to be on my mind, and since I..." I tried to find the right word that didn't expose too much, "cared about you, I'd work myself into a tizzy trying to tone it down. Willing to do anything to make sure I don't drive you away, drive you to do what my dad does to my mom."

"I'm not your dad," he returned instantly.

"That doesn't matter, either, Hopper. It's just who I am, how I work, what I do," I shared.

"What your dad does to your mom is not on your mom. It's on your dad. He's a dick, he does that to his family, and a bigger dick, he does it for decades," Hop continued like I didn't speak.

"That's true. But that's not the point."

"Yeah, it fuckin' is. You think you gotta tone down you so you won't drive your man to another woman's pussy. That shit's whacked, Lanie."

"Well, it's how I've been conditioned to think."

"Then stop thinking it."

"It's not that easy."

"Then let me help you work that shit out."

"God!" I cried, throwing up both my hands. I'd tried, I'd really tried to tamp down the drama but he wouldn't shut up! "Hopper, we don't work!"

"Lanie, that's total fuckin' bullshit and you know it."

"How, if you look back from start to finish, is *any* of the mess that was us a good thing? Fighting. Drama. Me pushing you away, you pushing back. You cutting me out then thinking you can just say you fucked up and all would be okay. It's lunacy."

"That's a goddamned relationship, Lanie."

"Well it *hurts*," I hissed. "And I didn't spend seven *fucking* years guarding myself from that pain only to have it shoved down my throat!" I ended on a shout.

"Jesus, lady, are you seriously gonna stand there and tell me you don't remember all the good we had, and there was a lot of good in there, Lanie, good so good it was the best and it totally fuckin' outweighed the bad in time and importance, and you're gonna throw us away just because you're shit scared?"

"Yes, I'm seriously going to stand here and tell you just that, Hop," I shot back.

"So you're okay, in taking that away from you, taking it away from me."

My breath pressed out of my lungs on a wheeze and I stared.

Hop continued.

"On the road groupie pussy. Biker pussy. Fuckin' Mitzi. I've had a lot, and some of the women in there, they were good. Fine women. Sweet women. Excellent lays. But never, not in forty fuckin' years of life, have I had a woman who I felt about like I feel about you. You tell me you care about me and yet, we *both* fuck up and hurt *each other*, you won't make the effort it takes to forgive and get back on track? In doing that, taking away the only shot I've ever had in forty fuckin' years of being genuinely happy?"

I didn't say anything because I hadn't thought of it like that and thinking of it like that made the pain I'd been feeling for nearly two weeks unbearable.

So unbearable, it was a wonder I stayed standing.

Unfortunately, I battled the pain too long. It gave Hopper the time to jump to a conclusion.

And Hop, being Hop, did just that.

"I did not fuck around on you. I did not use you to shield me from bullets. I did not lead you to heartbreak. I did none of that shit, Lanie, and you're makin' me pay for all *your*," he jabbed a finger at me, "mistakes. You wanna stand with an island between us, not touch me in weeks, not talk to me for days and be done, baby? You got it. We're done."

My body listed to the side, preparing to go after him, my mouth opening to call his name, but he stopped in the opened sliding glass door, turned to me and landed his last blow.

"You know, this reminds me of Mom and my old man. All this bullshit fighting about fuckin' nothin', two people just so shit scared of the love they feel for each other, they'd rather drive each other away than take a risk on feeling the fullness of that feeling." And if that wasn't enough, then came the coup de grâce. "So I guess that means I *didn't* fuckin' learn after Mitzi."

Did Hop just kind of say he loved me?

"You love me?" I breathed.

"You'll never know," he replied, turned, slid the door closed, and walked away.

CHAPTER SIXTEEN

The Best

Two weeks and three days later...

I WAS AT the Chaos hog roast, freaking out.

Hop had not yet showed, and the longer I was there, the longer I courted running into him.

I had not called, texted, or hung out at Chaos for a second chance at a second chance with Hop. Hop's finale was final. The pain was immense. I couldn't do it, not again.

I had to let it go. Try to find a way to survive. Not court more pain I wasn't strong enough to endure.

I had to move on.

I hated it.

I missed him so badly, it was an ache. I fell asleep with it. I woke up in the middle of the night feeling it. I pushed through the day suffering it.

But I had to hope it would dull. Someday.

And maybe it would. In about fifty years.

I had not told Tyra about what happened between Hop and me. Not yet.

I was not procrastinating.

We were gearing up at work for a couple of campaigns

going live so work was insanely busy. And I'd found a short-term counselor I liked so I started seeing her.

This was, surprisingly, working, and it had from the very first visit. That was to say, before talking to Tyra and going to the counselor, I didn't have that dream about Kansas City every night, but it came frequently. I hadn't had it now since talking to Tyra.

So that was one bit of good.

I still wasn't sleeping well, but the reason wasn't Elliott and Kansas City.

The reason was that Hop wasn't lying beside me, and I ached for him to be close to me.

But, as Hop said, we were done.

Also taking my headspace, Tyra had told Mitch's wife, Mara, to get Mitch to give that guy my number, and he'd called, four times.

His name was Jed. He had an unbelievably attractive voice and, back in the day when I was the old Lanie, I would have jumped on meeting him for coffee and, if his face or personality equaled the beauty of his voice, I would have hoped he'd jumped on me (and not end up being a jerk).

Alas, I was in love with another man and I felt terrible since I was going through the motions with Jed. I had absolutely no intention of taking it any further, but I had to do it for Tyra.

I had a feeling Jed knew I wasn't into it about two minutes into the first conversation, when getting-to-know-you discussions that might lead to coffee, a date, and maybe sex turned into getting-to-know-you discussions that would lead to just getting to know you.

In other words, he didn't only have a beautiful voice, he seemed like a nice guy who was giving me what I needed to keep my friend happy without putting on any pressure or blowing me off when he could totally do that. He just didn't. I didn't know why. I just knew it made him a nice guy.

If that wasn't enough, I spent a goodly amount of time licking the wounds I'd opened myself by having and then losing Hop.

So there wasn't time to sit down with Tyra and tell her about Hop.

Therefore, when Ty-Ty called to tell me there was a hog roast, asked me to come and I demurred, since I hadn't yet told her, I knew just how deeply I'd worried her and I knew she wanted me to live my life, so when she pressed me to go, I had no excuse not to.

So here I was.

Though I did tell her I couldn't stay long.

My out. I went but I intended to leave as soon as it was seemly.

It wasn't time yet for Hop and me to have moved past what Hop and I were and lapse into distant acquaintances that had to share each other's space on occasion.

With the number of times I'd turned to wine and Bob Seger the last couple of weeks, torturing myself and barely containing the pain, I knew that would take about seventy-five years.

The good thing about the hog roast was that I got to see Tabby and Shy together for the first time and meet Shy's good-looking, very nice brother Landon. Tab and Shy were cute together, and someone would have to be blind not to see they were over-the-moon in love and happy.

I was thrilled for her. She was so young, and still her road to love had been bumpier than most that had decades on her. But she was Tabby. She had been a good kid who grew into a lovely woman, funny and sweet. She deserved that.

And seeing her happy with Shy, it made it worth coming

to the hog roast and possibly seeing Hop, having those fes-
tering wounds I was trying and failing to anesthetize with
work, wine, and the stylings of the Silver Bullet Band open
further, spreading the pain, lacerating my heart.

So the time had come. I'd had a couple of beers, a pulled
pork sandwich, gabbed with Tyra, Tack, Sheila, Brick, Big
Petey, saw and was seen.

And Hop hadn't showed.

So now it was time to go.

I was moving through the forecourt of Ride, avoiding
people and skirting big drums filled with fire when I felt a
vice-like grip clamp around my arm.

I gave a small cry of surprise and my head whipped
around just as my body started moving without me moving it.

Hop had hold of me and, if his profile was any indication,
he was *ticked*.

This wasn't good.

"Hopper, let go," I hissed, struggling and losing as he
yanked me around the outskirts of the party toward the
garage.

"Shut it," he growled.

"Let me go!" I snapped.

He let me go after forcing me into the corner in the area
behind the concrete steps that led up to Tyra's office and
then pinning me there with his body.

With no escape route available, I glared at him. "Are you
crazy?"

"You're talkin' to that guy," he snarled.

Oh dear.

I should have known this would happen. It was nearly
impossible to keep anything under wraps in families.

And Chaos was family.

Damn.

"Hop—"

"Scrape me off, in just *weeks* you replace me?" he bit out, and I felt my eyes get wide.

"No!" I clipped. "I didn't *scrape you off* for one, and for two, it's a few phone calls, nothing more. I haven't even met him! And it won't *be* anything more. I'm just doing it to make Ty-Ty happy."

He moved forward, which was a miracle since I was already pressed into the cinderblocks that made up the garage and he didn't have much room to move.

"Stand back," I demanded.

"No fuckin' way," he replied.

With him that close, that spicy scent of him in my nostrils, his badass gorgeousness all I could see, I lost it.

"God, Hop! Move away! It's not a big deal and anyway, even if it was, it wouldn't be any of your business."

He lost it, too. I knew it when he pressed even closer, changed the subject and growled, "Can't sleep. Not hungry. Can't concentrate. If I don't pay attention, my mind wanders to you." His face dipped close as I started hyperventilating at his words. "I tried to give you what you needed, to stay away, let you live your fucked-up life, but I can't. Taste you in my mouth, lady. See you in my dreams."

Oh God.

He was killing me.

I couldn't bear this, therefore I whispered, "Stop it."

"No," he replied.

"We cause each other pain," I reminded him.

"I get it," he returned. "I get that you bury the good we got that's way fuckin' bigger than the bad to protect yourself from losin' it, seein' as you've lost everything you had that matters, startin' with your mom and dad."

Why did he have to be so *smart?*

"You aren't gonna lose me," he promised.

"You can't promise that," I snapped.

"Yeah, I fuckin' can," he shot back.

"Life happens, Hop," I told him.

"It doesn't if you don't live it," he retorted.

See? Smart!

Gah!

"Well, this isn't going to happen," I declared.

"Fuck yeah, it is. I'm done with this shit. Weeks, nothin' on my mind but you. Weeks, goin' to bed alone when you're a fuckin' twenty-minute drive away. Heard you were talkin' to that fuckin' guy and lost it. I ate shit, did shit I hated, scored marks on my goddamned soul to fight for the life I wanted. Bein' that man, do you think I'm gonna let the first woman in my life who makes me happy slip through my fingers?"

Uh-oh.

That was beautiful. No matter how crazy scared I was, I couldn't deny the beauty of what he said.

"I'm not," he stated.

"Hopper—"

I got no more out because Hop pulled me in his arms and kissed me. It was hungry, even desperate.

And gorgeous.

Still, I fought him, pushing at his shoulders.

This lasted about five seconds before the taste of him, the feel of him, his scent penetrated, and it hit me I was getting my fix. It hit me I'd gone cold turkey, and that ache I carried with me was me jonesing for nearly a month. It hit me all I needed to reach that unbelievable high that beat out everything in sheer beauty was holding me in his arms.

I slid my hands from his shoulders, wrapped my arms around him, and I kissed him back.

When I did, Hop growled down my throat, the sound

shooting through me, bursting in pure goodness between my legs. He bent into me, twisting me, and deepened the kiss.

Ecstasy.

I was gone, coasting on bliss when he tore his mouth from mine, stepped back, let me go but curled his fingers in a tight grip around mine and started walking, dragging me with him.

In my high-heeled boots, I hustled after him.

He kept us to the shadows rimming the revelry. We hit the Compound and he continued to waste no time pulling me through to the back hall and into his room.

He closed and locked the door as I threw my purse on the floor and yanked off my pashmina. Then he turned to me. Herding me backward to the bed as his hands went to my sweater, he pulled it up and it was gone.

His lips hit mine and a second later, my back hit bed.

We kissed deep and wet as I tugged at his cut to yank it down his arms. Hop broke the kiss to arch back, yank it off, then tug off his black thermal.

Yes.

My hands went to the skin of his chest, my fingers curling in, nails scraping down, one scoring through the denser hair along the line between his abs.

He growled, took my mouth in another kiss as he jerked down the cup of my bra, and his thumb and forefinger homed in.

I moaned into his mouth.

Hop pressed his hard hips into my soft ones.

I couldn't wait any longer.

I tore my lips away. "Now, Hop, honey. I need you now," I begged.

"You got it, lady," he replied, his voice thick, his hand moving from my breast to my belt buckle.

I tugged and pulled at his. He did the same with mine. My hands were shaking with need so he got his task completed faster, and I lost purchase on his jeans when he pulled mine down my legs.

"Fuck. Your boots," he grunted. "How do I get these fuckers off?"

"Zip at the side," I wheezed, pulling down my panties.

Off went my boots then Hop curled his fingers in my panties and they were gone.

"Lay back. Open," he ordered.

I did as asked.

Hop covered me then Hop entered me.

Even as my back arched, I rounded him with all my limbs. Oh yes. *God,* yes.

This was what I needed. I couldn't live without this. I couldn't beat this habit.

I didn't even want to.

"Beauty, fuck, missed how beautiful you feel," Hop murmured, pounding hard and deep.

"Yes, but the beauty is you," I gasped, lifting my head, shoving my face in his neck.

"Head back, baby. You know I like havin' your eyes."

I did know that.

I dropped my head back.

Hop thrust fast and hard, lifting a hand to frame my face, his thumb swept out to press against my lips, dragging at the lower one, claiming what he already owned.

I roamed his skin with my hands, scoring my nails into it, tightening my legs around his hips, claiming, in my way, what was mine.

All mine.

Suddenly, what he was giving me between my legs started overwhelming me.

"Hop," I breathed.

"Yeah, baby, I feel it," he grunted.

"Hop!" I cried.

"Fuck, so beautiful," he groaned, and it hit me, I climaxed, my head going back, my body arching into him, my arms and legs convulsing around him as I heard him growl, "Yeah, so fuckin' beautiful."

Then I had his mouth on mine and the grunts of his orgasm driving down my throat.

He was right.

So fucking beautiful.

I knew his climax left him when his tongue swept my mouth then his lips moved away, down to my jaw to stop at my neck and work there.

I turned my head and whispered in his ear, "You're right. I'm shit scared of taking the risk of feeling the fullness of how much I love you."

His mouth stopped working, his body went still, except his hips pressed into mine.

Then his head came up and I felt his eyes on me in the dark but he didn't say a word.

So I did.

"I've never loved anyone the way I love you."

"Fuck me," he murmured, his voice gruff, and not from just having come.

"My mom loves my dad like that. She took that risk. And she's lived a lifetime of paying for that decision."

"Baby."

"I'm scared, Hop. I have been since I was eleven and I understood. And everything that happened with men all my life ending in what happened in Kansas City proved me right."

"Fuck, baby," he groaned, dropping his head so his forehead rested on mine.

"I pushed you away. I jerked you around. I built walls and held onto stupid excuses to keep us apart all because I was scared," I admitted, and he slanted his head, his lips brushed mine then gently, he pulled out of me.

He rolled, taking me with him as he scooted us up the bed and settled on his back with me in his arms.

I pressed closer. Winding an arm around his middle, I rested my cheek on his pec.

"I didn't want just one night," I shared.

"I know," he said softly.

"I'd been watching you for years."

"I know, baby."

"I was ready to take the risk again. I just wasn't ready to admit it until just now, outside, when you said the things you said, which were exactly what I was going through then you kissed me, and I knew I couldn't live without you. But all that happened before, I put you through hell."

"Lanie—"

I closed my eyes tight then opened them. "I'm sorry I put you through that."

"I'm not, lady, because I loved every fuckin' second."

I blinked in the dark then lifted my head to look at him. "What?"

"Not havin' you these past weeks sucked, but it led to me comin' that hard, that fast and givin' that same thing to you, it was worth it. And here you are in my bed, tellin' me you love me and I'm gonna keep you here, so fuck yeah. It was worth it."

He caught my chin with his finger and thumb to hold my face toward his as he went on.

"But before that, I loved every fuckin' second, Lanie. Even when we were fightin'. And babe, you're too hard on yourself. I threw my punches too and I know I can be a dick when I do. So don't do what you do, take all this shit on your shoulders."

"You were always up-front. I didn't know it but I was playing games."

"Your head was messed up, Lanie. That wasn't games. That was your way of straightening shit out."

I liked that he thought that and I hoped he was right.

Still.

"We fight dirty, honey," I noted.

"No, we fight honest. Trust me, I know when fighting comes from someplace ugly, someplace cold, someplace jacked. I got that shit from Mitzi. I also know when it comes from someplace else, feelings that are good, fights that are worth it to get past shit and learn about each other and I know that because that's what we got."

"Do you think so?" I asked.

"I know so," Hop answered, and his words were firm.

I pulled my chin from his grip and pressed my face in his neck.

"It hurts," I told him.

"It hurts because you give a shit."

This made sense but still.

"You said I made you genuinely happy," I reminded him.

"Yeah, I said that," he confirmed.

I lifted my head to look at him again. "How? I jacked you around. I lied about what I wanted from the very beginning. Even though I didn't do it consciously, I still did it. I screwed things up and then did it again and again and—"

"Baby," he interrupted me, his body suddenly shaking with laughter, "didn't you hear me when I said I like a challenge?"

"There's a challenge, Hop, and then there's a pain in the ass."

Still laughing, he rolled us again so I was on my back and he was pressed into me.

"You're beautiful, fuck me, seriously, so goddamned beautiful sometimes, swear to God, I think I can't look at you any longer because if I do, your beauty will burn out my eyes."

Oh my God!

That was *so* sweet.

"You're funny. You're crazy," he carried on. "You're just you and to hell with what people think. You're total class. You could be a snob because you come from money and you got your kind of beauty, but because you're you, you fit anywhere. You treat my kids good. You're a fantastic fuckin' cook. You let go in bed and come hard, givin' me even more beauty. I lie in bed with you, tellin' you stories about bitches I used to date and you giggle your ass off, you don't get in my face about reminding you I used to date those bitches. I lie in bed, tellin' you stories about my life and you look at me with those beautiful eyes of yours and listen like I'm tellin' you God's secret plan for harmony. And I sing you a song and you stand on a goddamned chair and shout I'm the shit then jump me when we get home. None of that, none of it, lady, is a pain in the ass. All of it, every bit, is worth fighting for."

Oh.

My.

God!

That was *so* sweet!

"Hopper," I whispered.

"Babe, hear this. I figured something out about Mitzi. She didn't want that guy because he had her heart. She wanted that guy because her dad made shit but they lived in a part of town where she went to school with kids that had serious money. Don't know but I guess, for her, bein' poor around the rich fucked with her head. And that guy's dad made money.

The kind of money that meant he had it easy in life, doors opened for him. So by the time I met him, he had a wife who couldn't give him kids but he still had a six-bedroom house in Cherry Creek. He drove a BMW. She drove a Merc. He wore fuckin' loafers shined so bright I fought against puttin' on shades to battle the glare. And she was so tricked out, it didn't take a psychologist to figure out she was usin' money to buy her happiness. Mitzi wanted that. She wanted the Merc and designer gear. She didn't want him."

I didn't know where he was leading with this so I just said, "Okay."

Hop got I didn't understand so he explained.

"What I'm sayin' is, fucks with a man's pride, his woman steps out on him. But when Mitzi sorted her shit and figured out she'd wasted most of her life on a dream she wouldn't live because she wasn't woman enough to keep a decent man, she came crawlin' back to me. She didn't step out on me. She didn't give a shit about me. I was just there to keep her from bein' lonely and to get her off. She was steppin' out on our life. She understood, too late, that flashy cars and big houses were not where it was at. A man in your bed who's gonna be true to you and whose highest priority in life is lookin' after you and the kids you make together is."

Well, that was the God's honest truth.

And I loved, loved, *loved* it that Hop thought that way.

"Life is fucked up," Hop continued. "First it leads me to a bitch who wants the high life and fucks me over while she's tryin' to get it. And then it leads me to a good woman who had the high life and knew better what was important." He lifted a hand to cup my jaw before he finished, "Thank fuck it came in that order, babe, or I'd be fucked."

"Funny," I said quietly, "I was thanking fuck because you came into my life at all."

After I spoke my words, the room went still and it stayed that way for so long, it began to freak me out.

"Hop?" I called.

"Do you have any fuckin' clue how much I love you?"

After his growled words I stopped breathing. Therefore it took effort to wheeze out, "I do now."

I felt his lips hit mine, where he said, "Every step, every breath, every second I lived on this earth, I'm thankful for, no matter how fucked up or whacked or hard or good, 'cause all that shit led me to you."

Oh dear.

I was going to cry.

Damn!

I was crying.

In fact, I burst into tears on a muffled sob, twisting my head and shoving my face in Hop's neck.

His arms closed around me, he rolled us to our sides and he held me close, one hand stroking my spine as the goodness I felt from his words flowed from my eyes and into his skin.

"I'm giving you a key to my house," I announced stupidly, my words breaking, my breath hitching.

"Good," he muttered, his words breaking because he was stifling laughter.

"We need to speed up the easing Cody and Molly into things gig because I don't want to sleep without you, even if it might be inappropriate Dad's girlfriend spends the night," I declared.

"I'll work on that with them right away," Hop replied, still sounding amused.

"If it takes time, when they're asleep, I'll crawl through the window."

Even more humor in his tone when he stated, "Babe,

seein' as my room is on the top floor, I'd like to see how you pull that off, but I'll save you that hassle and let you in the front door."

I belatedly fell silent and stopped acting like an idiot but kept crying.

Hop asked, "Easing the Cody and Molly into things... *gig?*"

I pulled my head back and looked at him. "What?"

"You don't say words like 'gig', lady."

"My man's a biker. Shit rubs off."

The minute I finished speaking, Hop's arms spasmed around me as he burst out laughing.

I watched and listened through the dark, loving every second.

Still laughing, he bent his head and took my lips, laughing into my mouth as he kissed me.

Amazing.

Then he made love to me, a lot slower this time.

Even better.

And last, I fell asleep, naked in his arms.

No dreams.

Just Hop.

CHAPTER SEVENTEEN

Glad to have you back, darlin'

THE POUNDING AT the door woke us. Hop's arm convulsed around me and I lifted my head from where it lay on his chest to stare at the door.

"Open this goddamned door, brother!"

Oh God.

That was Tack.

And he sounded really, *really* angry.

"Fuck," Hop muttered.

"Fuckin' now!" Tack shouted.

"Fuck," Hop repeated.

"Oh dear," I mumbled.

"Not a good time!" Hop yelled.

"Open it or I kick it in!" Tack shouted, and I felt my eyes get wide. I'd never heard Tack angry like that.

"Oh dear," I whispered.

"Fuck," Hop grumbled, rolled into me, kissed me quickly then he rolled out of bed.

Tack pounded at the door.

Hop tossed his thermal to me and I tugged it on as he pulled up a pair of jeans and moved to the door.

"Jesus, brother, cool it! Fuck! I'm comin'!" Hop yelled,

made it to the door, unlocked it and opened it. I had the thermal down to my waist, the covers up it and I watched as Hop took a quick step back because Tack pushed in.

Tack scowled at me in bed for a nanosecond before his head swung Hop's way.

"Seriously?" he asked. "I just get done dealin' with that shit with Tabby and you, *another brother,* are nailin' *my other girl* in ... fuckin' ... *secret?*"

How sweet. I loved it that I was his other girl.

"Tack, breathe, brother, and give me a second to explain," Hop stated calmly.

Tack pointed my way. "Her head's messed up. You go in there when her head's messed up?"

"My head isn't messed up," I butted in, and Tack turned his scowl back to me.

"Darlin', you're in my heart, you know that, so no offense, but you're right, it isn't messed up. It's *fucked up.*"

Oh wow. I was in his heart.

"Tack, listen to me," Hop called Tack's attention to him and Tack sliced his gaze to Hop. "There's a reason we kept it under wraps, a good one I'm not gonna explain, because it's Lanie's and she gets to explain it if she wants. What you gotta know right now is this is real," he stated just as my phone rang from inside my purse.

"It better fuckin' be real, brother. I know you. I know you wouldn't pull shit on me, Red, Lanie, but what I *don't* know is why it's a goddamned secret," Tack returned.

I'd scooted up to my knees to reach the side of the bed where my purse was, grabbed it, and pulled my phone out while Hop replied, "Lanie had some things to work through and I thought we should focus on that without outside distractions."

It was my request we keep it a secret, but Hop was setting it up so if there was a fall, he would be taking it for me.

I was feeling all warm inside, thinking that was nice, still feeling the glow of Tack calling me his girl (regardless of this tense situation; however, I knew Hop would sort it out) as I put my phone to my ear.

I wouldn't have answered right then, but the display said it was Lis. She knew everything that was going on, including my break up with Hop. She had been trying to understand why we broke up since she told me she liked him and thought he was good for me. She was also worried about me, so I didn't want to miss a phone call from her to make her more worried about me. I'd done enough of that to people who cared about me.

"Hey, sweetie. Now's not a good time," I said in greeting. "I'll call you back in an hour or so and we'll talk."

"You think maybe her best fuckin' friend and *your* fuckin' friend, brother, might have been able to take your back on that?" Tack asked a very good question.

I didn't hear Hop's answer because Lis spoke in my ear.

"Lanie, honey...*God*. I don't know how to say this so I'm just going to say it. The bubble burst last night at Mom and Dad's. Dad is in the hospital. Mom's in jail."

I blinked at the covers.

"What?" I whispered.

"Apparently, this is a guess," she began, "but I figure Dad stewed on what you said then finally pulled his finger out and made his decision. From what I could get from Mom's hysterical phone call, Dad informed her he couldn't keep hurting her and his other chick, so he made a decision and he picked the other chick. Mom finally grew a backbone, lost her nut, grabbed a bottle of wine, and conked him on the head with it. He started bleeding. She started yelling. They started scrapping. The neighbors freaked, the cops were called, then the ambulance. Now Dad is under observation for a concussion and Mom needs a cosigner for a bond since Dad's seriously pissed and he's pressing charges."

"Oh my God," I said.

"Lady, what is it?" Hop asked.

"I know," my sister agreed.

"Oh my God," I repeated.

"No shit," my sister replied.

"Lanie, baby, *what is it?*" Hop asked.

"Oh my God!" I cried.

"Jesus, Lanie," Hop clipped, and I felt his hand under my chin lifting my eyes to his where he was standing by the bed, looking worried. "What the fuck is it?"

"Oh my God," Lis said in my ear. "Please tell me that's Hop."

I ignored her and the fact that Tack was standing there, and told Hop, "My dad told my mom he picked the other woman. She lost it. Conked him on the head with a wine bottle. He's in the hospital and pressing charges. She's in jail and looking for a cosigner for her bond."

Hop's hand fell away as he straightened, all the while doing a slow blink.

Then he asked, "Say again?"

"My dad told my mom he picked the other woman. She attacked him with a wine bottle. She needs a cosigner on a bond."

Hop stared at me. Then his whole torso shot back as he burst out laughing.

"Hop!" I shouted. "This isn't funny!"

He tipped his eyes to me, still laughing. "Oh, fuck yeah it is, baby."

"You know, he's right," Lis said in my ear.

"Please, babe, tell me, since he's in the hospital, she did some damage," Hop begged.

"Hop!" I snapped.

"I totally like him," Lis declared. "I already liked him considering he never missed the opportunity to give my little sister an orgasm, but now I *really* like him."

"Lis!" I hissed into the phone, rethinking how much I should share with my sister.

"Just sayin'," she mumbled. "Dad's a dick."

"He might have a concussion!" I cried.

"Yeah, shit happens when you're a dick," Lis replied, then went back to mumbling. "Long time coming."

"Oh my God!" I shouted, and suddenly I didn't have a phone in my hand because Hopper had it in his and was talking into it.

"Gotta have a meet with the brothers, babe, but you want, and you don't have the collateral, thinkin' my boys won't have a problem with Chaos covering her bond. We're not real big on motherfuckers steppin' out on their families then pressin' charges when they get their due, their woman clocks them with a wine bottle."

I looked to Tack, who was standing, arms crossed on his chest, lips twitching, sapphire-blue eyes dancing, earlier pique vaporized, and announced, "Those are the first words my man has ever spoken to my sister." Then I asked, "How's *that* for an introduction?"

"FYI, darlin', need to vote but Hop ain't wrong. Sounds like Chaos will cover her bond," Tack shared, and my mouth fell open.

Then I closed it to request, "Can *you* at least *try* to be a normal person in a crazy situation?"

"No." Tack denied my request.

Argh!

"You need to leave," I ordered. "I need to go ape-shit on my old man and I'm not wearing any underwear."

Tack burst out laughing.

Ugh!

Bikers!

"Right, we'll call you back," Hop said to my sister. "Yeah, nice to meet you, too."

Seriously?

I flopped back on the bed.

"We need to call a meet, brother. Lanie's mom's a banker's wife. According to the sister, she's flippin' out and Lis's old man isn't hip on puttin' up collateral for what he calls 'that nutcase' so he refuses to do it. We gotta get her ass outta jail," Hop shared.

"I'll make the calls," Tack agreed.

"Obliged," Hop replied.

"Lanie," Tack called.

"What?" I snapped to the ceiling.

"Look at me, babe."

I got up on my elbows and glared at Tack.

"You're right. Your head isn't messed up," Tack stated, then his face got soft when he finished, "Glad to have you back, darlin'."

Damn.

I was going to cry.

"Stop being nice when I'm ticked," I demanded, but my words were shaky.

Tack just grinned.

I deep breathed.

Hop moved to him, they did a fingers-wrapped-around-wrists biker, badass handshake and I heard Tack mutter, "She's good. You did good, brother."

To which Hop muttered back, "In more ways than one."

They smiled at each other while I fought off tears.

Tack left.

I decided to focus on being angry in order not to let loose the tears, so I glared at Hop as he moved to the end of the bed.

"I'm ticked at you," I declared.

He hit the bed with his hands then his knees and crawled up it toward me, and he looked so hot doing that, suddenly I wasn't ticked anymore.

He also ignored my declaration and asked, "You wanna go to Connecticut?"

"Heck no," I answered as he made it up my body and lowered his weight on me.

"Babe, your mom's in jail, your dad's in the hospital."

"Their tangled web," I replied. "I have campaigns going live. I've got meetings with my counselor I'd rather not put off because they're working. I've got a cop I need to explain some things to. And I've got to have a key cut so my man can come to my place whenever he wants. I don't have time to fly to Connecticut to sort out the lives of two adults who should have sorted themselves out three decades ago."

"Fair enough, but you missed somethin' in listing all your obligations," Hop said.

"And what's that?" I asked.

"Wrappin' that mouth of yours around your man's cock."

I did a top-to-toe shiver.

Hop felt it and grinned.

Then he dropped his lips to mine and kissed me. It lasted a while and I was holding on, fairly hot and very bothered, when he lifted his head.

"You're seein' a counselor and it's workin'?" he asked quietly.

"Yeah," I answered.

"Proud of you, lady."

I smiled.

Hop's eyes dropped to my mouth and he kissed me again.

About five minutes later, I got down to seeing to one of my obligations.

I worked hard at it, enjoying every second and, pleased to report, my endeavors were a success.

* * *

"You're such a pain!"

This was shouted by Cutter one second after Rider shoved him in the shoulder. Half a second after he shouted, Cut took a step back then lunged forward and tackled Ride, whereupon they both hit my rug and started wrestling.

Tack, who was enjoying a beer in my living room with Hop, and Tyra, who was in the kitchen preparing dinner with me, totally ignored them.

This was often their tactic.

"As long as they aren't close to somethin' that can hurt them or somethin' breakable, we let 'em duke it out," Tack had told me.

I wasn't certain this was an optimal parental choice, but I'd never seen bikers raised from womb to badass. It was probably good they knew their way around a slug fest from a young age.

Needless to say, Tack had told Tyra about Hop and me, and Tyra had wasted no time phoning me. We had a conversation that was uncomfortable for both of us, since she'd shared the BeeBee information and I hadn't shared anything at all. I'd had to explain, without giving away too much of Hop's business he didn't want spread around, that she'd been mistaken. He didn't cheat, he'd been on a break. Then I'd used Hop's words to tell her what he and I had was "real," figuring she'd lived in the biker world longer than me, she would understand.

She did but she was my best friend. I knew she'd want physical evidence.

So of course she told me she, Tack, and the boys were coming for dinner. "So I can see for myself that this is all good."

Considering the fact that they'd walked up to my back door while Hop was laying a hot and heavy one on me in the kitchen—so hot and heavy we hadn't heard their SUV parking in my back drive—Tyra got an eyeful of how good it was.

So did Tack, Ride, and Cut, with Rider not thinking much of what he'd seen, something that he shared upon entering by yelling at me, "That's gross! Mister Hop had his tongue in your mouth!" After which he instantly turned to his father and kept yelling, "You do that to Mom, too, and it's *sick!*"

Hop chuckled.

Ty-Ty gazed at her son with a smile twitching at her mouth.

Tack didn't miss a beat and muttered, "I'll remind you of those words when we have our first pregnancy scare."

To this Hop chuckled more. I joined in but Tyra cut narrowed eyes to her man while Rider looked confused and Cut shouted, "La-La, I want blue Powerade! Now!"

I set the kids up with Powerade. The men got beers and firmly planted themselves in the living room, not in my family room, which was too close to the kitchen and thus might mean they'd be called on to do something like open jars or chop onions. Tyra and I got down to cooking.

"So, let me get this straight. The bondsman accepted an out-of-state cosigner. Your mom was released. She went home and tossed all your dad's shit out on the lawn and called a locksmith. He got released from the hospital, came home and couldn't get into the house but found his crap in the yard and a note on the door telling him she was going to clean him out during the divorce proceedings. The police were called again when he kept pounding on the door and shouting. He was told to find elsewhere to stay. Your mom asked your sister to find her an A.A. meeting. And you're in love with Hopper Kincaid," Tyra stated, and I smiled at her.

"That about sums it up," I confirmed.

"Holy crap," she replied.

"I know," I agreed then went on. "Wish I was there when she was tossing all Dad's stuff on the lawn. Lis was. My sister is all over this. She's liking a jailbird mom with a backbone, so she's decided she's talking to Mom again and dragging her husband, Bart, along with her. So they were there when Mom was doing an extreme clean of the house. Bart thought it was a scream and took all Dad's pictures of him with senators and congressmen off the wall of his study and flung them out the window. Lis said she wanted to throw stuff too but she was laughing too hard, and by the time she got herself together, they'd already taken care of business."

"That's crazy, Lanie," Tyra told me.

"That's the Heron Family, Ty-Ty. If there's a statement to be made, you might as well do it with flair."

She started giggling and I did it right along with her.

She sobered and caught my eye. "You okay with all this?"

I looked back down to the mushrooms I was slicing. "Yeah." I pressed my lips together then turned to her and said softly, "Especially the A.A. part."

"You think she means it?" Tyra asked.

"I think she's never, not once, not even back in the day when Lis told them she didn't want to speak to either of them until Mom sorted herself out, admitted she had a problem. They say admitting it is a not only the first step but the most important one so, yeah. I think she means it."

"Happy for you," she told me.

"Me too," I replied and watched her eyes slide to the living room and back to me.

"How happy should I be for you?"

I understood what she was asking so I gave it to her.

"He's gentle. He's understanding. He's proved over and over he has my back. He's mellow, which is good to come home to when my mind is a mess and work is crazy. His kids are great, they like me, and I love watching him with them. He sang 'You'll Accomp'ny Me' to me at a biker bar. And he loves me."

Her eyes shot up at Hop singing to me and she breathed, "No joke? He sang to you?"

I shook my head. "No joke."

"Tack told me he used to be in a band. Is he good?"

I smiled. "He's a rock star."

"I mean, is he good when you aren't looking through love glasses," she teased, and I locked eyes with her.

"He should never have given it up. He's phenomenal," I stated firmly.

"Wow," she whispered.

"You don't know wow until you've seen Hopper onstage with a microphone and a guitar. Then you'll know wow."

Tyra grinned.

I went back to slicing mushrooms.

"'You'll Accomp'ny Me?'" she asked quietly.

I looked back at her. "It was the best moment of my life until he said last night, 'Do you have any fuckin' clue how much I love you?'"

Her eyes got big.

"Wow," she repeated.

"Yes. Now *that* was *wow*." I pulled in a deep breath and turned to her. "He's mine. I'm terrified. Love hasn't gone

real well for me. He gets that. He's patient. We fight. It hurts.
But somehow, after each fight, we come out stronger."

"If it's right, that's how it works," Tyra shared.

"I'm getting that now."

"I wish you would have told me," she said carefully and I
shook my head.

"I don't know how it happened, Ty-Ty. I don't know what
I saw that led me to him, but I'm glad I followed my gut and
my heart because it was Hop I needed to guide me through
letting the past go. It couldn't be you. I was blaming myself
for you getting hurt. It had to be someone else and there isn't
anyone in my life, even my sister, who could do it with the
tenderness and understanding Hop gave me."

Her eyes got bright but her lips smiled and she again said,
"Wow."

"Absolutely," I replied. "Wow."

My phone rang.

Rider shouted, "Mom! Cut poked me in the eye!"

I grabbed my phone as Tack called, "Boy, get your butt
over here. You know, the rare happens and your mother's in
the kitchen, you don't disturb her."

Tyra rolled her eyes at me and headed to the living room.

I put my phone to my ear. "Hey."

"You're banging a biker?"

It was Elvira.

"Elvira—" I began only to be cut off.

"Okay, I been around those hot boys and I got me a fine
piece of goodness in my bed, but that don't mean I don't
notice the goodness all around me when I'm on Chaos. So I
get you, goin' there with a brother. What I *don't* get is your
two sisters sat there, eatin' up tasty morsels about your man,
and you just stood there like a deer caught in headlights and
didn't say shit?"

"Elvira—" I tried but failed.

"Tyra called me, told me she got the wrong end of the stick and shared Hop was on a break with his ex-bitch when he was doin' the nasty with a biker groupie. Still, girl, what the fuck?"

"Well—"

"I *knew* he was a good guy. I can sniff 'em out. The assholes. He didn't smell like no asshole. So it threw me for a loop, thinkin' he was a cheater. Thought my radar had gone screwy. Good to know I still got it goin' on."

"I'm glad that—"

"But you standin' there, not sayin' a word? *Girl*, you crazy?"

"Actually, yes," I got out.

"Yeah, you are. Always knew that. Don't know why I'm askin'," she took a breath then changed subjects. "Chaos bonded out your mom?"

"Yeah. She's good."

"Sistah," she drew this word out, "you've had a helluva day," she declared and she was not wrong. I heard her shout, "What?" Then nothing, then, "Be right there, baby." She came back to me. "Date night. Movie, dinner, and a little somethin' somethin'. Pray for me that work doesn't call him in the middle of our entrée. That happens a lot and it never fails to shit me but what am I gonna do? My man serves and protects. It's my sacrifice for the population of Denver."

I grinned at my phone. "I'm praying."

"Good," she stated, then, "You happy?"

"Yeah, Elvira, I'm happy."

"Good," she whispered. "Finally."

She was right about that.

Then I heard her shout, "Keep your pants on!" And back to me, "Gotta go. I'm pourin' martinis in you sometime next week. I want it all but only the PG-rated parts. I do not want to know what that 'tache feels like on your skin."

Even if she did, I wouldn't share that.

That was all for me.

She continued, "It'll give me ideas, and it'll mean I can't come over for dinner with you and Hop the week after next 'cause I won't be able to look him in the eye if I know what that 'tache feels like on my skin. I'll text you with a night Malik and I can make it. I'm ordering your fried chicken and pecan pie so be prepared."

I guessed Hop and I were entertaining Elvira and Malik.

That worked for me. I just hope it worked for Hop.

"Right. I'll wait for your text."

"Lanie?" she called.

"Right here, sweetie."

"Keep hold of happy. You deserve it. It's found you. Don't let go," she ordered.

I really loved Elvira.

"I'll keep hold, honey."

"Good," she stated then, "Later, girl."

"Later."

She disconnected and I looked through the kitchen to the living room.

Tyra was bent at the waist, Cutter in front of her, and she was talking in his ear.

Tack was lounged back on my couch, motorcycle boots on my coffee table, arm thrown wide, bottle of beer in his hand, Rider on his knees beside his dad, leaning in but his hands were wrapped around a video game that he was resting on his dad's chest.

But Tack's eyes were aimed at his woman and he had that look in them.

The look of love.

My gaze drifted to Hop. He was seated almost exactly like Tack except his neck was twisted to look over the back of the couch, his eyes on me.

He had the same look in his eyes as Tack.

But it was all for me.

I felt my face get soft and I smiled.

I watched his face get soft and he smiled back.

Keep hold of happy... It's found you. Don't let go.

Finally, I understood.

I was wrong and Hopper was right.

You didn't avoid having something beautiful because you were terrified of losing it.

You fought to keep it.

And when you got it, you kept hold.

I was going to keep hold.

Always.

CHAPTER EIGHTEEN

At My Mercy

Five months later...

I WAS DONE, coming down from my climax and grinding into Hop. He had his hands on my hips, fingers digging into my flesh, grinding me down harder when he groaned into my chest.

I was astride him, he was sitting up, my fingers were in his hair, and as he came I wrapped my arms around his shoulders.

When he was done, he slid his hands up my back and glided his lips and mustache up my chest to my neck where his mouth worked.

I let the sweet feeling of Hop's mouth moving on my skin sink in and decided it was time. Friday night. The weekend. Hop was mellow. He'd just come. I'd just come. I'd known for a week. He had to know.

I had to do it now.

"Uh...honey?" I called.

"Right here, lady," he murmured into my neck.

"How are you, um...feeling?" I asked, seeking confirmation he was in a good place before I laid it out.

His head tipped back and I saw his lips tipped up.

"You seriously askin' that shit?"

It was, perhaps, a stupid question.

Then again, my news was huge and it could bring on a variety of responses and I wanted a good one.

"Well—" I started.

He wrapped his arms around me as he answered. "My dick is buried in my woman's wet tight cunt and I just came. How you think I'm feelin'?"

Okay, it was a stupid question.

"I need to tell you something," I shared.

He registered the look on my face and stopped smiling. "What?"

Here we go.

"Well, remember when I started having those headaches and we thought it was about me going to counseling and dealing with all that stuff, but you made me go to the doctor and he did some tests and told me to try going off the pill for a while and then, after that, there were those two times things got, uh . . . *heated* and we didn't exactly—"

I didn't finish because Hop pulled me off his cock, flung me onto his waterbed and covered me with his body. Before I got my breath back, he framed my head with both his hands and dipped his face close.

"You tellin' me you're havin' my baby?" he asked on a growl.

"Uh . . . yeah?" I answered, but it came out like a question just in case this wasn't happy news. I couldn't tell by the growl or the body throw. I also rushed on, "I know this is soon. We haven't been together long, but I'm sure about us and I'm, like, *really* happy about this baby and—"

I didn't finish again, because Hopper rolled us, and he did this twice, testing the waveless capacity of his waterbed, so we ended up across the bed, and I was again on my back with Hop's weight pinning me down. He reached out an arm, pulled open the drawer to his nightstand, rummaged around, and suddenly my hand was up and he was sliding a classic, stunning, diamond solitaire set in a simple, slim white-gold band on my finger.

I stared at the ring and stopped breathing.

"At Christmas, got Cherry to bullshit you about buyin' you jewelry and got your ring size. Then I got that. Waited for a good time. Now sure as fuck is that good time," he declared while I deep breathed.

But he wasn't done.

"You're movin' in. Your house is nice, babe, but it's nice for entertaining. You don't raise a family in a house like that. You raise one in a house like this. So we're raisin' our family in this house. You're also movin' in and doin' it now. Like, this weekend. And you best put your girls to work. You're gonna have my name before you push out my daughter, and they got work to do, they wanna get the wedding planned in time."

There was a lot there but I started at the end.

"Your daughter?"

"God loves me. Proved it with Molly, Cody, and you. No way your beauty, He'd give me a boy when you can give that to a girl and I can look at both of you the rest of my life."

Oh my God.

That was so beautiful!

"Hopper," I whispered.

"So she's a girl," he declared.

Oh dear. He was being unbelievably sweet and I had to say what I had to say.

But this was Hop. He'd spent months proving he understood so I knew he'd understand.

"Hop, honey," I put my hand to his cheek and smiled a shaky smile. "I love the ring. It's gorgeous. I'll move in. I'm fine with that. Happy, no...*thrilled*, actually. That's all good. But we can't get married."

His eyebrows snapped together and he asked, "Come again?"

"We can't get married," I answered carefully.

"Lady, you want to keep your name for business, do it. Don't give a fuck. But everybody who lives under this roof has the name Kincaid. We're a unit in every way we can be, starting with our name."

God!

That was beautiful too.

He wasn't making this easy.

"Hop," I took in a breath then told him, "That's not it."

His eyes moved over my face for a second. I knew he again registered my look so he invited gently, "Tell me what it is."

"I don't really want this moment spoiled but, I had the ring, the gown, the whole big thing planned with Elliott and—"

"Okay."

I blinked.

"What?"

"Okay," he repeated.

Was he giving in?

"You're okay with us not being married?" I asked hesitantly.

"You gonna live the rest of your life with me?"

My heart warmed, my body softened under his, and I felt tears sting my eyes. "Absolutely."

"You're happy about our baby?"

Oh yes, but happy was an understatement.

"Over the moon," I whispered, though I didn't tell him then I wanted a boy.

A boy that looked like him.

His mouth went soft and he dropped his forehead to mine.

"Then okay, lady."

He was giving in.

"Okay, Hop."

"Now kiss me."

I lifted my head and kissed him.

After some time, he broke the kiss, his lips moving over my cheek to my ear as he lifted his hand up, palm cupping my cheek, thumb dragging at my lips.

"She's havin' my baby," he murmured in my ear and my arms, already around him, squeezed.

"Yeah."

"Makes me happy, Lanie."

"Good."

"You make me happy, lady."

A tear rolled out of my eye and my voice broke on my repeated, "Good."

He lifted his head and looked down at me. "Have it all now, I made a baby outta love."

He was killing me.

"Stop making me cry and kiss me."

Hop grinned.

It was the most beautiful thing I'd ever seen.

Then he did as ordered.

* * *

The next morning, way too early, I found myself with bed head, wearing the clothes I picked up from the floor, and in Hop's Ram on my way to get donuts with my man.

I had no idea why I had to go. If Hop wanted donuts, he

was perfectly capable of going alone, and he well knew by now my order and backups if they didn't have what I wanted, seeing as every weekend when his kids were at his house, Saturday morning we had LaMar's donuts.

I also had no idea why I had to get up so freaking early to go. It was Saturday, and anyway, LaMar's kept stocked all day every day, *especially* Saturday.

Hop was insistent so I hauled myself out of bed, got dressed and there we were.

I was groggily staring out the window, sipping at a travel mug of coffee Hop had planted in my hand on the way out of his house, and I watched LaMar's coming closer.

Then I blinked as we passed.

"You passed it, honey," I informed him, looking over my shoulder and watching LaMar's get smaller in the distance.

"Give me your hand," he said. Unthinking, I gave him my hand and looked at him.

"Are you going to a different LaMar's or did you find another bakery?" I asked, hoping he was going to a different LaMar's. If he was going to drag me out of the house to try a different bakery, I feared we'd have words.

Things with Hop remained good, great, *the best*, but that didn't mean we didn't fight, and LaMar's was definitely worth fighting for. If it was that early and I was out in the world with bed head in clothes I'd worn the day before, I wasn't taking chances on any old bakery.

"Got up early, went out, got donuts. They're in the back," he stated, and I blinked again.

Then I heard the ratchet of a handcuff. My head jerked down and I saw the bracelet on me and watched as Hop steered with his knee while he ratcheted the other bracelet on his own wrist.

My head jerked back up and I cried, "What are you doing?"

"Kidnapping my woman, takin' her to Vegas, and getting married."

My mouth dropped open.

I snapped it shut to ask, "What?"

He glanced at me then back at the road. "Babe, learnin'."

That didn't answer my question. That didn't even make sense!

"Hopper, what are you talking about? We can't go to Vegas!"

"Yeah, we can."

My eyes narrowed on him. "I thought you were okay with us not getting married."

"Never said that."

"Yes you did."

"You asked, 'You're okay with us not being married?' I asked, 'You gonna live the rest of your life with me?' You said, 'Absolutely.' Never said I was okay with it 'cause I'm not. So we're gettin' married in Vegas."

I stared at him then yanked my wrist, shouting, "You're crazy."

"Headin' drama off at the pass and doin' it using drama," he retorted.

"What?" I shrieked and got another glance.

"Babe, knew I fought it out with you then, we'd hit a drama. I love your drama, you know it, but just found out you have my baby inside you, just put a ring on your finger, which, by the way, you didn't take off."

I didn't.

I still had it on.

Gah!

"Didn't want to spoil the moment," he continued. "You passed out after our baby celebration last night. While you were sleepin', I decided to fight off drama with drama. Commence kidnapping, which, over the next few hours, will go over state lines. Twice."

"You still aren't making sense, Hop."

Suddenly, he pulled off the road, put the truck in neutral, and turned his full attention to me.

"You got somethin' twisted up there," he pointed at my head, "about a wedding. You didn't say shit about a marriage. You said we can't *get* married, not *be* married."

"You're kidnapping me on a technicality?" I shouted, and he grinned.

Then he used our hands cuffed together to pull me closer and went on.

"You talked about the dress, the rings, the plans. I get that. I get why. So no dress. No flowers. No big thing. We get hitched. We live our lives. I get you'd shy away from the big thing. I'm a man. I'm all about not havin' a big thing. What you gotta get is, no baby of mine made of love is comin' into this world with her momma not wearin' my rings and carrying my name. It's just not gonna happen, Lanie. What's gonna happen is, we're goin' to Vegas, we're getting married, we're comin' home, and you're moving in."

He was insane.

"What about the kids?"

"They love you. They love me. You're in my bed every night when they're there. Doesn't make a difference you have your clothes in my closet. Molly will be pissed she didn't get a dress but she'll get over it. Cody will be relieved he doesn't have to wear some monkey suit."

This was true. Molly and Cody had totally accepted the easing Lanie into their lives gig, and Cody would lose his little badass biker-in-the-making mind if he had to put on a suit.

"Hopper, I don't—"

"Don't care what you don't," he cut me off to say. "Got donuts in the backseat. Snacks. Packed you a bag. Got a full tank of gas. And you got a lot of time to come to terms you're takin' my name. You don't, I'm haulin' your ass out connected to me to pump gas and you gotta use the men's restroom 'cause I sure as fuck am not walkin' into the ladies'."

My eyes got wide. "You packed me a bag?"

He smiled. "Sure I missed something, seein' as the bag I packed for you doesn't weigh as much as normal. But if I did, we can pick it up in Vegas."

I hated it when he was amusing when I was ticked off.

"I'm moving in and we're living happily ever after, Hop. I'm also keeping the ring because it's gorgeous. But we are *not* getting married."

"Yeah we are."

"No we aren't."

He turned back to the wheel, put the truck in drive, and moved back onto the road muttering, "We'll see."

"We're not!" I shouted, yanking on my wrist cuffed to his.

He caught my hand and pressed it to his thigh. "Don't want my bride on her wedding day havin' bruises on her wrist."

Argh!

I went silent.

Hop drove.

I stewed.

We were heading into the mountains when I stated, "This isn't going to work if both of us pull dramas, Hopper Kincaid. You're supposed to be the mellow one."

"Rethinkin' that 'cause this is fun," he replied. "Now, get me a donut, babe."

I growled and noticed Hopper grinned.

But I was hungry, and if I had the donuts I could throw one at him.

With difficulty, since my wrist was cuffed to Hop's, I twisted to the backseat and got the donuts. I also didn't throw one at him, because the minute I opened them, their sugary, doughy goodness wafted out, and it would be a crime to waste even one.

I handed Hop his and started snarfing mine.

"Babe?" Hop called.

"As of now, I'm not talking to you," I announced with a mouth full of donut.

"Love you more than life."

God.

He just kept killing me.

I went back to silently stewing.

But after what he said, my heart wasn't in it.

*   *   *

That night, the Flamingo Hotel, Vegas…

"Oh my *God*," I breathed, digging my heels into Hop's back. My wrists, cuffed to the bed, jerked, and suddenly Hop's mouth wasn't between my legs.

He'd shifted and I felt him kiss the sensitive skin where my leg met my pelvis, and my head shot up to look down at him.

He'd lifted up on his forearms, my legs still over his shoulders, and I got a good look at the new tattoo that was inked in his skin over his heart. Something he came home with as a surprise a couple of months ago.

It was a shield, its outline made of a kickass length of chain, inside in beautiful script it said *For my Lanie*.

I loved that tattoo almost as much as I loved my shield.

But right then, I couldn't think about how much I loved his tattoo.

"Don't stop," I begged.

"You gonna marry me?" he asked.

Totally killing me.

"Yes," I stated instantly, and he smiled a sexy smile.

"You sayin' that 'cause you wanna come or are you gonna marry me 'cause you want my name?"

"Both."

"Promise that, Lanie."

I held his eyes even as I squirmed. "Promise, Hop."

"You love me?"

"Until I die."

His face got soft but his lips ordered, "Say it."

Again. Killing me.

"Hop, please—"

"Say it, baby."

"Say what?"

"You want my name."

"Uncuff me."

"No. Say it."

"I want to touch you," I told him quietly and I did. I definitely wanted to touch him when I told him I wanted his name.

"Burying my face back in that pussy then fuckin' it, all with you at my mercy, babe. You can touch me later. Say what I want to hear now."

I dropped my head back to the bed and looked at the ceiling as I let the heat his words caused flash through my body. At the same time, I quickly sorted through my thoughts.

He was mine, I was his, he wanted this.

And I wanted him to have everything he wanted.

So I could let go of this one last thing and give it to him.

At the same time, having it myself.

When I had it together, I lifted up again and locked eyes with my man.

"I want to be your wife. I want your name. I want the name our son is going to have. I want to get married."

His face got dark, his eyes hot, but his lips curved before he corrected, "Daughter."

"Son."

He shook his head then I watched him dip his face between my legs.

Yes.

My heels dug into his back.

Hop slid his hands under my behind and he pulled me deeper into his mouth.

Keep hold of happy.

I was.

Every second.

Even if I had to do it with just my legs.

*   *   *

The next night...

"We need to have dinner as soon as possible," I told Tyra, my phone to my ear, my cheek to Hop's chest, my naked body entwined with his in our bed at the Flamingo in Vegas.

We'd been married by a fake Liberace.

We both wore jeans.

We found Hop's wedding band in an outpost on the way (though we did this shopping while I was under fake duress). It was wide, silver, with a thick ebony band in the middle. It didn't look like a traditional wedding ring, but it did look like a biker one.

Perfect for Hop.

He bought me a bouquet of red roses at fake Liberace's wedding chapel.

And when Liberace told Hop he could kiss the bride, Hop dipped me in an arched-back make-out session to end all make-out sessions. When he was done, he pulled me straight, crouched in front of me, wrapped his arms around my thighs, lifted me up, and roared, *"This is my woman!"*

I burst out laughing at the same time I burst into tears. It was the happiest moment of my life.

Bar none.

I'd done the right thing, marrying Hop.

And evidence was suggesting it was the same for my man.

Liberace told us no one had ever shouted like that after a ceremony. He did this making it clear he wished everyone did.

Liberace with his purple pompadour was also in some of our wedding photos. He was grinning like a lunatic. It was hilarious. But there was no doubt he genuinely loved his job.

Hop was right.

The dress, ring, flowers, all of it terrified me because that was what had led me and Elliott to Kansas City.

But jeans, roses, and Liberace were *perfect.*

"Is everything okay?" Tyra asked.

"Yes," I answered in a massive understatement. "Just, can you call Tabby and Shy and ask them to watch the boys so you and Tack can go out to dinner with us?"

"Sure, honey."

"I gotta go," I told her, and I did. I had to call my assistant at home on a Sunday and tell her I wouldn't be back in the office until Tuesday.

But first, I had to cuddle a little bit more with my husband.

"Okay. See you soon."

"Right. Bye, sweetie."

"Bye, Lanie."

I tossed my phone on the bed then moved my fingers to Hop's forearm and traced the pattern of fire. After I did that a while, I moved my finger to trace my shield.

"My name is Lanie Kincaid," I told his chest.

"Sure the fuck is," Hop replied on a growl, and I lifted my head to look at him.

His handsome face was set hard, determined, much like he looked when he talked about what he did to get Chaos out of the bad place they were in to a good place of family.

Family.

"Are you genuinely happy, Hopper Kincaid?" I asked softly.

"Abso-fuckin'-lutely, Lanie Kincaid," he stated firmly.

Wow.

That sounded beautiful.

I lifted a hand to his face and traced the side of his mustache with my thumb, watching it go before I lifted my eyes to him.

"For the first time since I was eleven, and for the first time in my whole life, it being totally honest and completely real, I am too."

He knifed up, his arms going around me, and he rolled us so he was on top then he kissed me.

"I think I have a clue how much you love me now, Hop," I told him when he broke the kiss.

"Good to know, baby," he said through a grin.

"Thank you," I whispered.

"So far from a hardship it isn't funny, lady, but you're welcome."

I lifted my head, sifting my fingers in his overlong hair,

smelling his spicy scent, feeling his 'tache tickle my skin, and I kissed my husband.

It was the best kiss of my life.

Up until then.

I would find that Hop, as ever, would keep making them better.

EPILOGUE

Waffles

Hop

One week later...

HIS PHONE RANG and Hop opened his eyes feeling his wife's weight pressed to his side, their legs tangled, and her cheek on his pec.

She shifted sleepily as he reached out a hand to the nightstand to grab his phone, seeing from the alarm clock it was early morning. As in *way* early morning. He looked at his display and saw it was Tack calling. They'd had dinner with him and Cherry the night before, where they shared their good news.

All of it. Tack and Tyra had been happy for them, Tyra over the moon. So much so Hop didn't know if she was happier about the baby than the marriage.

It didn't matter.

His woman had beamed through dinner, showing off her ring, touching her hand to her stomach, and Hop again didn't know if Lanie was happier about their baby or their marriage.

That was what mattered.

All was good in the family.

But a middle-of-the-night phone call was never good news. Ever.

He put the phone to his ear and muttered, "You got me."

"Callout, brother," Tack replied. "Benito."

Fuck, he thought

"Be there in fifteen," he said.

"Later."

"Later."

He tossed his phone to the nightstand as he felt Lanie stretch, pressing into him.

"Is everything okay?" she murmured, her voice drowsy and sweet.

"Yeah," he lied.

His woman was good in all the ways she could be. The short-term therapy counselor had suggested long-term therapy and Lanie had found someone she liked working with. They were winding things up seeing as his woman...no, his *wife*...had moved beyond the heavy shit and had been given the tools to deal with how her thoughts and memories twisted themselves and tortured her.

She still threw dramas, but they were not embedded in dysfunction.

She came home from work and ranted about shit that was fixable, thus mostly unimportant, but was important to get off her chest.

She hilariously lost it when she got caught up in something and burned her first attempt at making Cody's birthday cake.

And she bitched while he bit back laughter at the antics of her mother and father—strike that, her *sober,* seriously pissed off mother and her asshole father. Lanie and Lis were Team Joellyn all the way as Joellyn made maneuvers to take her husband to the cleaners. Edward had backtracked, saying he wanted her back, and none of the Heron women could tell if he said that because he knew he'd lose a vast chunk of his fortune or he was falling back in love with the woman he'd married now that she was sober. None of them cared, either. It was an all-out female Heron offensive to make that dirtbag pay.

Hop was loving it, and even if she bitched, he knew Lanie was too. She had one parent back, and she'd learned the hard way how precious life was. She wasn't wasting any of it on an unnecessary grudge.

But the business with Benito Valenzuela was something else.

He wouldn't let her worry. He wouldn't let her think anything about Benito if he could control it.

So he was going to control it.

Even if he had to lie.

But he was worried about it. The one thing that could set her to sliding back was this, if she found out how bad it was, and how it kept getting worse.

"Gotta go do something with Chaos," he told her, rolling her to her back and leaning in to kiss her throat but bracing for her reaction.

"Okay, honey."

Okay?

He lifted his head up and looked at her shadowed face.

She turned to her side, curled her legs up but stretched her neck to brush her lips against his collarbone.

Then she settled back in.

He stared at her.

Fuck. She trusted him.

Fuck. She was good with letting him go out in the middle of the night on unknown business for Chaos.

Hop gave it a beat to let that settle then bent and kissed her neck again, smoothing a hand over her hip then in, up her nightie and to her stomach. "Take care of Ellie while I'm gone."

"Happy to take care of Butch while you're gone," she mumbled dozily, and he felt his lips tip up.

He wanted a daughter who looked like his wife. His wife had informed him she wanted a son who looked like her husband.

God would decide, but it was fun arguing about something that meant everything knowing neither of them really cared which way it went.

But "Butch" was new.

"Butch?" he asked.

"Ty-Ty took all the cute baby boy biker names. I'm calling him Butch until I can come up with something else."

Fuck yeah, she was sleepy and joking.

She trusted him.

Hop stifled laughter and told her, "Ellie's a girl, Lanie."

"Butch is a boy, Hopper."

"We'll see," he muttered, leaning in to give his wife another light kiss.

"Yeah. We will," she replied, cuddled deeper into the bed and he rolled out.

Hop got dressed and went back to find his woman sleeping. He reached out, pulled the covers high and tucked her in.

Then he grabbed his phone, went downstairs to the locked cabinet, got his knife, moved to his safe and tagged his gun.

Then he walked out to his garage and hopped on his bike.

*   *   *

"Do not fire! Chaos, do not fire!" Tack roared, and Hop, crouched behind a hospital bed on a goddamned fucking

porno set of all fucking places, with his arms up and resting on the bed, gun pointed at one of Benito's men, stayed still but kept his finger on the trigger.

He took his eyes off his mark to look at Tack, who had his mouth tight. His gaze was on Shy, who had blood oozing down his neck because he just got winged by a ricochet bullet from one of Benito's men's guns.

Tack looked back at Benito and Hop looked back at his mark as he heard Tack growl, "Jesus Christ, are you shittin' me?"

They were there to rescue Tabby's best friend, Natalie. Tabby had been tight with Natalie for years. Hop knew her. The girl had been on Chaos and he'd seen her around. She was bad news in that sad way you knew, just looking into her eyes, that she'd chosen her path in life to numb some pain she didn't have the courage to face.

They'd been briefed, before they went to extract her from her film debut, that she got herself a habit to numb that pain. Then she got in deep with Benito and he was taking it out in trade. In other words, she had a bit part that was very active in his latest porno flick.

She wasn't big on doing this, so she called Tabby for a Chaos rescue. Shy stepped up for his woman and the boys rolled out.

Strategically, this was not good. Benito kept pushing; Chaos kept pushing back. So far, they had been able to keep Benito and his pushers and whores out of Chaos territory, but it was an ongoing battle. Regardless, hostilities had not escalated.

But for Tab, for Shy, for family, every man was there.

Tack and the Club hitting a porno set in the dead of night, demanding the actress who was meant to make her debut, and outing fucking *Elvira*—who had absolutely no fucking business being there undercover for some shit Hawk Delgado was working—did not go over big with Benito. Things got heated. Tack sent Elvira out for her own protection and he also sent away the Chaos recruits because they didn't need this experience. Not yet.

Things got more heated after that, and one of Benito's men jumped the gun.

Literally.

"Tack—" Benito started.

"Your man fuckin' fired," Hop clipped.

"Warning shot, he was closing in," Benito returned, jerking his head Shy's way. "It was a ricochet. He meant no harm."

"I don't give a fuck. My brother is bleeding and *your man fired*," Tack snarled. "And for once in your life, seein' as we got this many armed men in a faceoff, pay attention. He was approaching *me*."

"I will remind you, you were not invited to this party," Benito bit back.

"And I'll repeat what I've said five fuckin' times. Chaos will cover her debt. She's family. We agreed a long fuckin' time ago, man, family is off-limits," Tack returned.

"Not when they owe me a great deal of money," Benito shot back.

"Jesus, are you listening? Chaos is covering her debt," Tack replied.

"I prefer my method of payment," Benito retorted.

"That is not gonna happen. Con one of your other junkies into eatin' pussy for payback. This girl belongs to Chaos," Tack bit out.

Benito leaned toward Tack, his face twisting in anger. "She is not family. She is not blood or old lady. You lay claim to pussy on a whim, you can claim any-fuckin'-body. You do that, no rules and anything goes."

The entire room, already tense, went electric. They all knew what that meant.

If it came to war, Benito would play dirty, and it would not just be the brothers in the trenches.

Hop came out of his crouch, strode directly to Benito. Benito was concentrating on Tack, so he reacted to the advancing threat too late.

Hop had disarmed him and had his hand curled around Benito's throat, shoving him back with speed and force, so when he hit the hospital bed, he went down on it on his back. Hop kept squeezing as he put his gun to Benito's temple and listened vaguely to the scuffling maneuvers of the men around him who became antsy after a direct attack on Benito.

"Those rules *never* change," Hop declared. "Your beef is with Chaos, motherfucker. Any member of our family even fuckin' *shivers* 'cause they feel you close, you're eating my bullet."

Benito held his eyes but called out, "Tack, call off your dog."

"Say you get me," Hop growled.

"You're making a mistake," Benito hissed.

"Say. You. *Get* Me," Hop ground out.

He felt a presence and knew it was Tack before Tack spoke.

"I suggest you say you get him, man, 'cause you pull family into this shit you're stirrin', swear to fuckin' God, you won't eat Hop's bullet 'cause that would be too quick. I'll skin you alive, Benito. Do not mistake me. You harm any member of my family, and by that I mean all of Chaos, inch by inch you'll bleed and scream."

Benito's eyes were aimed over Hop's shoulder at Tack. He made a noise low in his throat before he looked at Hop and snapped, "I get you."

Hop instantly let him go and took two steps away.

Benito scrambled off the bed and faced Hop. "You just declared war."

"Motherfucker. Seriously?" Hop asked. "My brother's bleedin'. No paper signed but you spill Chaos blood, you do not come out of that shit unscathed. We had war five minutes ago."

"Five square miles," Tack cut in, and Benito looked to him. "I do not get it. You can have all of Denver—it sucks, but you can have it—no Chaos beef. All you gotta stay clear of is five fuckin' miles. What is it with you?"

"You can't claim what isn't yours," Benito returned.

"Your crew has been workin' Denver for seven years, motherfucker. Chaos claimed that territory fuckin' decades ago. How is it not ours?"

"Nothing is yours, you can't protect it," Benito retorted, and Tack shook his head.

"Man, trust me, Chaos lore is watered down. I get, you keepin' this shit up, you think we're no threat but, hear me, you do not wanna go to war with us," Tack advised.

"Soft," Benito whispered, his eyes lighting in a freaky way Hop did not like. "Everyone knows, you got out of the trade, you all went soft."

"I see you don't get this, seein' as you probably only get off jackin' off on a mountain of twenty-dollar bills, but a man protecting his home never goes soft."

"We'll see," Benito replied.

"No, *we'll* see," Tack fired back. "You and your boys do this, you'll be under dirt so you won't see shit."

Benito grinned.

Tack turned his eyes to Hop and shook his head.

Then he moved to exit while ordering, "Chaos, mount up."

The brothers moved out.

Tack tagged Shy and Hop on their way to the bikes. "Meet. Early. I'm callin' in the boys."

Hop jerked his chin up. He knew what Tack meant. He wasn't wasting time calling in reinforcements, and by that he meant Hawk Delgado, Brock Lucas, and Mitch Lawson.

Commandos and cops.

Benito should have listened.

After years undercover with the DEA, Brock Lucas knew the bowels of Denver like the back of his hand. Living with filth, to survive, he'd learned to embrace the wild inside. He might be married to a pretty baker who made unbelievably good cupcakes, and they were raising two boys, but he was still good with getting in touch with his wild side.

Mitch Lawson had proved without doubt that no matter how clean a cop he was, he had Chaos's back. He was cautious but far from dumb, and willing to go the distance, therefore a worthy ally and a surprisingly scary adversary.

And it was debatable but Hawk Delgado might be a functioning lunatic. But he got the job done, no matter how nasty that job might be. He didn't mind mess while doing it, and he had an army of commandos at his back. He paid them well, but he earned their loyalty another way and every one of them would lay down their lives for their leader.

Tack's eyes locked on Shy. "You and me now, to Baldy."

Shy nodded.

Baldy was a biker and a doctor. He would be in a Club if he had the time. Seeing as he took cash for his services, and the underbelly of Denver found themselves in need of a physician more than occasionally, he didn't have the time.

Shy gave Hop a handshake then headed to his bike.

Hop waylaid Tack.

"He touches family, brother, you won't get your chance to skin him," Hop warned. "Lanie never again feels fear. Not like that."

"I think he got that message," Tack replied.

"Hope he did, Tack. Swear to Christ, he didn't—"

Tack lifted a hand and curled his fingers around Hop's shoulder. "Calm. Patience. Natalie wasn't Chaos until we claimed her, so he isn't wrong to be pissed. We'll pay the money, which is all he cares about, he'll fall back and when he strikes, it won't be courting Armageddon. He's greedy but he's not stupid."

Hop stared into his brother's eyes. Then he did what he always did and he had never been wrong. He trusted his friend, nodded, and moved to his bike.

He had a text with the details on the meet by the time he pulled into his drive.

When he slid back into bed with his wife, she was still out.

He curled into her, pulling her close, splaying his hand on her still-flat stomach, and he pulled in a deep breath.

Smelling Lanie's perfume, he relaxed when he let it out.

Three hours later, he woke up, rolled carefully away from his still-sleeping woman, got dressed, and headed back out.

*　　*　　*

"Lanie," Hop muttered, using her name to tell his brothers it was time to get back to their women.

Tack turned and nodded to Hop.

"Right," he said. "Later, brothers. Have a mind, it's early, he won't move this quick, but watch your backs."

Hop nodded. Shy did too.

They swung on their bikes and roared off. They'd just had a meet with "the boys": Tack and his two lieutenants, Hop and Shy, as well as Hawk Delgado, Mitch Lawson, and Brock Lucas. War was declared. Reinforcements had been called. They were all in.

The meeting was tense, as it would be.

Now they waited.

As they rode away, Hop shouted, "Yo!" and Shy turned his head to look at his brother.

Hop jerked his head to the side. They both rode to the shoulder, stopped, put their feet down, and Hop looked back through the buildings from where they'd come.

Tack was standing there, motionless.

He was worried.

Hop closed his eyes.

When he opened them, Hop looked to Shy to see Shy looking back at Tack.

Then Shy's gaze came to him. "My guess, four hours ago, on a scale of one to ten of how bad this shit is, I would have said eleven. Now, I'm guessin' twenty-three."

"We may be at twenty-five," Hop corrected.

Shy's lips twitched.

This was his brother, Shy Cage. He'd never been to war but he still showed no fear.

Hop looked back to Tack to see he was moving to his bike.

"Brace, brother," Hop advised, then said, "Let's ride."

Shy jerked up his chin, they put on the gas, and they rode.

*　　*　　*

"Jesus, what is this?" Hop asked as he walked into the kitchen to see his woman in an un-fucking-believably amazing pair of knit yoga pants that were loose in the right places but clung to better places and a casual wraparound top that just clung to the right places, in other words every inch of her torso. Her hair was in a messy knot on top her head. Her face had no makeup.

And honest to Christ, she never looked so beautiful.

His kids were in the kitchen with her and it looked like a pancake batter bomb had exploded.

Needless to say, his kids had taken the news that their
father had a new wife and they had a new sister on the way
without even blinking. Hop wasn't surprised. It was good,
and kids sucked up good just as much as bad, so they had no
problem settling into it.

Molly especially. Cody, thank Christ, had come into this
world shielded by invisible steel. Not much affected him.
But Molly had a mind to her dad since she could form coher-
ent thought. Not close with her mother, Molly was Daddy's
little girl from the beginning. She wasn't old enough to process it, but that didn't mean she wanted her old man alone
and coasting on the scraps of goodness life could give him.
She seemed to relax when she got the news that Lanie was
legally bound to her father and they were cinching that with
a kid. Then again, his girl been relaxing since Lanie came
into the picture.

Yeah, kids totally sucked up the good.

"We're teaching Cody to make waffles, Dad!" Molly
shouted with excitement.

"Don't know why," Cody stated, but did this from his station manning the waffle iron. "I get a woman, she's doin' all
the cookin'."

Hop stared at his son then cut his eyes to his wife to see
her body shaking with silent laughter.

He had to stop himself from staring as his whole
fucked-up night melted away at seeing his woman laughing.

She trusted him. Totally trusted him.

He'd left their bed in the middle of the night to do Chaos
business. She'd gone back to sleep and stayed asleep, waking
up alone, and there she was, making waffles with his kids
and laughing.

Not anxious. Not freaked. Not wound up.

Laughing.

He'd done it. Pulled her out of the shadows and brought her into the light of family.

And she was basking in it.

He let that feeling smooth through him and turned back to his son.

"You plannin' on shackin' up soon, boy?" Hop asked.

"Soon's I graduate high school so I don't ever have to do laundry, clean, or cook," Cody answered.

Hop bit back laughter.

Lanie didn't bother. She giggled out loud, so Hop turned his head to watch her beautiful face beaming bright with happiness and he did it until he was sure he'd go blind.

"You're stupid," Molly declared, and Hop tore his gaze from Lanie to look at his daughter. "Everyone knows women don't do all the cooking and cleaning anymore."

"Lanie does it for Dad," Cody shot back. "*And* she works. *And* she has an ace ride." Cody looked to his father. "I'm gonna get a Lanie, 'cept," he screwed up his mouth as he narrowed his eyes on Lanie then looked back at his old man, "blonde," he finished. Then he thought better of his conclusion and said to Lanie, "Not bein' mean. You got pretty hair, too."

Lanie opened her mouth to say something but she was laughing too hard to get it out.

"Someone kill me. My son is already ordering up his woman," Hop muttered, and Cody looked at him.

"When did you have your first girlfriend?" he asked.

Hop wasn't going to answer that. Instead, he homed in on the point his son was not making.

"Do you have a girlfriend?"

"Oh dear," Lanie mumbled.

"Totally, Dad!" Molly gave it away. "He has *three*."

"Oh dear," Lanie repeated, but this time those two words shook with amusement.

"Three?" Hop asked, his eyebrows shooting up.

Cody lifted up the lid on the waffle maker to check progress all the while talking, "Seein' as I already decided to hook up early, I figure I gotta get my experience in now."

This time, Hop bit back a curse.

Molly cried, "Gross!"

Lanie kept laughing.

"Son, look at me," Hop called, and Cody decided the waffle wasn't done yet so he dropped the top back on and looked at his dad. "You are way too young for me to be sharin' this but seein' as you're jumpin' the gun, I gotta lay it out. You want a Lanie, one at a time. You never, and hear me, boy, *never* jack a girl around. You jack her around, you live with doin' that to a girl who doesn't deserve it, but you also answer to me. Are you hearin' me?"

Cody nodded solemnly. "I hear you, Dad."

Hop felt something in the room. He looked to his wife and he saw she wasn't laughing anymore. Her face was soft, her eyes were warm and he felt that warmth deep down, straight into his bones.

He returned the look then aimed his gaze back at his son.

"More advice," he started. "You can get your experience in about seven years. Now, concentrate on kickball or something."

"I already kill at kickball," Cody bragged. "Don't need no practice at that."

"Right, whatever," Hop replied, "I think you get me."

Cody studied him before giving in by mumbling, "I get you."

"Good," Hop stated. "Now, feed me. I'm starved."

Cody grinned.

Lanie got him a cup of coffee and gave it to him with a kiss on his jaw before she turned her attention back to supervising waffles.

Then they all sat at the kitchen table, Hopper Kincaid at the head with his family around, talking, laughing, giggling, shooting the shit over waffles.

It wasn't a birthday. It wasn't a holiday.

It still felt like a celebration.

And, even though it started shit, it was the best day of his life.

Just like every day after he won the love of Elaine Heron Kincaid.

But especially the day, seven months later, when his wife gave him his second son.

Nash Kane Kincaid.

Get lost in the Chaos!

Kristen Ashley's captivating series continues…

Please see the next page
for a preview of

RIDE STEADY

I FROZE BECAUSE I saw one of those bikers on his big, loud motorcycle riding down the shoulder my way.

And he wasn't one of those recreational bikers. I knew this at a glance. His black hair was very long, *too* long, and wild. He had a full black beard on his face. It was trimmed but not trimmed enough (as in, the beard being nonexistent). He had black wraparound sunglasses that made him look sinister (as bikers, in my mind, were wont to be). He also was wearing a black leather jacket that looked both beat-up and kind of new, faded jeans, and those clunky black motorcycle boots.

He stopped as I held my breath. He turned off the motorcycle and put down the stand to lean his bike on it before he swung a long leg with its heavy thigh and clunky boot off the bike.

Travis squealed.

Letting go of my necklace, he twisted in my arms and was pumping his fists excitedly.

I started breathing, feeling my heart beat fast, as the biker walked toward me, his sunglasses aimed my way, then he abruptly stopped with a strange jerk.

He studied me, his face impassive, standing like he was caught in suspended animation, and I studied him right back while he did.

I didn't know bikers. I'd never met a biker. Bikers scared me. They did this because they looked scary. They also did this because I'd heard they *were* scary. They had girlfriends who wore tube tops and they had knives on their belts and they drove too fast and too dangerously and got in bar brawls and held grudges against other bikers and did things to be put in jail and all sorts of stuff that wasn't normal but *was* scary.

As these thoughts tumbled through my head, he came unstuck, started moving my way, and in a deep, biker voice, he called, "You got a problem?"

Travis squealed again, pumping his arms, then he giggled as the big biker guy continued coming our way.

And as he did, slowly, my eyes moved to the traffic. It was bumper-to-bumper, crawling along at what couldn't be over twenty miles an hour. Looking at it, I knew I'd stood there for at least ten minutes, on the phone, then not, baby on my hip, car with a flat.

And not one single person had stopped to help.

Not one.

I turned my head back to the biker, who was now standing three feet away, his eyes downcast, his sunglasses aimed at my baby boy.

He'd stopped to help.

"I . . . have a flat," I forced out.

The sunglasses came to me and I felt my head tip to the side when they did because I got a look at him up close.

And what I saw made me feel strange.

Did I know him?

It felt like I knew him.

I screwed up my eyes to look closer at him.

He was a biker. I didn't know any bikers, so I didn't know him. I couldn't.

Could I?

"You got Triple A?" he asked.

I wished.

"No," I answered.

He lifted a black leather-gloved hand. "Give me the keys, stand back from the road. I'll take care of it."

He'd take care of it?

Just like that?

Should I let a biker change my tire?

Better question: Did I have any choice?

Since the answer to the better question was definite, I said, "I... well, that's very kind."

At this point, Travis made a lunge toward the biker. I struggled to keep him close, but my boy was strong and he tended to get what he wanted, and not only because he was strong.

Just then, he got what he wanted.

The biker came forward, gloved hands up, caught Travis at his sides and pulled him gently from my arm.

He settled him against his black T-shirt and leather jacket-clad chest with an ease and natural confidence that made my breath go funny.

Taking them in, biker and baby, for some reason, that vision filed itself into my memory banks. The ones I kept unlocked. The ones I liked to open and sift through. The ones that included making cookies with my mom. The ones that included Dad teaching me how to ride a bike and how he'd looked at me when I'd peddled away without training wheels, so proud, so happy. The ones that included the Easter before Althea died when she won the Easter egg hunt and Dad got that awesome picture of us in our frilly, pastel Easter dresses, wearing our Easter bonnets, holding our beribboned Easter baskets, hugging each other and giggling little girl giggles.

He didn't belong there. Not in those files. Not this biker.

But somehow, he did.

"Got the kid. Free hands, you can get the keys," he said, and I knew how he said it that it was an order, just a gently (kind of) worded one.

"Uh…right," I murmured, tearing my eyes away from him still holding a Travis who had become mesmerized by the biker's beard and was tugging on it. Tugging hard. Tugging with baby boy strength that I knew was already a force to be reckoned with.

But the biker didn't yank his face back. His chin jerked slightly with the tugs but he didn't seem to care.

Not even a little bit.

His eyes just stayed aimed to me until I took mine away.

I dug in my purse that was looped over my shoulder and came out with the keys.

I did this just in time to see the biker had tipped his chin to Travis and his resonant biker voice asked, "You gonna leave any whiskers for me, kid?"

Travis giggled, punched him in the lips with his baby fist, then tore off the biker's sunglasses.

I drew in a quick breath, hoping that wouldn't anger him. It didn't.

He just muttered, "Yeah, kid, hold those for me."

Then he transferred Travis to my arms, took my keys, and sauntered to my car.

He had the trunk open by the time I got myself together and took two steps forward.

"Uh…sir—"

His head twisted, just that, he didn't move a muscle of the rest of his body, and he said in a low rumble, "Stand back from the road."

I took three hasty steps back.

He returned his attention to my trunk.

"I just wondered," I called, juggling an active Travis, who was trying to get away since he clearly preferred leather and whiskers to his mommy, "your name."

"Joker," he answered, his hand appearing from the trunk holding tools that he tossed to the tarmac of the shoulder with a loud clang. I winced as he went back in and pulled out my spare.

Joker. His name was Joker.

No, I didn't know him. I knew no Jokers.

And anyway, who would name their child Joker?

"I'm Carissa. This is Travis," I yelled as he moved around the other side of the car and I saw the back of his jacket. On it was stitched a really interesting patch that included an eagle, an American flag, flames, and at the bottom, the word *Chaos*.

Oh dear. He belonged to the Chaos motorcycle gang.

Even I knew about the biker gang Chaos. This was because when I was growing up, Dad got all his stuff for our cars at their auto store on Broadway, a store called Ride. Pretty much everyone did who knew about cars and didn't want folks to mess them around.

"They're bikers, but they're honest," Dad had said. "They don't have a part, they don't tell you another part will work when it won't. They tell you they'll get it, it'll be there in a week, and then it's there in a week. Don't know about that gang. Do know they know how to run a business."

As this memory filtered through my head, at the end of it, I realized the man called Joker made no response.

"This is really nice!" I called as he disappeared in a crouch on the other side of my car. The other side of the car meaning right by the traffic.

That concerned me. It wasn't going fast and I'd pulled so far over, my passenger side tires were in the turf and scrabble at the edge of the shoulder, but it was still dangerous.

He again didn't respond so I yelled, "Please be careful!"

His deep voice came back. "I'm good."

"Okay, but stay that way. Okay?" I shouted back.

Nothing from Joker.

I fell silent. Well, not really. I turned my attention to my tussle with my son and did my all to turn his attention from the biker he could no longer see but very much wanted to get to.

"He's busy, baby, helping us out, fixing our car."

Travis looked at me and shouted an annoyed "Goo gah!" and then shoved the arm of Joker's sunglasses in his mouth.

I balanced him on my hip and tried gently to take the sunglasses away so Travis didn't get drool all over them or worse, break them.

Travis shrieked.

"We can't thank Joker for his help by breaking his sunglasses," I explained.

Travis yanked the sunglasses free from my tentative grip, and so they wouldn't break, I let him. He then brandished them in the air with victorious glee for a couple of seconds before bringing them down and shoving the lens against his mouth whereupon he tongued it.

I sighed and looked to where Joker was working, even though I still couldn't see him, and cautiously (but loudly, to be heard over the distance and traffic) shared, "Travis is drooling on your sunglasses."

Joker straightened, lugging my tire with him and tossing

it with a swing of his broad, leather jacket–covered shoulders into the trunk (something he did one-handed, which was impressive), this making my entire car bounce frighteningly.

His eyes came to me. "Got about a dozen pairs. He fucks those up, not a problem."

Then he crouched down again.

I bit back my admonishment that he shouldn't use the *f*-word. Aaron cursed all the time. I found it coarse, eventually annoying and finally ended concerned he'd use that language around our son.

I had no idea if he did.

But he probably did.

Instead of focusing on that, I focused on the fact that Joker seemed really nice.

Not seemed, he just was.

All the people who passed me, not helping, but he stopped.

Now he was changing a tire and, except for the time my dad made me do it so he could be assured I'd know how if the time came when I'd have to, I'd never done it again. But I knew it wasn't a lot of fun.

He'd let Travis pull his whiskers, yank off his glasses, and even let slide the good possibility some baby he didn't know would break them.

I looked to the glasses and knew they were expensive. They said *Liberty* on the side. They were attractive yet sturdy. I didn't think he got them off a revolving rack.

And I didn't want him to stop, help us, lose his expensive glasses, even though he was very nice and didn't seem to care.

"Please, baby boy, don't break those glasses," I whispered.

Like my eight-month-old understood me, he stopped licking the lens and shoved the glasses to me.

I grinned, murmured, "Thank you, my googly-foogly," took the glasses and bent into him to blow on his neck.

He squealed with glee.

Since he liked that so much, like I always did, I did it again. Then again. And since I didn't have anywhere else to put them, I shoved Joker's sunglasses in my hair so I could adjust Travis in order to tickle him.

He squirmed in my arms and squealed louder.

Goodness, that sound was beautiful.

No better sound in the world.

Not one.

I kept playing with my boy, and in doing so, I was suddenly unconcerned I was standing on I-25 with a biker from a biker gang changing my tire, and soon I'd be handing my baby off to my ex and *Tory*, so I wouldn't have him for a whole week.

Right then, it was just him and me.

It had been just him and me for a year and a half, part of that time he was in my belly, the rest he was my entire world.

I'd wanted a family. After Althea died, I'd started wanting that and made it with my dolls, then my Barbies, then in my dreams.

That's all I wanted. All I'd ever wanted.

A husband. A home. And lots of babies.

I didn't care what it said about me that I didn't want a career. That I didn't dream of cruises or tiaras or being important, carrying a briefcase, getting up and going to a high-powered job.

I wanted to do laundry.

I wanted to make cookies.

I wanted to have dinner ready for my husband and children when they got home.

I wanted to be a soccer mom (though, I didn't want a minivan, I wanted something like Aaron's Lexus SUV).

That's all I wanted.

I wanted to be a good wife and a *great* mother.

And again, I did not care even a little bit what people thought that said about me.

My mom worked. She'd worked even before Althea died. She'd worked after too.

I didn't mind that then. It made her happy.

But now, I wanted those moments back, the ones when she was at work. Those times she was away when I got home after school.

I wanted them back.

I wanted my dad to have them back.

And that was what I was going to give my husband. I was going to give my children the same.

That's all I wanted, to give my family that.

All I'd ever dreamed.

That dream had to change. Aaron killed it, so I had to revise it.

So now it was just Travis and me, every other week.

That was my new dream and if I tried real hard, I could convince myself I was living it.

Even though I wasn't.

Not even close.

But I'd make do.

"Done."

My head jerked up and I saw Joker standing in the turf a few feet away.

"Looked at your tire, hoped it was a nail," he informed me. "It wasn't. It blew. Your tread is low on all of them. They all need to be replaced."

My bubble of joy with me and my baby burst as life

pressed into it, the pressure, as always, way too much for that bubble of goodness to bear.

The tires might need it but I didn't need them to need it.

I also couldn't afford four new tires.

"Can't drive on that spare." Joker kept speaking, but he was doing it eyeing me closely. "Not for long. You need to see to that, soon's you can."

I stopped thinking about tires, my inability to afford them, and the absence of time I had to deal with it, and stared into his eyes.

They were gray. A strange, blunt steel gray.

It was far from unattractive.

It was also very familiar.

"Yeah?" he asked on a prompt and my body jolted.

Travis lunged.

And yet again, surprisingly Joker instantly lifted his now bare hands to my son and took him from me, curling him close, natural, taking that beautiful load on like he'd done it since the moment Travis was born.

Something warm washed through me.

"Yeah?" Joker repeated.

"Uh, yes. New tires. Don't drive on the spare," I replied.

"You go to Ride, I'll give them your name. They'll give you a discount."

And that was when something dirty washed through me.

The dirty was the fact that my car was twenty years old, faded, rusted, worn-out, and probably only still working because God loved me (I hoped), and all that was not lost on him.

This was embarrassing.

And as that washed through me, more did. Suddenly, gushes of nasty poured all over me.

The fact that I hadn't shifted off the last fifteen pounds of baby weight.

The fact that I hadn't been able to afford highlights for the last seven months so my hair did not look all that great, the golden blond streaks starting four inches down from my roots in a way that was *not* an attractive ombré.

The fact that I was dressed to go to work in a polo shirt, khakis, and sneakers, and not in a cute dress and cuter shoes.

The fact that he had expensive glasses, an expensive bike, a leather jacket, and he might be ill-groomed, but he was tall, broad, had interesting eyes, was nice, generous with his time, great with kids, and a Good Samaritan.

"You got time to do it and can hang," he went on. "I'll ask them to go over the car. Make sure it's good."

Oh no.

He was taking pity on me.

More dirty washed through me.

"No...no." I shook my head, reaching out to take Travis from him. It was a feat, Travis didn't want to let go, but I bested it and tucked my son firmly on my hip. "I...you've already been very nice. I should..." I flipped out my free hand, "I have money..."

I trailed off and twisted to get to my purse, thinking the twenty-dollar bill in it was not enough, but it was all I had. I was also thinking that I was unfortunately going to have to use my credit card to get gas.

"No need. Just get to Ride. Sort out that spare, yeah?"

I turned back to him. "You sure?"

"Don't want your money."

That was firm in a way that sounded like he was offended, something I really didn't want, so, hesitantly, I nodded. "You've been really kind."

"Yeah," he muttered. "Be safe."

And then he turned toward his bike.

He just turned toward his bike!

I couldn't let him just turn toward his bike and *walk away*.

I had no idea why but there was no denying in that second that I knew into my bones I couldn't allow the biker named Joker to walk away.

"Joker!" I called.

He turned back.

When I got his eyes, I didn't know what to do so I didn't do anything.

"Right," he said, walked to me and got closer than he had before.

Even as Travis tried to make a lunge at him, he lifted up his hand and I held my breath.

I felt his sunglasses slide out of my hair.

"Thanks," he murmured and turned back.

"Really, thank you," I blurted, this a hopefully not blatant effort to detain him (although it was an effort to detain him), and he again turned to me. "I don't know what to say. I feel like I should do something. You helped me out a lot."

"Get you and your kid off the side of the highway and get safe, that's all you gotta do."

"Oh. Yes. Of course. I should do that," I babbled.

"Later," he said and moved to his bike.

"Later," I called as he did, not wanting him to go.

I didn't understand this.

Okay, he helped me out and he was very nice about it.

And okay, I was alone. Like *really* alone. No family. No friends. No husband. New baby. New life I didn't like all that much (except said presence of my new baby). Dad far away.

And he stopped and helped me out making a problem I would have had to sort into one of those now nonexistent times when I got to let someone else sort it and I could play with my son, even if that time was on the side of a traffic-clogged interstate.

That meant a lot.

But I didn't want him to go in a way that wasn't just not wanting to see the last of a person who did me a kindness.

It was different.

And it was frightening.

But what was more frightening was that he was on his bike and making it roar.

It was almost over.

He'd be gone.

And I'd be alone.

It wasn't that (or just that).

It was that *he'd be gone*.

I opened my mouth to yell something over the noise of his motorcycle and Travis hit me in the jaw.

I looked down at my son.

I needed to get him to safety.

And then get him to his dad.

I closed my eyes, opened them, and saw Joker jerk his chin in an impatient way to my car.

So I hurried there, opened the passenger-side door, got my son safely in his car seat, rounded the car and got in.

Joker didn't merge into traffic until I did. He also didn't leave the interstate until I did. He followed me off the ramp to Speer Boulevard.

Then he turned off.

And was gone.

Tabitha Allen grew up in the thick of the Chaos MC, and the club has always had her back. But one rider was different from the start, and now Tabby wants more than friendship with the one man she can't have.

Please turn this page for an excerpt from

OWN THE WIND

"I Dreamed a Dream"

Three and a half months later...

HIS CELL RANG and Parker "Shy" Cage opened his eyes.

He was on his back in his bed in his room at the Chaos Motorcycle Club's Compound. The lights were still on and he was buried under a small pile of women. One was tucked up against his side, her leg thrown over his thighs, her arm over his middle. The other was upside down, tucked to his other side, her knee in his stomach, her arm over his calves.

Both were naked.

"Shit," he muttered, twisting with difficulty under his fence of limbs. He reached out to his phone.

He checked the display, his brows drew together at the "unknown caller" he saw on the screen as he touched his thumb to it to take the call.

"Yo," he said into the phone.

"Shy?" a woman asked, she sounded weird, far away, quiet.

"You got me," he answered.

"It's Tabby."

He shot to sitting in bed, limbs flying and they weren't his.

"Listen, I'm sorry," her voice caught like she was trying to stop crying or, maybe, hyperventilating, then she whispered, "So, so sorry but I'm in a jam. I think I might even be kinda...um, in trouble."

"Where are you?" he barked into the phone, rolling over the woman at his side and finding his feet.

"I...I...well, I was with this old friend and we were. Damn, um..." she stammered as Shy balanced the phone between ear and shoulder and tugged on his jeans.

"Babe, where are you?" he repeated.

"In a bathroom," she told him, as he tagged a tee off the floor and straightened, waiting for her to say more.

When she didn't, gently, he prompted, "I kinda need to know where that bathroom is, sugar."

"I, uh...this guy is...um, I didn't know it, obviously, but I think he's—" another hitch in her breath before she whispered so low he barely heard "—a bad dude."

Fuck.

Shit.

Fuck.

He nabbed his boots off the floor and sat on the bed to yank them on with his socks, asking, "Do I need backup?"

"I don't want anyone..." she paused. "Please, don't tell anyone. Just...can you please just text me when you're here? I'll stay in the bathroom, put my phone on vibrate so no one will hear, and I'll crawl out the window when you get here."

"Tab, no one is gonna think shit. Just give me the lay of the land. Are you in danger?"

"I'll crawl out the window."

He gentled his voice further and stopped putting on his boots to give her his full attention.

"Tabby, baby, are you in danger?"

"I... well, I don't know really. There's a lot of drugs and I saw some, well, a lot of guns."

Shit.

"Address, honey," he urged, and she gave it to him.

Then she said, "Don't tell anyone, please. Just text."

"I'll give you that if you keep me notified and often. Text me. Just an 'I'm okay' every minute or so. I don't get one, I'll know you're not and I'm bringin' in the boys."

"I can do that," she agreed.

"Right, hang tight, I'll be there."

"Uh... thanks, Shy."

"Anytime, Tab. Yeah?"

He waited, and it felt like years before she whispered, "Yeah."

He disconnected, pulled on his last boot, and stood, tugging on his tee as he turned to his bed. One of the women was up on an elbow and blinking at him. The other was still out.

As he found his knife in the nightstand and shoved the sheath into his belt, he ordered, "Get her ass up. Both of you need to get dressed and get gone." He reached into the nightstand and grabbed his gun, shoving it into the back waistband of his jeans and pulling his tee over it. "You got fifteen minutes to get out. You're not gone by the time I get back, I will not be happy."

"Sure thing, babe," the awake one muttered. She lifted a hand to shove at the hip of her friend.

Jesus.

Slicing a glance through them he knew he was done. Some of the brothers, a lot older than him, enjoyed as much as they could get, however that came, and they didn't limit it to two pieces of ass.

He'd had that ride and often.

It hit him right then it went nowhere.

He'd never, not once, walked up to a woman who looked lost without him and became found the second she saw him. Who leaned into him the minute he touched her. Who made him laugh so hard, his head jerked back with it. Whose mouth he could take and the world melted away for him just as he made that same shit happen for her.

And he would not get that if he kept this shit up.

He jogged through the Compound to his bike and rode with his cell in his hand.

She texted, *I'm okay*, and Shy took in a calming breath and turned his eyes back to the road.

She texted again. This time, *I'm still okay*, and, getting closer to her, Shy felt his jaw begin to relax.

A few minutes later she texted again. This time it was *I'm still okay but this bathroom is seriously gross*.

When Shy got that, after his eyes went back to the road, he was flat-out smiling.

She kept texting her ongoing condition of *okay*, with a running commentary of how much she disliked her current location, until he was outside the house. He turned off his bike and scanned. Lights on in a front room, another one beaming from a small window at the opposite side at the back. The bathroom.

He bent his head to the phone and texted, *Outside, baby*.

Seconds later he saw a bare foot coming out the small window and another one, then legs. He kicked down the stand, swung off his bike, and jogged through the dark up the side of the house.

He caught her legs and tugged her out the rest of the way, putting her on her feet.

She tipped her head back to him, her face pale in the dark.

"Thanks," she said softly.

He, unfortunately, did not have all night to look in her shadowed but beautiful face. He had no idea what he was dealing with. He had to get them out of there.

He took her hand and muttered, "Let's go."

She nodded and jogged beside him, her hand in his, her shoes dangling from her other hand. He swung on his bike, she swung on behind him. A child born to the life, she wrapped her arms around him without hesitation.

He felt her tits pressed to his back and closed his eyes.

Then he opened them and asked, "Where you wanna go?"

"I need a drink," she replied.

"Bar or Compound?" he offered, knowing what she'd pick. She never came to the Compound anymore.

"Compound," she surprised him by answering.

Thank Christ he kicked those bitches out. He just hoped they followed orders.

He rode to the Compound, parked outside, and felt the loss when she pulled away and swung off. He lifted a hand to hold her steady as she bent to slide on her heels, then he took her hand and walked her into the Compound.

Luckily, it was deserted. Hopefully, his room was too. He didn't need one of those bitches wandering out and fucking Tab's night even worse.

"Grab a stool, babe. I'll get you a drink," he muttered, shifting her hand and arm out to lead her to the outside of the bar while he moved inside.

Tabby, he noted, took direction. She rounded the curve of the bar and took a stool.

Shy moved around the back of it and asked, "What're you drinking?"

"What gets you drunk the fastest?" she asked back, and he stopped, turned, put his hands on the bar and locked eyes on her.

"What kind of trouble did I pull you out of?" he asked quietly.

"None, now that I'm out that window," she answered quietly.

"You know those people?" he asked.

She shrugged and looked down at her hands on the bar. "An old friend. High school. Just her. The others..." She trailed off on another shrug.

Shy looked at her hands.

They were visibly shaking.

"Tequila," he stated, and her eyes came to his.

"What?"

"Gets you drunk fast."

She pressed her lips together and nodded.

He grabbed the bottle and put it in front of her.

She looked down at it then up at him, and her head tipped to the side when he didn't move.

"Glasses?" she prompted.

He tagged the bottle, unscrewed the top, lifted it to his lips and took a pull. When he was done, he dropped his arm and extended it to her.

"You can't get drunk fast, you're fuckin' with glasses," he informed her.

The tip of her tongue came out to wet her upper lip and, Jesus, he forgot how cute that was.

Luckily, she took his mind off her tongue when she took the bottle, stared at it a beat then put it to her lips and threw back a slug.

The bottle came down with Tabby spluttering and Shy reached for it.

Through a grin, he advised, "You may be drinking direct, sugar, but you still gotta drink smart."

"Right," she breathed out like her throat was on fire.

He put the bottle to his lips and took another drag before he put it to the bar.

Tabby wrapped her hand around it, lifted it, and sucked some back, but this time she did it smart, and her hand with the bottle came down slowly, although she was still breathing kind of heavy.

When she recovered, he leaned into his forearms on the bar and asked softly, "You wanna talk?"

"No," she answered sharply, her eyes narrowing, the sorrow shifting through them slicing through his gut. She lifted the bottle, took another drink before locking her gaze with his. "I don't wanna talk. I don't wanna share my feelings. I don't wanna *get it out*. I wanna *get drunk*."

She didn't leave any lines to read through, she said it plain, so he gave her that out.

"Right, so we gonna do that, you sittin' there sluggin' it back and me standin' here watchin' you, or are we gonna do something? Like play pool."

"I rock at pool," she informed him.

"Babe, I'll wipe the floor with you."

"No way," she scoffed.

"Totally," he said through a grin.

"You're so sure, darlin', we'll make it interesting," she offered.

"I'm up for that," he agreed. "I win, you make me cookies. You win, you pick."

He barely finished speaking before she gave him a gift the likes he'd never had in his entire fucking life.

The pale moved out of her features as pink hit her cheeks, life shot into her eyes, making them vibrant, their startling color rocking him to his fucking core before she bested all that shit and burst out laughing.

He had no idea what he did, what he said, but whatever it

was, he'd do it and say it over and over until he took his last breath just so he could watch her laugh.

He didn't say a word when her laughter turned to chuckles and continued his silence, his eyes on her.

When she caught him looking at her, she explained, "My cooking, hit and miss. Sometimes, it's brilliant. Sometimes, it's..." she grinned "...*not*. Baking is the same. I just can't seem to get the hang of it. I don't even have that"—she lifted up her fingers to do air quotation marks—"*signature dish* that comes out great every time. I don't know what it is about me. Dad and Rush, even Tyra, they rock in the kitchen. Me, no." She leaned in. "*Totally* no. So I was laughing because anyone who knows me would not think cookies from me would be a good deal for a bet. Truth is, they could be awesome but they could also seriously suck."

"How 'bout I take my chances?" he suggested.

She shrugged, still grinning. "Your funeral."

Her words made Shy tense, and the pink slid out of her cheeks, the life started seeping out of her eyes.

"Drink," he ordered quickly.

"What?" she whispered, and he reached out and slid the tequila to her.

"Drink. Now. Suck it back, babe. Do it thinkin' what you get if you win."

She nodded, grabbed the bottle, took a slug, and dropped it to the bar with a crash, letting out a totally fucking cute "Ah" before she declared, "You change my oil."

His brows shot up. "That's it?"

"I need my oil changed and it costs, like, thirty dollars. I can buy a lot of stuff with thirty dollars. A lot of stuff *I want*. I don't want *oil*. My car does but I don't."

"Tabby, sugar, your dad part-owns the most kick-ass

garage this side of the Mississippi and most of the other side, and you're paying for oil changes?"

Her eyes slid away and he knew why.

Fuck.

She was doing it to avoid him. Still.

Serious as shit, this had to stop.

So he was going to stop it.

"We play pool and we get drunk and we enjoy it, that's our plan, so let's get this shit out of the way," he stated. Her eyes slid back to him and he said flat out, "I fucked up. It was huge. It was a long time ago but it marked you. You were right. I was a dick. I made assumptions, they were wrong and I acted on 'em and I shouldn't have and that was more wrong. I wish you would have found the time to get in my face about it years ago so we could have had it out, but that's done. When you did get in my face about it, I should have sorted my shit, found you, and apologized. I didn't do that either. I'd like to know why you dialed my number tonight, but if you don't wanna share that shit, that's cool too. I'll just say, babe, I'm glad you did. You need a safe place just to forget shit and escape, I'll give it to you. Tonight. Tomorrow. Next week. Next month. That safe place is me, Tabby. But I don't want that old shit haunting this. Ghosts haunt until you get rid of them. Let's get rid of that fuckin' ghost and move on so I can beat your ass at pool."

As he spoke, he saw the tears pool in her eyes but he kept going, and when he stopped he didn't move even though it nearly killed him. Not to touch her, even her hand. Not to give her something.

It killed.

Before he lost the fight to hold back, she whispered, "You are never gonna beat my ass at pool."

That was when he grinned, leaned forward, and wrapped his hand around hers sitting on the bar.

"Get ready to have your ass kicked," he said softly.

"Oil changes for a year," she returned softly.

"You got it but cookies for a year," he shot back.

"Okay, but don't say I didn't warn you," she replied.

He'd eat her cookies, they were brilliant or they sucked. If Tabitha Allen made it, he'd eat anything.

Shy didn't share that.

He gave her hand a squeeze, nabbed the bottle, and took off down the bar toward the cues on the wall.

Tabby followed.

*   *   *

They were in the dark, in his bed, in his room in the Compound.

Shy was on his back, eyes to the ceiling.

Tabby was three feet away, on her side, her chin was tipped down.

She was obliterated.

Shy wasn't even slightly drunk.

She'd won four games, he'd won five.

Cookies for a year.

Now, he was winning something else, because tequila didn't make Tabitha Allen a happy drunk.

It made her a talkative one.

It also made her get past ugly history and trust him with absolutely everything that mattered right now in her world.

"DOA," she whispered to the bed.

"I know, sugar," he whispered to the ceiling.

"Where did you hear?" she asked.

"Walkin' into the Compound, boys just heard and they were taking off."

"You didn't come to the hospital."

He was surprised she'd noticed.

"No. I wasn't your favorite person. Didn't think I could help. Went up to Tack and Cherry's, helped Sheila with the boys," he told her.

"I know. Ty-Ty told me," she surprised him again by saying. "That was cool of you to do. They're a handful. Sheila tries but the only ones who can really handle them are Dad, Tyra, Rush, Big Petey, and me."

Shy didn't respond.

"So, uh...thanks," she finished.

"No problem, honey."

She fell silent and Shy gave her that.

She broke it.

"Tyra had to cancel all the wedding plans."

"Yeah?" he asked quietly.

"Yeah," she answered. "Second time she had to do that. That Elliott guy wasn't dead when she had to do it for Lanie, but still. Two times. Two weddings. It isn't worth it. All that planning. All that money..." she pulled in a shaky breath "...not worth it. I'm not doing it again. I'm never getting married."

At that, Shy rolled to his side, reached out and found her hand lying on the bed.

He curled his hand around hers, held tight and advised, "Don't say that, baby. You're twenty-two years old. You got your whole life ahead of you."

"So did he."

Fuck, he couldn't argue that.

He pulled their hands up the bed and shifted slightly closer before he said gently, "If he was in this room right now, sugar, right now, he wouldn't want this. He wouldn't want to hear you say that shit. Dig deep, Tabby. What would he want to hear you say?"

She was silent then he heard her breath hitch before she whispered, "I'd give anything..."

She trailed off and went quiet.

"Baby," he whispered back.

Her hand jerked and her body slid across the bed to slam into his, her face in his throat, her arm winding around him tight, her voice so raw, it hurt to hear. His own throat was ragged just listening.

"I'd give anything for him to be in this room. *Anything.* I'd give my hair, and I *like* my hair. I'd give my car, and Dad fixed that car up for me. I *love* that car. I'd swim an ocean. I'd walk through arrows. I'd *bleed* for him to be here."

She burrowed deeper into him and Shy took a deep breath, pressing closer, giving her his warmth. He wrapped an arm around her and pulled her tighter as she cried quietly, one hand holding his tight.

He said nothing but listened, eyes closed, heart burning, to the sounds of her grief.

Time slid by and her tears slowly stopped flowing.

Finally, she said softly, "I dreamed a dream."

"What, sugar?"

"I dreamed a dream," she repeated.

He tipped his head and put his lips to the top of her hair but he had no reply. He knew it sucked when dreams died. He'd been there. There were no words to say. Nothing made it better except time.

Then she shocked the shit out of him and started singing, her clear, alto voice wrapping around a song he'd never heard before, but its words were gutting, perfect for her, what she had to be feeling, sending that fire in his heart to his throat so high, he would swear he could taste it.

"*Les Mis,*" she whispered when she was done.

"What?"

"The musical. *Les Misérables.* Jason took me to go see it. It's very sad."

If that was a song from the show, it fucking had to be.

She pressed closer. "I dreamed a dream, Shy."

"You'll dream more dreams, baby."

"I'll never dream," she whispered, her voice lost, tragic.

"We'll get you to a dream, honey," he promised, pulling her closer.

She pressed in, and he listened as her breath evened out, felt as her body slid into sleep, all the while thinking her hair smelled phenomenal.

Shy turned into her, trapping her little body under his and muttering, "We'll get you to a dream."

Tabby held his hand in her sleep.

Shy held her but didn't sleep.

The sun kissed the sky and Shy's eyes closed.

When he opened them, she was gone.

Fall in Love with Forever Romance

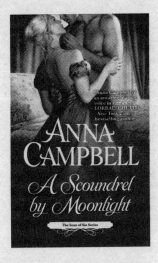

A SCOUNDREL BY MOONLIGHT
by Anna Campbell

Justice. That's all Nell Trim wants—for the countless young women the Marquess of Leath has ruined with his wildly seductive ways. But can she resist the scoundrel's temptations herself? Check out this fourth sensual historical romance in the Sons of Sin Regency series from bestselling author Anna Campbell!

SINFULLY YOURS
by Cara Elliott

Secret passions are wont to lead a lady into trouble... The second rebellious Sloane sister gets her chance at true love in the next Hellions of High Street Regency romance from bestselling author Cara Elliott.

Fall in Love with Forever Romance

A GOOD ROGUE IS HARD TO FIND
by Kelly Bowen

The rogue's life has been good to William Somerhall, until he moves in with his mother and her paid companion, Miss Jenna Hughes. To keep the eccentric dowager duchess from ruin, he'll have to keep his friends close—and the tempting Miss Hughes closer still. Fans of Sarah MacLean and Tessa Dare will fall in love with the newest book in Kelly Bowen's Lords of Worth series!

WILD HEAT
by Lucy Monroe

The days may be cold, but the nights are red-hot in *USA Today* bestselling author Lucy Monroe's new Northern Fire contemporary romance series. Kitty Grant decides that the best way to heal her broken heart is to come back home. But she gets a shock when she sees how sexy her childhood friend Tack has become. Before she knows it, they're reigniting sparks that could set the whole state of Alaska on fire.

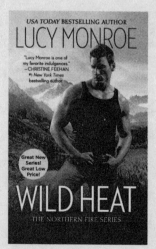

Fall in Love with Forever Romance

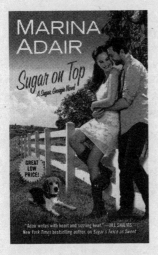

SUGAR ON TOP
by Marina Adair

It's about to get even sweeter in Sugar! When scandal forces Glory Mann to co-chair the Miss Sugar Peach Pageant with sexy single dad Cal MacGraw, sparks fly. Fans of Carly Phillips, Rachel Gibson, and Jill Shalvis will love the latest in the Sugar, Georgia series!

A MATCH MADE
ON MAIN STREET
by Olivia Miles

When Anna Madison's high-end restaurant is damaged by a fire, there's only one place she can cook: her sexy ex's diner kitchen. But can they both handle the heat? The second book of the Briar Creek series is "sure to warm any reader's heart" (*RT Book Reviews* on *Mistletoe on Main Street*).

Fall in Love with Forever Romance

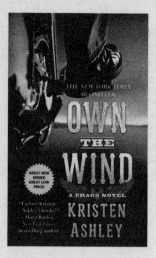

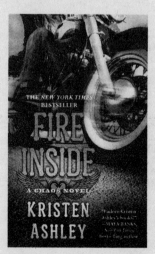